Baen Books by Lois McMaster Bujold

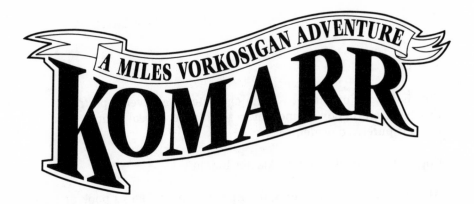

A MILES VORKOSIGAN ADVENTURE

KOMARR

LOIS McMASTER BUJOLD

BAEN

KOMARR

Copyright © 1998 by Lois McMaster Bujold

A Baen Books Original

Baen Publishing Enterprises
P.O. Box 1403
Riverdale, NY 10471

ISBN: 0-671-87877-8

Cover art by Gary Ruddell

First printing, June 1998

Distributed by Simon & Schuster
1230 Avenue of the Americas
New York, NY 10020

Library of Congress Cataloging-in-Publication Data

Bujold, Lois McMaster
    Komarr / Lois McMaster Bujold.
        p.   cm. — (A Miles Vorkosigan adventure)
    "A Baen Books original" — T.p. verso.
    ISBN 0-671-87877-8
    I. Title. II. Series: Bujold, Lois McMaster. Vorkosigan adventure.
PS3552.U397K66   1998   98-14345
813'.54—dc21   CIP

Typeset by Windhaven Press, Auburn, NH
Printed in the United States of America

CHAPTER ONE

The last gleaming sliver of Komarr's true-sun melted out of sight beyond the low hills on the western horizon. Lagging behind it in the vault of the heavens, the reflected fire of the solar mirror sprang out in brilliant contrast to the darkening, purple-tinged blue. When Ekaterin had first viewed the hexagonal soletta-array from downside on Komarr's surface, she'd immediately imagined it as a grand Winterfair ornament, hung in the sky like a snowflake made of stars, benign and consoling. She leaned now on her balcony overlooking Serifosa Dome's central city park, and gravely studied the lopsided spray of light through the glassy arc overhead. It sparkled deceptively in contrast to the too-dark sky. Three of the six disks of the star-flake shone not at all, and the central seventh was occluded and dull.

Ancient Earthmen, she had read, had taken alterations in the clockwork procession of their heavens—comets, novae, shooting stars—for disturbing omens, premonitions of disasters natural or political; the very word, *disaster*, embedded the astrological source of the concept. The collision two weeks ago of an out-of-control inner-system ore freighter with the insolation mirror that supplemented Komarr's solar energy was surely most literally a disaster, instantly so for the half-dozen Komarran members of the soletta's station-keeping crew who had been killed. But it seemed to be playing out in slow motion thereafter; it had so far barely affected the sealed arcologies

1

that housed the planet's population. Below her, in the park, a crew of workers was arranging supplemental lighting on high girders. Similar stopgap measures in the city's food-producing greenhouses must be nearly complete, to spare them and this equipment to such an ornamental task. No, she reminded herself; no vegetation in the dome was merely ornamental. Each added its bit to the biological reservoir that ultimately supported life here. The gardens in the domes would live, cared for by their human symbiotes.

Outside the arcologies, in the fragile plantations that labored to bio-transform a world, it was another question altogether. She knew the math, discussed nightly at her dinner table for two weeks, of the percentage loss of insolation at the equator. Days gone winter-cloudy—except that they were planetwide, and going on and on, until when? When would repairs be complete? When would they *start*, for that matter? As sabotage, if it had been sabotage, the destruction was inexplicable; as half-sabotage, doubly inexplicable. *Will they try again?* If it was a *they* at all, ghastly malice and not mere ghastly accident.

She sighed, and turned away from the view, and switched on the spotlights she'd put up to supplement her own tiny balcony garden. Some of the Barrayaran plants she'd started were particularly touchy about their illumination. She checked the light with a meter, and shifted two boxes of deerslayer vine closer to the source, and set the timers. She moved about, checking soil temperature and moisture with sensitive and practiced fingers, watering sparingly where needed. Briefly, she considered moving her old bonsai'd skellytum indoors, to provide it with more controlled conditions, but it was all indoors here on Komarr, really. She hadn't felt wind in her hair for nearly a year. She felt an odd twinge of identification with the transplanted ecology outside, slowly starving for light and heat, suffocating in a toxic atmosphere . . . *Stupid. Stop it. We're lucky to be here.*

"Ekaterin!" Her husband's inquiring bellow echoed, muffled, inside the residence tower.

She poked her head through the door to the kitchen. "I'm on the balcony."

"Well, come down here!"

She set her gardening tools in the box seat, closed the lid, sealed the transparent doors behind her, and hurried across the room into the hall and down the circular staircase. Tien was standing impatiently beside the double doors from their apartment to the building's corridor, a comm link in his hand.

"Your uncle just called. He's landed at the shuttleport. I'll get him."

"I'll get Nikolai, and go with you."

"Don't bother, I'm just going to meet him at the West Station locks. He said to tell you, he's bringing a guest. Another Auditor, some sort of assistant to him, it sounded like. But he said not to worry, they'll both take pot luck. He seemed to imagine we'd feed them in the kitchen or something. Eh! *Two* Imperial Auditors. Why ever did you have to invite him, anyway?"

She stared at him in dismay. "How can my Uncle Vorthys come to Komarr and not see us? Besides, you can't say your department isn't affected by what he's investigating. Naturally he wants to see it. I thought you liked him."

He slapped his hand arrhythmically on his thigh. "Back when he was just the old weird Professor, sure. Eccentric Uncle Vorthys, the Vor tech. This Imperial appointment of his took the whole family by surprise. I can't imagine what favors he called in to get it."

Is that your only idea of how men advance? But she did not speak the weary thought aloud. "Of all political appointments, surely Imperial Auditor is the least likely to be gained that way," she murmured.

"Naïve Kat." He smiled shortly, and hugged her around the shoulders. "No one gets something for nothing in Vorbarr Sultana. Except, perhaps, your uncle's assistant, whom I gather is closely related to *the* Vorkosigan. He apparently got his appointment for breathing. Incredibly young for the job, if he's the one I heard about who was sworn in at Winterfair. A lightweight, I presume, although all your Uncle Vorthys said was that he was sensitive about his height and not to mention it. At least some part of this mess promises to be a show."

He tucked his comm link away in his tunic pocket. His hand was shaking slightly. Ekaterin grasped his wrist and turned it over. The tremula increased. She raised her eyes, dark with worry, in silent question to his.

"No, dammit!" He jerked his arm away. "It's not starting. I'm just a little tense. And tired. And hungry, so see if you can't pull together a decent meal by the time we're back. Your uncle may have prole tastes, but I can't imagine they're shared by a Vorbarr Sultana lordling." He thrust his hands into his trouser pockets and looked away from her unhappy frown.

"You're older now than your brother was then."

"Variable onset, remember? We'll go soon. I promise."

"Tien . . . I wish you'd give up this galactic treatment

plan. They have medical facilities here on Komarr that are almost as good as, as Beta Colony or anywhere. I thought, when you won this post here, that you would. Forget the secrecy, just go openly for help. Or go discreetly, if you insist. But don't wait any longer!"

"They're not discreet enough. My career is finally on course, finally paying off. I have no desire to be publicly branded a mutant *now*."

If I don't care, what does it matter what anyone else thinks? She hesitated. "Is that why you don't want to see Uncle Vorthys? Tien, he's the least likely of my relatives—or yours, for that matter—to care if your disease is genetic or not. He will care about you, and about Nikolai."

"I have it under control," he insisted. "Don't you dare betray me to your uncle, this close to the real payoff. I have it under control. You'll see."

"Just don't . . . take your brother's way out. Promise me!" The lightflyer accident that hadn't been quite an accident: that had ushered in these years of chronic, subclinical nightmare waiting and watching. . . .

"I have no intention of doing anything like that. It's all planned. I'll finish out this year's appointment, then we'll take a long overdue galactic vacation, you and me and Nikolai. And it will all be fixed, and no one will ever know. If *you* don't lose your head and panic at the last minute!" He grasped her hand, and grimaced an unfelt smile, and strode out the doors.

Wait and I'll fix it. Trust me. That's what you said the last time. And the time before that, and the time before that. . . . Who is betrayed? Tien, you're running out of time, can't you see it?

She turned for her kitchen, mentally revising her planned family dinner to include a Vor lord from the Imperial capital. White wine? Her limited experience of the breed suggested that if you could get them sufficiently sloshed, it wouldn't matter what you fed them. She put another of her precious imported-from-home bottles in to chill. No . . . make that two more bottles.

She added another place to the table on the balcony off the kitchen that they routinely used for a dining room, sorry now she'd not engaged a servitor for the evening. But human servants on Komarr were so expensive. And she'd wanted this bubble of domestic privacy with Uncle Vorthys. Even the staid official newsvid reps were badgering everyone involved in the investigation; the arrival of not one but two Imperial Auditors on-site in Komarr orbit had not calmed the fever of speculation, but only redirected it. When she'd first spoken with him shortly after his arrival on-site, on a distance-delayed channel that defeated any attempt at long conversation, normally-patient Uncle Vorthys's description of the public briefings into which he'd been roped had been notably irritated. He'd hinted he would be glad to escape them. Since his years of teaching must have inured him to stupid questions, Ekaterin wondered if the true source of his irritation was that he couldn't answer them.

But mostly, she had to admit, she just wanted to recapture the flavor of a happier past, greedily for herself. She'd lived with Aunt and Uncle Vorthys for two years after her mother had died, attending the Imperial University under their casual supervision. Life with the Professor and the Professora had somehow been less constrained, and constraining, than in her father's conservative Vor household in the South Continent frontier town of her birth; perhaps because they'd treated her as the adult she aspired to be, rather than the child she had been. She'd felt, a bit guiltily, closer to them than to her real parent. For a while, any future had seemed possible.

Then she'd chosen Etienne Vorsoisson, or he had chosen her . . . *You were pleased enough at the time.* She'd said *Yes* to the marriage arrangements her father's Baba had offered, with all good will. *You didn't know. Tien didn't know. Vorzohn's Dystrophy. Nobody's fault.*

Nine-year-old Nikolai bounded into the kitchen. "I'm hungry, Mama. Can I have a piece of that cake?"

She intercepted fast-moving fingers attempting to sample frosting. "You can have a glass of fruit juice."

"Aw . . ." But he accepted the proffered substitute, cannily offered in one of the good wineglasses lined up waiting. He gulped it down, bobbing about as he drank. Excited, or was he picking up parental nerves? *Stop projecting,* she told herself. The boy had spent the last two hours in his room, tinkering intently with his models; he was due to shake out the knots.

"Do you remember Uncle Vorthys?" she asked him. "It's been three years since we visited him."

"Sure." He finished swallowing his snack. "He took me to his laboratory. I thought it would be beakers and bubbly things, but it was all big machines and concrete. Smelled funny, kind of dusty and sharp."

"From the welders and the ozone, that's right," she said, impressed with his recall. She rescued the glass. "Hold out your hand. I want to see how much you have left to grow. Puppies with big paws are supposed to grow up to be big dogs, you know." He held up his hand to hers, and they met, palm to palm. His fingers were within two centimeters of being as long as her own. "Oh, my."

He flashed her a self-conscious, satisfied grin, and stared briefly down at his feet, wriggling them in speculation. His right big toe poked through a new hole in his new sock.

His child-light hair was darkening; it might yet become as brown as hers. He was chest-high to her, though she could have sworn he had been only hip-high about fifteen minutes ago. His eyes were brown like his Da's. His grubby hand—where did he find so much dirt in this dome?—was as steady as his eyes were clear and guileless. *No tremula.*

The early symptoms of Vorzohn's Dystrophy were deceptive, mimicking half a dozen other diseases, and could strike any time from puberty to middle age. *But not today, not Nikolai.*

Not yet.

Sounds from the apartment's entryway, and low-pitched masculine voices, drew them out of her kitchen. Nikolai shot ahead of her. When she arrived behind him, he was already being half picked up by the stout, white-haired man who seemed to fill the space. "Oof!" He stopped short of swinging Nikolai around. "You've grown, Nikki!"

Uncle Vorthys hadn't changed, despite his awe-inspiring new title: same grand nose and big ears, same rumpled, oversized tunic and trousers that always looked slept-in, same deep laugh. He deposited his great-nephew on the flagstones, spared a hug for his niece, which was firmly returned, and bent and felt in his valise. "Something here for you, Nikki, I do believe . . ." Nikolai bounced around him; Ekaterin retreated temporarily to wait her turn.

Tien was shouldering through the door with baggage. Only then did she notice the man standing apart, smiling distantly, watching this homey scene.

She swallowed startlement. He was barely taller than nine-year-old Nikolai, but unmistakably not a child. He had a large head set on a short neck, and a faintly hunched stance; the rest of him looked lean but solid. He wore tunic and trousers in a subtle gray, the tunic open on a fine white shirt, and polished half-boots. His clothing was entirely without the pseudo-military ornamentation usually affected by the high Vor, but the perfection of the fit—it had to be hand-tailored, to fit that odd body—hinted a price Ekaterin didn't dare to estimate.

She was uncertain of his age; not much older than herself, perhaps? There was no gray in the dark hair, but laugh-lines around his eyes, and pain-lines around his mouth, scored his winter-pale skin. He moved stiffly, setting down his valise, wheeling to watch Nikolai monopolize his great-uncle, but did not otherwise appear very crippled. He was not a figure who blended in, but his air was notably unobtrusive. Socially uncomfortable? Ekaterin was recalled abruptly to her duties as a daughter of the Vor.

She advanced to him. "Welcome to my household . . ." ack, Tien hadn't mentioned his *name* " . . . my Lord Auditor."

He held out his hand and captured hers in a perfectly ordinary, businesslike grasp. "Miles Vorkosigan." His hand was dry and warm, smaller than her own, but bluntly masculine; clean nails. "And you, Madame?"

"Oh! Ekaterin Vorsoisson."

He released her hand without kissing it, to her relief. She stared briefly at the top of his head, level with her collarbone, realized he would be speaking to her cleavage, and stepped back a little. He looked up at her, still smiling slightly.

Nikolai was already dragging Uncle Vorthys's larger bag toward the guest room, proudly showing off his strength. Tien properly followed his senior guest. Ekaterin made a rapid recalculation. She couldn't possibly put this Vorkosigan fellow up in Nikolai's room; the child's bed would be such an embarrassingly good fit. Invite an Imperial Auditor to sleep on her living room couch? Hardly. She gestured him to follow her down the opposite hallway, into her planting-room-cum-office. One whole side was given over to a workbench and shelving, crammed with supplies; cascading lighting arrays climbing the corners nourished tender new plantings, in a riotous variety of Earth greens and Barrayaran red-browns. A large open area on the floor fronted a fine wide window.

"We haven't much space," she apologized. "I'm afraid even Barrayaran administrators here must accept what's assigned to them. I'll order in a grav-bed for you, I'm sure they'll have it delivered before dinner's over. But at least the room's private. My uncle snores so magnificently. . . . The bath's just down the hall to the right."

"It's fine," he assured her. He stepped to the window and stared out over the domed park. The lights in the encircling buildings gleamed warmly in the luminous twilight of the half-eclipsed mirror.

"I know it's not what you're used to."

One corner of his mouth twitched up. "I once slept for six

weeks on bare dirt. With ten thousand extremely grubby Marilacans, many of whom snored. I assure you, it's just fine."

She smiled in return, not at all certain what to make of this joke, if it was a joke. She left him to arrange his things as he saw fit, and scurried to call the rental company and finish setting up dinner.

They all rendezvoused, despite her best intentions for a more formal service, in her kitchen, where the little Auditor foiled her expectations again by only allowing her to pour him half a glass of wine. "I started today with seven hours in a pressure suit. I'd be asleep with my face in my plate before dessert." His gray eyes glinted.

She herded them all out to the table on the balcony and presented the mildly spicy stew based on vat-protein that she'd correctly guessed her uncle would like. By the time she handed round the bread and wine, she'd at last caught up enough to finally have a word with her uncle herself.

"What's happening now with your investigation? How long can you stay?"

"Not much more than what you've heard on the news, I'm afraid," he replied. "We can only take this downside break while the probable-cause crews finish collecting the pieces. We're still missing some fairly important ones. The freighter's tow was fully loaded, and had a tremendous mass. When the engines blew, bits of all sizes vectored off in every possible direction and speed. We desperately want any parts of its control systems we can find. They should have most of it retrieved in three more days, if we're lucky."

"So was it deliberate sabotage?" Tien asked.

Uncle Vorthys shrugged. "With the pilot dead, it's going to be very hard to prove. It might have been a suicide mission. The crews have found no sign yet of military or chemical explosives."

"Explosives would have been redundant," murmured Vorkosigan.

"The spinning freighter hit the mirror array at the worst possible angle, edge-on," Uncle Vorthys continued. "Half the damage was done by parts of the mirror itself. With that much momentum imparted to it by the assorted collisions, it just ripped itself apart."

"If all that result was planned, it had to have been a truly amazing calculation," Vorkosigan said dryly. "It's the one thing which inclines me to the belief it might have been a true accident."

Ekaterin watched her husband, watching the little Auditor

covertly, and read the silent disturbed judgment, *Mutant!* in his eyes. What was Tien going to make of the man, who openly bore, without apparent apology or even self-consciousness, such stigmata of abnormality?

Tien turned to Vorkosigan, his gaze curious. "I can see why Emperor Gregor dispatched the Professor, the Empire's foremost authority on failure analysis and all that. What's, um, your part in this, Lord Auditor Vorkosigan?"

Vorkosigan's smile twisted. "I have some experience with space installations." He leaned back, and jerked up his chin, and smoothed the odd flash of irony from his face. "In fact, as far as the probable-cause investigation goes, I'm merely along for the ride. This is the first really interesting problem to come along since I took oath as an Auditor three months ago. I wanted to watch how it was done. With his Komarran marriage coming up, Gregor is vitally interested in any possible political repercussions from this accident. Now would be a very awkward time for a serious downturn in Barrayar–Komarr relations. But whether accident or sabotage, the damage to the mirror impinges quite directly on the Terraforming Project. I understand your Serifosa Sector is fairly representative?"

"Indeed. I'll take you both on a tour tomorrow," Tien promised. "I'm having a full technical report prepared for you by my Komarran assistants, with all the numbers. But the most important number is still pure speculation. How fast is the mirror going to be repaired?"

Vorkosigan grimaced and held out a small hand, palm-up. "How fast depends in part on how much money the Imperium is willing to spend. And that's where things become very political indeed. With parts of Barrayar itself still undergoing active terraforming, and with the planet of Sergyar drawing off immigrants from both the worlds damned near as fast as they can board ship, some members of the government are wondering openly why we are spending so much Imperial treasure dinking with such a marginal world as Komarr."

Ekaterin could not tell from his measured tone whether he agreed with those members or not. Startled, she said, "The terraforming of Komarr was going on for three centuries before we conquered it. We can hardly stop *now*."

"So are we throwing good money after bad?" Vorkosigan shrugged, declining to answer his own question. "There's a second layer of thinking, a purely military one. Restricting the population to the domes makes Komarr more militarily vulnerable. Why give the citizenry of a conquered world extra territory in which to fall back and regroup? This line of thought makes the interesting assumption that three hundred or so years from *now*, when the terraforming is at last complete, the populations of Komarr and Barrayar will still not have assimilated each other. If they did, then they would be *our* domes, and we certainly wouldn't want them to be vulnerable, eh?"

He paused for a bite of bread and stew, washed down by wine, then went on, "Since assimilation is Gregor's avowed policy, and he's putting his Imperial person where his policy is . . . the question of motivation for sabotage becomes, er, complex. Could the saboteurs have been isolationist Barrayarans? Komarran extremists? Either, hoping to publicly throw the blame on the other? How emotionally attached is the average Komarran-in-the-dome to a goal whom none now living will ever survive to see realized, or would they rather save the money today? Sabotage versus accident makes no engineering difference, but does make a profound political one." He and Uncle Vorthys exchanged a wry look.

"So I watch, and listen, and wait," Vorkosigan concluded. He turned to Tien. "And how do you like Komarr, Administrator Vorsoisson?"

Tien grinned, and shrugged. "It's all right except for the Komarrans. I've found them a damned touchy bunch."

Vorkosigan's brows twitched up. "Have they no sense of humor?"

Ekaterin glanced up warily, wincing at that dry edge in his drawling voice, but apparently it slipped past Tien, who only snorted. "They're divided about equally between the greedy and the surly. Cheating Barrayarans is considered a patriotic duty."

Vorkosigan raised his empty wineglass to Ekaterin. "And you, Madame Vorsoisson?"

She refilled it to the top before he could stop her, cautious of her reply. If her uncle was the technical expert in this Auditorial duo, did that leave Vorkosigan as the . . . political one? Who was really the senior member of the team? Had Tien caught any of the subtle flashing implications in the little lord's speech? "It hasn't been easy to make Komarran friends. Nikolai goes to a Barrayaran school. And I have no work as such."

"A Vor lady hardly needs to work." Tien smiled.

"Nor a Vor lord," added Vorkosigan, almost under his breath, "yet here we are . . ."

"That depends on your ability to choose the right parents," said Tien, a touch sourly. He glanced across at Vorkosigan.

"Relieve my curiosity. *Are* you related to the former Lord Regent?"

"My father," Vorkosigan replied, with quelling brevity. He did not smile.

"Then you are *the* Lord Vorkosigan, the Count's heir."

"That follows, yes."

Vorkosigan was getting unnervingly dry, now. Ekaterin blurted, "Your upbringing must have been terribly difficult."

"He managed," Vorkosigan murmured.

"I meant for you!"

"Ah." His brief smile returned, and flicked out again.

The conversation was going dreadfully awry, Ekaterin could feel it; she hardly dared open her mouth on an attempt to redirect it. Tien stepped in, or stepped in it: "Was your father the great Admiral reconciled that you couldn't have a military career?"

"My grandfather the great General was more set on it."

"I was a ten-years man myself, the usual. In Administration, very dull. Trust me, you didn't miss much." Tien waved a kindly, dismissive hand. "But not every Vor has to be a soldier these days, eh, Professor Vorthys? You're living proof."

"I believe Captain Vorkosigan served, um, thirteen years, was it, Miles? In Imperial Security. Galactic operations. Did you find it dull?"

Vorkosigan's smile upon the Professor grew genuine, for an instant of time. "Not nearly dull enough." He jerked up his chin, evidently a habitual nervous tic. For the first time Ekaterin noticed the fine white scars on either side of his short neck.

Ekaterin fled to the kitchen, to serve the dessert and give the blighted conversation time to recover. When she came out again, things had eased, or at least, Nikolai had stopped being so supernaturally good, i.e., quiet, and had struck up a negotiation with his great-uncle for after-dinner attention in the form of a round of his current favorite game. This carried them through till the rental company arrived at the front door with the grav-bed, and the great engineer went off with the whole male mob to oversee its installation. Ekaterin turned gratefully to the soothing routine of cleaning up.

Tien returned to report success and the Vor lord suitably settled.

"Tien, were you watching that fellow closely?" asked Ekaterin. "A mutie, a mutie *Vor*, yet he carried on as if nothing were the least out of the ordinary. If he can . . ." she trailed off hopefully, leaving the *surely you can* for Tien to conclude.

Tien frowned. "Don't start that again. It's obvious he doesn't think the rules apply to him. He's Aral Vorkosigan's *son*, for God's sake. Practically the Emperor's foster brother. No wonder he got this cushy Imperial appointment."

"I don't think so, Tien. Were you listening to him at all?" *All those undercurrents* . . . "I think . . . I think he's the Emperor's hatchet man, sent to judge the whole Terraforming Project. Powerful . . . maybe dangerous."

Tien shook his head. "His father was powerful and dangerous. He's just privileged. Damned high Vor twit. Don't worry about him. Your uncle will take him away soon enough."

"I'm not worried about *him*."

Tien's face darkened. "I'm getting so tired of this! You argue with everything I say, you practically insult my intelligence in front of your so-noble relative—"

"I didn't!" *Did I?* She began a confused mental review of her evening's remarks. What in the world had she said, to set him on edge like this—

"Just because you're the great Auditor's niece doesn't make *you* anybody, girl! This is disloyalty, that's what it is."

"No—no, I'm sorry—"

But he was already stalking out. There would be a cold silence between them tonight. She almost ran after him, to beg his forgiveness. He was under a lot of pressure at work, it was very ill-timed of her to push for a resolution to his medical dilemma now. . . . But she was abruptly too weary to try anymore. She finished putting away the last of the food, and took the leftover half bottle of wine and a glass out onto the balcony. She turned off the cheery colored plant lights and just sat in the dim reflected illumination from the sealed Komarran city. The crippled star-flake of the insolation mirror had almost reached the western horizon, following the true-sun into night as the planet turned.

A white shape moved silently in the kitchen, briefly startling her. But it was only the mutie lord, who had shed his elegant gray tunic and, apparently, his boots. He stuck his head through the unsealed doors. "Hello?"

"Hello, Lord Vorkosigan. I'm just out here watching the mirror set. Would you, um, care for some more wine . . . ? Here, I'll get you a glass—"

"No, don't get up, Madame Vorsoisson. I'll fetch it." His pale smile winked out of the shadows at her. A few muted clinks came from within, then he trod silently onto the balcony. She poured, good hostess, generously into the glass he set beside her own, then he took it up again and went to the railing to study what could be seen of the sky past the girders of the dome.

"It's the best aspect of this location," she said. "This bit of western view." The mirror-array was magnified by the atmosphere close to the horizon, but its normal evening color-effects in the wispy clouds were dimmed by its damage. "Mirror-set's usually much prettier than this." She sipped her wine, cool and sweet on her tongue, and felt herself finally starting to become a little furry in the brain. Furry was good. Soothing.

"I can see that it must be," he agreed, still staring out. He drank deeply. Had he switched, then, from resisting sleep through alcohol to pursuing it?

"This horizon is so crowded and cluttered, compared to home. I'm afraid I find these sealed arcologies a touch claustrophobic."

"And where is home, for you?" He turned to watch her.

"South Continent. Vandeville."

"So you grew up around terraforming."

"The Komarrans would say, that wasn't terraforming, that was just *soil conditioning*." He chuckled along with her, at her deadpan rendition of Komarran techno-snobbery. She continued, "They're right, of course. It wasn't as though we had to start by spending half a millennium altering an entire planet's atmosphere. The only thing that made it hard for us, back in the Time of Isolation, was trying to do it with practically no technology. Still . . . I loved the open spaces at home. I miss that wide sky, horizon to horizon."

"That's true in any city, domed or not. So you're a country girl?"

"In part. Though I liked Vorbarr Sultana when I was at university. It had other kinds of horizons."

"Did you study botany? I noticed the library rack on the wall of your plant room. Impressive."

"No. It's just a hobby."

"Oh? I could have mistaken it for a passion. Or a profession."

"No. I didn't know what I wanted, then."

"Do you know now?"

She laughed a little, uneasily. When she didn't answer, he merely smiled, and strolled along the balcony examining her plantings. He stopped before the skellytum, squatting in its pot like some bright red alien Buddha, tendrils raised in a pose of placid supplication. "I have to ask," he said plaintively, "what *is* this thing?"

"It's a bonsai'd skellytum."

"Really! *That's* a—I didn't know you could do that to a skellytum. They're usually five meters tall. And a really ugly brown."

"I had a great aunt, on my father's side, who loved gardening. I used to help her when I was a girl. She was very much a crusty old frontier woman, *very* Vor—she'd come to the South Continent right after the Cetagandan War. Survived a succession of husbands, survived . . . well, everything. I inherited the skellytum from her. It's the only plant I brought to Komarr from Barrayar. It's over seventy years old."

"Good God."

"It's the complete tree, fully functional."

"And—ha!—short."

She was afraid for a moment that she'd inadvertently offended him, but apparently not. He finished his inspection, and returned to the railing, and his wine. He stared out again at the western horizon, and the sinking mirror, his brows lowering.

He had a presence which, by ignoring his elusive physical peculiarities himself, defied the observer to dare comment. But the little lord had had all his life to adjust to his condition. Not like the hideous surprise Tien had found among his late brother's papers, and subsequently confirmed for himself and Nikolai through carefully secret testing. *You can get tested anonymously*, she had argued. *But I can't get treated anonymously*, he had countered.

Since coming to Komarr, she'd been so close to defying custom, law, and her lord-and-husband's orders, and unilaterally taking his son and heir for treatment. Would the Komarran doctors know a Vor mother was not her son's legal guardian? Maybe she could pretend the genetic defect had come from her, not from Tien? But the geneticists, if they were any good, would surely figure out the truth.

After a while, she said elliptically, "A Vor man's first loyalty is supposed to be to his Emperor, but a Vor woman's first loyalty is supposed to be to her husband."

"Historically and legally, that's so." His voice was amused, or bemused, as he turned again to watch her. "This was not always to her disadvantage. When he was executed for treason, she was presumed to be only following orders, and got off. Actually, I wonder if the underlying practical reason was that an underpopulated world just couldn't spare her labor."

"Haven't you ever found that oddly asymmetrical?"

"But simpler for her. Most women usually only had one husband at a time, but the Vor were all too frequently presented with a choice of emperors, and where was your loyalty then? Bad guesses could be lethal. Though when my grandfather General Piotr—and his army—abandoned Mad Emperor Yuri for Emperor Ezar, it was lethal for Yuri. Good for Barrayar, though."

She sipped again. From where she sat, he was silhouetted against the darkening dome, shadowed, enigmatic. "Indeed. Is your passion politics, then?"

"God, no! I don't think so."

"History?"

"Only in passing." He hesitated. "It used to be the military."

"Used to be?"

"Used to be," he repeated firmly.

"And now?"

It was his turn to not answer. He stared down at his glass, tilting it to make the last of the wine swirl about. He finally said, "In Barrayaran political theory, it all connects. The ordinary subjects are loyal to their Counts, the Counts are loyal to the Emperor, and the Emperor, presumably, is loyal to the whole Imperium, the body of the Empire in the form of all its, er, bodies. Here I find it grows a trifle abstract for my taste; how can he be answerable to all, yet not answerable to each? And so we arrive back at square one." He drained his glass. "How do we be true to one another?"

I don't know anymore. . . .

Silence fell, as they both watched the last glint of mirror slip behind the hills. A pale glow in the sky still haloed its passing for a minute or two longer.

"Well. I'm afraid I'm getting rather drunk." He did not seem that drunk to her, but he rolled his glass between his hands and pushed off from the balcony rail against which he'd been leaning. "Goodnight, Madame Vorsoisson."

"Goodnight, Lord Vorkosigan. Sleep well."

He carried his glass in with him and vanished into the darkened apartment.

CHAPTER TWO

Miles floundered from a dream of his hostess's hair which, if not exactly erotic, was embarrassingly sensual. Unbound from the severe style she'd favored yesterday, it had revealed itself a rich dark brown with amber highlights, a mass of silk flowing coolly through his stubby hands—he presumed they were his hands, it had been his dream, after all. *I woke up too soon. Rats.* At least the vision had not been tinged with any of the gory grotesqueries of his occasional nightmares, from which he came awake cold and damp, with heart racing. He was warm and comfortable, in the silly elaborate gravbed she had insisted on producing for him.

It wasn't Madame Vorsoisson's fault that she happened to belong to a certain physical type that set off old resonances in Miles's memory. Some men harbored obsessions about much stranger things . . . his own fixation, he had long ago ruefully recognized, was on long cool brunettes with expressions of quiet reserve and warm alto voices. True, on a world where people altered their faces and bodies almost as casually as they altered their wardrobes, there was nothing in the least unusual about her beauty. Till one remembered she wasn't from here, and realized her ivory-skinned features were almost certainly untouched by modification. . . . Had she recognized his idiot-babble, last night on her balcony, as suppressed sexual panic? Had that odd remark about a Vor woman's duties been an oblique warning to him to back off? But he hadn't been *on*, he didn't think. Was he that transparent?

Miles had realized within five minutes of his arrival that he should probably not have let the genial and expansive Vorthys bully him into accompanying him downside, but the man seemed constitutionally incapable of not sharing a treat. That the pleasures of this family reunion might not be equally enjoyed by an awkward outsider—or the family into which he'd been thrust—had clearly never occurred to the Professor.

Miles sighed envy of his host. Administrator Vorsoisson seemed to have achieved a perfect little Vor clan. Of course, he'd had the wit to start a decade ago. The arrival of galactic sex-selection technologies had resulted in a shortage of female births on Barrayar. This dearth of women had reached its lowest ebb in Miles's generation, though parents seemed to be coming back to their senses now. Still, every Vor woman Miles knew close to his own age was already married, and had been for years. Was he going to have to wait another twenty years for his own bride?

If necessary. No lusting after married women, boy. You're an Imperial Auditor now. The nine Imperial Auditors were expected to be models of rectitude and respectability. He could not recall ever hearing of any kind of sex scandal touching one of Emperor Gregor's handpicked agent-observers. *Of course not. All the rest of the Auditors are eighty years old and have been married for fifty of 'em.* He snorted. Besides, she probably thought he was a mutant, though thankfully she'd been too polite to say so. To his face.

So find out if she has a sister, eh?

He wallowed out of the grav-bed's indolence-inducing clutches and sat up, forcing his mind to switch gears. At a conservative guess, a couple hundred thousand words of new data on the soletta accident and its consequences would be incoming this shift. He would, he decided, start with a cold shower.

No comfortable ship-knits today. After selecting among the three new formal civilian suits he'd packed along from Barrayar—in shades of gray, gray, and gray—Miles combed his damp hair neatly and sauntered out to Madame Vorsoisson's kitchen, from which voices and the perfume of coffee wafted. There he found Nikolai munching Barrayaran-style groats and milk, Administrator Vorsoisson fully dressed and apparently on the verge of leaving, and Professor Vorthys, still in pajamas, sorting through a new array of data disks and frowning. A glass of pink fruit juice sat untasted at his elbow. He looked up and said, "Ah, good morning, Miles. Glad you're up," seconded by Vorsoisson's polite, "Good morning, Lord Vorkosigan. I trust you slept well?"

"Fine, thanks. What's up, Professor?"

"Your comm link arrived from ImpSec's local office." Vorthys pointed to the device beside his plate. "I notice they didn't send *me* one."

Miles grimaced. "Your father was not so famous in the Komarran conquest."

"True," agreed Vorthys. "The old gentleman fell in that odd generation between the wars, too young to fight the Cetagandans, too old to aggress on the poor Komarrans. This lack of military opportunity was a source of great personal regret to him, we children were given to understand."

Miles strapped the comm link onto his left wrist. It represented a compromise between himself and ImpSec Serifosa, which would otherwise be responsible for his health here. ImpSec had wanted to err on the side of caution and surround him with an inconvenient mob of bodyguards. Miles had ventured to test his Imperial Auditor's authority by ordering them to stay out of his hair; to his delight, it had worked. But the link gave him a straight line to ImpSec, and tracked his location—he tried not to feel like an experimental animal released into the wild. "And what are those?" He nodded to the data disks.

Vorthys spread the disks like a bad hand of cards. "The morning courier also brought us recordings of last night's haul of new bits. And something especially for you, since you kindly volunteered to take over the review of the medical end of things. A new preliminary autopsy."

"They finally found the pilot?" Miles relieved him of the disks.

Vorthys grimaced. "Parts of her."

Madame Vorsoisson entered from the balcony in time to hear this. "Oh, dear." She was dressed as yesterday in Komarran-style street wear in dull earthy tones: loose trousers, blouse, and long vest, muffling whatever figure she possessed. She would have been brilliant in red, or breathtaking in pale blue, with those blue eyes . . . her hair this morning was soberly tied back again, rather to Miles's relief. It would have been unnerving to think he was developing some form of precognition as a result of his late injuries, along with his damned seizures.

Miles nodded good morning to her and carefully returned his attention to Vorthys. "I must have been sleeping well. I didn't hear the courier come in. You've reviewed them already?"

"Just a glance."

"What parts of the pilot did they find?" asked Nikolai, interested.

"Never you mind, young man," said his great-uncle firmly.

"Thank you," murmured Madame Vorsoisson to him.

"That makes the last body, though. Good," said Miles. "It's so distressing for the relatives when they lose one altogether. When I was—" He cut off the rest, *When I was a covert ops fleet commander, we'd move the heavens to try and get the bodies of our casualties back to their people.* That chapter of his life was closed, now.

Madame Vorsoisson, splendid woman, handed him black coffee. She then inquired what her guests would like for breakfast; Miles maneuvered Vorthys into answering first, and volunteered for groats along with him. As she bustled around serving, and mopping up after Nikolai, Administrator Vorsoisson said, "My department's presentation will be ready for you this afternoon, Auditor Vorthys. This morning Ekaterin wondered if you would like to see Nikolai's school. And after the presentation, perhaps there will be time for a flyover of some of our projects."

"Sounds like a fine itinerary." Professor Vorthys smiled at Nikolai. In all the hustle of their hurried departure from Barrayar, he—or perhaps the Professora—had not forgotten a gift for his great-nephew. *I should have brought something for the kid,* Miles decided belatedly. *Surest way to please a mother.* "Ah, Miles . . .?"

Miles tapped the stack of data disks beside his bowl. "I suspect I'll have enough to occupy myself here this morning. Madame Vorsoisson, I noticed a comconsole in your workroom; may I use it?"

"Certainly, Lord Vorkosigan."

With a polite murmur about getting things in order for them at his department, Vorsoisson took his leave, and the breakfast party broke up shortly thereafter, each to their assorted destinations. Miles, new disks in hand, returned to Madame Vorsoisson's workroom/guest room.

He paused before seating himself at her comconsole, to stare out the sealed window at the park, and the transparent dome arcing over it to let in the free solar energy. Komarr's wan sun was not directly visible, risen to the east behind this apartment block, but the line of its morning light crept across the far edge of the park. The damaged insolation mirror, following it, had not yet risen over the horizon to double the shadows it cast.

So does this mean seven thousand years bad luck?

He sighed, darkened the window's polarization—scarcely necessary—seated himself at the comconsole, and began feeding it data disks. A couple of dozen good-sized new pieces of wreckage had been retrieved overnight; he ran the vids of them turning in space as the salvage ships approached. Theory was, if you could find every fragment, take precise recordings of all their spins and trajectories, and then run them backward, you could end up with a computer-generated picture of the very moment of the disaster, and so diagnose its cause. Real life never worked out quite that neatly, alas, but every little bit helped. ImpSec Komarr was still canvassing the orbital transfer stations for any casual vid-carrying tourists who might have been panning that section of space at the time of the whatever-and-collision. Futilely by now, Miles feared; usually, such people came forward immediately, excited and wanting to be helpful.

Vorthys and the probable-cause crew were now of the opinion that the ore tow had already been in more than one piece at the moment it had struck the mirror, a speculation which had not yet been released to the general public. So had the evidence-destroying explosion of the engines been cause or consequence of that catastrophe? And at what point had those tortured fragments of metal and plastic acquired some of their more interesting distortions?

Miles reran, for the twentieth time that week, the computer's track of the freighter's course prior to the collision, and contemplated its anomalies. The ship had carried only its pilot, on a routine—indeed, dead boring—slow run in from the asteroid mining belt to an orbital refinery. The engines had not been supposed to be thrusting at the time of the accident; acceleration had been completed and deceleration was not yet due to begin. The tow ship had been running about five hours ahead of schedule, but only because it had departed early, not because it had boosted hotter than usual. It had been coasting off-course by about six percent, within normal parameters and not yet ready for course correction, though the pilot might have been amusing herself trying to achieve more precision with some unscheduled microboosting. Even with the minor course correction due, the tow ship's route had been several hundred comfortable kilometers from the soletta array, in fact farther away than if it had been precisely on course.

What the course variation *had* done was take the freighter's track almost directly across one of Komarr's unused wormhole jump points. Komarr local space was unusually rich in active jump points, a fact of strategic and historic consequence; one of the jumps was Barrayar's only gateway to the wormhole

nexus. It was for control of the jump points, not for possession of the chilly planet, that Barrayar's invasion fleet had
poured through here thirty-five years ago. As long as the
Imperium's military held that high ground, its interest in
Komarr's downside population and their problems was, at best,
mild.

This jump point, however, supported neither traffic nor trade
nor strategic threat. Explorations through it had dead-ended
either in deep interstellar space, or close to stars that did not
support either habitable planets or economically recoverable
system resources. Nobody jumped out through there; nobody
should have jumped in through there. The immediate vision
of some unmotivated pirate-villain popping out of the wormhole, potting the innocent ore freighter—by some weapon that
left no traces, mind you—and popping back in again was
currently unsupported by any evidence whatsoever, though the
area had been scoured for it. It was the news media's current favorite scenario. But none of the five-space trails generated by ships taking wormhole jumps had been detected,
either.

The five-space anomaly of the jump point was not even
observable by ordinary means from three-space; it should not,
just sitting there, have affected the freighter in any way even
if the ship had passed directly across its central vortex. The
freighter was a dedicated inner-system ship, and lacked Necklin
rods and jump capacity. Still . . . the jump point was there.
Nothing else was.

Miles rubbed his neck and turned to the new autopsy report.
Gruesome, as always. The pilot had been a Komarran woman
in her mid-fifties. Call it Barrayaran sexism, but female corpses
always bothered Miles more. Death was such a malicious
destroyer of dignity. Had he looked that disordered and exposed
when he'd gone down to the sniper's fire? The pilot's body
showed the usual progression: smashed, decompressed, irra-
diated, and frozen, all quite typical of deep-space impact
accidents. One arm torn off, somewhere in the initial crunch
rather than later, judging from the close-up vids of the freezing-
effects of liquids lost at the stump. It had been a quick death,
anyway. Miles knew better than to add, *Almost painless.* No
traces of illicit drugs or alcohol had been found in her frozen tissues.

The Komarran medical examiner, along with his six final
reports, included a message wanting to know if he had Miles's
permission to release the bodies of the six members of the
mirror's station-keeping crew back to their waiting families.

Good God, hadn't that been done yet? As an Imperial Auditor, he wasn't supposed to be running this investigation, just observing and reporting on it. He did not desire his mere presence to freeze anyone's initiative. He fired off the permission immediately, right from Madame Vorsoisson's comconsole.

He started working his way through the six reports. They were more detailed than the prelims he'd already seen, but contained no surprises. By this time, he wanted a surprise, something, anything beyond *Spaceship blows up for no reason, kills seven.* Not to mention the astronomical property damage bill. With three reports assimilated, and his bland breakfast becoming a regret in his stomach, he backed out for a short period of mental recovery.

Idly, while waiting for the queasiness to pass, he sorted through Madame Vorsoisson's data files. The one titled *Virtual Gardens* sounded pleasant. Perhaps she wouldn't mind if he took a virtual stroll through them. *The Water Garden* enticed him. He called it up on the holovid plate before him.

It was, as he had guessed, a landscape design program. One could view it from any distance or angle, from a miniature-looking total overview to a blown-up detailed inspection of a particular planting; one could program a stroll through its paths at any given eye level. He chose his own, at ahem-mumble-something under five feet. The individual plants grew according to realistic programs taking into account light, water, gravitation, trace nutrients, and even attacks by programmed pests. This garden was about a third filled, with tentative arrangements of grasses, violets, sedges, water lilies, and horsetails; it was currently suffering an outbreak of algae. The colors and shapes stopped abruptly at the unfinished edges, as if an invasion from some alien gray geometric universe were gobbling it all up.

His curiosity piqued, in best approved ImpSec style he dropped to the program's underlayer and checked for activity levels. The busiest recently, he discovered, was one labeled *The Barrayaran Garden.* He popped back up to the display level, selected his own eye-height again, and entered it.

It was not a garden of pretty Earth-plants set on some suitably famous site on Barrayar; it was a garden made up entirely and exclusively of native species, something he would not have guessed possible, let alone lovely. He'd always considered their uniform red-brown hues and stubby forms boring at best. The only Barrayaran vegetation he could identify and name offhand was that to which he was violently allergic. But Madame Vorsoisson had somehow used shape and texture to create a sepia-toned serenity. Rocks and running water framed the various plants—there was a low carmine mass of love-lies-itching, forming a border for a billowing blond stand of razor-grass, which, he had once been assured, botanically was not a grass. Nobody argued about the razor part, he'd noticed. Judging from the common names, the lost Barrayaran colonists had not loved their new xenobotany: damnweed, henbloat, goatbane . . . *It's beautiful. How did she make it beautiful?* He'd never seen anything like it. Maybe that kind of artist's eye was something you just had to be born with, like perfect pitch, which he also lacked.

In the Imperial capital of Vorbarr Sultana, there was a small and dull green park at the end of the block beside Vorkosigan House, on a site where another old mansion had been torn down. The little park had been leveled with more of an eye to security concerns for the neighboring Lord Regent than any aesthetic plan. Would it not be splendid, to replace it with a larger version of this glorious subtlety, and give the city-dwellers a taste of their own planetary heritage? Even if it would—he checked—take fifteen years to grow to this mature climax. . . .

The virtual garden program was supposed to help prevent time-consuming and costly design mistakes. But when all the garden you could have was what you could pack in your luggage, he supposed it could be a hobby in its own right. It was certainly neater, tidier, and easier than the real thing. So . . . why did he guess she found it approximately as satisfying as looking at a holovid of dinner instead of eating it?

Or maybe she's just homesick. Regretfully, he closed down the display.

In pure trained habit, he next called up her financial program, for a little quick analysis. It turned out to be her household account. She ran her home on a quite tight budget, given what Administrator Vorsoisson's salary ought to be, Miles thought; her biweekly allowance was rather stingy. She didn't spend nearly as much on her botanical hobbies as the results suggested she must. Other hobbies, other vices? The money trail was always the most revealing of people's true pursuits; ImpSec hired the Imperium's best accountants to find ingenious ways to hide their own activities, for that very reason. She spent damn little on clothes, except for Nikolai's. He'd heard parents of his acquaintance complain about the cost of dressing their children, but surely this was extraordinary . . . wait, that wasn't a clothing expenditure. Funds squeezed here, here, and there were all being funneled into a dedicated little private account labeled "Nikolai's Medical."

Why? As dependents of a Barrayaran bureaucrat on Komarr, weren't the Vorsoissons' medical expenses covered by the Imperium?

He called up the account. A year's worth of savings from her household budget did not make a very impressive pile, but the pattern of contributions was steady to the point of being compulsive. Puzzled, he backed out again and called up the whole program list. Clues?

One file, down at the end of the list, had no name. He called it up immediately. It turned out to be the only thing on her comconsole which required a password for entry. Interesting.

Her comconsole program was the simplest and cheapest commercial type. ImpSec cadets dissected files like this as a class warmup exercise. A touch of homesickness of his own twinged through him. He dropped to the underlayer and had its password choked out in about five minutes. *Vorzohn's Dystrophy?* Well, *that* wasn't a mnemonic he would have guessed offhand.

His reflexes overtook his growing unease. He had the file open simultaneously with belated second thoughts, *You're not in ImpSec anymore, you know. Should you be doing this?*

The file proved to contain a medical course's worth of articles, culled from every imaginable Barrayaran and galactic source, on the topic of one of Barrayar's rarer and more obscure home-grown genetic disorders. Vorzohn's Dystrophy had arisen during the Time of Isolation, principally, as its name suggested, among the Vor caste, but had not been medically identified as a mutation until the return of galactic medicine. For one thing, it lacked the sort of exterior markers that would have caused, well, *him* for example, to have had his throat cut at birth. It was an adult-onset disease, beginning with a bewildering variety of physical debilitations and ending with mental collapse and death. In the harsher world of Barrayar's past, carriers frequently met their deaths from other causes after bearing or engendering children, but before the syndrome manifested itself. Enough madness ran in enough families— *including some of my dear Vorrutyer ancestors*—from other causes that late onset was frequently identified as something else anyway. Thoroughly nasty.

But it's treatable now, isn't it?

Yes, albeit expensively; that went with the rare part, no economies of scale. Miles scanned rapidly down the articles. Symptoms were manageable with a variety of costly biochemical concoctions to flush out and replace the distorted molecules; retrogenetic true cures were available at a higher price. Well, almost true cures: any progeny would still have to be screened for it, preferably at the time of fertilization and before being popped into the uterine replicator for gestation.

Hadn't young Nikolai been gestated in a uterine replicator? Good God, Vorsoisson surely hadn't insisted his wife—and child—go through the dangers of old-fashioned body-gestation, had he? Only a few of the most conservative Old Vor families still held out for the old ways, a custom upon which Miles's own mother had vented the most violently acerbic criticism he'd ever heard from her lips. *And she should know.*

So what the hell is going on here? He sat back, mouth tight. If, as the files suggested, Nikolai was known or suspected to carry Vorzohn's Dystrophy, one or both of his parents must also. How long had they known?

He suddenly realized what he should have noticed before, in the initial illusion of smug marital bliss which Vorsoisson managed to project. That was always the hardest part, seeing the absent pieces. About three more children were missing, that was what. Some little sisters for Nikolai, please, folks? But no. *So they've known at least since shortly after their son was born.* What a personal nightmare. *But is he the carrier, or is she?* He hoped it wasn't Madame Vorsoisson; horrible to think of that serene beauty crumbling under the onslaught of such internal disruption. . . .

I don't want to know all this.

His idle curiosity was justly punished. This idiot snooping was surely not proper behavior for an Imperial Auditor, however much it had been inculcated in an ImpSec covert ops agent. Former agent. Where was all that shiny new Auditor's probity now? He might as well have been sniffing in her underwear drawer. *I can't leave you alone for a damn minute, can I, boy?*

He'd chafed for years under military regulations, till he'd come to a job with no written regs at all. His sense of having died and gone to heaven had lasted about five minutes. An Imperial Auditor was the Emperor's Voice, his eyes and ears and sometimes hands, a lovely job description till you stopped to wonder just what the hell that poetic metaphor was supposed to *mean.*

So was it a useful test to ask himself, *Can I imagine Gregor doing this or that thing?* Gregor's apparent Imperial sternness hid an almost painful personal shyness. The mind boggled. All right, should the question instead be, *Could I imagine Gregor in his office as Emperor doing this?* Just what acts, wrong for a private individual, were yet lawful for an Imperial Auditor carrying out his duties? Lots, according to the precedents he'd been reading. So was the real rule, "Ad lib till you make a mistake, and then we'll destroy you"? Miles wasn't sure he liked that one at all.

And even in his ImpSec days, slicing through someone's private files had been a treatment reserved for enemies, or at least suspects. Well, and prospective recruits. And neutrals in whose territory you expected to be operating. And . . . and . . . he snorted self-derision. Gregor at least had better manners than ImpSec.

Thoroughly embarrassed, he closed the files, erased all tracks of his entry, and called up the next autopsy report. He studied what telltales he could glean from the bodily fragmentation. Death had a temperature, and it was damned cold. He paused to turn up the workroom's thermostat a few degrees before continuing.

CHAPTER THREE

Ekaterin hadn't realized how much a visit from an Imperial Auditor would fluster the staff of Nikolai's school. But the Professor, a long-time educator himself, quickly made them understand this wasn't an official inspection, and produced all the right phrases to put them at their ease. Still, she and Uncle Vorthys didn't linger as long as Tien had suggested to her.

To burn a bit more time, she took him on a short tour of Serifosa Dome's best spots: the prettiest gardens, the highest observation platforms, looking out across the sere Komarran landscape beyond the sealed urban sprawl. Serifosa was the capital of this planetary Sector—she still had to make an effort not to think of it as a Barrayaran-style District. Barrayaran District boundaries were more organic, higgly-piggly territories following rivers, mountain ranges, and ragged lines where Counts' armies had lost historic battles. Komarran Sectors were neat geometric slices equitably dividing the globe. Though the so-called domes, really thousands of interconnected structures of all shapes, had lost their early geometries centuries ago, as they were built outward in random and unmatching spurts of architectural improvement.

Somewhat belatedly, she realized she ought to be dragging the engineer emeritus through the deepest utility tunnels, and the power and atmosphere cycling plants. But by then it was time for lunch. Her guided tour fetched up near her favorite restaurant, pseudo-outdoors with tables spilling out into a landscaped park under the glassed-in sky. The damaged soletta-array was now visible, creeping along the ecliptic, veiled today by thin high clouds as if ashamedly hiding its deformations.

The enormous power of the Emperor's Voice conferred upon an Auditor hadn't changed her uncle much, Ekaterin was pleased to note; he still retained his enthusiasm for splendid desserts, and, under her guidance, constructed his menu choices from the sweets course backwards. She couldn't quite say "hadn't changed him at all"; he seemed to have acquired more social caution, pausing for more than just technical calculations before he spoke. But it wasn't as if he could entirely ignore other people's new and exaggerated reactions to him.

They put in their orders, and she followed her uncle's gaze upward as he briefly studied the soletta from this angle. She said, "There's not really a danger of the Imperium abandoning the soletta project, is there? We'll have to at least repair it. I mean . . . it looks so unbalanced like that."

"In fact, it is unbalanced at present. Solar wind. They'll have to do something about that shortly," he replied. "*I* should certainly not like to see it abandoned. It was the greatest engineering achievement of the Komarrans' colonial ancestors, apart from the domes themselves. People at their best. If it was sabotage . . . well, that was certainly people at their worst. Vandalism, just senseless vandalism."

An artist describing the defacement of some great historic painting could hardly have been more vehement. Ekaterin said, "I've heard older Komarrans talk about how they felt when Admiral Vorkosigan's invasion forces took over the mirror, practically the first thing. I can't think that it had much tactical value, at the high speed at which the space battles went, but it certainly had a huge psychological impact. It was almost as if we had captured their sun itself. I think returning it to Komarran civilian control in the last few years was a very good political move. I hope this doesn't mess that up."

"It's hard to say." That new caution, again.

"There was talk of opening its observation platform to tourism again. Though now I imagine they're relieved they hadn't yet."

"They still have plenty of VIP tours. I took one myself, when I was here several years ago teaching a short course at Solstice University. Fortunately, there were no visitors aboard on the day of the collision. But it should be open to the public, to be seen and to educate. Do it up right, with maybe a museum on-site explaining how it was first built. It's a great work. Odd to think that its principal practical use is to make swamps."

"Swamps make breathable air. Eventually." She smiled. In

her uncle's mind the pure engineering aesthetic clearly over-shadowed the messy biological end view.

"Next you'll be defending the rats. There really are rats here, I understand?"

"Oh, yes, the dome tunnels have rats. And hamsters, and gerbils. All the children capture them for pets, which is likely where they came from in the first place, come to think of it. I do think the black-and-white rats are cute. The animal-control exterminators have to work in dead secret from their younger relatives. And we have roaches, of course, who doesn't? And—over in Equinox—wild cockatoos. A couple of pairs of them escaped, or were let loose, several decades ago. They now have these big rainbow-colored birds all over the place, and people *will* feed them. The sanitation crews wanted to get rid of them, but the Dome shareholders voted them down."

The waitress delivered their salads and iced tea, and there was a short break in the conversation while her uncle appre-ciated the fresh spinach, mangoes and onions, and candied pecans. She'd guessed the candied pecans would please him. The market-garden hydroponics production in Serifosa was among Komarr's best.

She used the break to redirect the conversation toward her greatest current curiosity. "Your colleague Lord Vorkosigan—did he really have a thirteen-year career in Imperial Security?" *Or were you just irritated by Tien?*

"Three years in the Imperial Military Academy, a decade in ImpSec, to be precise."

"How did he ever get in, past the physicals?"

"Nepotism, I believe. Of a sort. To give him credit, it seems to have been an advantage he used sparingly thereafter. I had the fascinating experience of reading his entire classified military record, when Gregor asked me and my fellow Auditors to review Vorkosigan's candidacy, before he made the appoint-ment."

She subsided in slight disappointment. "Classified. In that case, I suppose you can't tell me anything about it."

"Well," he grinned around a mouthful of salad, "there was the Dagoola IV episode. You must have heard of it, that giant breakout from the Cetagandan prisoner-of-war camp that the Marilacans made a few years ago?"

She recalled it only dimly. She'd been heads-down in moth-erhood, about that time, and scarcely paid attention to news, especially any so remote as galactic news. But she nodded encouragement for him to go on.

"It's all old history now. I understand from Vorkosigan that the Marilacans are engaged in producing a holovid drama on the subject. *The Greatest Escape*, or something like that, they're calling it. They tried to hire him—or actually, his cover identity—to be a technical consultant on the script, an opportunity he has regretfully declined. But for ImpSec to retain security classification upon a series of events that the Marilacans are simultaneously dramatizing planetwide strikes me as a bit rigid, even for ImpSec. In any case, Vorkosigan was the Barrayaran agent behind that breakout."

"I didn't even know we *had* an agent behind that."

"He was our man on-site."

So that odd joke about snoring Marilacans . . . hadn't been. Quite. "If he was so good, why did he quit?"

"Hm." Her uncle applied himself to mopping up the last of his salad dressing with his multigrain roll, before replying. "I can only give you an edited version of that. He didn't quit voluntarily. He was very badly injured—to the point of requiring cryo-freezing—a couple of years ago. Both the original injury and the cryo-freeze did him a lot of damage, some of it permanent. He was forced to take a medical discharge, which he—hm!—did not handle well. It's not my place to discuss those details."

"If he was injured badly enough to need cryo-freeze, he was dead!" she said, startled.

"Technically, I suppose so. 'Alive' and 'dead' are not such neat categories as they used to be in the Time of Isolation."

So, her uncle was in possession of just the sort of medical information about Vorkosigan's mutations she most wanted to know, if he had paid any attention to it. Military physicals were thorough.

"So rather than let all that training and experience go to waste," Uncle Vorthys went on, "Gregor found a job for Vorkosigan on the civilian side. Most Auditorial duties are not too physically onerous . . . though I confess, it's been useful to have someone younger and thinner than myself to send out-station for those long inspections in a pressure suit. I'm afraid I've abused his endurance a bit, but he's proved very observant."

"So he really is your assistant?"

"By no means. What fool said that? All Auditors are coequal. Seniority is only good for getting one stuck with certain administrative chores, on the rare occasions when we act as a group. Vorkosigan, being a well-brought-up young man, is polite to my white hairs, but he's an independent Auditor in his own right, and goes just where he pleases. At present it pleases him to study my methods. I shall certainly take the opportunity to study his.

"Our Imperial charge doesn't come with a manual, you see. It was once proposed the Auditors create one for themselves, but they—wisely, I think—concluded it would do more harm than good. Instead, we just have our archives of Imperial reports; precedents, without rules. Lately, several of us more recent appointees have been trying to read a few old reports each week, and then meet for dinner to discuss the cases and analyze how they were handled. Fascinating. And delicious. Vorkosigan has the most extraordinary cook."

"But this *is* his first assignment, isn't it? And . . . he was designated just like that, on the Emperor's whim."

"He had a temporary appointment as a Ninth Auditor first. A very difficult assignment, inside ImpSec itself. Not my kind of thing at all."

She was not *totally* oblivious to the news. "Oh, dear. Did he have anything to do with why ImpSec changed chiefs twice last winter?"

"I so much prefer engineering investigations," her uncle observed mildly.

Their vat-chicken salad sandwiches arrived, while Ekaterin absorbed this deflection. What kind of reassurance was she seeking, after all? Vorkosigan disturbed her, she had to admit, with his cool smile and warm eyes, and she couldn't say why. He did tend to the sardonic. Surely she was not subconsciously prejudiced against mutants, when Nikolai himself . . . *In the Time of Isolation, if such a one as Vorkosigan had been born to me, it would have been my maternal duty to the genome to cut his infant throat.*

Nikki, happily, would have escaped my cleansing. For a while. The Time of Isolation is over forever. Thank God.

"I gather you like Vorkosigan," she began once again to angle for the kind of information she sought.

"So does your aunt. The Professora and I had him to dinner a few times, last winter, which is where Vorkosigan came up with the notion of the discussion meetings, come to think of it. I know he's rather quiet at first—cautious, I think—but he can be very witty, once you get him going."

"Does he amuse you?" *Amusing* had certainly not been her first impression.

He swallowed another bite of sandwich, and glanced up again at the white irregular blur in the clouds now marking the position of the soletta. "I taught engineering for thirty years.

It had its drudgeries. But each year, I had the pleasure of finding in my classes a few of the best and brightest, who made it all worthwhile." He sipped spiced tea and spoke more slowly. "But much less often—every five or ten years at most— a true genius would turn up among my students, and the pleasure became a privilege, to be treasured for life."

"You think he's a genius?" she said, raising her eyebrows. *The high Vor twit?*

"I don't know him quite well enough, yet. But I suspect so, a part of the time."

"Can you be a genius part of the time?"

"All the geniuses I ever met were so just part of the time. To qualify, you only have to be great once, you know. Once when it matters. Ah, dessert. My, this is splendid!" He applied himself happily to a large chocolate confection with whipped cream and more pecans.

She wanted personal data, but she kept getting career synopses. She would have to take a more embarrassingly direct path. While arranging her first spoonful of her spiced apple tart and ice cream, she finally worked up her nerve to ask, "Is he married?"

"No."

"That surprises me." Or did it? "He's high Vor, heavens, the highest—he'll be a District Count someday, won't he? He's wealthy, or so I would assume, he has an important position . . ." She trailed off. What did she want to say? *What's wrong with him that he hasn't acquired his own lady by now? What kind of genetic damage made him like that, and was it from his mother or his father? Is he impotent, is he sterile, what does he really look like under those expensive clothes? Is he hiding more serious deformities? Is he homosexual? Would it be safe to leave Nikolai alone with him?* She couldn't say *any* of that, and her oblique hints weren't eliciting anything even close to the answers she sought. Drat it, she wouldn't have had this kind of trouble getting the pertinent information if she'd been talking to the *Professora.*

"He's been out of the Empire most of the past decade," he said, as if that explained something.

"Does he have siblings?" *Normal brothers or sisters?*

"No."

That's a bad sign.

"Oh, I take that back," Uncle Vorthys added. "Not in the usual sense, I should say. He has a clone. Doesn't look like him, though."

"That—if he's a—I don't understand."

"You'll have to get Vorkosigan to explain it to you, if you're curious. It's complicated even by his standards. I haven't met the fellow myself yet." Around a mouthful of chocolate and cream, he added, "Speaking of siblings, were you planning any more for Nikolai? Your family is going to be very stretched out, if you wait much longer."

She smiled in panic. Dare she tell him? Tien's accusation of betrayal seared her memory, but she was so tired, exhausted, sick to death of the stupid secrecy. If only her aunt were here . . .

She was dully conscious of her contraceptive implant, the one bit of galactic techno-culture Tien had embraced without question. It gave her a galactic's sterility without a galactic's freedom. Modern women gladly traded the deadly lottery of fertility for the certainties of health and result that came with the use of the uterine replicator, but Tien's obsession with concealment had barred her from that reward too. Even if he was somatically cured, his germ-cells would not be, and any progeny would still have to be genetically screened. Did he mean to cut off all future children? When she'd tried to discuss the issue, he'd put her off with an airy, *First things first*; when she'd persisted, he'd become angry, accusing her of nagging and selfishness. That was always effective at shutting her up.

She skittered sideways to her uncle's question. "We've moved around so much. I kept waiting for things to get settled with Tien's career."

"He does seem to have been rather, ah, restless." He raised his eyebrows at her, inviting . . . what?

"I . . . won't pretend that hasn't been difficult." That was true enough. Thirteen different jobs in a decade. Was this normal for a rising bureaucrat? Tien said it was a necessity, no bosses ever promoted from within or raised a former subordinate above them; you had to go around to move up. "We've moved eight times. I've abandoned six gardens, so far. The last two relocations, I just didn't plant anything except in pots. And then I had to leave most of the pots, when we came here."

Maybe Tien would stay with this Komarran post. How could he ever garner the rewards of promotion and seniority, the status he hungered for, if he never stuck with one thing long enough to earn any? His first few postings, she'd had to agree with him, had been mediocre; she'd had no problem understanding why he wanted to move on quickly. A young couple's early life was supposed to be unsettled, as they stretched into their new lives as adults. Well, as she'd stretched into hers;

she'd been only twenty, after all. Tien had been thirty when they'd married. . . .

He'd started every new job with a burst of enthusiasm, working hard, or at least, very long hours. Surely no one could work harder. Then the enthusiasm dwindled, and the complaints began, of too much work, too little reward, offered too slowly. Lazy coworkers, smarmy bosses. At least, so he said. That had become her secret danger signal, when Tien began offering sly sexual slander of his superiors; it meant the job was about to end, again. A new one would be found . . . though it seemed to take longer and longer to find a new one, these days. And his enthusiasm would flame up again, and the cycle would begin anew. But her hypersensitized ear had picked up no bad signs so far in this job, and they'd been here nearly a year already. Maybe Tien had finally found his— what had Vorkosigan called it? His passion. This was the best posting he'd ever achieved; perhaps things were finally starting to break into good fortune, for a change. If she just stuck it out long enough, it would get better, virtue would be rewarded. And . . . with this Vorzohn's Dystrophy thing hanging over them, Tien had good reason for impatience. His time was not unlimited.

And yours is? She blinked that thought away.

"Your aunt was not sure if things were working out happily for you. Do you dislike Komarr?"

"Oh, I like Komarr just fine," she said quickly. "I admit, I've been a little homesick, but that's not the same thing as not liking being here."

"She did think you would seize the opportunity to place Nikki in a Komarran school, for the, as she would say, cultural experience. Not that his school we saw this morning isn't very nice, of course, which I shall report back for her reassurance, I promise."

"I was tempted. But being a Barrayaran, an off-worlder, in a Komarran classroom might have been difficult for Nikki. You know how kids can gang up on anyone who's different, at that age. Tien thought this private school would be much better. A lot of the high Vor families in the Sector send their children there. He thought Nikki could make good connections."

"I did not have the impression that Nikki was socially ambitious." His dryness was mitigated by a slight twinkle.

How was she to respond to that? Defend a choice she did not herself agree with? Admit she thought Tien wrong? If she once began complaining about Tien, she wasn't sure she could stop before her most fearful worries began to pour out. And people complaining about their spouses always looked and sounded so ugly. "Well, connections for me, at least." Not that she had been able to muster the energy to pursue them as assiduously as Tien thought she ought.

"Ah. It's good you're making friends."

"Yes, well . . . yes." She scraped at the last of the apple syrup on her plate.

When she looked up, she noticed a good-looking young Komarran man who had stopped by the outer gate to the restaurant's patio and was staring at her. After a moment, he entered and approached their table. "Madame Vorsoisson?" he said uncertainly.

"Yes?" she said warily.

"Oh, good, I thought I recognized you. My name is Andro Farr. We met at the Winterfair reception for the Serifosa terraforming employees a few months ago, do you remember?"

Dimly. "Oh, yes. You were somebody's guest . . . ?"

"Yes. Marie Trogir. She's an engineering tech in the Waste Heat Management department. Or she was. . . . Do you know her? I mean, has she ever talked with you?"

"No, not really." Ekaterin had met the young Komarran woman perhaps three times, at carefully choreographed Project events. She had usually been too conscious of herself as a representative of Tien, of the need to cordially meet and greet everyone, to get into any very intimate conversations. "Had she intended to talk to me?"

The young man slumped in disappointment. "I don't know. I thought you might have been friends, or at least acquaintances. I've talked to all her friends I can find."

"Um . . . oh?" Ekaterin was not at all sure she wished to encourage this conversation.

Farr seemed to sense her wariness; he flushed slightly. "Excuse me. I seem to have found myself in a rather painful domestic situation, and I don't know why. It took me by surprise. But . . . but you see . . . about six weeks ago, Marie told me she was going out of town on a field project for her department, and would be back in about five weeks, but she wasn't sure exactly. She didn't give me any comconsole codes to reach her, she said she'd probably not be able to call, and not to worry."

"Do you, um, live with her?"

"Yes. Anyway, time went by, and time went by, and I didn't hear . . . I finally called her department head, Administrator Soudha. He was vague. In fact, I think he gave me a run-around. So I went down there in person and asked around.

When I finally pinned him, *he* said," Farr swallowed, "she'd resigned abruptly six weeks ago and left. So had her engineering boss, Radovas, the one she'd said she was going on the field project with. Soudha seemed to think they'd . . . left together. It makes no sense."

The idea of running away from a relationship and leaving no forwarding address made perfect sense to Ekaterin, but it was hardly her place to say so. Who knew what profound dissatisfactions Farr had failed to detect in his lady? "I'm sorry. I know nothing about this. Tien never mentioned it."

"I'm sorry to bother you, Madame." He hesitated, balanced upon turning away.

"Have you talked to Madame Radovas?" Ekaterin asked tentatively.

"I tried. She refused to talk with me."

That, too, was understandable, if her middle-aged husband had run off with a younger and prettier woman.

"Have you filed a missing person report with Dome Security?" Uncle Vorthys inquired. Ekaterin realized she hadn't introduced him and, on reflection, decided to leave it that way.

"I wasn't sure. I think I'm about to."

"Mm," said Ekaterin. Did she really want to encourage the fellow to persecute this girl? She had apparently got away clean. Had she chosen this cruel method of ending their relationship because she was a twit, or because he was a monster? There was no way to tell from the outside. You could never tell what secret burdens anyone carried, concealed by their bright smiles.

"She left all her things. She left her cats. I don't know what to do with them," he said rather piteously.

Ekaterin had heard of desperate women leaving everything up to and including their children, but Uncle Vorthys put in, "That does seem odd. I'd go to Security if I were you, if only to put your mind at ease. You can always apologize later, if necessary."

"I . . . I think I might. Good day, Madame Vorsoisson. Sir." He ran his hands through his hair, and let himself back out the little fake wrought-iron gate to the park.

"Perhaps we ought to be getting back," Ekaterin suggested as the young man turned out of sight. "Should we take Lord Vorkosigan some lunch? They'll make up a carry-out."

"I'm not sure he notices missing meals, when he's wound up in a problem, but it does seem only fair."

"Do you know what he likes?"

"Anything, I would imagine."

"Does he have any food allergies?"

"Not as far as I know."

She made a hasty selection of a suitably balanced and nutritious meal, hoping that the prettily-arranged vegetables wouldn't end up in the waste disposer. With males, you never knew. When the order was delivered, they took their leave, and Ekaterin led the way to the nearest bubble-car station to get back to her own dome section. She still had no clear idea how Vorkosigan had so successfully handled his mutant-status on their mutagen-scarred homeworld, except, perhaps, by pursuing most of his career off it. Was that likely to be any help to Nikolai?

CHAPTER FOUR

Etienne Vorsoisson's bureaucratic domain occupied two floors partway up a sealed tower otherwise devoted to local Serifosa Dome government offices. The tower, on the edge of the dome-sprawl, was not housed inside any other atmosphere-containing structure. Miles eyed the glass-roofed atrium with disfavor as they ascended a curving escalator within it. He swore his ear detected a faint, far off whistle of air escaping some less-than-tight seal. "So what happens if somebody lobs a rock through a window?" he murmured to the Professor, a step behind him.

"Not much," Vorthys murmured back. "It would vent a pretty noticeable draft, but the pressure differential just isn't that great."

"True." Serifosa Dome was not really like a space installation, despite occasional misleading similarities of architecture. They made the air in here *from* the air out there, for the most part. Vent shafts spotted all over the dome complex sucked in Komarr's free volatiles, filtered out the excess carbon dioxide and some trace nasties, passed the nitrogen through unaltered, and concentrated the oxygen to a humanly-bearable mix. The *percentage* of oxygen in Komarr's raw atmosphere was still too low to support a large mammal without the technological aid of a breath mask, but the absolute *amount* remained a vast reservoir compared to the volume of even the most extensive dome complexes. "As long as their power system keeps running."

They stepped from the escalator and followed Vorsoisson into a corridor branching off the central atrium. The sight of a case of emergency breath masks affixed to a wall next to

41

a fire extinguisher reassured Miles slightly, in passing, that the Komarrans here were not completely oblivious to their routine hazards. Though the case looked suspiciously dusty; had it ever been used since it had been installed, however many years ago? Or checked? If this were a military inspection, Miles could amuse himself by stopping the party right now, and tearing the case apart to determine if the masks' power and reservoir levels still fell within spec. As an Imperial Auditor, he could also do so, of course, or take any other action which struck his fancy. When a younger man, his besetting sin had been his impulsiveness. In the dark doubts of night, Miles sometimes wondered if Emperor Gregor had quite thought through his most recent Auditorial appointment. Power was supposed to corrupt, but this felt more like being a kid turned loose in a candy store. *Control yourself, boy.*

The mask case fell behind without incident. Vorsoisson, as tour guide, continued to point out the offices of his various subordinate departments, without, however, inviting his visitors inside. Not that there was that much to see in these administrative headquarters. The real interest, and the real work, lay outside the domes altogether, in experimental stations and plots and pockets of biota all over Serifosa Sector. All Miles would find in these bland rooms were . . . comconsoles. And Komarrans, of course, lots of Komarrans.

"This way, my lords." Vorsoisson shepherded them into a comfortably spacious room featuring a large round holovid projection table. The place looked, and smelled, like every other conference chamber Miles had ever been in for military and security briefings and debriefings during his truncated career. *More of the same. I predict my greatest challenge this afternoon will be to stay awake.* A half a dozen men and women sat waiting, nervously fingering recording pads and vid disks, and a couple more scurried in behind the two Auditors with murmured apologies. Vorsoisson indicated seats set aside for the visitors, at his right and left hand. With a brief general smile of greeting, Miles settled in.

"Lord Auditor Vorthys, Lord Vorkosigan, may I present the department heads of the Serifosa branch of the Komarr Terraforming Project." Vorsoisson went round the table, naming each attendee and their department, which under the three basic branches of Accounting, Operations, and Research included such evocative titles as Carbon Draw-down, Hydrology, Greenhouse Gases, Tests Plots, Waste Heat Management, and Microbial Reclassification. Native-born Komarrans, every one; Vorsoisson was the only Barrayaran expatriate among them.

Vorsoisson remained standing and turned to one of the new-comers. "My lords, may I also present Ser Venier, my administrative assistant. Vennie has organized a general presentation for you, after which my staff will be happy to answer any further questions."

Vorsoisson sat down. Venier nodded to each Auditor and murmured something inaudible. He was a slight man, shorter than Vorsoisson, with intent brown eyes and an unfortunate weak chin which, together with his nervous air, lent him the look of a slightly manic rabbit. He took the holovid control podium, and rubbed his hands together, and stacked and restacked his pile of data disks before selecting one, then putting it back down. He cleared his throat and found his voice. "My lords. It was suggested I start with a historical overview." He nodded to each of them again, his glance lingering for a moment on Miles. He inserted a disk in his machine, and started an attractive, i.e., artistically enhanced, view of Komarr spinning over the vid plate. "The early explorers of the wormhole nexus found Komarr a likely candidate for possible terraforming. Our almost point-nine-standard gravity and abundant native supply of gaseous nitrogen, the inert buffer gas of choice, and of sufficient water-ice, made it an immensely easier problem to tackle than such classic cold dry planets as, say, Mars."

They had indeed been early explorers, Miles reflected, to arrive and settle before more salubrious worlds were found to render such ambitious projects economically uninteresting, at least if you didn't already live there. But . . . then there were the wormholes.

"On the debit side," Venier continued, "the concentration of atmospheric CO_2 was high enough to be toxic to humans, yet insolation was so inadequate that no greenhouse effect, runaway or otherwise, captured the heat needed to maintain liquid water. Komarr was therefore a lifeless world, cold and dark. The earliest calculations suggested more water would be needed, and a few so-called low-impact cometary crashes were arranged, hence we can thank our ancestors for our southern crater lakes." A colorful, though out-of-scale, sprinkle of lights dusted the lower hemisphere of the planet-image, resolving into a string of blue blobs. "But the growing demand topside for cometary water and volatiles for the orbital and wormhole stations soon put a stop to *that*. And the early downside settlers' fears of poorly controlled trajectories, of course."

Demonstrated fears, as Miles recalled his Komarran history.

He stole a glance at Vorthys. The Professor appeared perfectly content with Venier's class lecture.

"In fact," Venier went on, "later explorations showed the water-ice tied up in the polar caps to be thicker than at first suspected, if not so abundant as on Earth. And so the drive for heat and light began."

Miles sympathized with the early Komarrans. He loathed arctic cold and dark with a concentrated passion.

"Our ancestors built the first insolation mirror, succeeded a generation later by another design." A holovid model, again out of scale, appeared to the side, and melted into a second one. "A century later, this was in turn succeeded by the design we see today." The seven-disk hexagon appeared, and danced attendance on the Komarr globe. "Insolation at the equator was boosted enough to allow liquid water and the beginnings of a biota to draw down the carbon and release much-needed O_2. Over the following decades, a full-spectrum mixture of artificial greenhouse gases was manufactured and released into the upper atmosphere to help trap the new energy." Venier moved his hand; four of the seven disks winked out. "Then came the accident." All the Komarrans around the table stared glumly at the crippled array.

"There was mention of a cooling projection? With figures?" Vorthys prodded gently.

"Yes, my Lord Auditor." Venier slid a disk across the polished surface toward the Professor. "Administrator Vorsoisson said you were an engineer, so I left in all the calculations."

The Waste Heat Management fellow, Soudha, also an engineer, winced and bit his thumb at this innocent ignorance of Vorthys's stature in his field. Vorthys merely said, "Thank you. I appreciate that."

So where's my copy? Miles did not ask aloud. "And can you please summarize your conclusions for us nonengineers, Ser Venier?"

"Certainly, Lord Auditor . . . Vorkosigan. Serious damage to our biota in the northernmost and southernmost latitudes, not just in Serifosa Sector but planetwide, will begin after one season. For every year after that, we lose more ground; by the end of five years, the destructive cooling curve rises rapidly towards catastrophe. It took twenty years to build the original soletta array. I pray that it will not take that many to repair it." On the vid model, white polar caps crept like pale tumors over the globe.

Vorthys glanced at Soudha. "And so other sources of heat suddenly take on new importance, at least for a stopgap."

Soudha, a big, square-handed man in his late forties, sat back and smiled a bit grimly. He, too, cleared his throat before beginning. "It was hoped, early on in the terraforming, that the waste heat from our growing arcologies would contribute significantly to planetary warming. Over time, this proved optimistic. A planet with an activating hydrology is a huge thermal buffering system, what with the heat of liquefaction load locked up in all that ice. At present—before the accident—it was felt the best use of waste heat was in the creation of microclimates around the domes, to be reservoirs for the next wave of higher biota."

"It sounds like insanity to an engineer to say, 'We need to waste more energy in heat loss,'" agreed Vorthys, "but I suppose here it's true. What's the feasibility of dedicating some number of fusion reactors to pure heat production?"

"Boiling the seas cup by cup?" Soudha grimaced. "*Possible*, sure, and I'd love to see some more done with that technique for small-area development in Serifosa Sector. Economical— no. Per degree of planetary warming, it's even more costly than repairing—or enlarging—the soletta array, something for which we've been petitioning the Imperium for years. Without success. And if you've built a reactor, you might as well use it to run a dome while you're at it. The heat will arrive outside eventually just the same." He slid data disks across to both Vorthys and Miles this time. "Here's our current departmental status report." He glanced across at one of his colleagues. "We're all anxious to move on to higher plant forms in our lifetimes, but at present the greatest, if not success, at least activity remains on the microbial level. Philip?"

The man who had been introduced as the head of Microbial Reclassification smiled, not entirely gratefully, at Soudha, and turned to the Auditors. "Well, yes. Bacteria are booming. Both our deliberate inoculations, and wild genera. Over the years, every Earth type has been imported, or at any rate, has arrived and escaped. Unfortunately, microbial life has a tendency to adapt to its environment more swiftly than the environment has adapted to us. My department has its hands full, keeping up with the mutations. More light and heat are needed, as always. And, bluntly, my lords, more funding. Although our microflora grow fast, they also die fast, rereleasing their carbon compounds. We need to advance to higher organisms, to sequester the excess carbon for the millennial timeframes required. Perhaps you could address this, Liz?" He nodded toward a pleasantly plump middle-aged lady who had been named head of Carbon Draw-down.

She smiled happily, by which Miles deduced her department's responsibilities were going well this year. "Yes, my lords. We've a number of higher forms of vegetation coming along both in major test plots, and undergoing genetic development or improvement. By far our greatest success is with the cold- and carbon-dioxide-hardy peat bogs. They do require liquid water, and as always, would do *better* at higher temperatures. Ideally, they should be sited in subduction zones, for *really* long-term carbon sequestration, but Serifosa Sector lacks these. So we've chosen low-lying areas which will, as water is released from the poles, eventually be covered with lakes and small seas, locking the captured carbon down under a sedimentary cap. Properly set up, the process will run entirely automatically, without further human intervention. If we could just get the funding to double or triple the area of our plantations in the next few years . . . well, here are my projections." Vorthys collected another data disk. "We've started several test plots of larger plants, to follow atop the bogs. These larger organisms are of course infinitely more controllable than the rapidly mutating microflora. They are ready to scale up to wider plantations right now. But they are even more severely threatened by the reduction in heat and light from the soletta. We really *must* have a reliable estimate of how long it will take to effect repairs in space before we dare continue our planting plans."

She gazed longingly at Vorthys, but he merely said, "Thank you, Madame."

"We plan a flyover of the peat plantations later this afternoon," Vorsoisson told her. She settled back, temporarily content.

And so it continued around the table: more than Miles had ever wanted to know about Komarran terraforming, interspersed with oblique, and not so oblique, pleas for increased Imperial funding. And heat and light. *Power corrupts, but we want energy.* Only Accounting and Waste Heat Management had managed to arrive at the meeting with duplicate copies of their pertinent reports for Miles. He stifled an impulse to point this out to somebody. Did he really *want* another several hundred thousand words of bedtime reading? His newer scars were starting to twinge by the time everyone had had their say, without even yesterday's excuse of the physical stresses of buzzing around wreckage in a pressure suit. He rose from his chair much more stiffly than he had intended; Vorthys made a gesture of a helping hand to his elbow, but at Miles's frown and tiny head shake, suppressed it. He didn't really need a drink, he just wanted one.

"Ah, Administrator Soudha," Vorthys said, as the Waste Heat department head stepped past them toward the door. "A word, please?"

Soudha stopped, and smiled faintly. "My Lord Auditor?"

"Was there some special reason you could not help that young fellow, Farr, find his missing lady?"

Soudha hesitated. "I beg your pardon?"

"The fellow who was looking for your former employee, Marie Trogir, I believe he said her name was. Was there some reason you could not help him?"

"Oh, him. Her. Well, uh . . . that was a difficult thing, there." Soudha looked around, but the room had emptied, except for Vorsoisson and Venier waiting to convey their high-ranking guests on the next leg of their tour.

"I recommended he file a missing person complaint with Dome Security. They may be making inquiries of you."

"I . . . don't think I'll be able to help them any more than I could help Farr. I'm afraid I really don't know where she is. She left, you see. Very suddenly, only a day's notice. It put a hole in my staffing at what has proved to be a difficult time. I wasn't too pleased."

"So Farr said. I just thought it was odd about the cats. One of my daughters keeps cats. Dreadful little parasites, but she's very fond of them."

"Cats?" said Soudha, looking increasingly mystified.

"Trogir apparently left her cats in the keeping of Farr."

Soudha blinked, but said, "I've always considered it out of line to intrude on my subordinate's personal lives. Men or pets, it was Trogir's business, not mine. As long as they're kept off project time. I . . . was there anything else?"

"Not really," said Vorthys.

"Then if you will excuse me, my Lord Auditor." Soudha smiled again, and ducked away.

"What was that all about?" Miles asked Vorthys as they turned down the corridor in the opposite direction.

Vorsoisson answered. "A minor office scandal, unfortunately. One of Soudha's techs—female—ran off with one of his engineers, male. Completely blindsided him, apparently. He's fairly embarrassed about it. However did you run across it?"

"Young Farr accosted Ekaterin in a restaurant," said Vorthys.

"He really has been a pest." Vorsoisson sighed. "I don't blame Soudha for avoiding him."

"I always thought Komarrans were more casual about such things," said Miles. "In the galactic style and all that. Not as casual as the Betans, but still. It sounds like a Barrayaran backcountry elopement." *Without, surely, the need to avoid backcountry social pressures, such as homicidal relatives out to defend the clan honor.*

Vorsoisson shrugged. "The cultural contamination between the worlds can't run one way all the time, I suppose."

The little party continued to the underground garage, where the aircar Vorsoisson had requisitioned was not in evidence. "Wait here, Venier." Swearing under his breath, Vorsoisson went off to see what had happened to it; Vorthys accompanied him.

The opportunity to interview a Komarran in apparently-casual mode was not to be missed. What kind of Komarran was Venier? Miles turned to him, only to find him speaking first: "Is this your first visit to Komarr, Lord Vorkosigan?"

"By no means. I've passed through the topside stations many times. I haven't got downside too often, I admit. This is the first time I've been to Serifosa."

"Have you ever visited Solstice?"

The planetary capital. "Of course."

Venier stared at the middle distance, past the concrete pillars and dim lighting, and smiled faintly. "Have you ever visited the Massacre Shrine there?"

A cheeky damned Komarran, that's what kind. The Solstice Massacre was infamous as the ugliest incident of the Barrayaran conquest. The two hundred Komarran Counselors, the then-ruling senate, had surrendered on terms—and subsequently been gunned down in a gymnasium by Barrayaran security forces. The political consequences had run a short range from dire to disastrous. Miles's smile became a little fixed. "Of course. How could I not?"

"All Barrayarans should make that pilgrimage. In my opinion."

"I went with a close friend. To help him burn a death offering for his aunt."

"A relative of a Martyr is a friend of yours?" Venier's eyes widened in a moment of genuine surprise, in what otherwise felt to Miles to be a highly choreographed conversation. How long had Venier been rehearsing his lines in his head, itching for a chance to try them out?

"Yes." Miles let his gaze become more directly challenging.

Venier apparently felt the weight of it, because he shifted uneasily, and said, "As you are your father's son, I'm just a little surprised, is all."

By what, that I have any Komarran friends? "Especially as I am my father's son, you should not be."

Venier's brows tweaked up. "Well . . . there is a theory that the massacre was ordered by Emperor Ezar without the knowledge of Admiral Vorkosigan. Ezar was certainly ruthless enough."

"Ruthless enough, yes. Stupid enough, never. It was the Barrayaran expedition's chief Political Officer's own bright idea, for which my father made him pay with his life, not that that did much good for anyone after the fact. Leaving aside every moral consideration, the massacre was a supremely stupid act. My father has been accused of many things, but stupidity has never, I believe, been one of them." His voice was growing dangerously clipped.

"We'll never know the whole truth, I suppose," said Venier.

Was that supposed to be a concession? "You can be told the whole truth all day long, but if you won't believe it, then no, I don't suppose you ever will know it." He bared his teeth in a non-smile. *No, keep control; why let this Komarran git see he's scored you off?*

The doors of a nearby elevator opened, and Venier abruptly dropped from Miles's attention as Madame Vorsoisson and Nikolai exited. She was wearing the same dull dun outfit she'd sported that morning, and carried a large pile of heavy jackets over her arm. She waved her hand around the jackets and stepped swiftly over to them. "Am I very late?" she asked a bit breathlessly. "Good afternoon, Venier."

Suppressing the first idiocy that came to his lips, which was, *Any time is a good one for you, milady,* Miles managed a, "Well, good afternoon, Madame Vorsoisson, Nikolai. I wasn't expecting you. Are you to accompany us?" *I hope?* "Your husband has just gone off to fetch an aircar."

"Yes, Uncle Vorthys suggested it would be educational for Nikolai. And I haven't had much chance to see outside the domes myself. I jumped at the invitation." She smiled, and pushed back a strand of dark hair escaping its confinement, and almost dropped her bundle. "I wasn't sure if we were to land anywhere and get outside on foot, but I brought jackets for everyone just in case."

A large two-compartment sealed aircar hissed around the corner and sighed to the pavement beside them. The front canopy opened, and Vorsoisson clambered out, and greeted his wife and son. The Professor watched from the front seat with some amusement as the question of how to distribute six passengers among the two compartments was taken over by Nikolai, who wanted to sit both by his great-uncle and by his Da.

"Perhaps Venier could fly us today?" Madame Vorsoisson suggested diffidently.

Vorsoisson gave her an oddly black look. "I'm perfectly capable."

Her lips moved, but she uttered no audible protest.

Take your pick, my Lord Auditor, Miles thought to himself. *Would you rather be chauffeured by a man just possibly suffering the first symptoms of Vorzohn's Dystrophy, or by a Komarran, ah, patriot, with a car full of tempting Barrayaran Vor targets?* "I have no preference," he murmured truthfully.

"I brought coats—" Madame Vorsoisson handed them out. She and her husband and Nikolai had their own; a spare of her husband's did not quite meet around the Professor's middle.

The heavily padded jacket she handed Miles had been hers, he could tell immediately by the scent of her, lingering in the lining. He concealed a deep inhalation as he shrugged it on. "Thank you, that will do very well."

Vorsoisson dove into the rear compartment and came up with a double handful of breath masks, which he distributed. Both he and Venier had their own, with their names engraved on the cheek-pieces; the others were all labeled "Visitor": one large, two medium, one small.

Madame Vorsoisson hung hers over her arm, and bent to adjust Nikolai's, and check its power and oxygen levels. "I already checked it," Vorsoisson told her. His voice hinted a suppressed snarl. "You don't have to do it again."

"Oh, sorry," she said. But Miles, running through his own check in drilled habit, noticed she finished inspecting it before turning to adjust her own mask. Vorsoisson noticed too, and frowned.

After a few more moments of Betan-style debate, the group sorted themselves out with Vorsoisson, his son, and the Professor in the front compartment, and Miles, Madame Vorsoisson, and Venier in the rear. Miles was uncertain whether to be glad or sorry with his lot in seatmates. He felt he could have engaged either of them in fascinating, if quite different, conversations, if the other had not been present. They all pulled their masks down around their necks, out of the way but instantly ready to hand.

They departed the garage's vehicle-lock without further delay, and the car rose in the air. Venier returned to his initial stiffly professional lecture mode, pointing out bits of project scenery. You *could* begin to see the terraforming from this modest altitude, in the faint smattering of Earth-green in the damp low places, and a fuzziness of lichen and algae on the rocks. Madame Vorsoisson, her face plastered to the canopy, asked enough intelligent questions of Venier that Miles did not have to strain his tired brain for any, for which he was very grateful.

"I'm surprised, Madame Vorsoisson, with your interest in botany, that you haven't leaned on your husband for a job in his department," said Miles after a while.

"Oh," she said, as if this was a new idea to her. "Oh, I couldn't do that."

"Why not?"

"Wouldn't it be nepotism? Or some kind of conflict of interest?"

"Not if you did your job well, which I'm sure you would. After all, the whole Barrayaran Vor system runs on nepotism. It's not a vice for us, it's a lifestyle."

Venier suppressed an unexpected noise, possibly a snort, and glanced at Miles with increased interest.

"Why should you be exempt?" Miles continued.

"It's only a hobby. I don't have nearly enough technical training. I'd need much more chemistry, to start."

"You could start in a technical assistant position—take evening classes to fill in your gaps. Bootstrap yourself up to something interesting in no time. They have to hire someone." Belatedly, it occurred to Miles that if she, not Vorsoisson, was the carrier of the Vorzohn's Dystrophy, there might be quelling reasons why she had not plunged into such a time- and energy-absorbing challenge. He sensed an elusive energy in her, as if it were tied in knots, locked down, circling back to exhaust itself destroying itself; had fear of her coming illness done that to her? Dammit, which of them *was* it? He was supposed to be such a hotshot investigator now, he ought to be able to figure this one out.

Well, he could do so easily; all he had to do was cheat, and call ImpSec Komarr, and request a complete background medical check on his hosts. Just wave his magical Auditor-wand and invade all the privacy he wanted to. *No.* All this had nothing to do with the accident to the soletta array. As this morning's embarrassment with her comconsole had demonstrated, he needed to start keeping his personal and professional curiosity just as strictly separated as his personal and Imperial funds. *Neither a peculator nor a voyeur be.* He ought to get a plaque engraved with that motto and hang it on his wall for a reminder. At least money didn't tempt him. He could smell her faint perfume, organic and floral against the plastic and metal and recycled air. . . .

To Miles's surprise, Venier said, "You really should consider it, Madame Vorsoisson."

Her expression, which during the flight had gradually become animated, grew reserved again. "I . . . we'll see. Maybe next year. After . . . if Tien decides to stay."

Vorsoisson's voice, over the intercom from the front compartment, interrupted to point out the upcoming peat bog, lining a long narrow valley below. It was a more impressive sight than Miles had expected. For one thing, it was a true and bright Earth-green; for another, it ran on for kilometers.

"This strain produces six times the oxygen of its Earth ancestor," Venier noted with pride.

"So . . . if you were trapped outside without a breath mask, could you crawl around in it and survive till you were rescued?" Miles asked practically.

"Mm . . . if you could hold your breath for about a hundred more years."

Miles began to suspect Venier of concealing a sense of humor beneath that twitchy exterior. In any case, the aircar spiraled down toward a rocky outcrop, and Miles's attention was taken up by their landing site. He'd had unpleasant and deep, so to speak, personal experience with the treachery of arctic bogs. But Vorsoisson managed to put the car down with a reassuring crunchy jar on solid rock, and they all adjusted their breath masks. The canopy rose to admit a blast of chill unbreathable outside air, and they exited for a clamber over the rocks and down to personally examine the squishy green plants. They were squishy green plants, all right. There were lots of them. Stretching to the horizon. Lots. Squishy. Green. With an effort, Miles stopped his back-brain from composing a lengthy Report to the Emperor in this style, and tried instead to appreciate Venier's highly technical disquisition on potential deep-freeze damage to the something-chemical cycle.

After a little more time spent regarding the view—it didn't change, and Nikki, though he sprang around like a flea, with his mother laboring after him, didn't quite manage to fall into the bog—they all reboarded the aircar. After a flyover of a neighboring green valley, and a pass across another dull brown unaltered one for comparison and contrast, they turned for the Serifosa Dome.

A largish installation featuring its own fusion reactor, and a riot of assorted greens spilling away from it, caught Miles's attention on the leftward horizon. "What's that?" he asked Venier.

"It's Waste Heat's main experiment station," Venier replied.

Miles touched the intercom. "Any chance of dropping in for a visit down there?" he called the forward compartment.

Vorsoisson's voice hesitated. "I'm not sure we could get back to the dome before dark. I don't like to take the chance."

Miles hadn't thought night flight was that hazardous, but perhaps Vorsoisson knew his own limitations. And he did have his wife and child aboard, not to mention all that Imperial load in the somewhat unprepossessing persons of Miles and the Professor. Still, surprise inspections were always the most fun, if you wanted to turn up the good stuff. He toyed with the idea of insisting, Auditorially.

"It would certainly be interesting," murmured Venier. "I haven't been out there in person in years."

"Perhaps another day?" suggested Vorsoisson.

Miles let it go. He and Vorthys were playing visiting firemen here, not inspectors general; the real crisis was topside. "Perhaps. If there's time."

Another ten minutes of flight brought Serifosa Dome up over the horizon. It was vast and spectacular in the gathering dusk, with its glittering strings of lights, looping bubble-car tubes, warm glow of domes, sparkling towers. *We humans don't do too badly,* Miles thought, *if you catch us at the right angle.* The aircar slid back through the vehicle lock and settled again to the garage pavement.

Venier went off with the aircar, and Vorsoisson collected the spare breath masks. Madame Vorsoisson's face was bright and glowing, exhilarated by her field trip. "Don't forget to put your mask back on the recharger," she chirped to her husband as she handed him hers.

Vorsoisson's face darkened. "Don't. Nag. Me," he breathed through set teeth.

She recoiled slightly, her expression closing as abruptly as a shutter. Miles stared off through the pillars, politely pretending not to have heard or noticed this interplay. He was hardly an expert on marital miscommunication, but even he could see how that one had gone awry. Her perhaps unfortunately-chosen expression of love and interest had been received by the obviously tense and tired Vorsoisson as a slur on his competence. Madame Vorsoisson deserved a better hearing, but Miles had no advice to offer. *He* had never even come near to capturing a wife to miscommunicate with. Not for lack of trying. . . .

"Well, well," said Uncle Vorthys, also heartily pretending not to have noticed the byplay. "Everyone will feel better with a little supper aboard, eh, Ekaterin? Let me treat you all to dinner. Do you have another favorite place as splendid as the one where we ate lunch?"

The moment of tension was extinguished in another Betan debate over the dinner destination; this time, Nikki was successfully overruled by the adults. Miles wasn't hungry, and the temptation to relieve Vorthys of the day's collection of data disks and escape back to some comconsole was strong, but perhaps with another drink or three he could endure one more family dinner with the Vorsoisson clan. The last, Miles promised himself.

A trifle drunker than he had intended to be, Miles undressed for another night in the rented grav-bed. He piled the new stack of data disks on the comconsole to wait for morning, coffee, and better mental coherence. The last thing he did was rummage in his case and fish out his controlled-seizure stimulator. He sat cross-legged on the bed and regarded it glumly.

The Barrayaran doctors had found no cure for the post-cryonic seizure disorder that had finally ended his military career. The best they had been able to offer was this: a triggering device to bleed off his convulsions in smaller increments, in controlled private times and places, instead of grandly, randomly, and spectacularly in moments of public stress. Checking his neurotransmitter levels was now a nightly hygienic routine, just like brushing his teeth, the doctors had suggested. He felt his right temple for the implant and positioned the read-contact. His only sensation was a faint spot of warmth.

The levels were not yet in the danger zone. A few more days before he had to put in the mouth-guard and do it again. Having left his Armsman, Pym, who usually played valet and general servant, back on Barrayar, he would have to find another spotter. The doctors had insisted he have a spotter, when he did this ugly little thing. He would much prefer to be helpless and out-of-consciousness—and twitching like a fish, he supposed, though of course *he* was the one person who never got to watch—in complete privacy. Maybe he would ask the Professor.

If you had a wife, she could be your spotter.

Gee, what a treat for her.

He grimaced, and put the device carefully away in its case, and crawled into bed. Perhaps in his dreams the space wreckage would reassemble itself, just like in a vid reconstruction, and reveal the secrets of its fate. Better to have visions of the wreckage than the bodies.

CHAPTER FIVE

Ekaterin studied Tien warily as they undressed for bed. The frowning tension in his face and body made her think she had better offer sex very soon. Strain in him frightened her, as always. It was past time to defuse him. The longer she waited, the harder it would be to approach him, and the tenser he would become, ending in some angry explosion of muffled, cutting words.

Sex, she imagined wistfully, should be romantic, abandoned, self-forgetful. Not the most tightly self-disciplined action in her world. Tien demanded response of her and worked hard to obtain it, she thought; not like men she'd heard about who took their own pleasure, then rolled over and went to sleep. She sometimes wished he would. He became upset—with himself, with her?—if she failed to participate fully. Unable to act a lie with her body, she'd learned to erase herself from herself, and so unblock whatever strange neural channel it was that permitted flesh to flood mind. The inward erotic fantasies required to absorb her self-consciousness had become stronger and uglier over time; was that a mere unavoidable side-effect of learning more about the ugliness of human possibility, or a permanent corruption of the spirit?

I hate this.

Tien hung up his shirt and twitched a smile at her. His eyes remained strained, though, as they had been all evening. "I'd like you to do me a favor tomorrow."

Anything, to delay the moment. "Certainly. What?"

"Take the brace of Auditors out and show 'em a good time. I'm about saturated with them. This downside holiday of theirs has been incredibly disruptive to my department. We've lost a week altogether, I bet, pulling together that show for them yesterday. Maybe they can go poke at something else, till they go back topside."

"Take them where, show them what?"

"Anything."

"I already took Uncle Vorthys around."

"Did you show him the Sector University district? Maybe he'd like that. Your uncle is interested in lots of things, and I don't think the Vor dwarf cares what he's offered. As long as it includes enough wine."

"I haven't the first clue what Lord Vorkosigan likes to do."

"Ask him. Suggest something. Take him, I don't know, take him shopping."

"Shopping?" she said doubtfully.

"Or whatever." He trod over to her, still smiling tightly. His hand slipped behind her back, to hold her, and he offered a tentative kiss. She returned it, trying not to let her dutifulness show. She could feel the heat of his body, of his hands, and how thinly stretched his affability was. Ah, yes, the work of the evening, defusing the unexploded Tien. Always a tricky business. She began to pay attention to the practiced rituals, key words, gestures, that led into the practiced intimacies.

Undressed and in bed, she closed her eyes as he caressed her, partly to concentrate on the touch, partly to block out his gaze, which was beginning to be excited and pleased. Wasn't there some bizarre mythical bird or other, back on Earth, who fancied that if it couldn't see you, you couldn't see it? And so buried its head in the sand, odd image. While still attached to its neck, she wondered?

She opened her eyes, as Tien reached across her and lowered the lamplight to a softer glow. His avid look made her feel not beautiful and loved, but ugly and ashamed. How could you be violated by mere eyes? How could you be lovers with someone, and yet feel every moment alone with them intruded upon your privacy, your dignity? *Don't look, Tien.* Absurd. There really was something wrong with her. He lowered himself beside her; she parted her lips, yielding quickly to his questing mouth. She hadn't always been this self-conscious and cautious. Back in the beginning, it had been different. Or had it been she alone who'd changed?

It became her turn to sit up and return caresses. That was easy enough; he buried his face in his pillow, and did not talk for a while, as her hands moved up and down his body, tracing muscle and tendon. Secretly seeking symptoms. The tremula seemed reduced tonight; perhaps last evening's shakes really had been a false alarm, merely the hunger and nerves he had claimed.

She knew when the shift had occurred in her, of course, back about four, five jobs ago now. When Tien had decided, for reasons she still didn't understand, that she was betraying him—with whom, she had never understood either, since the two names he'd finally mentioned as his suspects were so patently absurd. She'd had no idea such a sexual mistrust had taken over his mind, until she'd caught him following her, watching her, turning up at odd times and bizarre places when he was supposed to be at work—and had that perhaps had something to do with why *that* job had ended so badly? She'd finally had the accusation out of him. She'd been horrified, deeply wounded, and subtly frightened. Was it stalking, when it was your own husband? She had not had the courage to ask who to ask. Her one source of security was the knowledge that she'd never so much as been alone in any private place with another man. Her Vor-class training had done her that much good, at least. Then he had accused her of sleeping with her women friends.

That had broken something in her at last, some will to desire his good opinion. How could you argue sense into someone who believed something not because it was true, but because he was an idiot? No amount of panicky protestation or indignant denial or futile attempt to prove a negative was likely to help, because the problem was not in the accused, but in the accuser. She began then to believe he was living in a different universe, one with a different set of physical laws, perhaps, and an alternate history. And very different people from the ones she'd met of the same name. Smarmy dopplegangers all.

Still, the accusation alone had been enough to chill her friendships, stealing their innocent savor and replacing it with an unwelcome new level of awareness. With the next move, time and distance attenuated her contacts. And on the move after that, she'd stopped trying to make new friends.

To this day she didn't know if he'd taken her disgusted refusal to defend herself for a covert admission of guilt. Weirdly, after the blowup the subject had been dropped cold; he didn't bring it up again, and she didn't deign to. Did he think her innocent, or himself insufferably noble for forgiving her for nonexistent crimes?

Why is he so impossible?

She didn't want the insight, but it came nonetheless. *Because he fears losing you.* And so in panic blundered about destroying her love, creating a self-fulfilling prophecy? It seemed so. *It's not as though you can pretend his fears have no foundation.* Love was long gone, in her. She got by on a starvation diet of loyalty these days.

I am Vor. I swore to hold him in sickness. He is sick. I will not break my oath, just because things have gotten difficult. That's the whole point of an oath, after all. Some things, once broken, cannot ever be repaired. Oaths. Trust. . . .

She could not tell to what extent his illness was at the root of his erratic behavior. When they returned from the galactic treatment, he might be much better emotionally as well. Or at least she would at last be able to tell how much was Vorzohn's Dystrophy, and how much was just . . . Tien.

They switched positions; his skilled hands began working down her back, probing for her relaxation and response. An even more unhappy thought occurred to her then. Had Tien been, consciously or unconsciously, putting off his treatment because he realized on some obscure level that his illness, his vulnerability, was one of the few ties that still bound her to him? *Is this delay my fault?* Her head ached.

Tien, still valiantly rubbing her back, made a murmur of protest. She was failing to relax; this wouldn't do. Resolutely, she turned her thoughts to a practiced erotic fantasy, unbeautiful, but one which usually worked. Was it some weird inverted form of frigidity, this thing bordering on self-hypnosis she seemed to have to do in order to achieve sexual release despite Tien's too-near presence? How could you tell the difference between not liking sex, and not liking the only person you'd ever done sex with?

Yet she was almost desperate for touch, mere affection untainted by the indignities of the erotic. Tien *was* very good about that, massaging her for quite unconscionable lengths of time, though he sometimes sighed in a boredom for which she could hardly blame him. The touch, the make-it-better, the sheer catlike comfort, eased her body and then her heart, despite it all. She could absorb hours of this—she slitted one eye open to check the clock. Better not get greedy. So mind-wrenching, for Tien to demand a sexual show of her on the one hand, and accuse her of infidelity on the other. Did he want her to melt, or want her to freeze? *Anything you pick is wrong.* No, this wasn't helping. She was taking much too long to cultivate her arousal. Back to work. She tried again to start her fantasy. He might have rights upon her body, but her mind was hers alone, the one part of her into which he could not pry.

✦ ✦ ✦

It went according to plan and practice, after that, mission accomplished all around. Tien kissed her when they'd finished. "There, all better," he murmured. "We're doing better these days, aren't we?"

She murmured back the usual assurances, a light, standard script. She would have preferred an honest silence. She pretended to doze, in postcoital lassitude, till his snores assured her he was asleep. Then she went to the bathroom to cry.

Stupid, irrational weeping. She muffled it in a towel, lest he, or Nikki, or her guests hear and investigate. *I hate him. I hate myself. I hate him, for making me hate myself. . . .*

Most of all, she despised in herself that crippling desire for physical affection, regenerating like a weed in her heart no matter how many times she tried to root it out. That neediness, that dependence, that love-of-touch must be broken first. It had betrayed her, worse than all the other things. If she could kill her need for love, then all the other coils which bound her, desire for honor, attachment to duty, above all every form of fear, could be brought into line. Austerely mystical, she supposed. *If I can kill all these things in me, I can be free of him.*

I'll be a walking dead woman, but I will be free.

She finished the weep, and washed her face, and took three painkillers. She could sleep now, she thought. But when she slipped back into the bedroom, she found Tien lying awake, his eyes a faint gleam in the shadows. He turned up the lamp at the whisper of her bare feet on the carpet. She tried to remember if insomnia was listed among the early symptoms of his disease. He raised the covers for her to slip beneath. "What were you doing in there all that time, going for seconds without me?"

She wasn't sure if he was waiting for a laugh, if that was supposed to be a joke, or her indignant denial. Evading the problem, instead she said, "Oh, Tien, I almost forgot. Your bank called this afternoon. Very strange. Something about requiring my countersignature and palm-print to release your pension account. I told them I didn't think that could be right, but that I would check with you and get back to them."

He froze in the act of reaching for her. "They had no business calling you about that!"

"If this was something you wanted me to do, you might have mentioned it earlier. They said they'd delay releasing it till I got back to them."

"Delayed, no! You idiot bitch!" His right hand clenched in a gesture of frustration.

The hateful and hated epithet made her sick to her stomach. All that effort to pacify him tonight, and here he was right back on the edge. . . . "Did I make a mistake?" she asked anxiously. "Tien, what's wrong? What's going on?" She prayed he wasn't about to put his fist through the wall again. The noise—would her uncle hear, or that Vorkosigan fellow, and how could she explain—

"No . . . no. Sorry." He rubbed his forehead instead, and she let out a covert sigh of relief. "I forgot about it being under Komarran rules. On Barrayar, I never had any trouble signing out my pension accumulation when I left any job, any job that offered a pension, anyway. Here on Komarr I think they want a joint signature from the designated survivor. It's all right. Call them back first thing in the morning, though, and clear it."

"You're not leaving your job, are you?" Her chest tightened in panic. Dear no, not another move so soon. . . .

"No, no. Hell, no. Relax." He smiled with one side of his mouth.

"Oh. Good." She hesitated. "Tien . . . do you have any accumulation from your old jobs back on Barrayar?"

"No, I always signed it out at the end. Why let them have the use of the money, when we could use it ourselves? It served to tide us over more than once, you know." He smiled bitterly. "Under the circumstances, you have to admit, the idea of saving for my old age is not very compelling. And you wanted that vacation to South Continent, didn't you?"

"I thought you said that was a termination bonus."

"So it was, in a sense."

So . . . if anything horrible happened to Tien, she and Nikolai would have nothing. *If he doesn't get treatment soon, something horrible is going to happen to him.* "Yes, but . . ." The realization struck her. Could it be . . . ? "Are you getting it out for—we're going for the galactic treatment, yes? You and me and Nikolai? Oh, Tien, good! Finally. Of course. I should have realized." So that's what he needed the money for, yes, at last! She rolled over and hugged him. But would it be enough? If it was less than a year's worth . . . "Will it be enough?"

"I . . . don't know. I'm checking."

"I saved a little out of my household allowance, I could put that in," she offered. "If it will get us underway sooner."

He licked his lips, and was silent for a moment. "I'm not sure. I don't like to let you . . ."

"This is exactly what I saved it for. I mean, I know I didn't earn it in the first place, but I managed it—it can be my contribution."

"How much do you have?"

"Almost four thousand Imperial marks!" She smiled, proud of her frugality.

"Oh!" He looked as though he were making an inner calculation. "Yes, that would help significantly."

He dropped a kiss on her forehead, and she relaxed further. She said, "I never thought about raiding your pension for the medical quest. I didn't realize we could. How soon can we get away?"

"That's . . . the next thing I'll have to find out. I would have checked it out this week, but I was interrupted by my department suffering a severe outbreak of Imperial Auditors."

She smiled in brief appreciation of his wit. He'd used to make her laugh more. If he had grown more sour with age, it was understandable, but the blackness of his humor had gradually come to weary her more than amuse her. Cynicism did not seem nearly so impressively daring to her now as it had when she was twenty. Perhaps this decision had lightened his heart, too.

Do you really think he'll do what he says, this time? Or will you be a fool? Again. No . . . if suspicion was the deadliest possible insult, then trust was always right, even if it was mistaken. Provisionally relieved by his new promise, she snuggled into the crook of his body, and for once his heavy arm flung across her seemed more comfort than trap. Maybe this time, they would finally be able to put their lives on a rational basis.

"Shopping?" Lord Vorkosigan echoed over the breakfast table the next morning. He had been the last of the household to arise; Uncle Vorthys was already busy on the comconsole in Tien's study, Tien had left for work, and Nikki was off to school. Vorkosigan's mouth stayed straight, but the laugh lines at the corners of his eyes crinkled. "That's an offer seldom made to the son of my mother. . . . I'm afraid I don't need— no, wait, I do need something, at that. A wedding present."

"Who do you know who's getting married?" Ekaterin asked, relieved her suggestion had taken root, primarily because she didn't have a second one to offer. She prepared to be helpful.

"Gregor and Laisa."

It took her a moment to realize he meant the Emperor and his new Komarran fiancée. The surprising betrothal had been announced at Winterfair; the wedding was to be at Midsummer. "Oh! Uh . . . I'm not sure you can find anything in the Serifosa Dome that would be appropriate—maybe in Solstice they would have the kind of shops . . . oh, dear."

"I have to come up with something, I'm supposed to be Gregor's Second and Witness on their wedding circle. Maybe I could find something that would remind Laisa of home. Though possibly that's not a good idea—I'm not sure. I don't want to chance making her homesick on her honeymoon. What do you think?"

"We could look, I suppose . . ." There were exclusive shops she'd never dared enter in certain parts of the dome. This could be an excuse to venture inside.

"Duv and Delia, too, come to think of it. Yes, I've gotten way behind on my social duties."

"Who?"

"Delia Koudelka's a childhood friend of mine. She's marrying Commodore Duv Galeni, who is the new Chief of Komarran Affairs for Imperial Security. You may not have heard of him yet, but you will. He's Komarran-born."

"Of Barrayaran parents?"

"No, of Komarran resistance fighters. We seduced him to the service of the Imperium. We've agreed it was the shiny boots that turned the trick."

He was so utterly deadpan, he had to be joking. Hadn't he? She smiled uncertainly.

Uncle Vorthys lumbered into her kitchen then, murmuring, "More coffee?"

"Certainly." She poured for him. "How is it going?"

"Variously, variously." He sipped, and gave her a thank-you smile.

"I take it the morning courier has been here," said Vorkosigan. "How was last night's haul? Anything for me?"

"No, happily, if by that you mean more body parts. They brought back quite a bit of equipment of various sorts."

"Does it make any difference in your pet scenarios so far?"

"No, but I keep hoping it will. I dislike the way the vector analysis is shaping up."

Vorkosigan's eyes became notably more intent. "Oh? Why?"

"Mm. Take Point A as all things a moment before the accident—intact ship on course, soletta passively sitting in its orbital slot. Take Point B to be some time after the accident, parts of all masses scattering off in all directions at all speeds. By good old classical physics, B must equal A plus X, X being whatever forces—or masses—were added during the accident.

We know A, pretty much, and the more of B we collect, the more we narrow down the possibilities for X. We're still missing some control systems, but the topside boys have by now retrieved most of the initial mass of the system of ship-plus-mirror. By the partial accounting done so far, X is . . . very large and has a very strange shape."

"Depending on when and how the engines blew, the explosion could have added a pretty damned big kick," said Vorkosigan.

"It's not the magnitudes of the missing forces that are so puzzling, it's their direction. Fragments of anything given a kick in free fall generally travel in a *straight* line, taking into account local gravities of course."

"And the ore ship pieces didn't?" Vorkosigan's brows rose. "So what do you have in mind for an outside force?"

Uncle Vorthys pursed his lips. "I'm going to have to contemplate this for a while. Play around with the numbers and the visual projections. My brain is getting too old, I think."

"What's the . . . the *shape* of the force, then, that makes it so strange?" asked Ekaterin, following all this with deep interest.

Uncle Vorthys set his cup down and placed his hands side by side, half open. "It's . . . a typical mass in space creates a gravitational well, a funnel if you will. This looks more like a *trough*."

"Running from the ore ship to the mirror?" asked Ekaterin, trying to picture this.

"No," said Uncle Vorthys. "Running from that nearby wormhole jump point to the mirror. Or vice versa."

"And the ore ship, ah, fell in?" said Vorkosigan. He looked momentarily as baffled as Ekaterin felt.

Uncle Vorthys did not look much better. "I should not like to say so in public, that's certain."

Vorkosigan asked, "A gravitational force? Or maybe . . . a gravitic imploder lance?"

"Eh," said Uncle Vorthys neutrally. "It's certainly not like the force map of any imploder lance I've ever seen. Ah, well." He picked up his coffee, and prepared to depart for his comconsole again.

"We were just planning an outing," said Ekaterin. "Would you like to see some more of Serifosa? Pick up a present for the Professora?"

"I would, but I think it's my turn to stay in and read this morning," said her uncle. "You two go and have a good time. Though if you do see anything you think would please your aunt, I'd be extremely grateful if you'd purchase it, and I'll reimburse you."

"All right . . ." Go out with Vorkosigan alone? She'd assumed she would have her uncle along as chaperone. Still, if they stayed in public places, it should be enough to assuage any incipient suspicion on Tien's part. Not that Tien seemed to see Vorkosigan as any sort of threat, oddly. "You didn't need to see any more of Tien's department, did you?" Oh, dear, she hadn't phrased that well—what if he said yes?

"I haven't even reviewed their first stack of reports yet." Her uncle sighed. "Perhaps you'd care to take those on, Miles . . . ?"

"Yeah, I'll have a go at them." His eyes flicked up to Ekaterin's anxious face. "Later. When we get back."

Ekaterin led Lord Vorkosigan across the domed park that fronted her apartment building, heading for the nearest bubble-car station. His legs might be short, but his steps were quick, and she found she did not have to moderate her pace; if anything, she needed to lengthen her stride. That stiffness which she had seen impede his motion seemed to be something that came and went over the course of the day. His gaze, too, was quick, as he looked all around. At one point he even turned and walked backward a moment, studying something that had caught his eye.

"Is there anyplace in particular you would like to go?" she asked him.

"I don't know a great deal about Serifosa. I throw myself on your mercy, Madame, as my native guide. The last time I went shopping in any major way, it was for military ordnance."

She laughed. "That's very different."

"It's not as different as you might think. For the really high-ticket items they send sales engineers halfway across the galaxy to wait upon you. It's exactly the way my Aunt Vorpatril shops for clothes—in her case, come to think of it, also high-ticket items. The couturiers send their minions to her. I've become fond of minions, in my old age."

His old age was no more than thirty, she decided. A new-minted thirty much like her own, still worn uncomfortably. "And is that the way your mother the Countess shops, too?" How had *his* mother dealt with the fact of his mutations? Rather well, judging from the results.

"Mother just buys whatever Aunt Vorpatril tells her to. I've always had the impression she'd be happier in her old Betan Astronomical Survey fatigues."

The famous Countess Cordelia Vorkosigan was a galactic expatriate, of the most galactic possible sort, a Betan from Beta Colony. Progressive, high-tech, glittering Beta Colony, or corrupt, dangerous, sinister Beta Colony, take your pick of political views. No wonder Lord Vorkosigan seemed tinged with a faint galactic air; he literally was half galactic. "Have you ever been to Beta Colony? Is it as sophisticated as they say?"

"Yes. And no."

They arrived at the bubble-car platform, and she led them to the fourth car in line, partly because it was empty and partly to give herself an extra few seconds to select their destination. Quite automatically, Lord Vorkosigan hit the switch to close and seal the bubble canopy as soon as they'd settled into the front seat. He was either accustomed to his privacy, or just hadn't yet encountered the "Share the Ride" campaign now going on in Serifosa Dome. In any case, she was glad not to be bottled up with any Komarran strangers this trip.

Komarr had been a galactic trade crossroads for centuries, and the bazaar of the Barrayaran Empire for decades; even a relative backwater like Serifosa offered an abundance of wares at least equal to Vorbarr Sultana. She pursed her lips, then slotted in her credit chit and punched up the Shuttleport Locks District as their destination on the bubble-car's control panel. After a moment, they bumped into the tube and began to accelerate. The acceleration was slow, not a good sign.

"I believe I've seen your mother a few times on the holovid," she offered after a moment. "Sitting next to your father on reviewing platforms and the like. Mostly some years ago, when he was still Regent. Does it seem strange . . . does it give you a very different view of your parents, to see them on vid?"

"No," he said. "It gives me a very different view of holovids."

The bubble-car swung into a walled darkness lit by side-strips, flickering past the eye, then broke abruptly into sunlight, arching toward the next air-sealed complex. Halfway up the arc, they slowed still further; ahead of them, in the tube, Ekaterin could see other bubble-cars bunching to a crawl, like pearls on a string. "Oh, dear, I was afraid of that. Looks like we're caught in a blockage."

Vorkosigan craned his neck. "An accident?"

"No, the system's just overloaded. At certain times of day on certain routes, you can get held up from twenty to forty minutes. They're having a local political argument over the bubble-car system funding right now. One group wants to shorten the safety margins between cars and increase speeds.

Another one wants to build more routes. Another one wants to ration access."

His eyes lit with amusement. "Ah, yes, I understand. And how many years has this argument been ongoing without issue?"

"At least five, I'm told."

"Isn't local democracy wonderful," he murmured. "And to think the Komarrans imagined we were doing them a *favor* to leave their downside affairs under their traditional sector control."

"I hope you don't mind heights," she said uncertainly, as the bubble-car moaned almost to a halt at the top of the arc. Through the faint distortions of the canopy and tube, half of Serifosa Dome's chaotic patchwork of structures seemed spread out to their view. Two cars ahead of them, a couple seized this opportunity to indulge in some heavy necking. Ekaterin studiously ignored them. "Or . . . small enclosed spaces."

He smiled a little grimly. "As long as the small enclosed space is above freezing, I can manage."

Was that a reference to his cryo-death? She hardly dared ask. She tried to think of a way to work the conversation back to his mother, and thence to how she'd dealt with his mutations. "Astronomical Survey? I thought your mother served in the Betan Expeditionary Force, in the Escobar War."

"Before the war, she had an eleven-year career in their Survey."

"Administration, or . . . She didn't go out on the blind wormhole jumps, did she? I mean, all spacers are a little strange, but wormhole wildcatters are supposed to be the craziest of the crazy."

"That's quite true." He glanced out, as with a slight jerk the bubble-car began to move once more, descending toward the next city section. "I've met some of 'em. I confess, I never thought of the government Survey as in the same league with the entrepreneurs. The independents make blind jumps into possible death hoping for a staggering fortune. The Survey . . . makes blind jumps into possible death for a salary, benefits, and a pension. Hm." He sat back, looking suddenly bemused. "She made ship captain, before the war. Maybe she had more practice for Barrayar than I'd realized. I wonder if she got tired of playing wall, too. I'll have to ask her."

"Playing wall?"

"Sorry, a personal metaphor. When you've taken chances a few too many times, you can get into an odd frame of mind. Adrenaline is a hard habit to kick. I'd always assumed that my, um, former taste for that kind of rush came from the *Barrayaran* side of my genetics. But near-death experiences tend to cause you to reevaluate your priorities. Running that much risk, that long . . . you'd end up either damn sure who you were and what you wanted, or you'd be, I don't know, anesthetized."

"And your mother?"

"Well, she's certainly not anesthetized."

She grew more daring still. "And you?"

"Hm." He smiled a small, elusive smile. "You know, *most* people, when they get a chance to corner me, try to pump me about my *father.*"

"Oh." She flushed with embarrassment, and sat back. "I'm sorry. I was rude."

"Not at all." Indeed, he did not look or sound annoyed, his posture open and inviting as he leaned back and watched her. "Not at all."

Thus encouraged, she decided to be daring again. When would she ever repeat such a chance, after all? "Perhaps . . . what happened to you was a different kind of wall for her."

"Yes, it makes sense that you would see it from her point of view, I guess."

"What . . . exactly did happen . . . ?"

"To me?" he finished. He did not grow stiff as he had in that prickly moment over dinner the other night, but instead regarded her thoughtfully, with a kind of attentive serious-ness that was almost more alarming. "What do you know?"

"Not a great deal. I'd heard that the Lord Regent's son had been born crippled, in the Pretender's War. The Lord Regent was noted for keeping his private life very private." Actually, she'd heard his heir was a mutie, and kept out of sight.

"That's *all*?" He looked almost offended—that he wasn't more famous? Or infamous?

"My life didn't much intersect that social set," she hastened to explain. "Or any other. My father was just a minor pro-vincial bureaucrat. Many of Barrayar's rural Vor are a lot more rural than they are Vor, I'm afraid."

His smile grew. "Quite. You should have met my grandfa-ther. Or . . . perhaps not. Well. Hm. There's not a great deal to tell, at this late date. An assassin aiming for my father managed to graze both my parents with an obsolete military poison gas called soltoxin."

"During the Pretendership?"

"Just prior, actually. My mother was five months pregnant with me. Hence this mess." A wave of his hand down his body, and that nervous jerk of his head, both summed himself and defied the viewer. "The damage was actually teratogenic, not genetic." He shot her an odd sidelong look. "It used to be very important to me for people to know that."

"Used to be? And not now?" Ingenuous of him—he'd managed to tell *her* quickly enough. She was almost disappointed. Was it true that only his body, and not his chromosomes, had been damaged?

"Now . . . I think maybe it's all right if they think I'm a mutie. If I can make it *really* not matter, maybe it will matter less for the next mutie who comes after me. A form of service that costs me no additional effort."

It cost him something, evidently. She thought of Nikolai, heading into his teens soon, and what a hard time of life that was even for normal children. "Were you made to feel it? Growing up?"

"I was of course somewhat protected by Father's rank and position."

She noted that *somewhat*. *Somewhat* was not the same as *completely*. Sometimes, *somewhat* was the same as *not at all*.

"I moved a few mountains, to force myself into the Imperial Military Service. After, um, a few false starts, I finally found a place for myself in Imperial Security, among the irregulars. The rest of the irregulars. ImpSec was more interested in results than appearances, and I found I could deliver results. Except—a slight miscalculation—all the achievements upon which I'd hoped to be rejudged disappeared into ImpSec's classified files. So I fell out at the end of a thirteen-year career, a medically discharged captain whom nobody knew, almost as anonymous as when I started." He actually sighed.

"Imperial Auditors aren't anonymous!"

"No, just discreet." He brightened. "So there's some hope yet."

Why did he make her want to laugh? She swallowed the impulse. "Do you wish to be famous?"

His eyes narrowed in a moment of introspection. "I would have said so, once. Now I think . . . I just wanted to be someone in my own right. Make no mistake, I like being my father's son. He is a great man. In every sense, and it's been a privilege to know him. But there is, nevertheless, a secret fantasy of mine, where just once, in some history somewhere, Aral Vorkosigan gets introduced as being principally important because he was Miles Naismith Vorkosigan's father."

She did laugh then, though she muffled it almost immediately with a hand over her mouth. But he did not seem to take offense, for his eyes merely crinkled at her. "It is pretty amusing," he said ruefully.

"No . . . no, not that," she hastily denied. "It just seems like some kind of hubris, I guess."

"Oh, it's all kinds of hubris." Except that he did not look in the least daunted by the prospect, merely calculating.

His thoughtful look fell on her then; he cleared his throat, and began, "When I was working on your comconsole yesterday morning—" The deceleration of the bubble-car interrupted him. The little man craned his neck as they slid to a halt in the station. "Damn," he murmured.

"Is something wrong?" she asked, concerned.

"No, no." He hit the pad to raise the canopy. "So, let's see this Docks and Locks district . . ."

Lord Vorkosigan seemed to enjoy their stroll through the organized chaos of the Shuttleport Locks district, though the route he chose was decidedly nonstandard; he zig-zagged by preference down to what Ekaterin thought of as the underside of the area, where people and machines loaded and unloaded cargo, and where the less well-off sorts of spacers had their hostels and bars. There were plenty of odd-looking people in the district, in all colors and sizes, wearing strange clothes; snatches of conversations in utterly strange languages teased her ear in passing. The looks they gave the two Barrayarans were noted but ignored by Vorkosigan. Ekaterin decided that his lack of offense wasn't because the galactics stared less—or more—at him, it was that they stared equally at everybody.

She also discovered that he was attracted by the dreadful, among the galactic wares cramming the narrow shops into which they ducked. He actually appeared to seriously consider for several minutes what was claimed to be a genuine twentieth-century reproduction lamp, of Jacksonian manufacture, consisting of a sealed glass vessel containing two immiscible liquids which slowly rose and fell in the convection currents. "It looks just like red blood corpuscles floating in plasma," Vorkosigan opined, staring in fascination at the underlit blobs.

"But as a *wedding* present?" she choked, half amused, half appalled. "What kind of message would people take it for?"

"It would make Gregor laugh," he replied. "Not a gift he gets much. But you're right, the wedding present proper needs to be, er, proper. Public and political, not personal." With a regretful sigh, he returned the lamp to its shelf. After another moment, he changed his mind again, bought it, and had it shipped. "I'll get him *another* present for the wedding. This can be for his birthday."

After that, he let Ekaterin lead him into the more sophisticated end of the district, with shops displaying well-spread-out and well-lit jewelry and artwork and antiques, interspersed with discreet couturiers of the sort, she thought, who might send minions to his aunt. He seemed to find it much less interesting than the galactic rummage sale a few streets and levels away, the animation fading from his face, until his eye was caught by an unusual display in a jeweler's kiosk.

Tiny model planets, the size of the end of her thumb, turned in a grav-bubble against a black background. Several of the little spheres were displayed under various levels of magnification, where they proved to be perfectly-mapped replicas of the worlds they represented, right down to the one-meter scale. Not just rivers and mountains and seas, but cities and roads and dams, were represented in realistic colors. Furthermore, the terminator moved across their miniature landscapes in real-time for the planetary cycle in question; cities lit the night side like living jewels. They could be hung in pairs as earrings, or displayed in pendants or bracelets. Most of the planets in the wormhole nexus were available, including Beta Colony and an Earth that included as an option its famous moon circling a handspan away, though how this pairing was to be hung on someone's body was not entirely clear. The prices, at which Vorkosigan did not even glance, were alarming.

"That's rather fine," he murmured approvingly, staring in fascination at the little Barrayar. "I wonder how they do that? I know where I could have one reverse-engineered. . . ."

"They seem more like toys than jewels, but I have to admit, they're striking."

"Oh, yes, a typical tech toy—high-end this year, everywhere next year, nowhere after that, till the antiquarians' revival. Still . . . it would be fun to make up an Imperial set, Barrayar, Komarr, and Sergyar. I don't know any women with three ears . . . two earrings and a pendant, perhaps, though then you'd have the socio-political problem of how to rank the worlds."

"You could put all three on a necklace."

"True, or . . . I think my mother would definitely like a Sergyar. Or Beta Colony . . . no, might make her homesick. Sergyar, yes, very apropos. And there's Winterfair, and birthdays coming up—let's see, there's Mother, Laisa, Delia, Aunt Alys, Delia's sisters, Drou—maybe I ought to order a dozen sets, and have a couple to spare."

"Uh," said Ekaterin, contemplating this burst of efficiency, "do all these women know each other?" Were any of them his lovers? Surely he wouldn't mention such in the same breath with his mother and aunt. Or might he be a suitor? But . . . to *all* of them?

"Oh, sure."

"Do you really think you ought to get them all the *same* present?"

"No?" he asked doubtfully. "But . . . they all know *me.* . . ."

In the end, he restrained himself, purchasing only two earring sets, one each of Barrayars and Komarrs, and swapping them out, for the brides of the two mixed marriages. He added a Sergyar on a fine chain for his mother. At the last moment, he bolted back for another Barrayar, for which woman on his lengthy list he did not say. The packets of tiny planets were made up and gift-wrapped.

Feeling a little overwhelmed by the Komarran bazaar, Ekaterin led him off for a look at one of her favorite parks. It bounded the end of the Locks district, and featured one of the largest and most naturally landscaped lakes in Serifosa. Ekaterin mentally planned a stop for coffee and pastry, after they circumnavigated the lake along its walking trails.

They paused at a railing above a modest bluff, where a view across the lake framed some of the higher towers of Serifosa. The crippled soletta array was in full view overhead now, through the park's transparent dome, creating dim sparkles on the lake's wavelets. Cheerful voices echoed distantly across the water, from families playing on an artificially-natural swimming beach.

"It's very pretty," said Ekaterin, "but the maintenance cost is terrific. Urban forestry is a full-time specialty here. Everything's consciously created, the woods, the rocks, the weeds, everything."

"World-in-a-box," murmured Vorkosigan, gazing out over the reflecting sheet. "Some assembly required."

"Some Serifosans think of their park system as a promise for the future, ecology in the bank," she went on, "but others, I suspect, don't know the difference between their little parks and real forests. I sometimes wonder if, by the time the atmosphere is breathable, the Komarrans' great-grandchildren will all be such agoraphobes, they won't even venture out in it."

"A lot of Betans tend to think like that. When I was last there—" His sentence was shattered by a sudden crackling boom; Ekaterin started, till she identified the noise as a load dropped from a mag-crane working on some construction, or reconstruction, back over their shoulders beyond the trees. But Vorkosigan jumped and spun like a cat; the package in his right hand went flying, his left made to push her behind him, and he drew a stunner she hadn't even known he was carrying half out of his trouser pocket before he, too, identified the source of the bang. He inhaled deeply, flushed, and cleared his throat. "Sorry," he said to her wide-eyed look. "I overreacted a trifle there." Though they both surreptitiously examined the dome overhead; it remained placidly intact. "Stunner's a pretty useless weapon anyway, against things that go bump like that." He shoved it back deep into his pocket.

"You dropped your planets," she said, looking around for the white packet. It was nowhere in sight.

He leaned out over the railing. "Damn."

She followed his gaze. The packet had bounced off the boardwalk, and fetched up a meter down the bluff, caught on a bit of hanging foliage, a thorny bittersweet plant dangling over the water.

"I think maybe I can reach it . . ." He swung over the railing past the sign admonishing CAUTION: STAY ON THE TRAIL and flung himself flat on the ground over the edge before she could squeak, *But your good suit*— Vorkosigan was not, she suspected, a man who routinely did his own laundry. But his blunt fingers swung short of the prize they sought. She had a hideous vision of an Imperial Auditor under her guest-hold landing head-down in the pond. Could she be accused of treason? The bluff was barely four meters high; how deep was the water here?

"My arms are longer," she offered, climbing after him.

Temporarily thwarted, he scrambled back to a sitting position. "We can fetch a stick. Or better yet, a minion with a stick." He glanced dubiously at his wrist comm.

"I *think*," she said demurely, "calling ImpSec for this might be overkill." She lay prone, and reached as he had. "It's all right, I think I can . . ." Her fingers too swung short of the packet, but only just. She inched forward, feeling the precarious pull of the undercut slope. She stretched . . .

The root-compacted soil of the edge sagged under her weight, and she began to slide precipitously forward. She yelped; pushing backward fragmented her support totally. One wildly backgrappling arm was caught suddenly in a viselike grip, but the rest of her body turned as the soil gave way beneath her, and she found herself dangling absurdly feet-down over the pond. Her other arm, swinging around, was caught, too, and she looked up into Vorkosigan's face above her. He was lying prone on the slope, one hand locked around each of her wrists. His teeth were clenched and grinning, his gray eyes alight.

"Let go, you idiot!" she cried.

The look on his face was weirdly, wildly exultant. "Never," he gasped, "again—"

His half-boots were locked around . . . nothing, she realized, as he began to slide inexorably over the edge after her. But his death-grip never slackened. The exalted look on his face melted to sudden horrified realization. The laws of physics took precedence over heroic intent for the next couple of seconds; dirt, pebbles, vegetation, and two Barrayaran bodies all hit the chilly water more or less simultaneously.

The water, it turned out, was a bit over a meter deep. The bottom was soft with muck. She wallowed upright onto her feet, one shoe gone who knew where, sputtering and dragging her hair from her eyes and looking around frantically for Vorkosigan. *Lord* Vorkosigan. The water came to her waist, it ought not to be over his head—no half-booted feet were sticking up like waving stumps anywhere—could he *swim*?

He popped up beside her, and blew muddy water out of his mouth, and dashed it from his eyes to clear his vision. His beautiful suit was sodden, and a water-plant dangled over one ear. He clawed it away, and located her, his hand going toward her and then stopping.

"Oh," said Ekaterin faintly. "Drat."

There was a meditative pause before Lord Vorkosigan spoke. "Madame Vorsoisson," he said mildly at last, "has it ever occurred to you that you may be just a touch oversocialized?"

She couldn't stop herself; she laughed out loud. She clapped her hand over her mouth, and waited fearfully for some masculine explosion of wrath.

None came; he merely grinned back at her. He looked around till he spotted his packet, now dangling mockingly overhead. "Ha. Now gravity's on our side, at least." He waded underneath the remains of the overhang, disappeared into the water again, and came up holding a couple of rocks. He shied them at the thorn plant till he dislodged his package, and caught it one-handed as it fell, before it could hit the water. He grinned again, and splashed back to her, and offered her his other arm for all the world as though they were about to enter some ambassadorial reception. "Madame, will you wade with me?"

His humor was irresistible; she found herself laying her hand upon his sleeve. "My pleasure, my lord."

She abandoned her surreptitious toe-prodding for her lost shoe. They sloshed off toward the nearest low place on shore, with the most serenely cockeyed dignity Ekaterin had ever experienced. Packet in his teeth, he scrambled ahead of her, grabbed a narrow out-leaning tree trunk for support, and handed her up through the mud with the air of an Armsman-driver helping his lady from the rear compartment of her groundcar. To Ekaterin's intense relief, no one across the lake appeared to have noticed their show. Could Vorkosigan's Imperial authority save them from arrest for swimming in a no-swimming zone?

"You aren't upset about the accident?" she inquired timor-ously as they regained the path, still hardly able to believe her good fortune in his admittedly odd reaction. A passing jogger stared at them, turning and bouncing backward a moment, but Vorkosigan waved him genially onward.

He tucked his packet under his arm. "Madame Vorsoisson, trust me on this one. Needle grenades are accidents. *That* was just an amusing inconvenience." But then his smile slipped, his face stiffened, and his breath drew in sharply. He added in a rush, "I should mention, I've lately become subject to occasional seizures. I pass out and have convulsions. They last about five minutes, and then go away, and I wake up, no harm done. If one should occur, don't panic."

"Are you about to have one now?" she asked, panicked.

"I feel a little strange all of a sudden," he admitted.

There was a bench nearby, along the trail. "Here, sit down—" She led him to it. He sat abruptly, and hunched over with his face in his hands. He was beginning to shiver with the wet cold, as was she, but his shudders were long and deep, traveling the length of his short body. Was a seizure starting now? She regarded him with terror.

After a couple of minutes, his ragged breathing steadied. He rubbed his face, hard, and looked up. He was extremely pale, almost gray-faced. His pasted-on smile, as he turned toward her, was so plainly false that she almost would rather he'd have frowned. "I'm sorry. I haven't done anything like that in quite a while, at least not in a waking state. Sorry."

"Was that a seizure?"

"No, no. False alarm entirely. Actually, it was a, um, com-bat flashback, actually. Unusually vivid. Sorry, I don't usually . . . I haven't done . . . I don't usually do things like this, really." His speech was scrambled and hesitant, entirely unlike himself, and failed signally to reassure her.

"Should I go for help?" She was sure she needed to get him somewhere warmer, as soon as possible. He looked like a man in shock.

"Ha. No. Worlds too late. No, really, I'll be all right in a couple of minutes. I just need to think about this for a minute." He looked sideways at her. "I was just stunned by an insight, for which I thank you."

She clenched her hands in her lap. "Either stop talking gibberish, or stop talking at all," she said sharply.

His chin jerked up, and his smile grew a shade more genuine. "Yes, you deserve an explanation. If you want it. I warn you, it's a bit ugly."

She was so rattled and exasperated by now, she'd have cheerfully choked explanations out of his cryptic little throat. She took refuge in the mockery of formality which had extracted them so nobly from the pond. "If you please, my lord!"

"Ah, yes, well. Dagoola IV. I don't know if you've heard much about it . . . ?"

"Some."

"It was an evacuation under fire. It was an unholy mess. Shuttles lifting with people crammed aboard. The details don't matter now, except for one. There was this woman, Sergeant Beatrice. Taller than you. We had trouble with our shuttle's hatch ramp, it wouldn't retract. We couldn't dog the hatch and lift above the atmosphere till we'd jettisoned it. We were airborne, I don't know how high, there was thick cloud cover. We got the damaged ramp loosened, but she fell after it. I grabbed for her. Touched her hand, even, but I missed."

"Did . . . was she killed?"

"Oh, yes." His smile now was utterly peculiar. "It was a long way down by then. But you see . . . something *I* didn't see until about five minutes ago. I've spent five, six years walking around with this picture in my head. Not all the time, you understand, just when I chanced to be reminded. If only I'd been a little quicker, grabbed a little harder, hadn't lost my grip, I might have pulled her in. Instant replay on an endless repeat. In all those years, I never once pictured what would *really* have happened if I'd made my grab good. She was almost twice my weight."

"She'd have pulled you out," said Ekaterin. For all the simplicity of his words, the images they evoked were intense and immediate. She rubbed at the deep red marks aching now on her wrists. *Because you would not have let go.*

He looked for the first time at the marks. "Oh. I'm sorry."

"It's all right." Self-conscious, she stopped massaging them.

This didn't help, because *he* took her hand, and rubbed gently at the blotches, as if he might erase them. "I think there must be something askew with my body image," he said.

"Do you think you're six feet tall, inside your head?"

"Apparently my dream-self thinks so."

"Does that—realizing the truth—make it any better?"

"No, I don't think so. Just . . . different. Stranger."

Both their hands were freezing cold. She sprang to her feet, eluding his arresting touch. "We have to go get dry and warm, or we'll both . . . be in a state." *Catch your death*, was her great-aunt's old phrase for it, and a singularly inept phrase it would be to use just now. She dropped her useless remaining shoe in the first trash bin they passed.

On their way to the bubble-car stop near the public beach, Ekaterin darted into a kiosk and bought a stack of colorful towels. In the bubble-car, she turned the heat up to its stingy maximum.

"Here," she said, shoving towels at Lord Vorkosigan as the car accelerated. "Get out of that sopping tunic, at least, and dry off a bit."

"Right." Tunic, silk shirt, and thermal undershirt hit the floor with a wet splat, and he rubbed his hair and torso vigorously. His skin had a blotched purple-blue tinge; pink and white scars sprang out in high contrast to their darkened background. There were scars on scars on scars, mostly very fine and surgically straight, in criss-crossing layers running back through time, growing fainter and paler: on his arms, on his hands and fingers, on his neck and running up under his hair, circling his ribcage and paralleling his spine, and, most pinkly and recently, an unusually ragged and tangled mess centered on his chest.

She stared in covert astonishment; his glance caught hers. By way of apology, she said, "You weren't joking about needle grenades, were you?"

His hand touched his chest. "No. But most of this is old surgery, from the brittle bones the soltoxin gifted me with. I've had practically every bone in my body replaced with synthetics, at one time or another. Very piecemeal, though I suppose it would not have been medically practical to just whip me off my skeleton, shake me out like a suit of clothes, and pop me back on over another one."

"Oh. My."

"Ironically enough, all this show represents the successful repairs. The injury that really took me out of the Service you can't even see." He touched his forehead and wrapped a couple of towels around himself like a shawl. The towels had giant yellow daisies on them. His shivering was diminishing now, his skin growing less purple, though still blotchy. "I didn't mean to alarm you, back there."

She thought it through. "You should have told me sooner." Yes, what if one of his seizures had taken him by surprise, sometime along their route this morning? What in the world would she have done? She frowned at him.

He shifted uncomfortably. "You're quite right, of course. Um . . . quite right. Some secrets are unfair to keep from . . . people on your team." He looked away from her, looked back, smiled tensely, and said, "I started to tell you, earlier, but I rather lost my nerve. When I was working on your comconsole yesterday morning, I accidentally ran across your file on Vorzohn's Dystrophy."

Her breath seemed to freeze in her suddenly-paralyzed chest. "Didn't I—how could you accidentally . . ." Had she somehow left it open last time? Not possible!

"I could show you how," he offered. "ImpSec basic training is pretty basic. I think you could pick up that trick in about ten minutes."

The words blurted out before she could stop and think. "You opened it deliberately!"

"Well, yes." His smile now was false and embarrassed. "I was curious. I was taking a break from looking at vids of autopsies. Your, um, gardens are lovely, too, by the way."

She stared at him in disbelief. A mixture of emotions churned in her chest: violation, outrage, fear . . . and relief? *You had no right.*

"No, I had no right," he agreed, watching her obviously too-open expression; she tried to school her face to blankness. "I apologize. I can only plead that ImpSec training inculcates some pretty bad habits." He took a deep breath. "What can I do for you, Madame Vorsoisson? Anything you need to ask, or ask about . . . I am at your service." The little man half-bowed, an absurdly archaic gesture, sitting wrapped in his towels like some wizened old Count from the Time of Isolation in his robes of office.

"There's nothing you can do for me," Ekaterin said woodenly. She became aware that her legs and arms were tightly crossed, and she was starting to hunch over; she straightened with a conscious effort. Dear God, how would Tien react to her spilling, however inadvertently, his deadly—well, *he* acted as though it were deadly—secret? Now of all times, when he seemed on the verge of overcoming his denial, or whatever it was, and taking effective action at last?

"I beg your pardon, Madame Vorsoisson, but I'm afraid I'm still uncertain exactly what your situation is. It's obviously very private, if even your uncle doesn't know, and I'd give odds he doesn't—"

"Don't tell him!"

"Not without your permission, I assure you, Madame. But . . . if you are ill, or expect to become ill, there is a great *deal* that can be done for you." He hesitated. "The contents of that file tell me you already know this. Is *anyone* helping you?"

Help. What a concept. She felt as though she might melt through the floor of the bubble car at the mere thought. She retreated from the terrible temptation. "I'm not ill. We don't require assistance." She raised her chin defiantly, and added with all the frost she could muster, "It was very wrong of you to read my private files, Lord Vorkosigan."

"Yes," he agreed simply. "A wrong I do not care to compound by either concealing my breach of trust, or failing to offer what help I can command."

Just *how much* help Imperial Auditor Vorkosigan might command . . . was not to be thought about. Too painful. Belatedly, she realized that declaring herself unaffected was tantamount to naming Tien afflicted. She was rescued from her confusion by the bubble-car sliding to a stop at her home station. "This is very much not your business."

"I beg you will think of your uncle as a resource, then. I'm certain he would wish it."

She shook her head, and hit the canopy release sharply.

They walked in stiff and chilled silence back to her apartment building, in awkward contrast, Ekaterin felt, to their earlier odd ease. Vorkosigan didn't look happy either.

Uncle Vorthys met them at the apartment door, still in shirtsleeves and with a data disk in his hand. "Ah! Vorkosigan! Back earlier than I expected, good. I almost rang your comm link." He paused, staring at their damp and bizarre bedragglement, but then shrugged and went on, "We had a visit from a second courier. Something for you."

"A second courier? Must be something hot. Is it a break in the case?" Vorkosigan shrugged an arm free of his towel-shawl and took the proffered disk.

"I'm not at all sure. They found another body."

"The missing were all accounted for. A body part, surely— a woman's arm, perhaps?"

Uncle Vorthys shook his head. "A body. Almost intact. Male. They're working on the identification now. They *were* all accounted for." He grimaced. "Now, it seems, we have a spare."

CHAPTER SIX

Miles boiled himself in the shower for a long time, trying to regain control of his shocky body and scattered wits. He'd realized quickly, earlier, that all Madame Vorsoisson's anxious questions about his mother camouflaged oblique concerns about her son Nikolai, and he'd answered her as openly and carefully as he could. He'd been rewarded, through the extremely pleasant morning's expedition, by seeing her gradually relax and grow nearly open herself. When she'd laughed, her light blue eyes had sparkled. The animated intelligence had illuminated her face, and spilled over to loosen and soften her body from its original tight defensive density. Her sense of humor, creeping slowly out from hiding, had even survived his dropping them into that idiot pond.

Her brief appalled look when he'd half-stripped in the bubble-car had almost thrown him back into earlier modes of painful somatic self-consciousness, but not quite. It seemed he had grown comfortable at last in his own ill-used body, and the realization had given him a lunatic courage to try to clear things with her. So when all expression in her face shut down as he'd confessed his snooping . . . that had hurt.

He'd handled a bad situation as well as he could, hadn't he? Yes? No? He wished now he'd kept his mouth shut. *No. His false stance with Madame Vorsoisson had been unbearable. Unbearable? Isn't that a little strong? Uncomfortable*, he revised this hastily downward. Awkward, anyway.

But confession was supposed to be followed by absolution. If only the damned bubble-car had been delayed again, if only he'd had ten more minutes with her, he might have made it come out right. He shouldn't have tried to pass it off with that stupid joke, *I could show you how* . . .

Her icy, armored *We don't require assistance* felt like . . . missing a catch. He would be forced onward, she would spin down into the fog and never be seen again.

You're overdramatizing, boy. Madame Vorsoisson wasn't in a combat zone, was she?

Yes, she is. She was just falling toward death in exquisitely slow motion.

He wanted a drink desperately. Preferably several. Instead he dried himself off, dressed in another of his Auditor-suits, and went to see the Professor.

Miles leaned on the Professor's comconsole in the guest room which doubled as Tien Vorsoisson's home office, and studied the ravaged face of the dead man in the vid. He hoped for some revelation of expression, surprise or rage or fear, that would give a clue as to how the fellow had died. Besides suddenly. But the face was merely dead, its frozen distortions entirely physiological and familiar.

"First of all, are they sure he's really ours?" Miles asked, pulling up a chair for himself and settling in. On the vid, the anonymous medtech's examination recording played on at low volume, her voice-over comments delivered in that flat clinical tone universally used at moments like this. "He didn't drift in from somewhere else, I suppose."

"No, unfortunately," Vorthys said. "His speed and trajectory put him accurately at the site of our accident at the time of the smash-up, and his initial estimated time of death also matches."

Miles had wished for a break in the case, some new lead that would take him in a more speedily fruitful direction. He hadn't realized his desires were so magically powerful. *Be careful what you wish for* . . .

"Can they tell if he came from the ship, or the station?"

"Not from the trajectory alone."

"Mm, I suppose not. He shouldn't have been aboard either one. Well . . . we wait for the ID, then. News of this find has not yet been publicly released, I trust."

"No, nor leaked yet either, amazingly."

"Unless the explanation for his being there turns out to be rock-solid, I don't think secondhand reports are going to be enough on this one." He had read, God knew, enough reports in the last two weeks to saturate him for a year.

"Bodies are your department." The Professor ceded this one

to him with a wave of his hand and a good will clearly laced with relief. Above the vid-plate, the preliminary examination wound to its conclusion; no one reached for the replay button.

Well, strictly speaking, political consequences were Miles's department. He really ought to visit Solstice soon, though in the planetary capital a visiting Auditor was more likely to get *handled*; he'd wanted this open provincial angle of view first, free of VIP choreographing.

"Engineering equipment," Vorthys added, "is mine. They've also just retrieved some of the ship's control systems I was waiting for. I'm think I'm going to have to go back topside soon."

"Tonight?" Miles could move out, and into a hotel, under the cover of that avuncular withdrawal. That would be a relief.

"If I went up now, I'd get there just in time for bed. I'll wait till morning. They've also found some odd things. Not accounted for in inventory."

"Odd things? New or old?" There had been tons of poorly inventoried junk equipment on the station, a century's accumulation of obsolete and worn-out technology that had been cheaper to store than haul away. If the probable-cause techs had the unenviable task of sorting it now, it must mean the highest-priority retrieval tasks were almost done.

"New. That's what's odd. And their trajectories were associated with this new body."

"I hardly ever saw a ship where somebody didn't have an unauthorized still or something operating in a closet somewhere."

"Nor a station either. But our Komarran boys are sharp enough to recognize a still."

"Maybe . . . I'll go up with you, tomorrow," Miles said thoughtfully.

"I would like that."

Gathering up the remains of his nerve, Miles went to seek out Madame Vorsoisson. This would be, he guessed, his last chance to ever have a conversation alone with her. His footsteps echoed hollowly through the empty rooms, and his tentative speaking of her name went unanswered. She had left the apartment, perhaps to pick up Nikolai from school or something. *Missed again. Damn.*

Miles took the examination recording off to the comconsole in her workroom for a more careful second run-through, and stacked up the terraforming reports from yesterday next in line. With a self-conscious twinge, he keyed on the machine. His guilty conscience irrationally expected she might pop in at any moment to check up on him. But no, more likely she would avoid him altogether. He vented a depressed sigh and started the vid.

He found little to add to the Professor's synopsis. The mysterious eighth victim was middle-aged, of average height and build for a Komarran, if he was a Komarran. It was not possible at this point to tell if he had been handsome or ugly in life. Most of his clothing had been ripped or burned off in the disaster, including any handy pockets containing traceable credit chits, etcetera. The shreds that were left appeared to be anonymous ship-knits, common wear for spacers who might have to slide into a pressure suit at a moment's notice.

What was delaying the man's identification? Miles deliberately held in check the dozen theories his mind wanted to generate. He longed to gallop up immediately to the orbital station where the body had been taken, but his arrival in person topside, to breathe over the actual investigators' shoulders, would only distract them and slow things down. Once you had delegated the best people to do a job for you, you had to trust both them and your judgment.

What he could do without admitting impediment was go bother another useless high-level supervisor like himself. He punched up the private code for the Chief of Imperial Security–Komarr at his office in Solstice, which the man had properly sent him upon the Imperial Auditors' first arrival in Komarr local space.

General Rathjens appeared at once. He looked middle-aged, alert, and busy, all appropriate qualities for his rank and post. Interestingly, he took advantage of the latter and wore civilian Komarran-style street wear rather than Imperial undress greens, suggesting he was either subtly politically-minded, or preferred his comfort. Miles guessed the former. Rathjens was the ImpSec's top man on Komarr, reporting directly to Duv Galeni at ImpSec HQ in Vorbarr Sultana. "Yes, my Lord Auditor. What can I do for you?"

"I'm interested in the new corpse they found this morning topside in association, apparently, with our soletta disaster. You've heard of it?"

"Only just. I haven't had a chance to view the preliminary report yet."

"I just did. It's not very informative. Tell me, what's your standard operating procedure for identifying this poor fellow? How soon do you expect to have anything substantive?"

"The identification of a victim of an ordinary accident,

topside or downside, would normally be left to the local civil security. Since this one came within our orbit as possible sabotage, we're running our own search in parallel with the Komarran authorities."

"Do you cooperate with each other?"

"Oh, yes. That is, they cooperate with us."

"I understand," said Miles blandly. "How long is ID likely to take?"

"If the man was Komarran, or if he was a galactic who came through Customs at one of the jump point stations, we should have something within hours. If he was Barrayaran, it may take a little longer. If he was somehow unregistered . . . well, that becomes another problem."

"I take it he hasn't been matched with any missing person report?"

"That would have sped things up. No."

"So he's been gone for almost three weeks, but nobody's missed him. Hm."

General Rathjens glanced aside at some readout on his own comconsole desk. "Do you know you are calling from an unsecured comconsole, Lord Vorkosigan?"

"Yes." That was why all his and the Professor's reports and digests from topside were being hand-carried to them from the local Serifosa ImpSec office. They hadn't expected to be here long enough to bother having ImpSec install their own secured machine. *Should have.* "I'm only seeking background information just now. When you do find out who this fellow is, how are the relatives notified?"

"Normally, local dome security sends an officer in person, if at all possible. In a case like this with potential ImpSec connections, we send an agent of our own with them, to make an initial evaluation and recommend further investigation."

"Hm. Notify me first, please. I may want to ride along and observe."

"It could come at an odd hour."

"That's fine." He wanted to feed his back-brain on something besides second-hand data; he wanted action for his restless body. He wanted out of this apartment. He'd thought it had been uncomfortable that first night because the Vorsoissons were strangers, but that was as nothing to how awkward it had become now he'd begun to know them.

"Very well, my lord."

"Thank you, General. That's all for now." Miles cut the com.

With a sigh, he turned again to the stack of terraforming reports, starting with Waste Heat Management's excessively complete report on dome energy flows. It was only in his imagination that the gaze from a pair of outraged light blue eyes burned into the back of his head.

He had left the workroom door open with the thought— hope?—that if Madame Vorsoisson just happened to be passing by, and just happened to want to renew their truncated conversation, she might realize she had his invitation to do so. The awareness that this left him sitting alone with his back to the door came to Miles simultaneously with the sense that he was no longer alone. At a surreptitious sniff from the vicinity of the doorway, he fixed his most inviting smile on his face and turned his chair around.

It was Nikki, hovering in the frame and staring at him in uncertain calculation. He returned Miles's misdirected smile shyly. "Hello," the boy ventured.

"Hello, Nikki. Home from school?"

"Yep."

"Do you like it?"

"Naw."

"Ah? How was today?"

"Boring."

"What are you studying, that's so dull?"

"Nothin'."

What a joy such monosyllabic exchanges must be to his parents, paying for that exclusive private school. Miles's smile twisted. Reassured, perhaps, by the glint of humor in his eye, the boy ventured within. He looked Miles up and down more openly than he had done heretofore; Miles bore being Looked At. *Yes, you can get used to me, kiddo.*

"Were you really a spy?" Nikki asked suddenly.

Miles leaned back, brows rising. "Now, wherever did you get that idea?"

"Uncle Vorthys *said* you were in ImpSec. Galactic operations," Nikki reminded him.

Ah, yes, that first night at the dinner table. "I was a courier officer. Do you know what that is?"

"Not . . . 'zactly. I thought a courier was a jumpship . . . ?"

"The ship is named after the job. A courier is a kind of glorified delivery man. I carried messages back and forth for the Imperium."

Nikki's brow wrinkled dubiously. "Was it dangerous?"

"It wasn't supposed to be. I generally got places only to have to turn around immediately and go back. I spent a lot of time en route reading. Composing reports. And, ah, studying. ImpSec would send these training programs along, that you were supposed to complete in your spare time, and turn back in to your superiors when you got home."

"Oh," said Nikki, sounding a little dismayed, possibly at the thought that even grownups weren't spared from home-work. He regarded Miles more sympathetically. Then a spark rose in his eye. "But you got to go on *jumpships*, didn't you? Imperial fast couriers and things?"

"Oh, yes."

"*We* went on a jumpship, to come here. It was a Vorsmythe *Dolphin*-class 776 with quadruple-vortex outboard control nacelles and dual norm-space thrusters and a crew of twelve. It carried a hundred and twenty passengers. It was full up, too." Nikki's face grew reflective. "Kind of a barge, compared to Imperial fast couriers, but Mama got the jump pilot to let me come up and see his control room. He let me sit in his station chair and put on his headset." The spark had become a flame in the memory of this glorious moment.

Miles could recognize imprinting when he saw it. "You admire jumpships, I take it."

"I want to be a jump pilot when I grow up. Didn't you ever? Or . . . or wouldn't they let you?" A certain wariness returned to Nikki's face; had he been cautioned by the adults not to mention Miles's mutoid appearance? *Yes, let us all pretend to ignore the obvious. That ought to clarify the kid's worldview.*

"No, I wanted to be a strategist. Like my Da and my Gran'da. I couldn't have passed the physical for jump pilot anyway."

"My Da was a soldier. It sounded boring. He stayed on one base for practically the whole time. *I* want to be an Imperial pilot, in the fastest ships, and go places."

Very far away from here. Yes. Miles understood *that* one, all right. It occurred to him suddenly that even if nothing else was done between now and then, a military physical would reveal Nikki's Vorzohn's Dystrophy. And even if it was suc-cessfully treated, the defect would disqualify him for military pilot's training.

"Imperial pilot?" Miles let his brows rise in apparent sur-prise. "Well, I suppose . . . but if you really want to go places, the military's not your best route."

"Why not?"

"Except for a very few courier or diplomatic missions, the military jump pilots just go from Barrayar to Komarr to Sergyar and back. Same old routes, round and round. And you have to wait forever for your turn on the roster, my pilot acquaintances tell me. Now, if you really want experience, going out with the Komarran trade fleets would take you much farther afield—all the way to Earth, and beyond. And they go out for much longer, and there are many more berths to be had. There are more kinds of ships. Pilots get a lot more time in the hot-seat. *And* when you get to the interesting places, you're a lot freer to look around."

"Oh." Nikki digested this thoughtfully. "Wait here," he commanded abruptly, and darted out.

He was back in moments cradling a box jammed with model jumpships. "This is the *Dolphin*-776 we went on," he held one up for Miles's inspection. He rummaged for another. "Did you ride on fast couriers like this one?"

"The Falcon-9? Yes, a time or two." A model caught Miles's eye; automatically, he slid down onto the floor beside Nikki, who was arranging his collection for fleet inspection. "Good God, is that an RG freighter?"

"It's an antique." Nikki held it out.

Miles took it, his eye lighting. "I owned one of the very last of these, when I was seventeen. Now, *that* was a barge."

"A . . . a model like this?" asked Nikki uncertainly.

"No, a jumpship."

"You owned a real jumpship? Your*self*?" He inhaled alarmingly.

"Mm, me and a bunch of creditors." Miles smiled in reminiscence.

"Did you get to pilot it? In normal space, I mean, not in jump space."

"No, I wasn't even up to piloting shuttles then. I learned how to do that later, at the Academy."

"What happened to the RG? Do you still have it?"

"Oh, no. Or . . . well, I'm not just sure. It met with an accident in Tau Verde local space, ramming, um, colliding with another ship. Twisted hell out of its Necklin field generator rods. It was never going to jump again after that, so I leased it as a local-space freighter, and we left it there. If Arde— he's a jump pilot friend of mine—ever finds a set of replacement rods, I told him he can have the old RG."

"You had a *jumpship* and you *gave it away*?" Nikki's eyes widened in astonishment. "Do you have any *more*?"

"Not at present. Oh, look, a *General*-class cruiser." Miles reached for it. "My father commanded one of those, once, I believe. Do you have any Betan Survey ships . . . ?"

Heads bent together, they laid out the little fleet on the floor. Nikki, Miles was pleased to find, was well-up on all the tech-specs of every ship he owned; he expanded wonderfully, his voice, formerly shy around Miles-the-weird-adult-stranger, growing louder and faster in his unselfconscious enthusiasm as he detailed his machinery. Miles's stock rose as he was able to claim personal acquaintance with nearly a dozen of the originals for the models, and add a few interesting nonclassified jumpship anecdotes to Nikki's already impressive fund of knowledge.

"But," said Nikki after a slight pause for breath, "how do you get to be a pilot if you're not in the military?"

"You go through a training school and an apprenticeship. I know of at least four schools right here on Komarr, and a couple more at home on Barrayar. Sergyar doesn't have one yet."

"How do you get in?"

"Apply, and give them money."

Nikki looked daunted. "A lot of money?"

"Mm, no more than any other college or trade school. The biggest cost is getting your neurological interface surgically installed. It pays to get the best on that one." Miles added encouragingly, "You can do anything, but you have to make your chances happen. There are some scholarships and indenture-contracts that can grease your way in, if you hustle for them. You do have to be at least twenty years old, though, so you have lots of time to plan."

"Oh." Nikki seemed to contemplate this vast span of time, equal again to his whole life so far, stretching out before him. Miles could empathize; suppose someone told him he had to wait thirty more years for something he passionately desired? He tried to think of something he passionately desired. That he could have. The field was depressingly blank.

Nikki began to replace his models in their padded box. As he nestled the Falcon-9 into its space, his fingers caressed its Imperial military decals. He asked, "Do you still have your ImpSec silver eyes?"

"No, they made me give 'em back when I was fi—when I resigned."

"Why d'you quit?"

"I didn't want to. I had health problems."

"So they made you be an Auditor instead?"

"Something like that."

Nikki groped around for some way to continue this polite adult conversation. "Do you like it?"

"It's a little early to tell. It seems to involve a lot of homework." He glanced up guiltily at the stack of report disks waiting for him on the comconsole.

Nikki gave him a look of sympathy. "Oh. Too bad."

Tien Vorsoisson's voice made them both jump. "Nikki, what are you doing in here? Get up off the floor!"

Nikki scrambled to his feet, leaving Miles sitting cross-legged and abruptly conscious that his recently-chilled body had stiffened up again.

"Are you pestering the Lord Auditor? My apologies, Lord Vorkosigan! Children have no manners." Vorsoisson entered and loomed over them.

"Oh, his manners are fine. We were having an interesting discussion on the subject of jump ships." Miles contemplated the problem of standing gracefully in front of a fellow Barrayaran, without any unfortunate lurch or stumble to give a false impression of disability. He stretched, sitting, by way of preparation.

Vorsoisson grimaced wryly. "Ah, yes, the most recent obsession. Don't step barefoot on one of those damn things, it'll cripp—it'll hurt. Well, every boy goes through that phase, I suppose. We all outgrow it. Pick up all that mess, Nikki."

Nikki's eyes were downcast, but narrowed in brief resentment at this, Miles could see from his angle of view. The boy bent to scoop up the last of his miniature fleet.

"Some people grow into their dreams, instead of out of them," Miles murmured.

"That depends on whether your dreams are reasonable," said Vorsoisson, his lips twitching in rather bleak amusement. Ah, yes. Vorsoisson must be fully aware of the secret medical bar between Nikki and his ambition.

"No, it doesn't." Miles smiled slightly. "It depends on how hard you grow." It was difficult to tell just how Nikki took that in, but he heard it; his eyes flicked back to Miles as he carried his treasure box toward the door.

Vorsoisson frowned, suspicious of this contradiction, but said only, "Kat sent me to tell everyone supper is ready. Go wash your hands, Nikki, and tell your Uncle Vorthys."

Miles's last family dinner with the Vorsoisson clan was a strained affair. Madame Vorsoisson made herself very busy with serving admittedly excellent food, her faintly harried pose as effective as a placard saying *Leave me alone.* The conversation was left to the Professor, who was abstracted, and Tien, who, bereft of direction, spoke forcefully and without depth of local Komarran politics, authoritatively explaining the inner workings of the minds of people he had never, so far as Miles could discern, actually met. Nikolai, wary of his father, did not pursue the subject of jumpships in front of him.

Miles wondered now how he could have mistaken Madame Vorsoisson's silence for serenity, that first night, or Etienne Vorsoisson's tension for energy. Until seeing those brief glimpses of her animation earlier today, he had not guessed how much of her personality was missing from view, or how much went underground in the presence of her husband.

Now that he knew what clues to look for, he could see the faint grayness underlying Tien's dome-pallor, and spot his betraying tiny physical twitches masked as a big man's clumsiness with small objects. At first Miles had feared the illness was hers, and he'd been nearly ready to challenge Tien to a duel for his failure to take immediate and massive measures to solve the problem. If Madame Vorsoisson had been *his* wife . . . But apparently Tien was playing these little delaying headgames with his own condition. Miles knew, none better, the bone-deep Barrayaran fear of any genetic distortion. *Mortal embarrassment* was more than a turn of phrase. He didn't exactly go around advertising his own invisible seizure-disorder, either—though he'd been privately relieved to have that secret out with her. Not that it mattered, now that he was leaving. Denial was Tien's choice, stupid though it seemed; maybe the man was hoping to be hit by a meteor before his disease manifested itself. Miles's stifled impulse toward homicide was renewed with the thought, *But he's chosen the same for her Nikolai.*

Halfway through the main course—exquisitely aromatic vat-raised fish fillets baked on a bed of garlic potatoes—the door chimed. Madame Vorsoisson hastily rose to answer it. Feeling obscurely that it was bad security to send her off by herself, Miles followed. Nikolai, perhaps sensing adventure, tried to accompany them, but was roped back to face the remains of his dinner by his father. Madame Vorsoisson glanced at Miles over her shoulder, but said nothing.

She checked the welcome monitor beside the door. "It's another courier. Oh, it's a captain this time. Usually you get a sergeant." Madame Vorsoisson keyed open the hall door to reveal a young man in Barrayaran undress greens, with ImpSec's eye-of-Horus pins on his collar. "Do come in."

"Madame Vorsoisson." The man nodded to her, trod inside, and shifted his gaze to Miles. "Lord Auditor Vorkosigan. I'm Captain Tuomonen. I head up ImpSec's office here in Serifosa." Tuomonen appeared to be in his late twenties, dark haired and brown eyed like most Barrayarans, and a bit more trim and fit than the average desk soldier, though with dome-pale skin. He had a disk case in one hand and a larger case in the other, so nodded cordially rather than offering any salutelike gesture.

"Yes, General Rathjens mentioned you. We're honored to have such a courier."

Tuomonen shrugged. "ImpSec Serifosa is a very small office, my lord. General Rathjens directed you were to be informed as soon as possible after the new body was identified."

Miles's eye took in the secured disk case in the captain's hand. "Excellent. Come sit down." He led the captain to the conversation circle, a deeply-padded sunken bench which was the centerpiece of the Vorsoisson's living room. Like most of the rest of the furnishings, it was Komarran dome standard-issue. Did Madame Vorsoisson sometimes feel she was camping in a hotel, rather than making a home here? "Madame Vorsoisson, would you ask your uncle to join us? Let him finish eating first, though."

"I would like to speak with Administrator Vorsoisson, also, when he's finished," Tuomonen called after her. She nodded and withdrew, eyes dark with interest but posture still self-effacing, self-erasing, as if she wished she might become invisible to Miles's eyes.

"What do we have?" continued Miles, settling himself. "I told Rathjens I might like to accompany and observe the first ImpSec contact on this matter." He could pack his bag and take it along tonight, and not have to come back.

"Yes, my lord. That's why I'm here. Your mysterious body turns out to be a local fellow, from Serifosa. He is, or was, listed as an employee of the Terraforming Project here."

Miles blinked. "Not an engineer named Dr. Radovas, is it?"

Tuomonen stared at him, startled. "How did you know?"

"Wild-ass guess, because he went missing a few weeks ago. Oh, hell, I'll bet Vorsoisson could have identified him at a glance. Or . . . maybe not. He was pretty battered. Hm. Radovas's boss thought he'd eloped with his tech, a young lady named Marie Trogir. *Her* body hasn't turned up topside, has it?"

"No, my lord. But it sounds as though we ought to start looking for it."

"Yes. A full ImpSec search and background check, I think. Don't assume she's dead—if she's alive, we surely want to question her. Do you need a special order from me?"

"Not necessarily, but I'll bet it would expedite things." A faint enthusiastic gleam lit Tuomonen's eye.

"You have it, then."

"Thank you, my lord. I thought you'd want this." He handed Miles the secured case. "I pulled the complete dossier on Radovas before I left the office."

"Does ImpSec keep files on every Komarran citizen, or was he special?"

"No, we don't keep universal files. But we have a search program that can pull records of good depth from the information net very quickly. The first part of this is his public biography, school records, medical records, financial and travel documents, all the usual. I only had time to glance over it. But Radovas also does have a small ImpSec file, dating back to his student days during the Komarr Revolt. It was closed at the amnesty."

"Is it interesting?"

"I would not draw too many inferences from it alone. Half the population of Komarr of that age group was part of some student protest or would-be revolutionary group back then, including my mother-in-law." Tuomonen waited stiffly to see what response Miles would make to this tidbit.

"Ah, you married a local girl, did you?"

"Five years ago."

"How long have you been posted to Serifosa?"

"About six years."

"Good for you." *Yes! That leaves one more Barrayaran woman for the rest of us.* "You get along well with the locals, I take it."

Tuomonen's stiffness eased. "Mostly. Except for my mother-in-law. But I don't think that's entirely political." Tuomonen suppressed a small grin. "But our little daughter has her under complete control, now."

"I see." Miles smiled back at him. With a more thoughtful frown, he turned the case over, dug his Auditor's seal out of his pocket, and keyed it open. "Has your Analysis section red-flagged anything in this for me?"

"I *am* Serifosa's Analysis section," Tuomonen admitted ruefully. His glance at Miles sharpened. "I understand you're former ImpSec yourself, my lord. I think I'd rather let you read it over first, before I comment."

Miles's brows twitched up. Did Tuomonen not trust his own judgment, had the arrival of two Imperial Auditors in his sector unnerved him, or was he merely seizing the opportunity for some mutual brainstorming? "And what sort of dossier did you pull off the net on one Miles Vorkosigan, and speed-read before you left the office just now?"

"I did that day before yesterday, actually, my lord, when I was notified you would be arriving in Serifosa."

"And what was your analysis of it?"

"About two-thirds of your career is locked under a need-to-know seal that requires clearance from ImpSec HQ in Vorbarr Sultana to access. But your publicly recorded awards and decorations appear in a statistically significant pattern following supposedly routine courier missions assigned to you by the Galactic Affairs office. At approximately five times the density of the next most decorated courier in ImpSec history."

"And your conclusion, Captain Tuomonen?"

Tuomonen smiled faintly. "You were never a bloody courier, Captain Vorkosigan."

"Do you know, Tuomonen, I believe I am going to enjoy working with you."

"I hope so, sir." He glanced up as the Professor entered the living room, flanked by Tien Vorsoisson.

Vorthys finished wiping his mouth with his dinner napkin, stuffed it absently into his pocket, and greeted Tuomonen with a handshake, then introduced his nephew-in-law. As they all sat again, Miles said, "Tuomonen has brought us the identification of our extra body."

"Oh, good," said Vorthys. "Who was the poor fellow?"

Miles watched Tuomonen watch Tien and say, "Strangely enough, Administrator Vorsoisson, one of your employees. Dr. Barto Radovas."

Tien's grayness became a shade paler. "Radovas! What the hell was he doing up *there*?" The shock and horror on Tien's face was genuine, Miles would have sworn, the surprise in his voice unfeigned.

"I was hoping you might have some ideas, sir," said Tuomonen.

"My God. Well . . . was he aboard the station, or the ship?"

"We haven't determined that yet."

"I really can't tell you that much about the man. He was in Soudha's department. Soudha never made any complaints about his work to me. He got all his merit raises right to schedule." Tien shook his head. "But what the hell was he doing . . ." He glanced worriedly at Tuomonen. "He's not actually my employee, you know. He resigned several weeks ago."

"Five days before his death, according to our calculations," said Tuomonen.

Tien's brows wrinkled. "Well . . . he couldn't have been aboard that ore ship, then, could he? How could he have gotten all the way out to the second asteroid belt and boarded it before he even left Komarr?"

"He might have joined the ore ship en route," said Tuomonen.

"Oh. I suppose that's possible. My God. He's married. Was married. Is his wife still here in town?"

"Yes," said Tuomonen. "I'll be meeting shortly with the dome civil security officer who's taking the official notification of death to her."

"She's waited three weeks with no word from him," said Miles. "Another hour can't matter much at this point. I think I'd like to review your report before we leave, Captain."

"Please do, my lord."

"Professor, will you join me?"

They all ended up trooping into Vorsoisson's study. Miles privately felt he could do without Tien, but Tuomonen made no move to exclude him.

The report was not yet an in-depth analysis, but rather a wad of raw data bundled logically, with hasty preliminary notes and summations supplied by Tuomonen. A full analysis would doubtless arrive eventually from ImpSec-Komarr HQ. They all pulled up chairs and crowded around the vid display. After the initial overview, Miles let the Professor follow the thread of Radovas's career.

"He lost two years out of the middle of his undergraduate schooling to the Revolt," Vorthys noted. "Solstice University was shut down entirely, for a time then."

"But it looks like he made up some points with that two-year postgraduate stint on Escobar," Miles said.

"Anything could have happened to him there," opined Tien.

"But not much did, according to this," said Vorthys a bit dryly. "Commercial work in their orbital shipyards . . . he didn't even get a good research topic out of it. Solstice University did not renew his contract. Not a man with a gift for teaching, one feels."

"He was refused a job in the Imperial Science Institute because of his associations in the Revolt," Tuomonen pointed out, "despite the amnesty."

"All the amnesty promised was that he'd never be taken out and shot," said Miles a shade impatiently.

"But he was not refused it on the basis of inadequate technical competence," murmured Vorthys. "Here he goes on to a job rather below his educational level, in the Komarran orbital yards."

Miles checked. "He had three small children by then. He had to go for the money."

"Several bland years follow," the Professor droned on.

"Changes companies only once, for a respectable increase in salary and position. Then he is hired by—Soudha was fairly new then, but hired by Soudha for the Terraforming Project, and moves downside permanently."

"No pay raise that time. Professor . . ." Miles said plaintively. He touched his finger to air on the vid display at this juncture in the late Dr. Radovas's career. "Doesn't this downside move strike you as odd for a man trained and experienced in jump technologies? He was a five-space-math man."

Tuomonen smiled tightly, by which Miles deduced he had put his finger rather literally upon the same point that had bothered the captain.

Vorthys shrugged. "There could be many compelling reasons. He could have felt stale in his old work. He could have grown into new interests. Madame Radovas might have refused to live on a space station for one more day. I think you'll have to ask her."

"But it is unusual," said Tuomanen tentatively.

"Maybe," said Vorthys. "Maybe not."

"Well," sighed Miles after a long silence. "Let's go do the hard part."

The Radovas's apartment proved to be about a third of the way across the city from the Vorsoissons', but at this hour of the evening there were no delays in the bubble-car system. With Tuomonen leading, Miles, Vorthys, and Tien—whom Miles did not remember inviting, but who somehow had attached himself to the expedition—entered the lobby, where they found a youngish woman in a Serifosa Dome Security uniform waiting for them, none too patiently.

"Ah, the dome cop is female," Miles murmured to Tuomonen. He looked back over their cavalcade. "Good. We'll seem less like an invading army."

"So I hoped, my lord."

After brief introductions all around, they took a lift tube to a hallway nearly identical to every other dome residence building Miles had so far seen. The dome cop, who was styled Group-Patroller Rigby, rang the door chime.

After a pause long enough to start Miles wondering, *Is she home?* the door slid open. The woman framed there was slender and neatly dressed, appearing to Miles's Barrayaran eye to be in her mid-forties, which probably meant she was in her late fifties. She wore the usual Komarran trousers and blouse, and hunched into a heavy sweater. She looked pale and chilled, but there was certainly nothing else in her appearance to repel any husband.

Her eyes widened as she took in the uniformed people facing her, radiating the message *bad news*. "Oh," she sighed wearily. Miles, who had braced himself for hysterics, relaxed a little. She was going to be the underreacting type, it appeared. Her response would likely emerge oddly, and obliquely, and later.

"Madame Radovas?" the dome cop said. The woman nodded. "My name is Group-Patroller Rigby. I regret to inform you that your husband, Dr. Barto Radovas, has been found dead. May we please come in?"

Madame Radovas's hand went to her lips; she said nothing for a moment. "Well." She looked away. "I am not so pleased as I thought I'd be. What happened to him? That young woman—is she all right?"

"May we come in and sit down?" Rigby reiterated. "I'm afraid we are going to have to trouble you with some questions. We'll try to answer yours."

Madame Radovas's eye warily took in Tuomonen, in his ImpSec greens. "Yes. All right." She gave way, stepping backward, and gestured them all inside.

Her living room featured another standard conversation circle; Miles seated himself to one side, letting Tuomonen share line-of-sight across from Madame Radovas with the Group-Patroller, who introduced the rest of them. Tien joined them, folding himself onto the bench, a picture of awkward discomfort. Professor Vorthys shook his head slightly and remained standing, his gaze taking in the room.

"What happened to Barto? Was there an accident?" Madame Radovas's voice was husky, barely controlled, now that the news was sinking in.

"We're not certain," said Rigby. "His body was found in space, apparently associated with the disaster to the soletta three weeks ago. Did you know he had gone topside? Had he said anything before he left that would shed some light on this?"

"I . . . ." She looked away. "He didn't speak to me before he left. I think he was not very brave about this. He left me a note on the comconsole. Until I found it, I thought this was an ordinary work trip."

"May we see it?" Tuomonen spoke for the first time.

"I erased it. Sorry." She frowned at him.

"The plan for this . . . leaving, do you think it was your husband's, or Marie Trogir's?" asked Rigby.

"You know all about them, I see. I have no idea. I was

surprised. I don't know." Her voice grew sharper. "I wasn't consulted."

"Did he often make work trips?" asked Rigby.

"He went out on field tests fairly often. Sometimes he went to the terraforming conferences in Solstice. I usually went along on those." Her voice fluttered raggedly, then came back under her control.

"What did he take with him? Anything unusual?" asked Rigby patiently.

"Just what he normally took on a long field trip." She hesitated. "He took all his personal files. That's how I first knew for sure that he wasn't coming back."

"Did you talk to anyone at his work about this absence?"

Tien shook his head, but Madame Radovas replied, "I spoke to Administrator Soudha. After I found the note. Trying to figure out . . . what had gone wrong."

"Was Administrator Soudha helpful to you?" asked Tuomonen.

"Not very." She frowned again. "He didn't seem to feel it was any of his business what happened after Barto resigned."

"I'm sorry," said Vorsoisson. "Soudha didn't tell me about that part of it. I'll reprimand him. I didn't know."

And you didn't ask. But much as Miles would like to, even he found it hard to blame Tien for steering clear of what had looked to be an embarrassing domestic situation. Madame Radovas's frown at Vorsoisson became almost a glower.

"I understand you and your husband moved downside about four years ago," said Tuomonen. "It seemed an unusual change of careers, from five-space to what is effectively a form of civil engineering. Did he have a long-time interest in terraforming?"

She looked momentarily nonplused. "Barto cared about the future of Komarr. I . . . we were tired of station life. We wanted something more settled for the children. Dr. Soudha was looking for people for his team with different backgrounds, different kinds of problem-solving experience. He considered Barto's station experience valuable. Engineering is engineering, I suppose."

Professor Vorthys had been wandering gently around the room during this, one ear cocked toward the conversation, examining the travel mementos and portraits of children at various ages that were its principal decorations. He stopped before the library case on one wall, crammed with disks, and began randomly examining their titles. Madame Radovas gave him a brief curious glance.

"Due to the unusual situation in which Dr. Radovas's body was found, the law requires a complete medical examination," Rigby went on. "Given your personally awkward circumstances, when it's concluded, do you wish to have his body or his ashes returned to you, or to some other relative?"

"Oh. Yes. To me, please. There should be a proper ceremony. For the children's sake. For everyone's sake." She seemed very close to losing control now, tears standing in her eyes. "Can you . . . I don't know. Do you take care of this?"

"The Family Affairs counselor in our department will be glad to advise and assist you. I'll give you her number before we leave."

"Thank you."

Tuomonen cleared his throat. "Due to the mysterious circumstances of Dr. Radovas's death, ImpSec Komarr has also been asked to take an interest in the matter. I wonder if we might have your permission to examine your comconsole and personal records, to see if they suggest anything."

Madame Radovas touched her lips. "Barto took all his personal files. There's not much left but my own."

"Sometimes a technical examination can uncover more."

She shook her head, but said, "Well . . . I suppose so." She added more tartly, "Though I didn't think ImpSec had to bother with my permission."

Tuomonen did not deny this, but said, "I like to salvage what courtesies I can, Madame, from our crude necessities."

Professor Vorthys added in a distant tone from the far wall, his hands full of disks, "Get the library, too."

With a flash of bewildered anger, Madame Radovas said, "Why do you want to take away my poor husband's *library*?"

Vorthys looked up and gave her a kindly, disarming smile. "A man's library gives information about the shape of his mind the way his clothing gives information about the shape of his body. The cross-connections between apparently unrelated subjects may exist only in his thoughts. There is a sad disconnectedness that overcomes a library when its owner is gone. I think I should have liked to meet your husband when he was alive. In this ghostly way, perhaps I can, a little."

"I don't see why . . ." Her lips tightened in dismay.

"We can arrange for it to be returned to you in a day or two," Tuomonen said soothingly. "Is there anything you need out of it right away?"

"No, but . . . oh . . . I don't know. Take it. Take whatever you want, I don't care any more." Her eyes began to spill over at last. Group-Patroller Rigby handed her a tissue from one of her many uniform pockets and frowned at the Barrayarans.

Tien shifted uncomfortably; Tuomonen remained blandly professional. Taking her outburst for his cue, the ImpSec captain rose and carried his case over to the comconsole in the corner by the dining ell, opened it, and plugged an ImpSec standard black box into the side of the machine. At Vorthys's gesture, Rigby and Miles went to assist him in removing the library case intact from the wall, and sealing it for transport. Tuomonen, after sucking dry the comconsole, ran a scanner over the library, which Miles estimated contained close to a thousand disks, and generated a vid-receipt for Madame Radovas. She crumpled the plastic flimsy into the pocket of her gray trousers without looking at it, and stood with her arms crossed till the invaders assembled to depart.

At the last moment, she bit her lip and blurted, "Administrator Vorsoisson. There won't be . . . will I get . . . will there be any of the normal survivor's benefits coming from Barto's death?"

Was she in financial need? Her two youngest children were still in university, according to Tuomonen's files, and financially dependent on their parents; of course she was. But Vorsoisson shook his head sadly.

"I'm afraid not, Madame Radovas. The medical examiner seems to be quite clear that his death took place after his resignation."

If it had been the other way around, this would be a much more interesting problem for ImpSec. "She gets nothing, then?" asked Miles. "Through no fault of her own, she's stripped of all normal widow's benefits just because of her," he deleted a few pejorative adjectives, "late husband's fecklessness?"

Vorsoisson shrugged helplessly, and turned away.

"Wait," said Miles. He'd been of damned little use to anyone today so far. "Gregor does not approve of widows being left destitute. Trust me on this one. Vorsoisson, go ahead and run the benefits through for her anyway."

"I can't—how—do you want me to alter the date of his resignation?"

Thus creating the curious legal spectacle of a man resigning the day after his own death? By what method, spirit writing? "No, of course not. Simply make it by an Imperial order."

"There are no places on the forms for an Imperial order!" said Vorsoisson, taken aback.

Miles digested this. Tuomonen, looking faintly suffused,

watched with wide-eyed fascination. Even Madame Radovas's eyebrows crimped with bemusement. She looked directly at Miles as if seeing him for the first time. At last, Miles said gently, "A design defect you shall have to correct, Administrator Vorsoisson."

Tien's mouth opened on some other protest, but then, intelligently, closed. Professor Vorthys looked relieved. Madame Radovas, her hand pressed to her cheek in something like wonder, said, "Thank you . . . Lord Vorkosigan."

After the usual If-you-think-of-anything-more-call-this-number farewells, the herd of investigators moved off down the hallway. Vorthys handed Tien the library case to lug. Back at the building's entrance lobby, the Group-Patroller prepared to go her own way.

"What, if anything, does ImpSec want us to do now?" she asked Tuomonen. "Dr. Radovas's death seems out of Serifosa's jurisdiction. Close relatives are automatically suspects in a mysterious death, but she's been here the whole time. I don't see any causal chain to that body in space."

"Neither do I, at present," Tuomonen admitted. "For now, continue with your normal procedures, and send my office copies of all your reports and evidence files."

"I don't suppose you'd care to return the favor?" Judging by the twist of her lips, Rigby thought she knew the answer.

"I'll see what I can do, if anything pertinent to Dome security turns up," Tuomonen promised guardedly. Rigby's brows rose at even this limited concession from ImpSec.

"I'm going to have to go back topside tomorrow morning," said Vorthys to Tuomonen. "I am not going to have time to do a thorough examination of this library myself. I shall have to trouble ImpSec for it, I'm afraid."

Tuomonen, his eye taking in the thousand-disk case, looked momentarily appalled. Miles added quickly, "On my authority, requisition a high-level analyst from HQ for that job. One of the basement boffins, with engineering and math certification, I think—right, Professor?"

"Yes, indeed, the best man you can get," said Vorthys.

Tuomonen looked very relieved. "What do you want him to look for, my Lord Auditor?"

"I don't quite know," said the Professor. "That's why I want an ImpSec analyst, eh? Essentially, I want him to generate an independent picture of Radovas from this data, which we may compare with impressions from other sources later."

"A candid view of the shape of the mind inside this library," mused Miles. "I see."

"I'm sure you do. Talk to the man, Miles, you know the kinds of things they do. And the kinds of things we want."

"Certainly, Professor."

They turned the library case over to Tuomonen, and Group-Patroller Rigby took her leave. It was approaching Komarran midnight.

"I'll take all this lot back to my office, then," said Tuomonen, looking at his assorted burdens, "and call HQ with the news. How much longer do you expect to be staying in Serifosa, Lord Vorkosigan?"

"I'm not sure. I'll stay on and have a talk with Soudha, and Radovas's other colleagues, at least, before I go up again. I, ah, think I'll move my things to a hotel tomorrow, after the Professor goes up."

"You are welcome to the hospitality of my home, Lord Vorkosigan," said Tien formally, and very unpressingly.

"Thank you anyway, Administrator Vorsoisson. Who knows, I may be ready to follow on topside as early as tomorrow night. We'll see what turns up."

"I'd appreciate it if you'd keep my office apprised of your movements," said Tuomonen. "It was of course your privilege to order no close security upon your person, Lord Vorkosigan, but now that your case seems to have acquired a local connection, I'd strongly request you reconsider that."

"ImpSec guards are generally charming fellows, but I really like not tripping over them every time I turn around," Miles replied. He tapped the ImpSec issue chrono-comm link, which looked oversized strapped around his left wrist. "Let's stick with our original compromise, for now. I'll yelp for help if I need you, I promise."

"As you wish, my lord," said Tuomonen disapprovingly. "Is there anything else you need?"

"Not tonight," said Vorthys, yawning.

I need all this to make sense. I need half a dozen eager informers. I want to be alone in a locked room with Marie Trogir and a hypo of fast-penta. I wish I might fast-penta that poor bitter widow, even. Rigby would require a court order for such an invasive and offensive step; Miles could do it on whim and his borrowed Imperial Voice, if he didn't mind being a very obnoxious Lord Auditor indeed. The justification was simply not yet sufficient. *But Soudha had better watch his step, tomorrow.* Miles shook his head. "No. Get some sleep."

"Eventually." Tuomonen smiled wryly. "Good night, my lords, Administrator."

They left the widow's building in opposite directions.

CHAPTER SEVEN

Ekaterin half-dozed, curled on the sunken living room couch, waiting for the men to return. She pushed back her sleeves and studied the deep bruises darkening on her wrists in the pattern of Lord Vorkosigan's grip.

She was not normally very body-conscious, she thought. She watched people's faces, giving a bare glance to anything below the neck beyond the social language of clothing. This . . . not aversion, screening . . . seemed a mere courtesy, and a part of her sexual fidelity as automatic as breathing. So it was doubly disturbing to find herself so very aware of the little man. And probably very rude, as well, given the oddness of his body. Vorkosigan's face, once she'd penetrated his first wary opacity, was . . . well, charming, full of dry wit only waiting to break into open humor. It was disorienting to find that face coupled with a body bearing a record of appalling pain. Was it some kind of perverse voyeurism, that her second reaction after shock had been a suppressed desire to persuade him to tell her all the stories about his war wounds? *Not from around here*, those hieroglyphs carved in his flesh had whispered, exotic with promise. And, *I have survived. Want to know how?*

Yes. I want to know how. She pressed her fingers to the bridge of her nose, as if she might press back the incipient headache gathering behind her eyes. Her body jolted at the faint *snick* and *shirr* of the hall door opening. But familiar voices, Tien's and her uncle's, reassured her it was only the expected return of the information-hunting party. She wondered what strange prey they had made a prize of. She sat up, and pushed down her sleeves. It was well after midnight.

Tuomonen was no longer with them, she found to her relief as she rounded the corner into the hallway. She could lock her household down for the night, like a proper chatelaine. Tien looked tense, Vorkosigan looked tired, and Uncle Vorthys looked the same as ever. Vorkosigan was murmuring, "I trust it goes without saying, Vorsoisson, that tomorrow will be a surprise inspection?"

"Certainly, my Lord Auditor."

"Did you find out anything interesting?" Ekaterin inquired generally, resetting the lock behind them.

"Mm, Madame Radovas had no suggestions as to how her wandering husband had wandered into our soletta wreck," said Uncle Vorthys. "I'd been hoping she might."

"It's so sad. They had seemed like such a nice couple, the few times I met them."

"Well, you know middle-aged men." Tien shrugged reprovingly, clearly excluding himself from the class.

Ah, Tien. Why couldn't you be the one to run off with a younger, richer woman? Maybe you'd be happier. You could scarcely be less happy. Why does your one virtue have to be fidelity? As far as she knew, anyway. Though she had wondered, during that thankfully-over weird period when he'd been accusing her, why an act she found unthinkable had so obsessed him. Maybe he didn't find it so unthinkable at all? She hardly had the energy to care.

She offered a late-night snack, an invitation only Uncle Vorthys accepted, and they all parted company for their respective sleeping quarters. By the time her uncle had finished eating and said good night, and she tidied up and made her way to her own bedroom, checking on Nikolai on the way, Tien was already in bed on his side with his eyes closed. Not sleeping yet; he had a very distinctive near-snore when he was truly asleep. When she slipped in beside him, he rolled over and flung his arm over her, and snugged her in tight.

He does love me, in some inept way. The thought almost made her want to weep. Yet what other human connections did Tien have, aside from her and Nikolai? His distant mother, remarried, and the ghost of his dead brother. Tien clutched her at night sometimes like a drowning man clutching his log.

If there was a hell, she hoped Tien's brother was in it. A Vor hell. He had done the proper thing, oh yes he had, cutting out his own mutation, and setting an example for Tien impossible to—so to speak—live up to. Tien had tried to emulate him, twice early on and once later, running up to suicide attempts so half-hearted as to barely qualify as gestures. The first two times she had been utterly terrified. For a period she had believed her loyalty and dependency were the only things holding him to life. By the third, she was numb. Much more of this, and she wouldn't be human at all. She felt barely human now.

Hoping to pretend her way to the real thing, she let her breathing slow, and feigned sleep. After a time, Tien, who was no more asleep than she, got up and went to the bathroom. But instead of returning to bed, he plodded quietly across the bedroom and out toward the kitchen. Maybe he'd changed his mind about that snack. Would he like it if she heated him some milk with brandy and spices in it? It was an old family recipe and remedy her great-aunt had brought to South Continent; comfort-drink for a visiting sick niece, though the larger of the generous portions had always somehow seemed to find its way into the old lady's own cup. Ekaterin smiled in memory, and padded after Tien.

Not the refrigerator but the kitchen comconsole terminal made the only faint light ahead of her. She paused in the doorway, puzzled. In her parents' household, the only allowable reason to call anyone at this hour of the night was to announce either a birth or a death, a rule she'd found she had internalized.

"What the hell was Radovas's body doing up there?" Tien, his back to her, spoke hoarsely and lowly to the torso over the vid-plate. Startled, Ekaterin recognized his subordinate, Administrator Soudha. Soudha was not, as she would have expected, in pajamas, but still dressed for the day. Working this late at home? Well, engineers were like that. She drew back a little more into the shadows in the hallway. "You told me he'd quit."

"He did," said Soudha. "It's not our problem what happened to him afterward."

"The hell it's not. We're going to have frigging ImpSec all over the department tomorrow. The real thing, not just a VIP tour we can run around in circles and feed dinner and wave good-bye to. I could see Tuomonen getting this shitty-eyed look just thinking about it."

"We'll handle them. Go back to bed, Vorsoisson."

Lord Auditor Vorkosigan told you point-blank he wanted to make a surprise inspection, Tien. He speaks with the Emperor's Voice. What are you doing? She began to breathe through her mouth, soundlessly, starting to feel sick to her stomach.

"They're going to find out all about your sweet little scheme, and then we'll all be in it to our eyebrows," said Tien.

"No, they won't. We're tight in town. Just keep them away from the experiment station, and we'll grease them in and out without a squeak."

"The experiment station is a hollow shell. You haven't *got* a department, except in the files. What if they want to interview one of your ghost employees?"

"Such as yourself?" Soudha's mouth twisted in a thin smile. "Relax."

"I am not going down with you."

"You think you have a choice?" Soudha snorted. "Look. It'll be all right. They can audit all day long, and all they'll find is a lot of columns that add perfectly. Lena Foscol in Accounting is the most meticulous thief I've ever met. We're so far ahead of them they'll never catch up."

"Soudha, they're going to ask to interview people who *don't exist*. Then what?"

"Gone on vacation. Out on field work. We can stall."

"For how long? And then what?"

"Go to *bed*, Vorsoisson, and stop twitching."

"Goddammit, I've had two Imperial Auditors in my *house* for the last three days." He stopped and took a gulping breath; Soudha offered him a sympathetic shrug. Tien went on again in a lowered tone. "That's . . . another thing. I need an advance on my stipend. I need another twenty thousand marks. And I need it now."

"*Now?* Oh, sure, with ImpSec looking on, no doubt. Vorsoisson, you are gibbering."

"Dammit, I *have* to have the money. Or else."

"Or else what? Or else you're going to ImpSec and turn *yourself* in? Look, Tien." Soudha ran his hands through his hair in a harried swipe. "Lie low. Keep your mouth shut. Be sweet like sugar to the nice ImpSec lads, give them to me, and we'll handle them. Let's just take this one day at a time, all right?"

"Soudha, I know you can produce the twenty thousand. There has to be at least fifty thousand marks a month flowing out of your department's budget and into your pockets from the dummy employees alone, and God knows how much from the rest of it—though I'm sure your pet accountant does— what if they decide to fast-penta *her*?"

Ekaterin stepped backward, her bare feet seeking silence from the floor near the wall. *Dear God. What has Tien done now?* It was all too easy to fill in the blanks. Embezzlement and bribery at the very least, and on a grand scale. *How long has this been going on?*

The muffled voices from the kitchen exchanged a few more

curt words, and the blue reflection from the holovid winked out, leaving the hallway obliquely lit only by the amber lights in the park outside. Heart pounding, Ekaterin slipped back down the hall into her bathroom and locked its door. She quickly flushed the commode and stood trembling at the sink, staring at her dim reflection in the glass. The faint nightlight made drowned sparks in her dilated eyes. After another minute, the bed creaked as Tien made his way back into it.

She waited a long time, but when she crept out, he was still awake.

"Hm?" he said muzzily as she slid under the covers again.

"Not feeling too well," she muttered. Truthfully.

"Poor Kat. Something you ate, you think?"

"Not sure." She curled up away from him, not having to pretend the sick ache in her belly.

"Take something, eh? If you're batting around all night, neither of us will get any sleep."

"I'll see." *I must know.* After a time she added, "Did you get anything arranged about our galactic trip today?"

"God, no. Much too busy."

Not too busy to complete the transfer of her funds to his own account, she'd noticed. "Would you . . . like me to take over making all the arrangements? There's no reason you should carry all that burden, I have plenty of time. I've already researched off-world medical facilities."

"Not *now*, Kat! We can deal with this later. Next week, after your uncle goes."

She let it drop, staring into the darkness. *Whatever it is he needs twenty thousand marks for, it's not to fulfill his word to me.*

Eventually, he slept, about two hours; Ekaterin watched the time ooze by, black and slow as tar. *I must know.*

And after you know, then what? Will you deal with it later, too? She lay waiting for the dawn's light.

The light is broken, remember?

The routine of dealing with Nikolai's needs steadied her in the morning. Uncle Vorthys left very early, to catch his orbital flight.

"Will you be coming back down?" she asked him a little wanly, helping him on with his jacket in the vestibule.

"I hope I might, but I can't promise. This investigation has already gone on longer than I expected, and has taken some peculiar turns. I really have no idea how long it will take to finish up." He hesitated. "If it drags on beyond the end of the term at the District University, perhaps the Professora might come out to join me for a time. Would you like that?"

Not trusting herself to speak, she nodded.

"Good. Good." He seemed about to say more, but then just shrugged and smiled, and hugged her good-bye.

She managed to evade almost all contact with Tien and Vorkosigan by accompanying Nikki to school in the bubble-car, an escort he scorned, and taking the long route home. As she had hoped, the apartment was empty on her return.

She washed down more painkillers with more coffee, then, with reluctant steps, entered Tien's office and sat before his comconsole. *I wish I'd taken Lord Vorkosigan up on his offer to teach me how to do this.* Her outrage at the mutie lord yesterday in the bubble-car now seemed to her all out of proportion. Misplaced. How much could her intimate knowledge of Tien make up for her lack of training in this sort of snooping? Not enough, she suspected, but she had to try.

Get started. You are deliberately delaying.

No. I am desperately delaying.

She keyed on the comconsole.

Tien's financial accounts, on this his personal machine, were not locked under a code seal. Income matched his salary; outgo . . . when all the routine outgo was accounted for, the amount left over should have been a modest respectable savings. Tien did not indulge himself with unshared luxuries. But the account was almost empty. Several thousand marks had disappeared without trace, including the transfer she had made to him yesterday morning. No, wait—that transfer was still on the list, hastily entered, not erased or hidden yet. And it was a transfer, not an expenditure, to a file that had appeared nowhere else.

She followed its transfer marker to a hidden account. The comconsole produced a palm-lock form above the vid-plate.

When she and Tien had first set up their accounts on Komarr, less than a year ago, they had taken prudent thought for one or the other parent being temporarily disabled; each had emergency access to the other's accounts. Had Tien set this up entirely separately, or as a daughter-cell of his larger financial program, letting the machine do the work for him? *Maybe ImpSec covert ops doesn't have all the advantages,* she thought grimly, and placed her right hand in the light box. *If only you were willing to betray a trust, why, the most amazing range of possible actions opened up to you.*

So did the file.

She took a deep breath, and started reading.

By far the largest portion of what was under the seal turned out to be a huge research clip-file much like her own on the subject of Vorzohn's Dystrophy. But Tien's new obsession, it appeared, was Komarran trade fleets.

Komarr's economy was founded, of course, on its wormholes, and providing services to the trade ships of other worlds that passed through them. But once you had amassed all those profits, how to reinvest them? There were, after all, a physically limited number of wormholes in Komarr local space. So Komarr had gone on to develop its own trade fleets, going out into the wormhole nexus on long complicated circuits of months or even years, and returning, sometimes, with fabulous profits.

And sometimes not. Stories of all the best, most legendary returns were highlighted in Tien's files. The failures, admittedly fewer in number, were brushed aside. Tien was nothing if not an optimist, always. Every day was going to bring him his lucky break, the shot that would take him directly to the top with no intervening steps. As if he really believed that was how it was done.

Some of the fleets were closely held to the famous family corporations, Komarr's oligarchy, such as the Toscanes; others sold shares on the public market to any Komarran who cared to place his bet. Almost every Komarran did, at least in a small way; she'd heard one Barrayaran bureaucrat joke that it replaced the need for most other sorts of gambling in the Komarran state.

And when on Komarr, do as the Komarrans do? With dread in her heart, she switched to the financial portion of the file.

Where in God's name did Tien get a hundred thousand marks to buy fleet shares? His salary was barely five thousand marks a month. And then—having done so—why had he put all hundred thousand on the *same* fleet?

She turned her attention to the first question, which was at least potentially answerable with reference to facts of record, without requiring psychological theory. It took her some time to break the credit stream apart into its various sources. The partial answer was, he'd borrowed sixty thousand marks on short term at a disturbingly high interest rate, secured with his pension fund and forty thousand marks worth of fleet shares he'd bought with—what? With money that came from nowhere, apparently.

From Soudha? Was that what he had meant by a *ghost employee?*

Ekaterin read on. The fleet upon which Tien had placed

this borrowed bet had departed with much hype and fanfare; shares had been trading on the secondary market at rising prices for weeks after it had departed Komarr. Tien had even made a multicolored graph to track his electronic gains. Then the fleet had encountered disaster: an entire ship, cargo, and crew lost hideously to a wormhole mishap. The fleet, now unable to complete many of its planned trade chains that had been based in the lost cargo, had rerouted and come home early, tail between its imaginary legs. Some fleets returned two for one to their investors, though the average was closer to ten percent; the Golden Voyage of Marat Galen in the previous century was famous for having returned a fabulous fortune of a hundred to one for every share its investors had purchased, founding at least two new oligarchic clans in the process.

Tien's fleet, however, had returned a loss of four for one.

With his twenty-five thousand marks of residue, Ekaterin's four thousand marks, his personal savings, and his meager pension fund, Tien had been placed to pay back only two-thirds of his loan, now due. Pressingly overdue, apparently, judging from the aggressively-worded dunning notices accumulating in the file. When he had cried to Soudha that he needed twenty thousand marks now, Tien had not been exaggerating. She could not help calculating how many years it would take to scrimp twenty thousand marks from her household budget.

What a nightmare. It was almost possible to feel sorry for the man.

Except for the little problem of the origin of that magical first forty thousand marks.

Ekaterin sat back and rubbed her numb face. She had a horrible feeling she could guess the hidden parts of this whole chain of reasoning. This apparently complex and deeply entrenched scam in the Terraforming Project had not, she thought, originated with Tien. All his previous dishonesties had been petty: wrong change not returned, a little padding here and there on expense reports, the usual minor erosion of character almost every adult suffered in weak moments. Not grand theft. Soudha had been here in his job for over five years. This was surely a home-grown Komarran crime. But Tien, newly made head of the Serifosa Sector, had perhaps stumbled upon it, and Soudha had bought his silence. So . . . had the previous Barrayaran Administrator whom Tien had replaced been on the take as well? A question for ImpSec, to be sure.

But Tien was in far over his head and must have realized it. Hence the gamble with the trade fleet shares. If the fleet had returned four for one, instead of the other way around, Tien would have been placed to return his bribe, make restitution, get out from under. Had some such panicked thought been in the back of his mind?

And if he had been lucky instead of unlucky, would the impulse have survived to become reality?

And if Tien had pulled a hundred thousand marks out of his hat, and told you he won them on trade fleet shares, would you have asked the first question about their origin? Or would you have been overjoyed and thought him a secret genius?

She sat now bent over, aching in every part of her body, up her back, her neck, inside and outside her head. In her heart. Her eyes were dry.

A Vor woman's first loyalty was supposed to be to her husband. Even unto treason, even unto death. The sixth Countess Vorvayne had followed her husband right up to the stocks in which he had been hung to die for his part in the Saltpetre Plot, and sat at his feet in a hunger strike, and died, in fact a day before him, of exposure. Great tragic story, that one—one of the best bloody melodramas from the history of the Time of Isolation. They'd made a holovid of it, though in the vid version the couple had died at the same moment, as if achieving mutual orgasm.

Has a Vor woman no honor of her own, then? Before Tien entered my life, did I not have integrity all the same?

Yes, and I laid it on my marriage oath. Rather like buying all your shares in one fleet.

If Tien had been afflicted with some great misguided political passion—thrown in his lot with the wrong side in Vordarian's Pretendership, whatever—if he had followed his convictions, she might well have followed him with all good will. But this was not allegiance to some greater truth, or even to some grandly tragic mistake.

It was just stupidity, piled on venality. It wasn't tragedy, it was farce. It was Tien all over. But if there was any honor to be regained by turning her own sick husband over to the authorities, she surely did not see it either.

If I grow much smaller, trying to keep my height under his, I believe I must soon disappear altogether.

But if she was not a Vor woman, what was she? To step away from her oath-sworn place at Tien's side was to step across a precipice into the dark, naked of any identity at all.

It was, what did they call it, a window of opportunity. If

she left before the crisis broke, before this whole hideous mess came out in some public way, she would not be deserting Tien in his hour of greatest need, would she?

Ask your soldier's heart, woman. Is deserting the night before the battle any better than deserting in the heat?

Yet if she did not go, she tacitly acquiesced to this farce. Only ignorance was innocence, was bliss. Knowledge was . . . anything but power.

No one else would save her. No one else could. And even to open her lips and whisper "help" was to choose Tien's destruction.

She sat still as stone, in silence, for a very long time.

CHAPTER EIGHT

Captain Tuomonen arranged to rendezvous with Miles and Tien in the lobby of the Vorsoissons' residence building, rather than at the Terraforming Project offices, a blandly sociable gesture that did not fool Miles for a moment. The Imperial Auditor was to be saddled with an ImpSec guard whether he'd ordered one or not, it appeared. Miles almost looked forward to seeing the test of Tuomonen's polite ingenuity this security determination was doubtless going to demonstrate.

At the bubble-car platform across the park, Miles seized the opportunity to shunt Tien into another car and claim a private one for himself and Tuomonen, the better to decant the night's news from him. A few early morning commuters crowded in with the administrator, and his car slid away into the tubes. But as soon as the next pair of Komarrans, already hesitant at the sight of the green Imperial uniform, got close enough to make out the ImpSec eyes on the captain's collar, they sheered off hastily from any attempt to join Miles's little party.

"Do you always get a bubble-car to yourself?" Miles inquired of Tuomonen as the canopy closed and the car began to move.

"When I'm in uniform. Works like a charm." Tuomonen smiled slightly. "But if I want to eavesdrop on Serifosans, I make sure to wear civvies."

"Ha. So what's the status on Radovas's library this morning?"

"I dispatched one of the compound guards last night to hand-carry it to HQ in Solstice. Solstice is three time zones ahead of us; their analyst should have started on it by now."

"Good." Miles's brow wrinkled. *Compound guards?* "Um . . . just how big is ImpSec Serifosa, Captain Tuomonen?"

"Well . . . there's myself, my desk sergeant, and two corporals. We keep the data base, coordinate information flow
to HQ, and provide support for any investigators HQ sends
out on special projects. Then there is my lieutenant who
commands the guards at the Sector Sub-Consulate compound.
He has a unit of ten men to cover security there."

The Imperial Counselor was how the Barrayaran Viceroy of
Komarr was styled, in deference to local custom. Miles's incog-
nito arrival in Serifosa had excused him, or so he'd chosen
to pretend, from a courtesy call on the Counselor's Serifosa
Sector regional deputy. "Only ten men? For around the clock,
all week?"

"I'm afraid so." Tuomonen smiled wryly. "Not much goes
on in Serifosa, my lord. It was one of the least active Domes
in the Komarr Revolt, a tradition of political apathy it has since
maintained. It was the first Sector to have its occupying
Imperial garrison withdrawn. One of my Komarran in-laws
facetiously blames the lack of urban renewal in the Dome's
central section on the previous generation's failure to arrange
for it to have been leveled by Imperial forces." That aging
and decrepit area was visible now in the distance, as the car
reached the top of an arc and bumped into an intersecting
tube. They rotated and began to descend toward Serifosa's
newer rim.

"Still—apathetic or not—how do you stay on top of things?"

"I have a budget for paid informers. We used to pay them
on a piecework-basis, till I discovered that when they had no
real news to sell, they'd make some up. So I cut their numbers in half and put the best ones on a part-time regular salary,
instead. We meet about once a week, and I give them a little
security workshop and we have a gossip swap. I try to get
them to think of themselves as low-level civilian analysts, rather
than merely informers. It seems to have significantly helped
the reliability of my information flow."

"I see. Do you have anyone planted in the Terraforming
Project?"

"No, unfortunately. Terraforming is not considered security-
critical. I do have people at the shuttleport, in the Locks district,
in the Dome police, and a few in the local Dome government
offices. We also cover the power plant, atmosphere cycling,
and water treatment both independently and in cooperation
with local authorities. They check their job applicants for
criminal records and psychological instability, we check them
for potentially dangerous political associations. Terraforming
has always been just too damn far down the list for my budget

to cover. I will say its employment background check standards are among the lowest in the civil service."

"Hm. Wouldn't that policy tend to concentrate the disaffected?"

Tuomonen shrugged. "Many intelligent Komarrans still do not love the Imperium. They have to do something for a living. To qualify for the Terraforming Project, it is perhaps enough that they love Komarr. They have simply no political motivation for sabotage there."

Barto cared about the future of Komarr, his widow had said. Might Radovas have been among the disaffected? And if he were, so what? Miles frowned in puzzlement as the car pulled into the stop in the station beneath the Terraforming Project offices.

As instructed, Tien Vorsoisson was waiting for them on the platform. He escorted them as before up through the atrium of his building to the floors of his domain; though a few doors were open on early morning activity in various departments as they passed, they were the first to arrive in Vorsoisson's office.

"Do you have any preference as to how to divide this up?" Miles asked Tuomonen, staring around meditatively as Vorsoisson brought up the lights.

"I managed to squeeze in a short interview with Andro Farr this morning," said Tuomonen. "He gave me some names of Marie Trogir's particular acquaintances at work. I believe I'd like to start with them."

"Good. If you want to start with Trogir, I'll start with Radovas, and we can meet in the middle. I want to begin by interviewing his boss, Soudha, I believe, Administrator Vorsoisson."

"Certainly, my Lord Auditor. Do you wish to use my office?"

"No, I think I want to see him in his own territory."

"I'll take you downstairs, then. I'll be at your disposal in just a moment, Captain Tuomonen."

Tuomonen seated himself at Vorsoisson's comconsole and eyed it thoughtfully. "Take your time, Administrator."

Vorsoisson, with a worried look over his shoulder, led Miles down one flight to the Department of Waste Heat Management. Soudha had not yet arrived; Miles dispatched Tien back to Tuomonen, then circled the engineer's office slowly, examining its decor and contents.

It was a rather bare place. Perhaps the department head had another, more occupied work area out at his experiment station. The book rack on the wall was sparsely filled, mostly with disks on management and technical references. There were works on space stations and their construction, to be sure close cousins of domes, but unlike Radovas's library, no more specialized texts on wormholes or five-space math than might be residue from Soudha's university days.

A heavy tread announced the room's owner; the curious look on Soudha's face to find his office open and lit as he entered gave way to understanding as he saw Miles.

"Ah. Good morning, Lord Auditor Vorkosigan."

"Good morning, Dr. Soudha." Miles replaced the handful of disks in their former slots.

Soudha looked a bit tired; perhaps he was not a morning person. He gave Miles a weary smile of greeting. "To what do I owe the honor of this visit?" He muffled a yawn, pulled a chair up near his desk, and gave Miles a gesture of invitation to it. "Can I get you some coffee?"

"No, thank you." Miles sat, and let Soudha settle himself behind his comconsole desk. "I have some unpleasant news." Soudha's face composed itself attentively. "Barto Radovas is dead." He watched for Soudha's response.

Soudha blinked, his lips parting in dismay. "That's a shock. I thought he was in good health, for his age. Was it his heart? Oh, my, poor Trogir."

"No one's health stands up to exposure to vacuum without a pressure suit, regardless of their age." Miles decided not to include the details of the corpse's massive trauma, for now. "His body was found in space."

Soudha glanced up, his brows rising. "Do they think it has some connection to the soletta accident, then?"

Or why else would Miles be taking an interest, right. "Perhaps."

"Have they—what about Marie Trogir?" Soudha's lips thinned thoughtfully. "You didn't say she . . . ?"

"She's not been found. Or not yet. The probable-cause crews are continuing search sweeps topside, and ImpSec is now looking everywhere else. Their next task, of course, is to try to trace the couple from the time and place they were last seen, which was several weeks ago and here, apparently. We'll be requesting the cooperation of your department, of course."

"Certainly. This is . . . this is really a very horrifying turn of events. I mean, regardless of one's opinion of the way they chose to pursue their personal choices . . ."

"And what is your opinion, Dr. Soudha? I'd really like to get a sense of the man, and of Trogir. Do you have any ideas?"

Soudha shook his head. "I confess, this turn in their relationship took me by surprise. But I don't pry into my employees' private lives."

"So you've said. But you worked closely with the man for five years. What were his outside interests, his politics, his hobbies, his obsessions?"

"I . . ." Soudha shrugged in frustration. "I can give you his complete work record. Radovas was a quiet sort of fellow, never made trouble, did first-rate technical work—"

"Yes, why did you hire him? Waste Heat Management does not appear to have been his previous specialty."

"Oh, he had a great deal of station expertise—as you may know, getting rid of excess heat topside is a standard engineering challenge. I thought his technical experience might bring some new perspectives to our problems, and I was right. I was very pleased with his work—Section Two of the reports I gave you yesterday was mostly his, if you would like to examine them to get a real sense of the man. Power generation and distribution. Hydraulics, in Section Three, was mostly mine. The basis of heat exchange through liquid transfer is most promising—"

"I've looked over your report, thanks."

Soudha looked startled. "All of it? I had really understood Dr. Vorthys would be wanting it. I'm afraid it's a bit thick on the technical detail."

Oh, sure, I speed-read all two hundred thousand words before bed last night. Miles smiled blandly. "I accept your evaluation of Dr. Radovas's technical competence. But if he was so good, why did he leave? Was he bored, happy, frustrated? Why did this change in his personal circumstances lead to change in his work? I don't see a necessary connection."

"For that," said Soudha, "I'm afraid you will have to ask Marie Trogir. I strongly suspect the driving force in this peculiar decision came from her, though they both resigned and left together. She had far less to lose, leaving here, in pay and seniority and status."

"Tell me more about her."

"Well, I truly can't. Barto hired her himself and worked with her on a daily basis. She barely came to my attention. Her technical ability appears to have been adequate—although, come to think of it, those evaluations were all supplied by Barto. I don't know." Soudha rubbed his forehead. "This is all pretty upsetting. Barto, dead. *Why?*" The distress in his voice seemed genuine to Miles's experienced ear, but his shock appeared more surprise than the deep grief from loss of a close friend;

Miles would, perhaps, have to look elsewhere for the insights into Radovas he now sought.

"I'd like to examine Dr. Radovas's office and work areas."

"Oh. I'm afraid his office was cleared and reassigned."

"Have you replaced him?"

"Not yet. I'm still collecting applications. I hope to start interviewing soon."

"Radovas must have been friends with somebody. I want to speak with his coworkers."

"Of course, my Lord Auditor. When would you like me to set up appointments?"

"I thought I'd just drop in."

Soudha pursed his lips. "Several of my people are on vacation, and several more are out at the experiment station, running a small test this morning. I don't expect them to be done before dark. But I can get you started with the people here, and have some more in by the time you're done with the first."

"All right. . . ."

With the air of a man throwing a sacrifice to the volcano god, Soudha called in two subordinates, whom Miles interviewed one at a time in the same conference chamber they'd used day before yesterday for the VIP briefing. Arozzi was a younger man, scarcely older than Miles, an engineer who was temporarily scrambling to take over Radovas's abandoned duties, and perhaps, he hinted, hoping for promotion into the dead man's shoes. Would my Lord Auditor like to see some of his work? No, he had not been close friends with his senior. No, the office romance had been a surprise to him, but then Radovas had been a private sort of fellow, very discreet. Trogir had been a bright woman, bright and beautiful; Arozzi had no trouble appreciating what Radovas had seen in her. What had she seen in Radovas? He had no idea, but then, he wasn't a woman. Radovas dead? Dear God . . . No, he had no idea what the man had been doing topside. Maybe the couple had been trying to emigrate?

Cappell, the department's resident mathematician, was hardly more useful. He was a bit older than Arozzi, and a trifle more cynical. He took in the news of Radovas's death with less change of expression than either Arozzi or Soudha. He hadn't been close to Radovas or Trogir either, not on a social basis, though he worked often with the engineer, yes, checking calculations, devising projections. He'd be glad to show my Lord Auditor a few thousand more pages of his work. No?

What was Trogir like? Well-enough looking, he supposed, but rather sly. Look what she'd done to poor Radovas, eh? Did he think Trogir might be dead as well? No, women were like cats, they landed on their feet. No, he'd never actually experimented with testing that old saying on live cats; he didn't have any pets himself. Nor a wife. No, he didn't want a kitten, thank you for the offer, my Lord Auditor. . . .

Miles met again with Tuomonen at lunchtime over mediocre cafeteria food in the executive dining room off the building's atrium; the displaced executives were forced to go elsewhere. They exchanged reports on their morning's conversations. Tuomonen hadn't found any breakthroughs either.

"No one expressed a dislike of Trogir, but she seems damned elusive," Tuomonen noted. "The Waste Heat department has a reputation for keeping itself to itself, apparently. The one woman in Waste Heat who was supposed to be her friend didn't have much to say. I wonder if I ought to get a female interrogator?"

"Mm, maybe. Though I thought Komarrans were supposed to be more egalitarian about such things. Maybe a Komarran female interrogator?" Miles sighed. "D'you know that according to the latest statistics, half of the Barrayaran women who take advanced schooling on Komarr don't go home again? There's a small group of alarmist bachelors who are trying to get the Emperor to deny them exit visas. Gregor has declined to hear their petition."

Tuomonen smiled slightly. "Well, there's more than one solution to that problem."

"Yes, how have your Komarran in-laws taken the announcement of the Emperor's betrothal to the Toscane heiress?"

"Some of them think it's romantic. Some of them think it's sharp business practice on Emperor Gregor's part. Coming from Komarrans, that's a warm compliment, by the way."

"Technically, Gregor owns the planet Sergyar. You might point that out to anyone who theorizes he's marrying Laisa for her money."

Tuomonen grinned. "Yes, but is Sergyar a *liquid* asset?"

"Only in the sense of Imperial funds gurgling down the drain, according to my father. But that's an entire other set of problems. And what do the Barrayaran expatriates around here think of the marriage?"

"In general, it's favored." Tuomonen smiled dryly into his coffee cup. "Five years ago, my colleagues thought I was cutting my career throat by my own marriage. I'd never get promoted out of Serifosa, they said. Now I am suspected of secret genius,

and they've taken to regarding me with wary respect. I think
. . . it's best if I be amused."

"Heh. You are a wise man, Captain." Miles finished off a
starchy and gelid square of pasta-and-something, and chased
it with the last of his cooling coffee. "So what did Trogir's
friends think of Radovas?"

"Well, he's certainly managed to give a consistent impression of himself. Nice, conscientious guy, didn't make waves,
kept to Waste Heat, his elopement a surprise to most. One
woman thought it was your math fellow Cappell who was sweet
on Trogir, not Radovas."

"He sounded more sour than sweet to me. Frustrated, perhaps?" Miles's back-brain sketched a nice, straightforward
scenario of jealous murder, involving pushing Radovas out an
airlock on a trajectory that only just by coincidence matched
that of some soletta debris. *You can wish.* And anyway, it
seemed more logical that any homicidal maniac wishing to
clear a path to Trogir's side ought to have started with Andro
Farr, and what the hell did any of this tragic romance have
to do with an ore freighter swinging off course and smash-
ing into the soletta array anyway? Unless the jealous maniac
was Andro Farr . . . the Serifosa Dome police were supposed
to be looking into that possibility.

Tuomonen grunted. "I will say, I got more of a sense of
Trogir's personality from the few minutes I spent with Farr
than I have from the rest of this crew all morning. I want
to talk with him again, I think."

"*I* want to go topside, dammit. But whatever the end of
the story is, up there, it certainly has to have begun here.
Well . . . onward, I guess."

Soudha supplied Miles with more human sacrifices in the
form of employees called back from the experiment station.
They all seemed more interested in their work than in office
gossip, but perhaps, Miles reflected, that was an observer-
effect. By late afternoon, Miles was reduced to amusing
himself wandering around the project offices and terroriz-
ing employees by taking over their comconsoles at random
and sampling data, and occasionally emitting ambiguous little
"Hm . . ." noises as they watched him in fearful fascination. This lacked even the challenge of dissecting Madame
Vorsoisson's comconsole, since the government-issue machines
all opened everything immediately to the overrides in his
Auditor's seal, regardless of their security classification. He
mainly learned that terraforming was an enormous project

with a centuries-long scientific and bureaucratic history, and that any individual who attempted to sort clues through sheer mass data assimilation had to be frigging insane.

Now, *delegating* that task, on the other hand . . . *Who do I hate enough in ImpSec?*

He was still pondering this question as he browsed through the files on Venier's comconsole in the Administrator's outer office. The nervous Venier had fled after about the fourth "Hm," apparently unable to stand the suspense. Tien Vorsoisson, who had intelligently left Miles pretty much to his own devices all day, poked his head around the corner and offered a tentative smile.

"My Lord Auditor? This is the hour at which I normally go home. Do you wish anything else from me?"

Departing employees had been trickling past the open door-way for the past several minutes, and office lights had been going out all down the corridor. Miles sat back and stretched. "I don't think so, Administrator. I want to look at a few more files, and talk to Captain Tuomonen. Why don't you go on. Don't wait your dinner." A mental picture of Madame Vorsoisson, moving gracefully about preparing delectable aromatic food for her husband's return, flashed unbidden in his brain. He suppressed it. "I'll be along later to collect my things." *Or better yet . . .* "Or I may send one of Tuomonen's corporals for them. Give your lady wife my best thanks for the hospitality of her household." There. That finished that. He wouldn't even have to say good-bye to her.

"Certainly, my Lord Auditor. Do you, ah, expect to be here again tomorrow?"

"That rather depends on what turns up overnight. Good evening, Administrator."

"Good evening, my lord." Tien withdrew quietly.

A few minutes later, Tuomonen wandered in, his hands full of data disks. "Finding anything, my lord?"

"I got all excited for a moment when I found a personal seal, but it turned out to be just Venier's file of Barrayaran jokes. Some of them are pretty good. Do you want a copy?"

"Is that the one that starts out: 'ImpSec Officer: What do you mean he got away? Didn't I tell you to cover all the exits?—ImpSec Guard: I did sir! He walked out through one of the entrances.'"

"Yep. And the next one goes, 'A Cetagandan, a Komarran, and a Barrayaran walked into a genetic counselor's clinic—'"

Tuomonen grimaced. "I've seen that collection. My mother-in-law sent it to me."

"Ratting on her disaffected Komarran comrades, was she?"

"I don't think that was her intent, no. I believe it was more of a personal message." Tuomonen looked around the empty office and sighed. "So, my Lord Auditor. When do we break out the fast-penta?"

"I've found nothing, here, really." Miles frowned thoughtfully. "I've found *too much* of nothing here. I may have to sleep on this overnight, let my back-brain play with it. The library analysis may provide some direction. And I certainly want to see Waste Heat's experiment station tomorrow morning, before I go back topside. Ah, Captain, it's tempting. Call out the guards, descend in force, freeze everything, full financial audit, fast-penta everyone in sight . . . turn this place upside down and shake it. But I need a *reason*."

"*I* would need a reason," said Tuomonen. "With full documentation, and my career on the line if I spent that much of ImpSec's budget and guessed wrong. But you, on the other hand, speak with the Emperor's Voice. *You* could call it a drill." There was no mistaking the envy in his voice.

"I could call it a quadrille." Miles smiled wryly. "It may come to that."

"I could call HQ, have them put a flying squad on alert," murmured Tuomonen suggestively.

"I'll let you know by tomorrow morning," Miles promised.

"I need to stop by my own office and tend to some routine matters," said Tuomonen. "Would you care to accompany me, my Lord Auditor?"

So you can guard me at your convenience? "I still want to potter around here a bit. There's something . . . something that's bothering me, and I haven't figured out what it is yet. Though I would like a chance to talk to the Professor on a secured channel before the evening is out."

"Perhaps, when you're ready to leave, you could call me and I can send one of my men to escort you."

Miles considered refusing this ingenuous offer, but on the other hand, they could swing by the Vorsoissons' apartment and collect Miles's clothes on the return trip; Tuomonen would have his security, and Miles would have a minion to carry his luggage, a win–win scenario. And having the guard in tow would give Miles an excuse not to linger. "All right."

Tuomonen, partially satisfied, nodded and took himself off. Miles turned his attention to the next layer of Venier's comconsole. Who knew, maybe there would be another joke list.

CHAPTER NINE

Ekaterin finished folding the last of Lord Vorkosigan's clothing into his travel bag, rather more carefully than their owner was wont to, judging from the stirred appearance of the layers beneath. She sealed his toiletries case and fitted it in, then the odd, gel-padded case containing that peculiar medical-looking device. She trusted it wasn't some sort of ImpSec secret weapon.

Vorkosigan's war story of his Sergeant Beatrice burned in Ekaterin's mind, as the marks on her wrists seemed to burn. O fortunate man, that his missed grasp had passed in a fraction of a second. What if he had had years to think about it first? Hours to calculate the masses and forces and the true arc of descent? Would it have been cowardice or courage to let go of a comrade he could not possibly have saved, to save himself at least? He'd had a command, he'd had responsibilities to others, too. *How much would it have cost you, Captain Vorkosigan, to have opened your hands and deliberately let go?*

She closed the bag and glanced at her chrono. Getting Nikolai settled at his friend's house "for overnight"—that first, before anything else—had taken longer than she'd planned, as had getting the rental company to come collect their grav-bed. Lord Vorkosigan had talked about removing to a hotel this evening, but done nothing toward it. When he returned with Tien, to find no dinner and his bed gone and his bags packed and waiting in the hall, surely he would take the hint and decamp at once. Their good-bye would be formal and permanent, and above all, brief. She was almost out of time and had not even begun on her own things.

She dragged Vorkosigan's bag to the vestibule and returned

to her workroom, staring around at the seedlings and cuttings, lights and equipment. It was impossible to pack all that in a bag she could carry. Another garden was going to be abandoned. At least they were getting smaller and smaller.

She'd once wanted to cultivate her marriage like a garden; one of the legendary great Vor parks that people came from Districts away to admire for color and beauty through the changing seasons, the sort that took decades to reach full fruition, growing richer and more complex each year. When all other desires had died, shreds of that ambition still lingered, to tempt her with, *If only I try one more time.* . . . Her lips twisted in bleak derision. Time to admit she had a black thumb for marriage. Plow it under, surface it with concrete, and be done.

She began as a minimum gesture to pull her library off the wall and fit it into a box. The urge to cram a few of her things hastily into some shopping bag and flee before Tien returned was strong. But sooner or later, she would have to face him. Because of Nikki, there would have to be negotiations, formal plans, eventually legal petitions, the uncertainty of which made her sick to her stomach. But she had been years coming to this moment. If she could not do this now, when her anger was high, how could she find the strength to face the rest in colder blood?

She walked through the apartment, staring at the objects of her life. They were few enough; the major furnishings had all come with the place and would stay with the place. Her spasmodic efforts at decoration, at creating some semblance of a Barrayaran home, the hours of work—it was like deciding what to grab in a fire, only slower. *Nothing. Let it all burn.*

The sole awkward exception was her great-aunt's bonsai'd skellytum. It was her one memento of her life before Tien, and it was in the nature of a sacred trust to the dead. Keeping something that foolish and ugly alive for seventy and more years . . . well, it was a typical Vor woman's job. She smiled bitterly, and brought it off the balcony into the kitchen, and began to look around for some way to transport it. At the sound of the hall door opening, she caught her breath, and schooled her features to as little expression as possible.

"Kat?" Tien ducked into the kitchen and stared around. "Where's dinner?"

My first question would have been, Where's Nikolai? I wonder how long it will take that thought to come to him. "Where is Lord Vorkosigan?"

"He stayed on at the office. He'll be along later, he said, to take his things away."

"Oh." She realized then that some tiny part of her had been hoping to conduct the impending conversation while Vorkosigan was still finishing up in her workroom or something; his presence providing some margin of safety, of social restraint upon Tien. Maybe it was better this way. "Sit down, Tien. I have to talk with you."

He raised dubious brows, but sat at the head of the table, around to her left. She would have preferred to have him opposite her.

"I am leaving you tonight."

"What?" His astonishment appeared genuine. *"Why?"*

She hesitated, reluctant to be drawn into argument. "I suppose . . . because I have come to the end of myself." Only now, looking back over the long draining years, did she become aware of how much of her there had been to use up. No wonder it had taken so long. *All gone now.*

"Why . . . why now?" At least he didn't say, *You must be joking.* "I don't understand, Kat." She could see him begin to grope, not toward understanding, but away from it, as far away as possible. "Is it the Vorzohn's Dystrophy? Damn, I knew—"

"Don't be stupid, Tien. If that was the issue, I'd have left years ago. I took oath to you in sickness and health."

He frowned and sat back, his brows lowering. "Is there someone else? There's someone else, isn't there!"

"I'm sure you wish there were. Because then it would be because of them, and not because of you." Her voice was level, utterly flat. Her stomach churned.

He was obviously shocked, and beginning to shake a little. "This is madness. I don't understand."

"I have nothing more to say." She began to rise, wishing nothing more than to be gone at once, away from him. *You could have done this over the comconsole, you know.*

No. I took my oath in the flesh. I will break it to pieces in the same way.

He rose with her, and his hand closed over hers, gripping it, stopping her. "There's more to it."

"You would know more about that than I would, Tien."

He hesitated now, beginning, she thought, to be really afraid. This might not be any safer for her. *He's never hit me yet, I'll give him that much credit.* Part of her almost wished he had. Then there would have been clarity, not this endless muddle. "What do you mean?"

"Let go of me."

"No."

She considered his hand on hers, tight but not grinding. But still much stronger than her own. He was half a head taller and outweighed her by thirty kilos. She did not feel as much physical fear as she had thought she would. She was too numb, perhaps. She raised her face to his. Her voice grew edged. "Let go of me."

A little to her surprise, he did so, his hand flexing awkwardly. "You have to tell me why. Or I'll believe it's to go to some lover."

"I no longer care what you believe."

"Is he Komarran? Some damned Komarran?"

Goading her in the usual spot, and why not? It had worked before to bring her into line. It half-worked still. She had sworn to herself that she wasn't even going to bring up the subject of Tien's actions and inactions. Complaint was a tacit plea for help, for reform, for . . . continuation. Complaint was to attempt to shuffle off the responsibility for action onto another. To act was to obliterate the need for complaint. She would act, or not act. She would not *whine*. Still in that dead-level voice, she said, "I found out about your trade shares, Tien."

His mouth opened, and shut again. After a moment he said, "I can make it up. I know what went wrong now. I can make the losses up again."

"I don't think so. Where did you get that forty thousand marks, Tien." Her lack of inflection made it not a question.

"I . . ." She could watch it in his face, as he ratcheted over his choice of lies. He settled on a fairly simple one. "Part I saved, part I borrowed. You're not the only one who can scrimp, you know."

"From Administrator Soudha?"

He flinched at the name, but said ingenuously, "How did you know?"

"It doesn't matter, Tien. I'm not going to turn you in." She stared at him in weariness. "I take no part in you anymore."

He paced, agitated, back and forth across the kitchen, his face working. "I did it for you," he said at last.

Yes. Now he will attempt to make me feel guilty. All my fault. It was as familiar as the steps of some well-practiced, poisonous dance. She watched silently.

"All for you. You wanted money. I worked my tail off, but it was never enough for you, was it?" His voice rose, as he tried to lash himself into a relieving, self-righteous anger. It fell a little flat to her experienced ear. "You pushed me into taking a chance, with your endless nagging and worrying. So it didn't work, and now you want to punish me, is that it? You'd have been quick enough to make up to me if it had paid off."

He was very good at this, she had to admit, his accusations echoing her own dark doubts. She listened to his patterned litany with a sort of detached appreciation, like a torture victim, gone beyond pain unbeknownst, admiring the color of her own blood. *Now he will attempt to make me feel sorry for him. But I'm done feeling sorry. I'm done feeling anything.*

"Money money money, is that what this is all about? What is it that you want to buy so damned much, Kat?"

Your health, as you may recall. And Nikki's future. And mine.

As he paced, sputtering, his eye fell on the bright red skellytum, sitting in its basin on the kitchen table. "You don't love me. You only love yourself. Selfish, Kat! You love your damned potted *plants* more than you love me. Here, I'll prove it to you."

He snatched up the pot and pressed the control for the door to the balcony. It opened a little too slowly for his dramatic timing, but he strode through nonetheless, and whirled to face her. "Which shall it be to go over the railing, Kat? Your precious plant, or me? Choose!"

She neither spoke nor moved. *Now he will attempt to terrify me with suicide gestures.* This made, what, the fourth time around for that ploy? His trump card, which had always before ended the game in his favor.

He brandished the skellytum high. "Me, or it?" He watched her face, waiting for her to break. An almost clinical curiosity prompted her to say *You*, just to see how he would wriggle out of his challenge, but she kept silent still. When she did not speak, he hesitated in confusion for a moment, then launched the ancient absurd thing over the side.

Five floors up. She counted the seconds in her head, waiting for the crash from below. It came as more of a distant, sodden thump, mixed with the crack of exploding pottery.

"You ass, Tien. You didn't even look to see if there was anyone below."

With a look of sudden alarm that almost made her want to laugh, he peeked fearfully over the side. Apparently he hadn't managed to kill anyone after all, for he inhaled deeply and turned back toward her, taking a few steps through the open airseal door into the kitchen, but not too near to her. "React, damn you! What do I have to do to get through to you?"

"Don't bother," she said levelly. "I cannot imagine anything you could do that would make me more angry than I am."

He had come to the end of his menu of tactics and stood at a loss. His voice grew smaller. "What do you want?"

"I want my honor back. But you cannot give it to me."

His voice grew smaller still; his hands opened in pleading. "I'm sorry about your aunt's skellytum. I don't know what . . ."

"Are you sorry about grand theft and petty treason, bribery and peculation?"

"I did it for *you*, Kat!"

"In eleven years," she said slowly, "you have apparently never figured out who I am. I don't understand that. How you can live with someone so intimately, so long, and yet never see them. Maybe you were living with some Kat holovid projection from your own mind, I don't know."

"What do you *want*, dammit? It's not like I can go back. I can't confess. That would be public dishonor! For me, you, Nikki, your uncle—you can't want that!"

"I want never to have to tell a lie again for as long as I live. What you do is your problem." She took a deep breath. "But know this. Whatever you do, or don't do, from now on had better be for yourself. Because it won't touch me." Done once, done for all time. She was never going through this again.

"I can—I can fix it."

Was he referring to her skellytum, their marriage, his crime? Wrong anyway, in all cases.

When she still did not respond, he blurted desperately, "Nikolai is mine, by Barrayaran law."

Interesting. Nikki was the one tactic he had never employed before, off limits. She knew then how deathly serious he knew her to be. Good. He glanced around, and added belatedly, "Where is Nikki?"

"Someplace safer."

"You can't keep him from me!"

I can if you're in prison. She didn't bother saying it aloud. Under the circumstances, Tien was perhaps unlikely to challenge her possession of Nikki before the law. But she wanted to keep Nikolai's concerns as far separated as possible from the ugliest part of this thing. She would not start that war, but if Tien dared to do so, she would finish it. She watched him more coldly than ever.

"I *will* fix it. I can. I have a plan. I've been thinking about it all day."

Tien with a plan was about as reassuring as a two-year-old with a charged plasma arc. *No. You are not to take responsibility for him anymore. That's what this is all about, remember? Let go.* "Do whatever you wish, Tien. I'm going to go finish packing now."

"Wait—" He swung around her. It disturbed her to have him between her and the door, but she did not let her fear show. "Wait. I'll make it up. You'll see. I'll fix it. Wait here!"

With an anxious wave of his hands, he made for the hall door, and was gone.

She listened to his retreating footsteps. Only when she heard the faint whisper from the lift tube did she step back onto the balcony and look over. Far below, the shattered remains of her skellytum made an irregular wet blotch on the pavement, the broken scarlet tendrils looking like spattered blood. A passer-by was staring curiously at it. After a minute, she saw Tien emerge from the building and stride across the park toward the bubble-car platform, almost breaking into a run from time to time. He twice looked back up toward their balcony, over his shoulder; she stepped back into the shadows. He disappeared into the station.

Every muscle of her body seemed to be spasming with tension. She felt close to vomiting. She returned to her—to the kitchen, and drank a glass of water, which helped settle her breathing and her stomach. She went to her work room to fetch a basket and some plastic sheeting and a trowel, to go scrape the mess off the walkway five floors down.

CHAPTER TEN

Miles sat at Administrator Vorsoisson's comconsole desk, methodically reading through the files of all the employees of the Waste Heat department. There seemed to be a lot of personnel, compared to some of the other departments; Waste Heat was definitely a favored child in the Project budget. Presumably most of them spent the bulk of their time out at the experiment station, since Waste Heat's offices here were modest. In hindsight, always acute, Miles wished he'd begun his survey of Radovas's life out there today, where there might have been some action to observe, instead of in this tower of bureaucratic boredom. More, he wished he'd dropped in on the experiment station during their first tour . . . well, no. He would not have known what to look for then.

And you know now? He shook his head in wry dismay and brought up another file. Tuomonen had taken a copy of the personnel list, and in due time would be interviewing most of these people, unless something happened to take the investigation off in another direction. Such as finding Marie Trogir—that was the first item now on Miles's wish list for ImpSec. Miles shifted to ease the twinge in his back; he could feel his body stiffening from sitting still in a cool room too long. Didn't these Serifosans know they needed to waste more heat?

Quick steps in the hallway paused and turned in at the outer office, and Miles glanced up. Tien Vorsoisson, a little out of breath, hung a moment in his office doorway, then plunged inside. He was carrying two heavy jackets, his own and the one of his wife's that Miles had used the other day, and a breath mask labeled *Visitor, Medium*. He smiled at Miles in suppressed agitation. "My Lord Auditor. So glad to still find you here."

Miles shut down the file and regarded Vorsoisson with interest. "Hello, Administrator. What brings you back tonight?"

"You, my lord. I need to talk with you right away. I have to . . . to show you something I've discovered."

Miles opened his hand, indicating the comconsole, but Vorsoisson shook his head. "Not here, my lord. Out at the Waste Heat experiment station."

Ah ha. "Right now?"

"Yes, tonight, while everyone is gone." Vorsoisson laid the spare breath mask on the comconsole, rummaged in a cabinet in the far wall, and came up with his own personal mask. He yanked the straps over his neck and hastily adjusted his chest harness to hold the supplementary oxygen bottle in place. "I've requisitioned a lightflyer, it's waiting downstairs."

"All right . . ." Now what was this going to be all about? Too much to hope Vorsoisson had found Marie Trogir locked in a closet out there. Miles checked his own mask—power and oxygen levels indicated it was fully recharged—and slipped it on. He took a couple of breaths in passing, to test its correct function, then slid it down out of the way under his chin and shrugged on the jacket.

"This way . . ." Vorsoisson led off with long strides, which annoyed Miles considerably; he declined to run to keep up with the man. The Administrator perforce waited for him at the lift tube, bouncing on his heels in impatience. This time, when they reached the garage sub-level, the vehicle was ready. It was a less-than-luxurious government issue two-passenger flyer, but appeared to be in perfectly good condition.

Miles was less certain of the driver. "What's this all about, Vorsoisson?"

Vorsoisson put his hand on the canopy and regarded Miles with an intensity of expression that was almost alarming. "What are the rules for declaring oneself an Imperial Witness?"

"Well . . . various, I suppose, depending on the situation." Miles was not, he realized belatedly, nearly as well up on the fine points of Barrayaran law as an Imperial Auditor ought to be. He needed to do more reading. "I mean . . . I don't think it's exactly something one does for oneself. It's usually negotiated between a potential witness and whatever prosecuting authority is in charge of the criminal case." *And rarely.* Since the end of the Time of Isolation, with the importation of fast-penta and other galactic interrogation drugs, the authorities no longer had to *bargain* for truthful testimony, normally.

"In this case, the authority is you," said Tien. "The rules are whatever you say they are, aren't they? Because you are an Imperial Auditor."

"Uh . . . maybe."

Vorsoisson nodded in satisfaction, raised the canopy, and slid into the pilot's seat. With reluctant fascination, Miles levered himself in beside him. He fastened his safety harness as the flyer lifted and glided toward the garage's vehicle lock.

"And why do you ask?" Miles probed delicately. Vorsoisson had all the air of a man anxious to spill something very interesting indeed. Not for three worlds did Miles wish to frighten him off at this point. At the same time, Miles would have to be extremely cautious about what he promised. *He's your fellow Auditor's nephew-in-law. You've just stepped onto an ethical tightrope.*

Vorsoisson did not answer right away, instead powering the lightflyer up into the night sky. The lights of Serifosa brightened the faint feathery clouds of valuable moisture above, which occluded the stars. But as they shot away from the dome city, the glowing haze thinned and the stars came out in force. The landscape away from the dome was very dark, devoid of the villages and homesteads that carpeted less climatically hostile worlds. Only a monorail streaked away to the southwest, a faint pale line against the barren ground.

"I believe," Vorsoisson said at last, and swallowed. "I believe I have finally accumulated enough evidence of an attempted crime against the Imperium for a successful prosecution. I hope I haven't waited too long, but I had to be sure."

"Sure of what?"

"Soudha has tried to bribe me. I'm not absolutely certain that he didn't bribe my predecessor, too."

"Oh? Why?"

"Waste Heat Management. The whole department is a scam, a hollow shell. I'm not really sure how long they've been able to keep this bubble going. They had *me* fooled for . . . for months. I mean . . . a building full of equipment on a quiet day, how was I supposed to know what it did? Or didn't do? Or that there weren't anything *but* quiet days?"

"How long—" *have you known*, Miles bit off. That question was premature. "Just what are they doing?"

"They're bleeding off money from the project. For all I know, it may have started small, or by accident—some departed employee mistakenly kept on the roster, an accumulation of pay that Soudha figured out how to pocket. Ghost employees—his department is full of fictitious employees, all drawing

pay. And equipment purchases for the ghost employees—
Soudha suborned some woman in Accounting to go along with
it. They have all the forms right, all the numbers match.
They've slid it through I don't know how many fiscal inspections, because the accountants HQ sends out don't know how
to check the science, only the forms."

"Who *does* check the science?"

"That's the thing, my Lord Auditor. The Terraforming Project
isn't *expected* to produce quick results, not in any immediately measurable way. Soudha produces technical reports, all
right, plenty of them, right to schedule, but I think he mostly
does them by copying other sectors' previous-period results
and fudging."

Indeed, the Komarran Terraforming Project was a bureaucratic backwater, far down the Barrayaran Imperium's urgent
list. Not critical: a good place to park, say, incompetent Vor
second sons out of the way of their families. Where they could
do no harm to anyone, because the project was vast and slow,
and they would cycle out and be gone again before the damage
could even be measured. "Speaking of ghost employees—how
does Radovas's death connect with this alleged scam?"

Vorsoisson hesitated. "I'm not sure it does. Except to draw
ImpSec down on it and burst the bubble. After all, he quit
days before he died."

"Soudha said he quit. Soudha, according to you, is a proven
liar and data artist. Could Radovas have, say, threatened to
expose Soudha and been murdered to assure his silence?"

"But Radovas was in on it. For years. I mean, all the technical people had to know. They couldn't *not* know they weren't
doing the work the reports said."

"Mm, that may depend on how much of an artistic genius
Soudha was, arranging his reports." Soudha's own personnel
file certainly suggested he was neither stupid nor second-rate.
Might he have cooked those records as well? *Oh, God. This
means I'm not going to be able to trust any data off any
comconsole in the whole damned department.* And he'd wasted
hours today, decanting comconsoles. "Radovas might have had
a change of heart."

"I don't *know*," said Vorsoisson plaintively. His glance flicked
aside to Miles. "I want you to remember, I found this. I turned
them in. Just as soon as I was sure."

His repeated insistence on that last point hinted broadly to
Miles's ear that his knowledge of this fascinating piece of pecu-
lation predated his assurance by a noticeable margin. Had
Soudha's bribe been not just offered, but accepted? Till the

bubble burst. Was Miles witnessing an outbreak of patriotic duty on Vorsoisson's part, or an unseemly rush to get Soudha and Company before they got him?

"I'll remember," Miles said neutrally. Belatedly, it occurred to him that going off alone in the night with Vorsoisson to some deserted outpost, without even pausing to inform Tuomonen, might not be the brightest thing he'd ever done. Still, he doubted Vorsoisson would be nearly this forthcoming in the ImpSec captain's presence. It might be as well not to be too blunt with Vorsoisson about his chances of slithering out of this mess till they were safely back in Serifosa, preferably in the presence of Tuomonen and a couple of nice big ImpSec goons. Miles's stunner was a reassuring lump in his pocket. He would check in with Tuomonen via his wrist comm link as soon as he could arrange a quiet moment out of Vorsoisson's earshot.

"And tell Kat," Vorsoisson added.

Huh? What had Madame Vorsoisson to do with any of this? "Let's see this evidence of yours, then talk about it."

"What you'll mainly see is an absence of evidence, my lord," said Vorsoisson. "A great empty facility . . . there."

Vorsoisson banked the lightflyer, and they began to descend toward the Waste Heat experiment station. It was well lit with plenty of outdoor floodlamps, switched on automatically at dusk Miles presumed, and in high contrast to the surrounding dark. As they drew closer, Miles saw that its parking lot was not deserted; half a dozen lightflyers and aircars clustered in the landing circles. Windows glowed warmly here and there in the small office building, and more lights snaked through the airsealed tubes between sections. There were two big lift vans, one backing now into an opened loading bay in the large windowless engineering building.

"It looks pretty busy to me," said Miles. "For a hollow shell."

"I don't understand," said Vorsoisson.

Vegetation which actually stood higher than Miles's ankle struggled successfully against the cold here, but it was not quite abundant enough to conceal the lightflyer. Miles almost told Vorsoisson to douse the flyer's lights and bring them down out of sight over a small rise, despite the hike back it would entail. But Vorsoisson was already dropping toward an empty landing circle in the parking lot. He landed and killed the engine, and stared uncertainly toward the facility.

"Maybe . . . maybe you had better stay out of sight, at first," said Vorsoisson in worry. "They shouldn't mind me."

He was apparently unconscious of the world of self-revelation in this simple statement. They both adjusted their breath masks, and Vorsoisson popped the canopy. The chill night air licked Miles's exposed skin, above his breath mask, and prickled in his scalp. He dug his hands into his pockets as if to warm them, touched his stunner briefly, and followed the Administrator, a little behind him. Staying out of sight was one thing; letting Vorsoisson out of his sight was another.

"Try looking in the Engineering building first," Miles called, his voice muffled by his mask. "See if we can get a look at what's going on before you make contact with the en—er, try to speak to anyone."

Vorsoisson veered toward the loading bay's vehicle lock. Miles wondered if there was a chance anyone glancing out in the uncertain lighting might mistake him at first for Nikolai. The combination of Vorsoisson's dramatic mystery and his own natural paranoia was making him twitchy indeed, despite a better part of his mind that calculated high odds on a harmless scenario involving Vorsoisson being wildly mistaken.

They entered the pedestrian lock into the loading dock and cycled through. The pressure differential in his ears was slight. Miles kept his breath mask up temporarily as they rounded the parked lift van. He would call Tuomonen as soon as he ditched—

Miles skidded to a halt a moment too late to avoid being spotted in turn by the couple who stood quietly next to a float-pallet loaded with machinery. The woman, who had the pallet's control lead in her hand as she maneuvered the silently hovering load into the van, was Madame Radovas. The man was Administrator Soudha. They both looked up in shock at their unexpected visitors.

Miles was torn for a moment between whacking his wrist-comm's screamer circuit or going for his stunner; but at Soudha's sudden movement toward his own vest Miles's combat reflexes took over, and his hand dove for his pocket. Vorsoisson half-turned, his mouth round with astonishment and the beginning of some warning cry. Miles would have thought *I've just been led into ambush by that idiot*, except that Vorsoisson was clearly much more surprised than he was.

Soudha managed to get his stunner out and pointed a half second before Miles did. *Oh, shit, I never asked Dr. Chenko what a stunner blast would do to my seizure stimulator—* the stunner beam took him full in the face. His head snapped back in an agony that was mercifully brief. He was unconscious before he hit the concrete floor.

✧   ✧   ✧

Miles woke with a stunner migraine pinwheeling behind his eyes, metallic splinters of pure pain seemingly stuck quivering in his brain from his frontal lobes to his spinal column. He closed his eyes immediately against the too-bright glare of lights. He was nauseated to the point of vomiting. The realization immediately following, that he was still wearing his breath mask, caused his spacer's training to cut in; he swallowed and breathed deeply, carefully, and the dangerous moment passed. He was cold, and held upright in an awkward position by restraints pulling on his arms. He opened his eyes again and looked around.

He was outdoors in the chill Komarran dark, chained to a railing along the walkway on the blank side of what appeared to be the Waste Heat engineering building. Colored floodlights positioned in the vegetation two meters below, prettily illuminating the building and raised concrete walk, were the source of the eye-piercing light. Beyond them, the view was singularly uninformative, the ground falling away from the building and then rising, beyond it, into blank barrenness. The railing was a simple one, metal posts set into the concrete at meter intervals and a round metal handrail running between them. He was slumped to his knees, the concrete hard and cold beneath them, and his wrists were chained—chained? yes, chained, the links fastened with simple metal locks—to two successive posts, holding him half-spread-eagled.

His ImpSec comm-link was still strapped to his left wrist. He could not, of course, reach it with his right hand. Or—he tried—his head. He twisted his wrist around, to press it against the railing, but the screamer-button was recessed to prevent accidental bumps setting it off. Miles swore under his breath, and his breath mask. The mask appeared to be tightly fitted to his face, and he could feel the oxygen bottle still firmly strapped to his chest under his jacket—who had fastened his jacket up to his chin?—but he would have to be exquisitely careful not to jostle the mask till he had his hands free again to readjust it.

So . . . had the stunner beam induced a seizure while he was unconscious, or was he still working up to one? His next was almost due. He stopped swearing abruptly and took a couple of deep, calming breaths that fooled his body not at all.

A couple of meters to his right, he discovered Tien Vorsoisson similarly chained between two upright posts. His head lolled forward; he evidently wasn't awake yet. Miles tried to convince the knot of stressed terror in his solar plexus that this bit of cosmic justice was at least one bright point in the affair. He smiled grimly under his mask. All things considered, he'd rather Vorsoisson were free and able to try for help. Better still, leave Vorsoisson fastened there, free *himself* to try for help. But twisting his hands in their tight chains merely scraped his wrists raw.

If they wanted to kill you, you'd be dead now, he tried to convince his hyperventilating body. Unless, of course, they were sadists, out for a slow and studied revenge. . . . *What did I ever do to these people?* Besides the usual offense of being Barrayaran in general and Aral Vorkosigan's son in particular. . . .

Minutes crept by. Vorsoisson stirred and groaned, then fell back into flaccid unconsciousness, at least assuring Miles he wasn't dead. Yet. At length, the sound of footsteps on the concrete made Miles turn his head carefully.

Because of the approaching figure's breath mask and padded jacket Miles was not at first sure if it was a man or a woman, but as it neared he recognized the curly gray-blond hair and brown eyes of a woman who'd been at that first VIP orientation meeting—it was the accountant, the meticulous one who'd been sure to have a duplicate copy of her department's records for Miles, hah. *Foscol,* read the name on her breath mask.

She saw his open eyes. "Oh, good evening, Lord Auditor Vorkosigan." She raised her voice to a good loud clarity, to be sure her words penetrated the muffling of her mask.

"Good evening, Madame Foscol," he managed in return, matching her tone. If only he could get her talking, and listening—

She drew her hand from her pocket, and held up something glittering and metallic. "This is the key to your wrist locks. I'll set it over here, out of the way." She placed it carefully on the concrete walkway about halfway between Miles and the Administrator, next to the wall of the building. "Don't let anyone accidentally kick it over the side. You'd have a heck of a time finding it down there." She glanced thoughtfully over the rail at the dark vegetation below.

Implying that someone might be expected: a rescue party? Also implying that Foscol, Soudha, and Madame Radovas— *Madame Radovas, what is she doing here?*—did not expect to be around to supply the key in person when that happened.

She rummaged in her pocket again and came up with a data disk wrapped in protective plastic. "This, my Lord Auditor, is the complete record of Administrator Vorsoisson's acceptance of bribes, in the amount of some sixty thousand marks over the last eight months. Account numbers, data trail, where his money was embezzled in the first place—everything you should need for a successful prosecution. I'd been going to mail it to Captain Tuomonen, but this is better." Her eyes crinkled in a smile at him, above her breath mask. She bent and taped it securely to the back of Vorsoisson's jacket. "With my compliments, my lord." She stepped back and dusted her hands in the gesture of a dirty job well done.

"What are you doing?" Miles began. "What are you people doing out here, anyway? Why is Madame Radovas with—"

"Come, come, Lord Vorkosigan," Foscol interrupted him briskly. "You don't imagine that I'm going to stand around and *chat* with you, do you?"

Vorsoisson stirred, groaned, and belched. Despite the utter contempt in her eyes, lingering on his huddled figure, she waited a moment to be sure he wasn't going to vomit into his breath mask. Vorsoisson stared blearily at her, blinking in bewilderment and, Miles had no doubt, pain.

Miles clenched his fists and jerked against his chains. Foscol glanced at him and added kindly, "Don't hurt yourself, trying to get loose. Someone will be along eventually to collect you. I only regret I won't be able to watch." She turned on her heel and strode away, down the walk and around the corner of the building. After another minute, the faint sounds of a lift-van taking to the air drifted around the building. But they were on the opposite side of the building to the approach from Serifosa, and the departing van did not cross into Miles's limited line of sight.

Soudha's a competent engineer. I wonder if he's set the reactor here to destroy itself? was the next inspired thought to enter Miles mind. That would erase all the evidence, Vorsoisson, and Miles, too. If he timed it just right, Soudha might be able to take out the ImpSec rescue squad as well . . . but it seemed Foscol meant the evidence pinned to Vorsoisson's back to survive, at least, which argued against a scenario that would turn the experiment station into a glowing glass hole in the landscape resembling the lost city of Vorkosigan Vashnoi. Soudha and Company did not seem to be thinking militarily. Thank God. This scene seemed engineered for maximum humiliation, and one could not embarrass the dead.

Their next-of-kin, however . . . Miles thought of his father and shuddered. And Ekaterin and Nikolai, and, of course, Lord Auditor Vorthys. Oh, yes.

Vorsoisson, coming to full consciousness at last, reared up

and discovered the limits of his bonds. He swore muzzily, then with increasing clarity of expression, and yanked his arms against their chains. After about a minute, he stopped. He stared around and found Miles.

"Vorkosigan. What the hell is going on here?"

"We appear to have been parked out of the way while Soudha and his friends finish decamping from the experiment station. They seem to have realized their time had run out." Miles wondered if he ought to mention to Vorsoisson what was taped to his back, then decided against it. The man was already breathing heavily from his struggles. Vorsoisson swore some more, monotonously, but after a bit seemed to become aware that he was repeating himself, and ran down.

"Tell me more about this embezzlement scheme of Soudha's," Miles said into the eerie silence. No insect or bird chirps enlivened the Komarran night, and no tree leaves rustled in the faint, chill breeze. No further sounds came from the buildings behind them. The only noise was the susurration of their breath masks' powered fans, filters, and regulators. "When did you find out about it?"

"Just . . . yesterday. A week ago yesterday. Soudha panicked, I think, and tried to bribe me. I didn't want to embarrass Kat's Uncle Vorthys by blowing it wide open while he was here. And I had to be sure, before I started accusing people right and left."

Foscol says you lie. Miles wasn't sure which of them he trusted least by now. Foscol could have invented her evidence against Vorsoisson using the same skills she had apparently called on to hide Soudha's thefts. He would have to let the ImpSec forensic specialists sort it out, and carefully.

Miles simultaneously sympathized with and was deeply suspicious of Vorsoisson's claimed hesitation, a dizzying state of mind to endure on top of a stunner migraine. He had never thought of fast-penta as a medicine for headache, but he wished he had a hypospray of it to jab in Vorsoisson's ass right now. *Later*, he promised himself. *Without fail.* "Is that all that's going on, d'you think?"

"What do you mean, all?"

"I don't quite . . . if I were Soudha and his group, fleeing the scene of our crime . . . they did have some lead time to prepare their retreat. Maybe as long as three or four weeks, if they knew Radovas's body was likely to be found topside." *And what the hell was Radovas's body doing up there anyway? I still don't have a clue.* "Longer, if they kept their emergency backup plans up to date, and Soudha is an engineer if ever I met one; he's got to have had fail-safes incorporated into his schemes. Wouldn't it make more sense to scatter, travel light, try to get out of the Empire in ones and twos . . . not leave in a bunch with two lift-vans full of . . . whatever the hell they needed two lift-vans to transport? Not their money, surely."

Vorsoisson shook his head, which shifted his breath mask slightly; he had to rub his face against the railing to reseat it. After a few minutes he said in a small voice, "Vorkosigan . . . ?"

Miles hoped from the humbler tone the man might be going to edge toward true confession after all. "Yes?" he said encouragingly.

"I'm almost out of oxygen."

"Didn't you check—" Miles tried to bring up the image in his pulsing brain of the moment Vorsoisson had snatched his breath mask out of the cabinet, back in his office, and donned it. No. He hadn't checked anything about it. A fully-charged mask would support twelve to fourteen hours of vigorous outdoor activity, under normal circumstances. Miles's visitor's mask had presumably been taken from a central store, where some tech had the job of processing and recharging used masks before setting them on the rack ready for reuse. *Don't forget to put your mask on the recharger*, Vorsoisson's wife had said to him, and been snapped at for nagging. Was Vorsoisson in the habit of stuffing his equipment away uncleaned? In his office, Madame Vorsoisson couldn't very well pick up after him the way she doubtless did at home.

At one time, Miles could have crushed his own fragile hand bones and drawn his hand out through a restraint before his flesh began to swell enough to trap it again. He'd actually done that once, on a hideously memorable occasion. But the bones in his hands were all sturdy synthetics now, less breakable even than normal bone. All that his applied strength could do was make his chafed wrists bleed.

Vorsoisson's wrists began to bleed too, as he struggled more frantically against his chains.

"Vorsoisson, hold still!" Miles called urgently to him. "Conserve your oxygen. There's supposed to be someone coming. Go limp, breathe shallowly, make it last." Why hadn't the idiot mentioned this earlier, to Miles, to *Foscol* even . . . had Foscol intended this result? Maybe she'd meant both Miles and Vorsoisson to die, one after the other . . . *how long* till the promised someone came to collect them? A couple of days? Murdering an Imperial Auditor in the middle of a case was considered an act of treason worse than murdering a ruling District Count and only barely short of assassinating the Emperor himself. Nothing could be more surely calculated to send ImpSec's entire forces in frenzied pursuit of the fleeing embezzlers, with an implacable concentration reaching, potentially, across decades and distance and diplomatic barriers. It was a suicidal gesture, or unbelievably foolhardy. "How much do you have left?"

Vorsoisson wriggled his chin and tried to peer down over his nose into the dim recesses of his jacket to see the top of the canister strapped there. "Oh, God. I think it's reading zero."

"Those things always have some safety margin. Stay still, man! Try for some self-control!"

Instead Vorsoisson began to struggle ever more frantically. He threw himself forward and backward with all his considerable strength, trying to break the railing. Blood drops flew from the flayed skin of his wrists, and the railing reverberated and bent, but it did not break. He pulled up his knees and then flung himself down through the meter-wide opening between the posts, trying to propel his full body weight against the chains. They held, and then his backward-scrambling legs could not regain the walkway. His boot heels scraped and scrabbled on the wall. His dizzied choking, at the last, led to vomiting inside his breath mask. When it slipped down around his neck in his final paroxysms, it seemed almost a mercy, except for the way it revealed his distorted, purpling features. But the screams and pleas stopped, and then the gasps and gulpings. The kicking legs twitched, and hung limply.

Miles had been right; Vorsoisson might have had a full twenty or thirty minutes more oxygen if he had hunkered down quietly. Miles stood very still, and breathed very shallowly, and shivered in the cold. Shivering, he recalled dimly, used more oxygen, but he could not make himself stop. The silence was profound, broken only by the hiss of Miles's regulators and filters, and the beating of the blood in his own ears. He had seen many deaths, including his own, but this was surely one of the ugliest. The shocky shudders traveled up and down his body, and his thoughts spun uselessly: they kept circling back to the spuriously calm observation that a barrel of fast-penta would be no damned use to him now.

If he went into a convulsion and dislodged his breath mask in the process, he could be well on his way to asphyxiating before he even returned to consciousness. ImpSec would find him hanging there beside Vorsoisson, choked identically on his own spew. And nothing was more likely to set off one of his seizures than stress.

Miles watched the slime begin to freeze on the sagging corpse's face, scanned the dark skies in the wrong direction, and waited.

CHAPTER ELEVEN

Ekaterin set down her cases next to Lord Vorkosigan's in the vestibule, and turned for one last automatic check of the premises, one last patrol of her old life. All lights were out. All windows were sealed. All appliances were off . . . the comconsole chimed just as she was leaving the kitchen.

She hesitated. *Let it go. Let it all go.* But then she reflected it might be Tuomonen or someone, trying to reach Lord Vorkosigan. Or Uncle Vorthys, though she was not sure she even wanted to talk to him, tonight. She turned back to the machine, but her hand hesitated again with the thought that it might be Tien. *In that case, I will simply cut the com.* If it was Tien, about to attempt some other plea or threat or persuasion, at least it was a guarantee he was someplace else, and not here, and she could still walk away.

But the face that formed over the vid-plate at her reluctant touch was that of a Komarran woman from Tien's department, Lena Foscol. Ekaterin had only met her in person a couple of times, but Soudha's words over this same vid-plate last night leapt to her mind: *Lena Foscol in Accounting is the most meticulous thief I've ever met.* Oh, God. She was one of *them.* The background was out of focus, but the woman was wearing a parka, thrown open over dome-wear, suggesting she was either on her way to or on her way back from some outside expedition. Ekaterin regarded her with concealed revulsion.

"Madame Vorsoisson?" Foscol said brightly. Without waiting for Ekaterin's answer, she went on, "Please come pick up your husband at the Waste Heat experiment station. He'll be waiting for you outside on the northwest side of the Engineering building."

"But—" What was Tien doing out there at this time of night? "How did he get out there, doesn't he have a flyer? Can't he get a ride back with someone else?"

"Everyone else has left." Her smile widened, and she cut the com.

"But—" Ekaterin raised a hand in futile protest, too late. "Drat." And then, after a moment, "*Damn* it!"

Retrieving Tien from the experiment station would be a two-hour chore, at least. She would first have to take a bubble-car to a public flyer livery, and rent a flyer, since she had no authority to requisition one from Tien's department. She'd been seriously considering sleeping on a park bench tonight, just to save her pittance of funds for the uncertain days to come until she found some form of paying work, except that the dome patrollers didn't permit vagrants to loiter in any of the places where she might feel safe. Foscol hadn't said if Lord Vorkosigan was with Tien, which suggested he was not, which meant that she'd have to fly back to Serifosa alone with Tien, who would insist on taking the controls, and what if he finally got serious about his suicide threats when they were halfway back, and decided to take her down with him? No. It wasn't worth the risk. Let him rot out there till morning, or let him call someone else.

Her hand upon her case again, she reconsidered. Still hostage to fortune in this mess, or at least to everyone's good behavior, was Nikki. Tien's relationship to his son was mostly neglectful, interspersed with occasional bullying, but with enough spasms of actual attention that Nikki, at least, still seemed to show attachment to him. The two of them were always going to have a relationship separate from her own. She and Tien would be forced to cooperate for Nikki's sake: an iron-cladding of surface courtesy that must never crack. Tien's anger or potential brutality were no more of a threat to her future than some belated attempt on his part at affection or placation. She could face down either, now, she thought, with equal stoniness.

I am not here to vent my feelings. I am here to achieve my goals. Yes. She could foresee that was going to be her new mantra, in the weeks to come. With a grimace, she opened her case and retrieved her personal breath mask, checked its reservoirs, pulled on her parka, and headed out for the bubble-car station.

The delays were every bit as aggravating as Ekaterin had foreseen. Komarrans sharing her bubble-car forced two extra stops. She suffered a thirty-minute clog in the system within

sight of her goal; by the time it spat her out at the westernmost
dome lock, she was quite ready to chuck her plan of courtesy and go back to the apartment, except for the thought of
facing another thirty-minute delay en route. The lightflyer they
issued to her was elderly and not very clean. Alone at last,
flying through the vast silence of the Komarran night, her heart
eased a little, and she toyed with the fantasy of flying somewhere *else*, anywhere, just to extend the heavenly solitude.
There might be more to pleasure than the absence of pain,
but she couldn't prove it just now. The absence of pain, of
other human beings and their needs pressing down upon her,
seemed paradise enough. A paradise just out of reach.

Besides, she had no *elsewhere*. She could not even return
to Barrayar with Nikki without first earning enough to pay
for their passage, or borrowing the money from her father,
or her distant brothers, or Uncle Vorthys. Distasteful thought.
What you feel doesn't count, girl, she reminded herself. *Goals.
You'll do whatever you have to do.*

The bright lights of the experiment station, isolated in this
barren wilderness, made a glow on the horizon that drew the
eye from kilometers off. She followed the black silky gleam
of the river that wound past the facility. As she neared, she
made out several vehicles grounded in the station's lot, and
frowned in anger. Foscol had lied about there being no one
left at the station to give Tien a lift. On the other hand, this
raised the possibility that Ekaterin might get a ride back to
Serifosa with someone else . . . she checked her impulse to
turn the flyer around in midair, and landed in the lot instead.

She adjusted her breath mask, released the canopy, and
walked to the office building, hoping to arrange another ride
before she saw Tien. The airlock opened to her touch on the
control pad. There was not much reason to leave anything
locked up way out here. She turned up the first well-lit hallway,
calling, "Hello?"

No one answered. No one appeared to be here. About half
the rooms were bare and empty; the rest were rather messy
and disorganized, she thought. A comconsole was opened up,
its insides torn out . . . melted, in fact. That must have been
a spectacular malfunction. Her footsteps echoed hollowly as
she crossed through the pedestrian tube to the engineering
building. "Hello? Tien?" No answer here, either. The two big
assembly rooms were shadowed and sinister, and deserted.
"Anyone?" If Foscol hadn't lied after all, why were all those
aircars and flyers in the lot? Where had their owners gone,
and in what?

He'll be waiting for you outside on the northwest side. . . .
She had only a vague idea which side of the building was the
northwest; she'd half-expected Tien to be waiting in the parking
lot. She sighed uneasily, and adjusted her breath mask again,
and stepped out through the pedestrian lock. It would only take
a few minutes to circle the building. *I want to fly back to
Serifosa, right now. This is weird.* Slowly, she started around
the building to her left, her footsteps sounding sharp on the
concrete in the chill and toxic night air. A raised walkway, really
the level edge of the building's concrete foundation, skirted the
wall, with a railing along the outside as the ground fell away
below. It made her feel as though she were being herded into
some trap, or a corral. She rounded the second corner.

Halfway down the walk, a small human shape huddled on
its knees, arms outflung, its forehead pressed against the railing.
Another bigger shape hung by its wrists between two wide-
spaced posts, its body dangling down over the edge of the
raised concrete foundation, feet a half-meter from the ground.
What is this? The dark seemed to pulsate. She swallowed her
panic and hastened toward the odd pair.

The dangling figure was Tien. His breath mask was off,
twisted around his neck. Even in the colored half-light from
the spots in the vegetation below, she could see his face was
mottled and purple, with a cold doughy stillness. His tongue
protruded from his mouth; his bulging eyes were fixed and
frozen. Very, very dead. Her stomach churned and knotted in
shock, and her heart lumped in her chest.

The kneeling figure was Lord Vorkosigan, wearing her sec-
ond-best jacket that she had been unable to find while packing
a short eternity ago. His breath mask was still up—he turned
his head, his eyes going wide and dark as he saw her, and
Ekaterin melted with relief. The little Lord Auditor was still
alive, at least. She was frantically grateful not to be alone with
two corpses. His wrists, she saw at last, were chained to the
railing's posts just as Tien's were. Blood oozed from them,
soaking darkly into the jacket's cuffs.

Her first coherent thought was unutterable relief that she
had not brought Nikki with her. *How am I going to tell him?*
Tomorrow, that was a problem for tomorrow. Let him play away
tonight in the bubble of another universe, one without this
horror in it.

"Madame Vorsoisson." Lord Vorkosigan's voice was muffled
and faint in his breath mask. "Oh, God."

Fearfully, she touched the cold chains around his wrists.
The torn flesh was swollen up around the links, almost burying

them. "I'll go inside and look for some cutters." She almost added, *Wait here*, but closed her lips on that inanity just in time.

"No, wait," he gasped. "Don't leave me alone—there's a key . . . supposedly . . . on the walk back there." He jerked his head.

She found it at once, a simple mechanical type. It was cold, a slip of metal in her shaking fingers. She had to try several times to get it inserted in the locks that fastened the chains. She then had to peel the chain out of Vorkosigan's blood-crusted flesh as if from a rubber mold, before his hand could fall. When she released the second one, he nearly pitched head-first over the edge of the concrete. She grabbed him and dragged him back toward the wall. He tried to stand, but his legs would not at first unbend, and he fell over again. "Give yourself a minute," she told him. Awkwardly, she tried to massage his legs, to restore circulation; even through the fabric of his gray trousers she could feel how cold and stiff they were.

She stood, holding the key in her hand, and stared in bewilderment at Tien's body. She doubted she and Vorkosigan together could lift that dead weight back up to the walk.

"It's much too late," said Vorkosigan, watching her. His brows were crooked with concern. "I'm s-sorry. Leave him for Tuomonen."

"What is this on his back?" She touched the peculiar arrangement, what appeared to be a plastic packet fixed in place with engineering tape.

"Leave that," said Lord Vorkosigan more sharply. "Please." And then, in more of a rush, stuttering in his shivering, "I'm sorry. I'm sorry. I c-couldn't b-break the chains. Hell, he couldn't either, and he's s-stronger than I am. . . . I thought I c-could break my hand and get it out, but I couldn't. I'm sorry. . . ."

"You need to come inside, where it's warm. Here." She helped pull him to his feet; with a last look over his shoulder at Tien, he suffered himself to be led, hunched over, leaning on her and lurching on his unsteady legs.

She led him through the airlock into the office building, and guided him to an upholstered chair in the lobby. He more fell than sat in it. He shivered violently. "B-b-button," he muttered to her, holding up his hands like paralyzed paws toward her.

"What?"

"Little button on the s-side of wrist-comm. Press it!"

She did so; he sighed and relaxed against the seat back. His stiff hands yanked at his breath mask; she helped him pull it off over his head, and pulled down her own mask.

"*God* I am glad to get out of that thing. Alive. I th-thought I was gonna have a seizure out there. . . ." He rubbed his pale face, scrubbing at the red pressure-lines engraved in the skin from the edges of the mask. "And it *itched*." Ekaterin spotted the control on a nearby wall and hastily tapped in an increase of the lobby's temperature. She was shivering too, though not from the cold, in suppressed shocky shudders.

"Lord Vorkosigan?" Captain Tuomonen's anxious voice issued thinly from the wrist com. "What's going on? Where the hell *are* you?!"

Vorkosigan lifted his wrist toward his mouth. "Waste Heat experiment station. Get out here. I need you."

"What are you— Should I bring a squad?"

"Don't need guns now, I don't think. You'll need forensics, though. And a medical team."

"Are you injured, my lord?" Tuomonen's voice grew sharp with panic.

"Not to speak of," he said, apparently oblivious to the blood still leaking from his wrists. "Administrator Vorsoisson is dead, though."

"What the hell—*you didn't check in with me before you left the dome, dammit!* What the hell is going on out there?!"

"We can discuss my failings at length, later. Carry on, Captain. Vorkosigan out." He let his arm fall, wearily. His shivering was lessening, now. He leaned his head back against the upholstery; the dark smudges of exhaustion under his eyes looked like bruises. He stared sadly at Ekaterin. "I am sorry, Madame Vorsoisson. There was nothing I could do."

"I would scarcely think so!"

He looked around, squinting, and added abruptly, "Power plant!"

"What about it?" asked Ekaterin.

"Gotta check before the troops arrive. I spent a lot of time wondering if it might have been sabotaged, when I was tied up out there."

His legs were still not working right. He almost fell over again as he tried to turn on his heel; she rose and just caught him, under his elbow.

"Good," he said vaguely to her, and pointed. "That way."

She was evidently drafted as support. He hobbled off in determination, clinging to her arm without apology. The forced action actually helped her to recover, if not calm, a sort of tenuous physical coherence; her shudders damped out, and her incipient nausea passed, leaving her belly feeling hot and odd. Another pedestrian tube led down to the power plant, next to the river. The river was the largest in the Sector, and the proximate reason for siting the experiment station here. By Barrayaran standards it would have been called a creek. Vorkosigan barged awkwardly around the power plant's control room, examining panels and readouts. "Nothing *looks* abnormal," he muttered. "I wonder why they didn't set it to self-destruct? *I* would have. . . ." He fell into a station chair.

She pulled up another one, and sat opposite him, watching him fearfully. "What *happened*?"

"I—we came out, Tien brought me out here—how the devil did *you* come here?"

"Lena Foscol called me at home, and told me Tien wanted a ride. She almost didn't catch me. I'd been about to leave. She didn't even tell me *you* were out here. You might still be . . ."

"No . . . no, I'm almost certain she'd have made some other arrangement, if she'd missed you altogether." He sat up straighter, or tried to. "What time is it now?"

"A little before 2100."

"I . . . would have guessed it was much later. They stunned us, you see. I don't know how long . . . What time did she call you?"

"It was just after 1900 hours."

His eyes squeezed shut, then opened again. "It was too late. It was already too late by then, do you understand?" he asked urgently. His hand jerked toward hers, on her knee as she leaned toward him to catch his hoarse words, but then fell back.

"No . . ."

"There was something questionable going on in the Waste Heat department. Your husband brought me out here to show me—well, I don't quite know what he thought he was going to show me, but we ran headlong into Soudha and his accomplices in the process of decamping. Soudha got the drop on me—stunned us both. I came to, chained to that railing out there. I don't think—I don't know. . . . I don't think they meant to kill your husband. He hadn't checked his breath mask, y'see. His reservoirs were almost empty. The Komarrans didn't check it either, before they left us. I didn't know, no one did."

"Komarrans wouldn't," Ekaterin said woodenly. "Their mask-check procedures are ingrained by the time they're three years old. They'd never imagine an adult would go outside the dome with deficient equipment." Her hands clenched, in her lap. She could picture Tien's death now.

"It was . . . quick," Vorkosigan offered. "At least that."

It was not. Neither quick nor clean. "Please do not lie to me. Please do not ever lie to me."

"All right . . ." he said slowly. "But I don't think . . . I don't *think* it was murder. To set up that scene, and then call *you* . . ." He shook his head. "Manslaughter at most. Death by misadventure."

"Death from stupidity," she said bitterly. "Consistent to the end."

He glanced up at her, his eyes not so much startled as aware, and questioning. "Ah?"

"Lord Auditor Vorkosigan." She swallowed; her throat was so tight it felt like a muscle spasm. The silence in the building, and outside, was eerie in its emptiness. She and Vorkosigan might as well have been the only two people left alive on the planet. "You should know, when I said Foscol called as I was leaving . . . I was *leaving*. Leaving Tien. I'd told him so, when he came home from the department tonight, and just before he went back, I suppose, to get you. What did he do?"

He took this in without much response at first, as if thinking it over. "All right," he echoed himself softly at last. He glanced across at her. "Basically, he came in babbling about some embezzlement scheme which had been going on in Waste Heat Management, apparently for quite some time. He sounded me out about declaring him an Imperial Witness, which he seemed to think would save him from prosecution. It's not quite that simple. I didn't commit myself."

"Tien would hear what he wanted to hear," she said softly.

"I . . . so I gathered." He hesitated, watching her face. "How long . . . what do you know about it?"

"And how long have I known it?" Ekaterin grimaced, and rubbed her face free of the lingering irritation of her own mask. "Not as long as I should have. Tien had been talking for months . . . You have to understand, he was irrationally afraid of anyone finding out about his Vorzohn's Dystrophy."

"I actually do understand that," he offered tentatively.

"Yes . . . and no. It's Tien's older brother's fault, in part. I've cursed the man for years. When *his* symptoms began, he took the Old Vor way out and crashed his lightflyer. It made an impression on Tien he never shook off. Set an impossible example. We'd had no idea his family carried the mutation, till Tien, who was his brother's executor, was going through the records and effects, and we realized both that the accident was deliberate, and why. It was just after Nikki was born . . ."

"But wouldn't it have . . . I'd wondered when I read your file—the defect should have turned up in the gene scan, before the embryo was started in the uterine replicator. Is Nikki affected, or . . . ?"

"Nikki was a body-birth. No gene scan. The Old Vor way. Old Vor have *good* blood, you know, no need to check anything."

He looked as if he'd bitten into a lemon. "Whose bright idea was *that?*"

"I don't . . . quite remember how it was decided. Tien and I decided together. I was young, we were just married, I had a lot of stupid romantic ideas . . . I suppose it seemed heroic to me at the time."

"How old were you?"

"Twenty."

"Ah." His mouth quirked in an expression she could not quite interpret, a sad mixture of irony and sympathy. "Yes."

Obscurely encouraged, she went on. "Tien's scheme for dealing with the dystrophy without anyone ever finding out he had it was to go get galactic treatment, somewhere far from the Imperium. It made it much more expensive than it needed to be. We'd been trying to save for years, but somehow, something always went wrong. We never made much progress. But for the past six or eight months, Tien's been telling me to stop worrying, he had it under control. Except . . . Tien always talks like that, so I scarcely paid attention. Then last night, after you went to sleep . . . I heard you tell him straight out you wanted to make a surprise inspection of his department today, I *heard* you—he got up in the night and called Administrator Soudha, to warn him. I listened . . . I heard enough to gather they had some sort of payroll falsification scheme going, and I'm very much afraid . . . no. I'm certain Tien was taking bribes. Because—" she stopped and took a breath "—I broke into Tien's comconsole this morning and looked at his financial records." She glanced up, to see how Vorkosigan would take this. His mouth renewed the crooked quirk. "I'm sorry I ripped at you the other day, for looking through mine," she said humbly.

His mouth opened, and closed; he merely gave her a little encouraging wave of his fingers and slumped down a bit more in his chair, listening with an air of uttermost attention. *Listening.*

She went on hurriedly, not before her nerve broke, for she

scarcely felt anything now, but before she dragged to a halt from sheer exhaustion. "He'd had at least forty thousand marks that I couldn't see where they'd come from. Not from his salary, certainly."

"Had?"

"If the information on the comconsole was right, he'd taken all forty thousand and borrowed sixty more, and lost it all on Komarran trade fleet shares."

"*All?*"

"Well, no, not quite all. About three-quarters of it." At his astonished look, she added, "Tien's luck has always been like that."

"I always used to say you made your own luck. Though I've been forced to eat those words often enough, I don't say it so much anymore."

"Well . . . I think it must be true, or how else could his luck have been so *consistently* bad? The only common factor in all the chaos *was* Tien." She leaned her head back wearily. "Though I suppose it might have been me, somehow." *Tien often said it was me.*

After a little silence, he said hesitantly, "Did you love your husband, Madame Vorsoisson?"

She didn't want to answer this. The truth made her ashamed. But she was done with dissimulation. "I suppose I did, once. In the beginning. I can hardly remember anymore. But I couldn't stop . . . caring for him. Cleaning up after him. Except my caring got slower and slower, and finally it . . . stopped. Too late. Or maybe too soon, I don't know." But if, of course, she had not broken from Tien just then, in just that way, he would not tonight have . . . and, and, and, along the whole chain of events that led to this moment. That *if-only* could, of course, be said equally for any link in the chain. Not more, not less. Not repairable. "I thought, if I let go, he would fall." She stared at her hands. "Eventually. I didn't expect it to happen so soon."

It began to be borne in upon her what a mess Tien's death was going to leave in her lap. She would be trading the painful legalities of separation for the equally painful and difficult legalities of sorting out his probably bankrupt estate. And what was she supposed to do about his body, or any kind of funeral, and how to notify his mother, and . . . yet solving the worst problem without Tien seemed already a thousand times easier than solving the simplest *with* Tien. No more deferential negotiations for permission or approval or consensus. She could just *do* it. She felt . . . like a patient coming out of some paralysis, stretching her arms wide for the first time, and surprised to discover they were strong.

She frowned in puzzlement. "Will there be charges? Against Tien?"

Vorkosigan shrugged. "It is not customary to try the dead, though I believe it was done occasionally in the Time of Isolation. Lord Vorventa the Twice-Hung springs to mind. No. There will be investigations, there will be reports, oh my head the reports, ImpSec's and my own and possibly the Serifosa Sector's security—I anticipate argument over jurisdiction—there may be testimony required of you in the prosecution of other persons . . ." He broke off, to hitch himself around with difficulty in his chair, and shove a now somewhat less stiff-from-cold hand into his pocket. "Persons who I suppose got away with my stunner . . ." His expression changed to one of dismay, and he spasmed to his feet and turned out both his trouser pockets, then checked his jacket, shucked it off, and patted his gray tunic. "*Damn.*"

"What?" asked Ekaterin in alarm.

"I think the bastards took my Auditor's seal. Unless it just fell out of my pocket, somewhere in all the horsing around tonight. Oh, God. It'll open any government or security comconsole in the Empire." He took a deep breath, then brightened. "On the other hand, it has a locator-circuit. ImpSec can trace it, if they're close enough—ImpSec can trace *them.* Ha!" With difficulty, he forced his red and swollen fingers to open a channel on his comm link. "Tuomonen?" he inquired.

"We're on our way, my lord," Tuomonen's voice came back instantly. "We're in the air, about halfway there I estimate. Will you *please* leave your channel open?"

"Listen. I think my assailants have taken off with my Auditor's seal. Delegate someone to start trying to track it at once. Find it and you'll find them, if it's not just been dropped around here somewhere. You can check that possibility when you get here."

Vorkosigan then insisted on a tour of the building, drafting Ekaterin once more as occasional support, though he stumbled very little now. He frowned at the melted comconsole, and at the empty rooms, and stared with narrowed eyes at the jumbles of equipment. Tuomonen and his men arrived just as they were reentering the lobby.

Lord Vorkosigan's lips twitched in bemusement as two half-armored guards, stunners at the ready, leaped through the airseal door. They gave Vorkosigan anxious nods, which he acknowledged with a wry salutelike gesture, then pelted after each other through the facility for a rather noisy security check. Vorkosigan hitched himself into a deliberately more relaxed posture, leaning against an upholstered chair. Captain Tuomonen, another Barrayaran soldier in half-armor, and three men in medical gear followed into the lobby.

"My lord!" said Tuomonen, pulling down his breath mask. His tone of voice sounded familiarly maternal to Ekaterin's ear, halfway between *Thank God you're safe* and *I'm going to strangle you with my bare hands.*

"Good evening, Captain," said Vorkosigan genially. "So glad to see you."

"You didn't notify me!"

"Yes, it was entirely my mistake, and I'll be certain to note your exoneration in my report," Vorkosigan said soothingly.

"It's not that, dammit!" Tuomonen strode over to him, motioning a medic in his wake. He took in Vorkosigan's macerated wrists and bloody hands. "Who did that to you?"

"I did it to myself, rather, I'm afraid." Vorkosigan's pose of studied ease slipped back into his original grimness. "It could have been worse, as I will show you directly. Around back. I want you to record everything, a complete scan. Anything you're in doubt of, leave for the experts from HQ. I want a top forensics team scrambled from Solstice immediately. Two teams, one for out here, one for those royally buggered comconsoles at the Terraforming offices. But first, I think," he glanced at the medtechs, and at Ekaterin, "we should get Administrator Vorsoisson's body down."

"Here's the key," said Ekaterin numbly, producing it from her pocket.

"Thank you," said Vorkosigan, taking it from her. "Wait here, please." He jerked up his chin, checked and pulled up his mask, and led the still-protesting Tuomonen back out the airseal doors, imperiously motioning the medics to follow. Ekaterin could still hear the clattering and strained sharp voices of the armed guards, echoing from distant corridors deeper in the office building.

She huddled into the chair Vorkosigan had vacated, feeling very odd not to be following the men to Tien. But someone else was going to be cleaning up the mess this time, it appeared. A few tears leaked from her eyes, residue of her body-shock she supposed, for she surely felt no more emotion than if she'd been a lump of lead.

After a long while, the men returned to the lobby, where Tuomonen finally persuaded Vorkosigan to sit down and let the senior medic attend to his injured wrists.

"This isn't the treatment I'm most concerned about just now," Vorkosigan complained, as a hypospray of synergine hissed into the side of his neck. "I have to get back to Serifosa. There's something I really need out of my luggage."

"Yes, my lord," said the medtech soothingly, and went on cleaning and bandaging.

Tuomonen went out to his aircar to relay some terse communication with his ImpSec superiors in Solstice, then returned to lean on the back of the chair and watch the medtech finish up.

Vorkosigan eyed Ekaterin, across the medtech. "Madame Vorsoisson. In retrospect, thinking back, did your husband ever say anything that indicated this scam had to do with something more than money?"

Ekaterin shook her head.

Tuomonen, in gruff tones, put in, "I'm afraid, Madame Vorsoisson, that ImpSec is going to have to take charge of your late husband's body. There must be a complete examination."

"Yes, of course," Ekaterin said faintly. She paused. "Then what?"

"We'll let you know, Madame." He turned to Vorkosigan, evidently continuing a conversation. "So what else did you think of, when you were tied up out there?"

"All I could really think about was when my next seizure was due," said Vorkosigan ruefully. "It became kind of an obsession, after a while. But I don't think Foscol knew about that hidden defect, either."

"I still want to call it murder and attempted murder, for the all-Sectors alert order," said Tuomonen, evidently continuing a debate. "And the attempted murder of an Imperial Auditor makes it treason, which disposes of any arguments about requisitions."

"Yes, very good," sighed Vorkosigan in acquiescence. "Make sure your reports have the facts clear, though, please."

"As I see them, my lord." Tuomonen grimaced, then burst out, "Damn, to think how long this thing must have been going on, right under my nose . . . !"

"Not your jurisdiction, Captain," observed Vorkosigan. "It was the Imperial Accounting Office's job to spot this kind of fraud in the civil service. Still . . . there's something very wrong here."

"I should say so!"

"No, I mean beyond the obvious." Vorkosigan hesitated. "They abandoned all their personal effects, yet took at least two air-vans of equipment."

"To . . . sell?" Ekaterin posited. "No, that makes no sense. . . ."

"Mm, and they left in a group, didn't split up. These people seemed to me to be Komarran patriots, of a sort. I can see where they might classify theft from the Barrayaran Imperium as something between a hobby and a patriotic duty, but . . . to steal from the Komarran Terraforming Project, the hope of their future generations? And if it wasn't just to line their pockets, what the *devil* were they using all the money *for*?" He scowled. "That will be for ImpSec's forensic accounting team to sort out, I suppose. And I want engineering experts in here, to see if they can make anything at all from the mess that's been left. And not left. It's clear Soudha's crew put *something* together in the Engineering building, and I don't think it had anything to do with waste heat." He rubbed his forehead, and muttered, "I'll bet Marie Trogir could tell us. *Damn* but I wish I'd fast-penta'd Madame Radovas when I had the chance."

Ekaterin swallowed a lump of dread and humiliation. "I'm going to have to tell my uncle."

Vorkosigan glanced up at her. "I'll take over that task, Madame Vorsoisson."

She frowned, torn between what seemed to her weak gratitude, and a dreary sense of duty, but could not muster the energy to argue with him. The medic finished winding the last medical tape around Vorkosigan's wrists.

"I must leave you in charge here, Captain, and return to Serifosa. I don't dare fly myself. Madame Vorsoisson, would you be so kind . . . ?"

"You *will* take a guard," said Tuomonen, a little dangerously.

"I have to get the flyer back," said Ekaterin. "It's rented." She squinted, realizing how stupid that sounded. But it was the only fragment of order in this mortal chaos it was presently in her power to restore. And then, belatedly, the realization came: *I can go home. It's safe to go home.* Her voice strengthened. "Certainly, Lord Vorkosigan."

The presence of the hulking young guard crowded into the flyer behind them, Vorkosigan's exhaustion, and Ekaterin's emotional disorientation combined to blunt conversation on the flight back to Serifosa. She drew stares, turning the flyer back in at the rental desk while trailed politely by a large, fully-armed, half-armored soldier and a dwarfish man with bloody clothes and bandages on his wrists, but on the other hand, they had a bubble-car all to themselves for the ride back to the apartment. There were no delays in the system on this return leg, Ekaterin noted with weary irony. She wondered if there would be any point, later when this all got sorted out, to check if Vorkosigan's insistence that it had already been too late for Tien when Foscol had called her was precisely true.

Her steps quickened in the hallway of her apartment; she felt like an injured animal, wanting nothing more than to go hide in her burrow. She came to an abrupt halt at her door, and her breath drew in. The palm-lock panel was hanging partway out of the wall, and the sliding door was not entirely closed. A thin line of light leaked along its edge. She backed up a step, and pointed.

Vorkosigan took it all in at once and motioned to the guard who, equally silently, stepped up to the door and drew his stunner. Vorkosigan put his finger to his lips, took her by the arm, and drew her back halfway to the lift-tubes. The automatic door wasn't working; the guard had to grasp it awkwardly and lean, to push it back into its slot. Stunner raised and visor lowered, he slipped inside. Ekaterin's heart hammered.

After a few minutes, the ImpSec guard, his visor up again, poked his head back out the door. "Someone's been through here right enough, m'lord. But they're gone now." Vorkosigan and Ekaterin followed him inside.

Both Vorkosigan's cases and her own, which she had left sitting by the door in the vestibule, had been broken open. Their clothing was scattered in mixed heaps all around on the floor. Little else in the apartment appeared to have been touched; some drawers were opened, their contents stirred, but aside from the disorder nothing had been vandalized. Was it a violation, when she herself had all but vacated this space, abandoned those possessions? She scarcely knew.

"This is not how I left my things," Vorkosigan observed mildly to her when they fetched up in the vestibule again after their first short survey.

"It's not how I left them either," she said a bit desperately. "I thought you would be coming back with Tien, and then leaving, so I'd packed them all for you, ready to take away."

"Touch nothing, especially the comconsoles, till the forensics folks get here," Vorkosigan told her. She nodded understanding. They both shucked their heavy jackets; automatically, Ekaterin hung them up.

Vorkosigan then proceeded to ignore his own dictate, and kneel in the vestibule to sort through the heaps. "Did you pack my code-locked data case?"

"Yes."

"It's gone now." He sighed, rose, and raised his wrist-comm to report these new developments to Captain Tuomonen, still at the experiment station. The overburdened Tuomonen, apprised, swore briefly and ordered his soldier to stick with the Lord Auditor like glue until relieved. For once, Vorkosigan didn't object.

Vorkosigan returned to the mess, turning over an untidy pile of Ekaterin's clothing. "Ha!" he cried, and pounced on the gel-pack case which contained that odd device. He opened it hurriedly, his hands shaking a little. "Thank God they didn't take *this*." He looked up at her, measuringly. "Madame Vorsoisson . . ." his normally forceful tone grew uncertain. "I wonder if I could trouble you to . . . assist me in this."

She almost said *Yes*, without thinking, but managed to alter the word to "What?" before it left her mouth.

He smiled tightly. "I mentioned my seizure disorder to you. It doesn't have a cure, unfortunately. But my Barrayaran doctors came up with a palliative, of sorts. I use this little machine to stimulate seizures, bleed them off in a controlled time and place, so they don't happen in an uncontrolled time and place. They tend to be exacerbated by stress." By his grimace, she could see him picturing the cold walkway on the backside of the Engineering building. "I suspect I'm now overdue. I would like to get it over with at once."

"I understand. But what do I do?"

"I'm supposed to have a spotter. To see I don't spit out my mouth guard, or, or injure myself or damage anything while I'm out. There shouldn't be much to it."

"All right . . ."

Under the dubious eye of the ImpSec guard, she followed him to the living room. He headed for the curved couch. "If you lie on the floor," Ekaterin suggested diffidently, still not sure how spectacular a show to expect, "you can't fall any further."

"Ah. Right." He settled himself on the carpet, the case open in his hand. She made sure the space around them was clear, and knelt beside him.

He unfolded the device, which resembled a set of head-phones with a pad on one end and a mysterious knob on the other. He fitted it over his head and adjusted it to his temples. He smiled at Ekaterin in what she belatedly realized was extreme embarrassment, and muttered, "I'm afraid this looks a little stupid," fitted a plastic mouthguard onto his teeth, and lay back.

"Wait," said Ekaterin suddenly as his hand reached for his temple.

"Wha'?"

"Could . . . whoever came in here have tampered with that thing? Maybe it ought to be checked first."

His wide eyes met hers; as certainly as if she had been telepathic, she knew she shared with him at that moment a vision of his head being blown off at the touch of his hand on the stimulator's trigger. He ripped it back off his head, sat up, spat out his mouthguard, and cried, "Shit!" He added after a moment, in a tone level but about half an octave higher than his norm, "You're quite right. Thank you. I wasn't thinking. I made . . . many cosmic promises, that if I made it back here, I'd do this first thing, and *never never never* put it off just one extra day again." Hyperventilating, he stared in consternation at the device clutched in his hand.

Then his eyes rolled up, and he fell over backwards. Ekaterin caught his head just before it banged into the carpet. His lips were drawn back in a strange grin. His body shuddered, in waves passing down to his toes and fingertips, but he did not flail wildly about as she'd half-expected. The guard hovered, looking panicked. She rescued the mouth guard, and fitted it back over his teeth, not as difficult a task as it at first appeared; despite an impression to that effect, he was not rigid.

She sat back on her heels, and stared. *Triggered by stress. Yes. I see.* His face was . . . altered, his personality clearly not present but in a way that resembled neither sleep nor death. It seemed terribly rude to watch him so, in all his vulnerability; courtesy urged her to look away. But he had explicitly appointed her to this task.

She checked her chrono. About five minutes, he'd said these things lasted. It seemed a small eternity, but was in fact less than three minutes when his body stilled. He lay slumped in alarmingly flaccid unconsciousness for another minute beyond that, then drew in a shuddering breath. His eyes opened and stared about in palpable incomprehension. At least his dilated pupils were the same size.

"Sorry. Sorry . . ." he muttered inanely. "Didn't mean to do that." He lay staring upward, his eyebrows crooked. He added after a moment, "What *does* it look like, anyway?"

"Really strange," Ekaterin answered him honestly. "I like your face better when you're at home in your head." She had not realized how powerfully his personality enlivened his features, or how subtly, until she'd seen it removed.

"I like my *head* better when I'm at home in it, too," he

breathed. He squeezed his eyes shut, and opened them again. "I'll get out of your way now." His hands twitched, and he tried to sit up.

Ekaterin didn't think he ought to be trying to do *anything* yet. She pressed him firmly back down with a hand on his chest. "Don't you dare take away that guard till my door gets fixed." Not that its expensive electronic lock had appeared to do the least good.

"Oh. No, of course not," he said faintly.

It was abundantly apparent that Vorkosigan's implicit claim that he bounced back out of his seizures with no ill effects was a, well, if not a lie, a gross exaggeration. He looked terrible.

She raised her gaze to catch that of the disturbed guard. "Corporal. Would you please help me to get Lord Vorkosigan to bed until he is more recovered. Or at least until your people arrive."

"Sure, ma'am." He seemed relieved to have this direction provided for him, and helped her pull Vorkosigan to his unsteady feet.

Ekaterin made a lightning calculation. Nikki's bed was the only one instantly available, and his room had no comconsole. If Vorkosigan went to sleep, which he obviously desperately needed to do after this night's ordeal, there was a chance he might be let to stay that way even when the ImpSec forensic invasion arrived. "This way," she nodded to the guard, and led them down the hall.

The incoherence of Vorkosigan's mumbled protests assured Ekaterin that she was doing precisely the right thing. He was shivering again. She helped him off with his tunic, made him lie down, dragged off his boots, covered him with extra blankets, turned the room's heat up to high, doused the lights, and withdrew.

There was no one to put *her* to bed, but she did not care to attempt conversation with the guard, who took up station in her living room to wait for his overextended reinforcements. Her whole body felt as though it had been beaten. She took some painkillers and lay down fully dressed in her own bedroom, a thousand uncertainties and conflicting scenarios for what she must do next jostling in her mind.

Tien's body, which had breathed beside her in this space last night, must be in the hands of the ImpSec medical examiner by now, laid out naked and still on a cold metal tray in some clinical laboratory here in Serifosa. She hoped they would treat his congealed husk with some measure of dignity, and not the nervous jocularity death sometimes evoked.

When this bed had been impossible to bear in the night, it had been her habit to sneak off to her workroom and fiddle with her virtual gardens. The Barrayaran garden had increasingly been her choice, of late. It lacked the texture, the smell, the slow dense satisfactions of the real, but it had soothed her mind nonetheless. But first Vorkosigan had occupied the room, and now he'd ordered her not to touch the comconsoles till ImpSec had drained them. She sighed and turned over, huddled in her accustomed corner of the bed even though the rest was unoccupied. *I want to leave this place as soon as I can. I want to be someplace where Tien has never been.*

She did not expect to sleep, but whether from the pain meds or exhaustion or the combination, she fell into a doze at last.

CHAPTER TWELVE

Miles could tell right away that he wasn't going to enjoy waking up. A bad seizure usually left him with hangover-like symptoms the following day, and the lingering effects of heavy stun included muscle aches, muscle spasms, and pseudo-migraines. The combination, it appeared, was downright synergistic. He groaned, and tried to regain unconsciousness. A gentle touch on his shoulder thwarted his intent.

"Lord Vorkosigan?"

It was Ekaterin Vorsoisson's soft voice. His eyes sprang open on thankfully-dim lighting. He was in her son Nikki's room, and could not remember how he'd arrived here. He rolled over and blinked up at her. She had changed clothes since his last memory of her, kneeling beside him on her living room floor; she now wore a soft, high-necked beige shirt and darker-toned trousers in the Komarran style. Her long dark hair lay loose in damp new-washed strands on her shoulders. *He* still had on his blood-stained shirt and wrinkled trousers from yesterday's nightmare.

"I'm sorry to wake you," she continued, "but Captain Tuomonen is here."

"Ah," said Miles thickly. He struggled upright. Madame Vorsoisson was holding out a tray with a large mug of black coffee and a bottle of painkiller tablets. Two tablets had already been extracted from the bottle, and lay ready for ingestion beside the cup. Only in his imagination did a heavenly choir supply background music. "Oh. My."

She didn't say anything more till he had fumbled the tablets to his lips and swallowed them. His swollen hands weren't working too well, but did manage to clutch the mug in

163

something resembling a death-grip. A second swallow scalded away a world of nastiness lingering in his mouth, well worth the challenge to the queasiness in his stomach. "Thank you." After a third gulp, he achieved, "What time is it?"

"It's about an hour after dawn."

He'd been out of the loop for about four hours, then. All sorts of events could occur in four hours. Not parting with the mug, he kicked his legs out of the bed. His sock-clad feet groped for the floor. Walking was going to be a chancy business for the first few minutes.

"Is Tuomonen in a hurry?"

"I can't tell. He looks tired. He says they found your seal."

That decided it; Tuomonen before a shower. He swallowed more coffee, handed the mug back to Ekater—to Madame Vorsoisson—and levered himself to his feet. After an awkward smile at her, he did a few bends and stretches, to be certain he could walk down the hall without falling over in front of ImpSec.

He had not the first idea what to say to her. *I'm sorry I got your husband killed* was inaccurate on a couple of counts. Up to the point he had been stunned, Miles might have done half a dozen different things to have altered last night's outcome; but if only Vorsoisson had checked his own damned breath mask before going out, the way he was supposed to, Miles was pretty certain he would still have been alive this morning. And the more he learned about the man, the less convinced he was that his death was any disservice to his wife. Widow. After a moment he essayed, "Are you all right?"

She smiled wanly, and shrugged. "All things considered."

Thin lines etched parallels between her eyes. "Did you, um . . ." he gestured at the bottle of tablets, "get any of those for yourself?"

"Several. Thank you."

"Ah. Good." *Harm has been done you, and I don't know how to fix it.* It was going to take a hell of a lot more than a couple of pills, though. He shook his head, regretted the gesture instantly, and staggered out to see Tuomonen.

The Imp Sec captain was waiting on the circular couch in the living room, also gratefully sucking down Madame Vorsoisson's coffee. He appeared to consider standing at some sort of quasi-attention when the Lord Auditor entered the room, but then thought better of it. Tuomonen gestured, and Miles seated himself across the table from the captain; they each mumbled their good-mornings. Madame Vorsoisson followed with Miles's half-empty coffee cup and set it before him, then, after a wary glance at Tuomonen, quietly seated herself. If Tuomonen wanted her to leave, he was going to have to ask her himself, Miles decided. And then justify the request.

In the event, Tuomonen merely nodded thanks to her, and shifted around and drew a plastic packet from his tunic. It contained Miles's gold-encased Auditor's electronic seal. He handed it across to Miles.

"Very good, Captain," said Miles. "I don't suppose you were so fortunate as to find it on the person of its thief?"

"No, more's the pity. You'll never guess where we *did* find it."

Miles squinted and held the plastic bag up to the light. A sheen of condensation fogged the inside. "In a sewer pipe halfway between here and the Serifosa Dome waste treatment plant, would be my first guess."

Tuomonen's jaw fell open. "How did you know?"

"Forensic plumbing was once a sort of hobby of mine. Not to sound ungrateful, but has anyone washed it?"

"Yes, in fact."

"Oh, thank you." Miles opened the packet and shook the heavy little device into his palm. It appeared undamaged.

Tuomonen said, "My lieutenant had its signal traced, or at any rate, triangulated, within half an hour of your call. He led an assault team down into the utility tunnels after it. I wish I could have seen it, when they finally figured out what was going on. You would have appreciated it, I'm almost certain."

Miles grinned despite his headache. "I was in no shape last night to appreciate anything, I'm afraid."

"Well, they made an impressive delegation when they went to wake up the Serifosa Dome municipal engineer. She's Komarran, of course. ImpSec coming for her in the middle of the night—her husband about had a heart spasm. My lieutenant finally got him calmed down, and got across to her what we needed . . . I'm afraid she found it an occasion for, er, considerable irony. We are all grateful that my lieutenant didn't yield to his first impulse, which was to have his team blast open the pipe section in question with their assault plasma rifles. . . ."

Miles almost choked on a swallow of coffee. "Exceedingly grateful." He stole a glance at Ekaterin Vorsoisson, who was leaning back against the cushions listening to this, eyes alight, a hand pressed to her lips. His painkillers were cutting in; she didn't look so blurry now.

"There was no sign by then of our human quarry, of course," Tuomonen finished with a sigh. "Long gone."

Miles stared at his distorted reflection in the dark surface of his drink. "One sees the scenario. You should be able to work out the timetable quite precisely. Foscol and an unknown number of accomplices pick my pocket, tie me and the Administrator to the railing, fly back to Serifosa, call Madame Vorsoisson. Probably from someplace nearby. As soon as she vacates her apartment, they break in, knowing they have at least an hour to explore before the alarm goes up. They use my seal to open the data case and access my report files. Then they flush the seal down the toilet and leave. Not even breathing hard."

"Too bad they weren't tempted to keep it."

"Mm, they clearly realized it was traceable. Hence their little joke." He frowned. "But . . . why my data case?"

"They might have been looking for something about Radovas. What all *was* in your data case, my lord?"

"Copies of all the classified technical reports and autopsies from the soletta accident. Soudha's an engineer. He doubtless had a very good idea what was in there."

"We're going to have an interesting time later this morning at the Terraforming Project offices," said Tuomonen glumly, "trying to figure out which employees are absent because they fled, and which ones are absent because they are fictional. I need to get over there as soon as possible, to supervise the preliminary interrogations. We'll have to fast-penta them all, I suppose."

"I predict it will be a great waste of time and drugs," agreed Miles. "But there's always the chance of someone knowing more than they think they know."

"Mm, yes." Tuomonen glanced at the listening woman. "Speaking of which—Madame Vorsoisson—I'm afraid I'm going to have to ask you to cooperate with a fast-penta interrogation as well. It's standard operating procedure, in a mysterious death of this nature, to question the closest relatives. The Dome police may also be wanting in on it, or at least demand a copy, depending on what decisions are made about jurisdiction by my superiors."

"I understand," said Madame Vorsoisson, in a colorless voice.

"There was nothing mysterious about Administrator Vorsoisson's death," Miles pointed out uneasily. "I was standing right next to him." Well, kneeling, technically.

"She's not a *suspect*," Tuomonen said. "A witness."

And a fast-penta interrogation would help to keep it that way, Miles realized with reluctance.

"When do you wish to do this, Captain?" Madame Vorsoisson asked quietly.

"Well . . . not immediately. I'll have a better set of questions after this morning's investigations are complete. Just don't go anywhere."

Her glance at him silently inquired, *Am I under house arrest?* "At some point, I have to go get my son Nikolai. He was staying overnight at a friend's home. He hasn't been told anything about this yet. I don't want to tell him over the comconsole, and I don't want him to hear it first on the news."

"That won't happen," said Tuomonen grimly. "Not yet, anyway. Though I expect I'll have the information services badgering us soon enough. Someone is bound to notice that the most boring ImpSec post on Komarr is suddenly boiling with activity."

"I must either go get him, or call and arrange for him to stay longer."

"Which would you prefer?" Miles put in before Tuomonen could say anything.

"I . . . if you are going to do the interrogation here, today, I'd rather wait till it's over with to get Nikki. I'll have to explain to his friend's mother something of the situation, at least that Tien was . . . killed in an accident last night."

"Have you bugged her comconsoles?" Miles asked Tuomonen bluntly.

Tuomonen's look queried this revelation, but he cleared his throat, and said, "Yes. You should be aware, Madame Vorsoisson, that ImpSec will be monitoring all calls in and out of here for a few days."

She looked blankly at him. "Why?"

"There is the possibility that someone, either from Soudha's group or some other connection we haven't yet discovered, not yet realizing the Administrator is dead, might try to communicate."

She accepted this with a slightly dubious nod. "Thank you for warning me."

"Speaking of calls," Miles added, "please have one of your people bring me a secured vid-link here. I have a few calls to make myself."

"Will you be staying here, my lord?" asked Tuomonen.

"For a while. Till after your interrogation, and until Lord Auditor Vorthys gets downside, as he will surely wish to do. That's the first call I want to make."

"Ah. Of course."

Miles looked around. His seizure stimulator, its case, and his mouthguard were still lying where they'd been dropped a few hours ago. Miles pointed. "And if you please, could you have your lab check my medical gear for any sign of tampering, then return it to me."

Tuomonen's brows rose. "Do you suspect it, my lord?"

"It was just a horrible thought. But I think it's going to be a very bad idea to underestimate either the intelligence or the subtlety of our adversaries in this thing, eh?"

"Do you need it urgently?"

"No." *Not anymore.*

"The data packet Foscol left on Administrator Vorsoisson's person—have you had a chance to look at it?" Miles went on. He managed to avoid glancing at Madame Vorsoisson.

"Just a quick scan," said Tuomonen. He did look at Madame Vorsoisson, and away, spoiling Miles's effort at delicacy. Her lips thinned only a little. "I turned it over to the ImpSec financial analyst—a colonel, no less—that HQ sent out to take charge of the financial part of the investigation."

"Oh, good. I was going to ask if HQ had sent you relief troops yet."

"Yes, everything you requested. The engineering team arrived on site at the experiment station about an hour ago. The packet Foscol left seems to be documentation of all the financial transactions relating to the, um, payments made by Soudha's group to the Administrator. If it's not all lies, it's going to be an amazing help in sorting out the whole embezzlement part of the mess. Which is really very odd, when you think about it."

"Foscol clearly had no love for Vorsoisson, but surely everything that incriminates him, incriminates the Komarrans equally. Quite odd, yes." If only his brain hadn't been turned to pulsing oatmeal, Miles felt, he could follow out some line of logic from this. Later.

An ImpSec tech wearing black fatigues emerged from the back of the apartment. He carried a black box identical to— in fact, possibly the same as—the one which Tuomonen had used at Madame Radovas's, and said to his superior, "I've finished all the comconsoles, sir."

"Thank you, Corporal. Go back to the office and transfer copies to our files, to HQ Solstice, and to Colonel Gibbs."

The tech nodded and trod out through the, Miles noticed, still-ruined door.

"And, oh yes, would you please detail a tech to repair Madame Vorsoisson's front door," Miles added to Tuomonen. "Possibly he could install a somewhat better-quality locking system while he's about it." She shot him a quietly grateful look.

"Yes, my lord. I will of course keep a guard on duty while you are here."

A duenna of sorts, Miles supposed. He must try to get Madame Vorsoisson something rather better. Suspecting he'd loaded poor sleepless Tuomonen with enough chores and orders for one session, Miles requested only that he be notified at once if ImpSec caught up with Soudha or any member of his group, and let the captain go off to his suddenly multiplied duties.

By the time he'd showered and dressed in his last good gray suit, the painkillers had achieved their full effect, and Miles felt almost human. When he emerged, Madame Vorsoisson invited him to her kitchen; Tuomonen's door guard stayed in the living room.

"Would you care for some breakfast, Lord Vorkosigan?"

"Have you eaten?"

"Well, no. I'm not really hungry."

Likely not, but she looked as pale and washed-out as he felt. Tactically inspired, he said, "I'll have something if you will. Something bland," he added prudently.

"Groats?" she suggested diffidently.

"Oh, yes please." He wanted to say, *I can get them*—mixing up a packet of instant groats was well within his ImpSec survival-trained capabilities, he could have assured her—but he didn't want to risk her going away, so he sat, an obedient guest, and watched her move about. She seemed uneasy, in what should have been this core place of her domain. Where *would* she fit? *Someplace much larger.*

She set up and served them both; they exchanged commonplace courtesies. When she'd eaten a few bites, she worked up an unconvincing smile, and asked, "Is it true fast-penta makes you . . . rather foolish?"

"Mm. Like any drug, people have varied reactions. I've conducted any number of fast-penta interrogations in the line of my former duties. And I've had it given to me twice."

Her interest was clearly piqued by this last statement. "Oh?"

"I, um . . ." He wanted to reassure her, but he had to be honest. *Don't ever lie to me*, she'd said, in a voice of suppressed passion. "My own reaction was idiosyncratic."

"Don't you have that allergy ImpSec is supposed to give to its—well, no, of course not, or you wouldn't be here."

ImpSec's defense against the truth drug was to induce a fatal allergic response in its key operatives. One had to agree to the treatment, but as it was a gateway to larger responsibilities and hence promotions, the security force had never lacked for volunteers. "No, in fact. Chief Illyan never asked me to undergo it. In retrospect, I can't help wondering if my father had a hand, there. But in any case, it doesn't make me truthful so much as it makes me hyper. I babble. Fast-foolish, I guess. The one, um, hostile interrogation I underwent, I was actually able to beat, by continually reciting poetry. It was a very bizarre experience. In normal people, the degree of, well, ugliness, depends a lot on whether you fight it or go along with it. If you feel that the questioner is on your side, it can be just a very relaxing way of giving the same testimony you would anyway."

"Oh." She did not look reassured enough.

"I can't claim it doesn't invade your reserve," and she possessed a reserve oceans-deep, "but a properly conducted interview ought not to," *shame you*, "be too bad." Though if last night's events had not shaken her out of her daunting self-control . . . He hesitated, then added, "How *did* you learn to underreact the way you do?"

Her face went blank. "Do I underreact?"

"Yes. You are very hard to read."

"Oh." She stirred her black coffee. "I don't know. I've been this way for as long as I can remember." A more introspective look stilled her features for a time. "No . . . no, there was a time . . . I suppose it goes back to . . . I had, I have, three older brothers."

A typical Vor family structure of their generation: too damned many boys, a token girl added as an afterthought. Hadn't any of those parents possessed a) foresight and b) the ability to do simple arithmetic? Hadn't any of them wanted to be *grandparents*?

"The eldest two were out of my range," she went on, "but the youngest was close enough in age to me to be obnoxious. He discovered he could entertain himself mightily by teasing me to screaming tantrums. Horses were a surefire subject; I was horse-mad at the time. I couldn't fight back—I hadn't the wits then to give as good as I got, and if I tried to hit him, he was enough bigger than me—I'm thinking of the time when I was about ten and he was about fourteen—he could just hold me upside down. He had me so well-trained after a while, he could set me off just by whinnying." She smiled grimly. "It was a great trial to my parents."

"Couldn't they stop him?"

"He usually managed to be witty enough, he got away with it. It even worked on me—I can remember laughing and trying to hit him at the same time. And I think my mother was starting to be ill by then, though neither of us knew it. What my mother told me—I can still see her, holding her head—was the way to get him to stop was for me to just not react. She said the same thing when I was teased at school, or upset about most anything. Be a stone statue, she said. Then it wouldn't be any fun for him, and he would stop.

"And he did stop. Or at least, he grew out of being a fourteen-year-old lout, and left for university. We're friends now. But I never unlearned to respond to attack by turning to stone. Looking back now, I wonder how many of the problems in my marriage were due to . . . well." She smiled, and blinked. "My mother was wrong, I think. She certainly ignored her own pain for far too long. But I'm stone all the way through, now, and it's too late."

Miles bit his knuckles, hard. Right. So at the dawn of puberty, she'd learned no one would defend her, she could not defend herself, and the only way to survive was to pretend to be dead. Great. And if there were a more fatally wrong move some awkward fellow could possibly make at this moment than to take her in his arms and try to comfort her, it escaped his wildest imaginings. If she needed to be stone right now because it was the only way she knew how to survive, let her be marble, let her be granite. *Whatever you need, you take it, Milady Ekaterin; whatever you want, you've got it.*

What he finally came up with was, "I like horses." He wondered if that sounded as idiotic as it . . . sounded.

Her dark brows crinkled in amused bafflement, so apparently it did. "Oh, I outgrew that years ago."

Outgrew, or gave up? "I was an only child, but I had a cousin—Ivan—who was as loutish as they come. And, of course, much bigger than me, though we're about the same age. But when I was a kid, I had a bodyguard, one of the Count-my-Father's Armsmen. Sergeant Bothari. He had no sense of humor at all. If Ivan had ever tried anything like your brother, no amount of wit would have saved him."

She smiled. "Your own bodyguard. Now, there's an idyllic childhood indeed."

"It was, in a lot of ways. Not the medical parts, though. The Sergeant couldn't help me there. Nor at school. Mind you, I didn't appreciate what I had at the time. I spent half of my time trying to figure out how to get away from his protection. But I succeeded often enough, I guess, to know I *could* succeed."

"Is Sergeant Bothari still with you? One of those crusty Old Vor family retainers?"

"He probably would be, if he were still alive, but no. We were, uh, caught in a war zone on a galactic trip when I was seventeen, and he was killed."

"Oh. I'm sorry."

"It was not exactly my fault, but my decisions were pretty prominent in the causal chain that led to his death." He watched for her reaction to this confession; as usual, her face changed very little. "But he taught me how to survive, and go on. The last of his very many lessons." *You have just experienced destruction; I know survival. Let me help.*

Her eyes flicked up. "Did you love him?"

"He was a . . . difficult man, but yes."

"Ah."

He offered after a time, "However you came by it, you are very level-headed in emergencies."

"I am?" She looked surprised.

"You were last night."

She smiled, clearly touched by the compliment. Dammit, she shouldn't take in this mild observation as if it were great praise. *She must be starving half to death, if such a scrap seems a feast.*

It was the most nearly unguarded conversation she'd ever granted him, and he longed to extend the moment, but they'd run out of groats to push around in the bottom of their dishes, their coffee was cold, and the tech from ImpSec arrived at this moment with the secured comconsole uplink Miles had requested. Madame Vorsoisson pointed out to the tech her late husband's office as a private space to set up the machine. The forensics people had been and gone while Miles slept; after briefly watching the new installation she retreated into housewifery like a red deer into underbrush, apparently intent on erasing all traces of their invasion of her space.

Miles turned to face the next most difficult conversation of the morning.

It took several minutes to establish the secure link with Lord Auditor Vorthys aboard the probable-cause team's mothership, now docked at the soletta array. Miles settled himself as comfortably as his aching muscles would allow, and prepared to cultivate patience in the face of the irritating several-second time lag between every exchange. Vorthys, when he at last appeared, was wearing standard-issue ship-knits, evidently in preparation for donning a pressure suit; the close-fitting cloth did not flatter his bulky figure. But he seemed to be well up for the day. The standard-meridian Solstice time kept topside was a few hours ahead of Serifosa's time zone.

"Good morning, Professor," Miles began. "I trust you've had a better night than we did. At the top of the bad news, your nephew-in-law Etienne Vorsoisson was killed last night in a breath-mask mishap at the Waste Heat experiment station. I'm here now at Ekaterin's apartment; she's holding up all right so far. I'll have a very long transmission in explanation. Over to you."

The trouble with the time lag was just how agonizingly long one had in which to anticipate the change of expression, and of people's lives, occasioned by the arrival of words one had sent but could no longer call back and edit. Vorthys looked every bit as shocked as Miles had expected when the message reached him. "My God. Go ahead, Miles."

Miles took a deep breath and began a blunt precis of yesterday's events, from the futile hours of being given the royal runaround at the Terraforming offices, to Vorsoisson's hasty return to drag him out to the experiment station, the revelation of his involvement with the embezzlement scheme, their encounter with Soudha and Madame Radovas, the waking up chained to the railing. He did not describe Vorsoisson's death in detail. Ekaterin's arrival. ImpSec teams called out in force, too late. The business with his seal. Vorthys's expression changed from shocked to appalled as the details mounted.

"Miles, this is horrible. I'll come downside as soon as I can. Poor Ekaterin. Do please stay with her till I get there, won't you?" He hesitated. "Before this came up, I was actually thinking of requesting you to come topside. We've found some very odd pieces of equipment up here, which have undergone some quite incredible physical distortions. I'd wondered if you might have seen anything like it in your galactic military experiences. There are some traceable serial numbers left here and there in the debris, though, which I'd hoped may prove a lead. I'll just have to leave them to my Komarran boys for the moment."

"Odd equipment, eh? Soudha and his friends left with a lot of odd equipment, too. At least two lift-vans full. Have your Komarran boys send those serial numbers to Colonel Gibbs, care of ImpSec Serifosa. He's going to be tracing a lot of serial numbers in Terraforming Project purchases that—may not be as bogus as I'd first assumed. There's got to be more connections between here and there than just poor Radovas's body. Look, um . . . ImpSec here wants to fast-penta Ekaterin, on account of Tien's involvement. Do you want me to delay that till you arrive? I thought you might wish to supervise her interrogation, at least."

Lag. Vorthys's brow wrinkled in worried thought. "I . . . dear God. No. I want to, but I should not. My niece—a clear conflict of interest. Miles, my boy, do you suppose . . . would you be willing to sit in on it, and see that they don't get carried away?"

"ImpSec hardly ever uses those lead lined rubber hoses anymore, but yes, I planned to do just that. If you do not disapprove, sir."

Lag. "I should be excessively relieved. Thank you."

"Of course. I also should very much like to have your evaluation of whatever the ImpSec engineering team turns up out at the experiment station. At the moment I have very little evidence and lots of theories. I'm itching to reverse the proportions."

Professor Vorthys smiled dry appreciation of this last line, when it arrived. "Aren't we all."

"I have another suggestion, sir. Ekaterin seems very alone, here. She doesn't seem to have any close Komarran women friends that I've seen so far, and of course, no female relatives . . . I wondered if it might not be a good idea for you to send for the Professora."

Vorthys's face lit when this one registered. "Not only good, but wise and kind. Yes, of course, at once. Given a family emergency of this nature, her assistant can surely supervise her final exams. The idea should have occurred to me directly. Thank you, Miles."

"Everything else can wait till you get downside, unless something breaks in the case on ImpSec's end. I'll get Ekaterin in here before I close the transmission. I know she longs to talk with you, but . . . Tien's involvement in this mess is pretty humiliating for her, I suspect."

The Professor's lips tightened. "Ah, Tien. Yes. I understand. It's all right, Miles."

Miles was silent for a time. "Professor," he began at last, "about Tien. Fast-penta interrogations tend to be a lot more controllable if the interrogator has some clue what he's getting into. I don't want . . . um . . . can you give me some sense of what Ekaterin's marriage looked like from her family's point of view?"

The time lag dragged, while Vorthys frowned. "I don't like to speak ill of the dead before their offering is even burned," he said at last.

"I don't think we're going to have a lot of choice, here."

"Huh," he said glumly when Miles's words reached him. "Well . . . I suppose it seemed like a good idea to everyone at the time. Ekaterin's father, Shasha Vorvayne, had known Tien's late father—he was recently deceased then. A decade ago already, my word the time has gone fast. Well. The two older men had been friends, both officers in the District government, the families knew each other . . . Tien had just quit the military, and had used his veteran's rights to obtain a job in the District civil service. Good-looking, healthy . . . seemed poised to follow in his father's footsteps, you know, though I suppose it ought to have been a clue that he had put in his ten years and never risen beyond the rank of lieutenant." Vorthys pursed his lips.

Miles reddened slightly. "There can be a lot of reasons—never mind. Go on."

"Vorvayne had begun to recover from my sister's untimely death. He had met a woman, nothing unseemly, an older woman, Violie Vorvayne is a charming lady—and begun to think of remarriage. He wanted, I suppose, to see Ekaterin properly settled—to honorably tie off the last of his obligations to the past, if you will. My nephews were all out on their own by then. Tien had called on him, in part as courtesy to his late father's friend, in part to get a reference for his District service application . . . they struck up as much of an acquaintance as might be between two men of such dissimilar ages. My brother-in-law doubtless spoke highly of Ekaterin. . . ."

"Settled in her father's mind equated with married, I take it. Not, say, graduated from University and employed at an enormous salary?"

"Only for the boys. My brother-in-law can be more Old Vor than you high Vor, in a lot of ways." Vorthys sighed. "But Tien sent a reputable Baba to arrange the contracts, the young people were permitted to meet . . . Ekaterin was excited. Flattered. The Professora was distressed that Vorvayne hadn't waited a few more years, but . . . young people have no sense of *time*. Twenty is old. The first offer is the last chance. All that nonsense. Ekaterin didn't know how attractive she was, but her father was afraid, I think, that she might settle on some inappropriate choice."

"Non-Vor?" Miles interpreted this.

"Or worse. Maybe even a mere tech, who knew?" Vorthys permitted himself one tiny ironic glint. Ah, yes. Until his Auditorial apotheosis three years ago, so startling to his relatives, Vorthys had had a most un-Vorish career himself. And marriage.

And he'd started both back when the Old Vor were a lot more Old Vor than they were now—Miles thought of his grandfather, by way of exemplar, and suppressed a shudder.

"And the marriage seemed to start out well," the Professor went on. "She seemed busy and happy, there was little Nikki come along . . . Tien changed jobs rather often, I thought, but he was new in his career; sometimes it takes a few false starts to find your legs. Ekaterin grew out of touch with us, but when we did see her, she was . . . quieter. Tien never did settle down, always chasing some rainbow no one else could see. I think all the moves were hard on her." He frowned, as if thinking back for missed clues.

Miles did not dare explain about the Vorzohn's Dystrophy without Ekaterin's express permission, he decided. It was not his right. He confined himself to remarking, "I think Ekaterin may feel free to explain more of it now."

The Professor squinted worriedly at him. "Oh . . . ?"

I wonder what answers I'd get to those same questions if I could ask the Professora? Miles shook his head, and went to call Ekaterin to the comconsole.

Ekaterin. He tasted the syllables of her name in his mind. It had been so easy, speaking with her uncle, to slip into the familiar form. But she had not yet invited him to use her first name. Her late husband had called her *Kat.* A pet name. A little name. As if he hadn't had time to pronounce the whole thing, or wished to be bothered. It was true her full array, *Ekaterin Nile Vorvayne Vorsoisson,* made an impractical mouthful. But *Ekaterin* was light on the teeth and the tip of the tongue, yet elegant and dignified and entirely worth an extra second of, of anyone's time.

"Madame Vorsoisson?" he called quietly down the hall.

She emerged from her workroom; he gestured to the secured vid-link. Her face was grave, and her steps reluctant; he closed the office door softly on her, and left her and her uncle in private. Privacy was going to be a rare and precious element for her in the days to come, he could foresee.

The repair tech arrived at last, along with another duty guard. Miles took them aside for a word.

"I want you both to stay here till I get back, understand? Madame Vorsoisson is not to be left unguarded. Um . . . when you're done with the door, find out from her if there are any other repairs she needs done around here, and take care of them for her."

"Yes, my lord."

Trailed by his own guard, Miles took himself off to the Terraforming Project offices. He passed ImpSec guards on the bubble-car platform, in the building lobby, and at the corridor entrances to Terraforming's floors. Miles was put glumly in mind of an Old Vor aphorism about posting a guard on the picket line after the horses were stolen. Once within, the ImpSec personnel shifted from steely-eyed goons to intent techs and clerks, efficiently downloading comconsoles and examining files. Terraforming Project employees watched them in suppressed terror.

Miles found Colonel Gibbs set up in Vorsoisson's outer office, with his own imported comconsole planted firmly therein; rather to his surprise, the rabbity Venier was dancing worried attendance upon the ImpSec financial analyst. Venier shot Miles a look of dislike as he strode in.

"Good morning, Vennie; I didn't expect to see you, somehow," Miles greeted him cordially. He was oddly glad the fellow hadn't been one of Soudha's. "Hello, Colonel. I'm Vorkosigan. Sorry for dragging you out on such short notice."

"My Lord Auditor. I am at your disposal." Gibbs stood, formally, and took Miles's proffered hand for a dry handshake. Gibbs was a delight to Miles's eye; a spare, middle-aged man with graying hair and a meticulous manner who despite his Imperial undress greens looked every bit an accountant. Even having held his new rank for almost three whole months, it still felt odd to Miles to accept the older man's deference.

"I trust Captain Tuomonen has briefed you, and passed on the interesting data packet we acquired last night."

Gibbs, drawing up a chair for the Lord Auditor, nodded. Venier took the opportunity to excuse himself, and fled without further prompting at Gibbs' wave of permission. They seated themselves, and Miles went on, "How are you doing so far?" He glanced at the stacks of flimsies the comconsole desk had already acquired.

Gibbs gave him a faint smile. "For the first three hours' work, I am reasonably pleased. We have managed to sort out most of Waste Heat Management's fictitious employees. I expect tracking their false accounts to go quickly. Your Madame Foscol's report on the late Administrator Vorsoisson's receipts is very clear. Verifying its truth should not present a serious problem."

"Be *very* cautious about any data which may have passed through her hands," Miles warned.

"Oh, yes. She's quite good. I suspect I am going to find it

a pleasure and a privilege to work with her, if you take my meaning, my lord." Gibb's eyes glinted.

So nice to meet a man who loves his job. Well, he'd asked Solstice HQ to send him their best. "Don't speak too soon about Foscol. I have what promises to be a tedious request for you."

"Ah?"

"In addition to fictitious employees, I have reason to believe Waste Heat made a lot of fictitious equipment purchases. Phony invoices and the like."

"Yes. I've turned up three dummy companies they appear to have used for them."

"Already? That was quick. How?"

"I ran a data match of all invoices paid by the Terraforming Project with a list of all real companies in the tax registry of the Empire. Not, you understand, routine for in-house audits, though I believe I'll forward a suggestion that it should be added to the list of procedures in future. There were three companies left over. My field people are checking them out. I should have confirmation for you by the end of today. It is, I believe, not excessively optimistic to hope we may track every missing mark in a week."

"My most urgent concern is not actually the money." Gibb's brows rose at this; Miles forged on. "Soudha and his co-conspirators also left with a large amount of equipment. It has crossed my mind that if we had a reliable list of Waste Heat's equipment and supply purchases, and subtracted from it the current physical inventory of what's out there at their experiment station, the remainder *ought* to include everything they took with them."

"So it should." Gibbs eyed him with approval.

"It's a brute-force approach," Miles said apologetically. "And not, alas, quite as simple as a data match."

"That," murmured Gibbs, "is why enlisted men were invented."

They smiled at each other in pleased understanding. Miles continued, "This will only work if the supply list is truly accurate. I want you to hunt particularly for phony invoices covering real, but nonstandard, nonaccounted equipment purchases. I want to know if Soudha smuggled in anything . . . odd."

Gibbs's head tilted in interest; his eyes narrowed thoughtfully. "Easy enough for them to have used their dummy companies also to launder those."

"If you find anything like that, red-flag it and notify myself or Lord Auditor Vorthys at once. And *especially* if you turn up any matches with the equipment Vorthys's probable-cause crew are presently finding at the site of the soletta accident."

"Ah! The connection begins to come clear. I must say, I had been wondering why this intense Imperial interest in a mere embezzlement scheme. Though it's a very *nice* embezzlement scheme," he hastened to assure Miles. "Professional."

"Quite. Consider that equipment list your top priority, please, Colonel."

"Very good, my lord."

Leaving Gibbs frowning—rather interestedly, Miles thought—at a fountain of data displays on his comconsole, Miles went to find Tuomonen.

The tired-looking ImpSec captain reported no surprises uncovered so far this morning. The field agents had not yet picked up Soudha's trail. HQ had sent in a major with an interrogation unit, who had taken over the systematic examination of the department's remaining employees; the inquisition was now going on in the conference chamber. "But it's going to take days to work through them all," Tuomonen added.

"Do you still want to do Madame Vorsoisson this afternoon?"

Tuomonen rubbed his face. "Yes, in all."

"I'll be sitting in."

Tuomonen hesitated. "That is your privilege, my lord."

Miles considered going to watch the employee interrogations, but decided that in his current physical state he would not contribute anything coherent. Everything seemed to be under control, for the moment, except for himself. The morning's painkillers were beginning to wear off, and the corridor was getting wavery around the edges. If he was going to be useful to anyone later in the day, he'd better give his battered body a rest. "I'll see you back at Madame Vorsoisson's, then," he told Tuomonen.

CHAPTER THIRTEEN

Ekaterin seated herself at the comconsole in her workroom and began to triage the shambles of her life. It was actually simpler than her first fears had supposed—there was so little of it, after all. *How did I grow so small?*

She made a list of her resources. At the top, and most vital: medical care for the dependents of a deceased project employee was guaranteed till the end of the quarter, a few weeks away yet. A time window, of sorts. She counted the days in her head. It would be time enough for Nikki, if she didn't waste any.

A few hundred marks remained in her household account, and a few hundred marks in Tien's. Her use of this apartment also ran till the end of the quarter, when she must vacate it to make way for the next administrator to be appointed to Tien's position. That was fine; she didn't want to stay here longer. No pension, of course. She grimaced. Guaranteed passage back to Barrayar, unavailable while Tien was alive, was due her and Nikki as another death benefit, and thank heavens Tien hadn't figured out how to cash *that* in.

The physical objects she owned were more burden than asset, given that she must transport them by jumpship. The free weight limit was not generous. She'd apportion Nikki the bulk of their weight allowance; his little treasures meant more to him than most of her larger ones did to her. It was stupid to let herself feel overwhelmed by a few rooms of things she'd been willing to abandon altogether bare hours ago. She could still abandon them, if she chose. She'd frequented a certain secondhand shop in a seedier part of the dome to clothe herself and Nikki. She could sell Tien's clothing and ordinary effects there, a chore which need only take a few hours. For herself, she longed to travel light.

On the other side of the ledger, her debts too were simple, if overwhelming. First were the twenty thousand marks Tien had borrowed and not paid back. Then—was she honor-bound, for the sake of Vor pride and Nikki's family name, to make restitution to the Imperium for the bribe money Tien had accepted? *Well, you can't do it today. Pass on to what you can do.*

She had researched the medical resources on Komarr for treating genetic disorders till the information had worn grooves in her brain, fantasized solutions that Tien's paranoias—and his legal control of his heir—had blocked her from carrying out. Technically, Nikki's legal guardian now was some male third cousin of Tien's back on Barrayar whom Ekaterin had never met. Nikki not being heir to a fortune or a Countship, the transfer of his guardianship back to her was probably hers for the asking. She would deal with that legal kink later, too. For now, it took her something under nine minutes to contact the top clinic on Komarr, in Solstice, and browbeat them into setting up Nikki's first appointment for the day after tomorrow, instead of the five weeks from today they first tried to offer her.

Yes.

So simple. She shook with a spasm of rage, at Tien, and at herself. This could have been done months ago, when they'd first come to Komarr, as easily as this, if only she'd mustered the courage to defy Tien.

Next she must notify Tien's mother, his closest living relative. Ekaterin could leave it to her to spread the news to Tien's more distant relatives back on Barrayar. Not feeling up to recording a vid message, she put it in writing, hoping it would not appear too cold. An accident with a breath mask, which Tien had failed to check. Nothing about the Komarrans, nothing about the embezzlement, nothing to which ImpSec could object. Tien's mother might never need to know of Tien's dishonor. Ekaterin humbly requested her preferences as to ceremonies and the disposition of the remains. Most likely she would want them returned to Barrayar to bury beside Tien's brother. Ekaterin could not help imagining her own feelings, in some future scene, if she entrusted Nikki to his bride with all bright promise only to have him returned to her later as a heap of ashes in a box. With a note. No, she would have to see this through in person. All that also must come later. She sent the message on its way.

The physical was easy; she could be finished and packed in a week. The financial was . . . no, not impossible, just not possible to solve at once. Presumably she must take out a loan on longer terms to pay off the first one—assuming anyone would loan money to a destitute and unemployed widow. Tien's antilegacy clouded the glimmerings of the new future she ached to claim for herself. She imagined a bird, released from ten years in a cage, told she could at last fly free—as soon as these lead weights were attached to her feet.

This bird's going to get there if she has to walk every step.

The comconsole chimed, startling her from this determined reverie. A man, soberly dressed in the Komarran style, appeared over the vid-plate at her touch. He wasn't anyone she knew from Tien's department.

"How do you do, ma'am," he said, looking at her uncertainly. "My name is Ser Anafi, and I represent the Rialto Sharemarket Agency. I'm trying to reach Etienne Vorsoisson."

She recognized the name of the company whose money Tien had lost on the trade fleet shares. "He's . . . not available. I'm Madame Vorsoisson. What is your question?"

Anafi's gaze at her grew more stern. "This is the fourth reminder notice of his outstanding loan balance, now overdue. He *must* either pay in full, or take immediate action to set up a new repayment schedule."

"How do you normally set up such a schedule?"

Anafi appeared surprised at this measured response. Had he dealt with Tien before this? He unbent slightly, leaning back in his chair. "Well . . . we normally calculate a percentage of the customer's salary, mitigated by any available collateral they may be able to offer."

I have no salary. I have no possessions. Anafi, she suspected, would not be pleased to learn this. "Tien . . . died in an accident last night. Things are in some disarray here today."

Anafi looked taken aback. "Oh. I'm sorry, Madame," he managed.

"I don't suppose . . . was the loan insured?"

"I'll check, Madame Vorsoisson. Let us hope . . ." Anafi turned to his comconsole; after a moment, he frowned. "I'm sorry to say, it was not."

Ah, Tien. "How should I pay it back?"

Anafi was silent a long moment, as if thinking. "If you would be willing to cosign for the loan, I could set up a payment schedule today for you."

"You can do that?"

At a tentative knock on the door frame of her workroom,

she glanced around. Lord Vorkosigan had returned and stood leaning in the opening. How long had he been standing there? He gestured inside, and she nodded. He walked in and eyed Anafi over her shoulder. "Who is this guy?" he murmured.

"His name's Anafi. He's from the company Tien owes for the fleet shares loan."

"Ah. Allow me." He stepped up to the comconsole and tapped in a code. The view split, and a gray-haired man with colonel's tabs and Eye-of-Horus pins on his green uniform collar appeared.

"Colonel Gibbs," said Lord Vorkosigan genially. "I have some more data for you regarding Administrator Vorsoisson's financial affairs. Ser Anafi, meet Colonel Gibbs. ImpSec. He has a few questions for you. Good day."

"ImpSec!" said Anafi in startled horror. "ImpSec? What does—" He blipped out at Lord Vorkosigan's flourishing gesture.

"No more Anafi," he said, with some satisfaction. "Not for the next several days, anyway."

"Now, was that nice?" asked Ekaterin, amused in spite of herself. "They loaned that money to Tien in all good faith."

"Nevertheless, don't sign anything till you take legal advice. If you knew nothing of the loan, it's possible Tien's estate is liable for it, and not you. His creditors must squabble with each other for the pieces, and when it's gone, it's gone."

"But there's nothing in Tien's estate but debts." *And dishonor.*

"Then the squabble will be short."

"But is it fair?"

"Death is an ordinary business risk—in some businesses more than others, of course. . . ." He smiled briefly. "Ser Anafi was getting ready to have you sign on the spot. This suggests to me that he was perfectly aware of his risk, and thought he might hustle you into taking over a debt not rightfully yours while you were still in shock. *Not* fair. In fact, not ethical at all. Yes, I think we can leave him to ImpSec."

This was all rather high-handed, but . . . it was hard not to respond to the enthusiastic glint in Vorkosigan's eye as he'd annihilated her adversary.

"Thank you, Lord Vorkosigan. But I really need to learn how to do these things for myself."

"Oh, yes," he agreed without the least hesitation. "I wish Tsipis were here. He's been my family's man of business for thirty years. He *adores* tutoring the uninitiated. If I could turn him loose on you, you'd be up to speed in no time, and he'd be just ecstatic. I'm afraid he found me a frustrating pupil in my youth. I only wanted to learn about the military. He finally managed to smuggle in some economic education by presenting it as logistics and supply problems." He leaned against the comconsole desk, and crossed his arms, and tilted his head. "Do you think you will be returning to Barrayar anytime soon?"

"Just as soon as I possibly can. I can hardly bear being in this place."

"I think I understand. Where, ah, would you go, on Barrayar?"

She stared broodingly at the empty vid-plate. "I'm not sure yet. Not to my father's household." To be crammed back into the status of a child again. . . . She pictured herself arriving penniless and without resources, to batten upon her father or one of her brothers. They'd let her batten, all right, generously, but they would also act as if her dependence deprived her of rights and dignity and even intelligence. They would then arrange her life for her own good. . . . "I'm sure I'd be welcome, but I'm afraid his solution to my problems would be to try to marry me off again. The idea makes me gag, just now."

"Oh," said Lord Vorkosigan.

A brief silence fell.

"What would you do if you could do anything?" he asked suddenly. "No limited resources to juggle, no practical considerations. Anything at all."

"I don't . . . I usually start with the possible, and pare away from there."

"Try for more scope." A vague wave of his arm taking in the planet from zenith to horizon indicated his idea of scope.

She thought back, all the way back, to the point in her life where she had made that fatal wrong turn. So many years lost. "Well. I suppose . . . I would go back to university. But *this* time, I'd know what I was about. Formal training in horticulture and in art, for garden design; chemistry and biochemistry and botany and genetic manipulation. *Real* expertise, the kind that means you can't be intimidated or, or . . . persuaded to go along with something stupid because you think everyone in the universe knows more than you do." She frowned ruefully.

"So you could design gardens for pay?"

"More than that." Her eyes narrowed, as she struggled for her inner vision.

"Planets? Terraforming?"

"Oh, good heavens. *That* training takes ten years, and

another ten years of internship beyond it, before you can even begin to grasp the complexities."

"So? They have to hire someone. Good God, they hired Tien."

"He was only an administrator." She shook her head, daunted.

"All right," he said cheerfully. "Bigger than a garden, smaller than a planet. That still leaves sufficient scope, I'd say. A Barrayaran District could be a good start. One with incomplete terraforming, say, and, and forestry projects, and, oh, damaged land reclamation, and a crying need for a touch of beauty. And," he went on, "you could work *up* to planets."

She had to laugh. "What is this obsession with planets? Will nothing smaller do, for you?"

"Elli Qu—a friend of mine used to say, 'Aim high. You may still miss the target but at least you won't shoot your foot off.'" His grin winked at her. He hesitated, then said more slowly, "You know . . . your father and brothers aren't your only relatives. The Professor and the Professora are boundless in their enthusiasm for education. You can't convince me they wouldn't be pleased to shelter you and Nikki in their home while you got your new start. And you'd be right there in Vorbarr Sultana, practically next door to the University and, um, everything. Good schools for Nikki."

She sighed. "It would be such a lovely change for him to stay in one place for a while. He could finally cultivate friends he wouldn't have to abandon. But . . . I've come to despise dependency."

He eyed her shrewdly. "Because it betrayed you?"

"Or lured me into betraying myself."

"Mm. But surely there is a qualitative difference between, um, a greenhouse and a cryochamber. Both provide shelter, but the first promotes growth, while the second merely, um . . ." He seemed to have become a little tangled in his metaphor.

"Retards decay?" Ekaterin politely tried to help unwind him.

"Just so." His brief grin again. "Anyway, I'm pretty sure the Professors are a human greenhouse. All those students— they're used to people growing up and moving on. They regard it as normal. I'd think you'd *like* it there." He wandered to her window and glanced out.

"I did like it there," she admitted wistfully.

"Then it all sounds perfectly possible to me. Good, that's settled. Have you had lunch?"

"What?" She laughed, and clutched her hair.

"Lunch," he repeated, deadpan. "Many people eat it at about this time of day."

"You're mad," she said with conviction, ignoring this willful piece of misdirection. "Do you always dispose of people's futures in that offhand fashion?"

"Only when I'm hungry."

She gave up. "I suppose I have something I can fix—"

"Certainly not!" he said indignantly. "I sent a minion. I just spotted him returning across the park, with a very promising large bag. The guards have to eat too, you see."

She contemplated, briefly, the spectacle of a man who casually sent ImpSec for carry-out. There probably were security concerns about meals on duty, at that. She let Vorkosigan shepherd her into her own kitchen, where they selected from a dozen containers. Ekaterin snitched a flaky apricot tart to set aside for Nikki, and they sent the remainder to the living room for the guards to picnic off. The only thing Vorkosigan permitted her to do was supply fresh tea.

"Did you find out anything new this morning?" she asked him, when they were settled at the table. She tried not to think about her last conversation here with Tien. *Oh, yes, I want to go home.* "Any word on Soudha and Foscol?"

"Not yet. Part of me expects ImpSec to catch up with them at any moment. Part of me . . . is not so optimistic. I keep wondering just how long they had to plan their departure."

"Well . . . I don't think they were expecting Imperial Auditors to arrive in Serifosa. That, at least, came as a surprise to them."

"Hm. Ah! *I* know why this whole thing feels so odd. It's as though my entire brain is suffering a time lag, and it's not just the bloody seizures. I'm on the wrong side. I'm on the damned defense, not the offense. One step behind all the time, reacting not acting—and I'm horribly afraid it may be an intrinsic condition of my new job." He downed a bite of sandwich. "Unless I can sell Gregor on the idea of an Auditor Provocateur . . . Well, anyway, I did have one idea, which I propose to spring on your uncle when he gets downside." He paused; silence fell. After a moment he added, "If you make an encouraging noise, I'll go on."

He'd caught her with her mouth full. "Hmm?"

"Lovely, yes. You see, suppose . . . suppose this thing of Soudha's is more than a mere embezzlement scheme. Maybe they were diverting all those Imperial funds to support a real research and development project, although nothing to do with Waste Heat Management. It may be a prejudice of my military background, but I keep thinking they might have been building a weapon. Some new variation on the gravitic imploder lance, I don't know." He gulped tea.

"I never had the impression that Soudha or any of the other Komarrans in the Terraforming Project were very military-minded. Quite the opposite."

"They needn't be, for an act of sabotage. Some grand stupid vile gesture—I keep worrying about Gregor's wedding coming up."

"Soudha isn't grandiose," said Ekaterin slowly. "Nor vile, particularly." She didn't doubt that Tien's death had been unintended.

"Nor stupid." Vorkosigan sighed regretfully. "I merely suggest that timetable to make myself nervous. Keeps me awake. But suppose it was a weapon. Did they perhaps *attack* that ore ship, as a test? Vile enough. Did their smoke test go very wrong? Was the subsequent damage to the mirror accidental, or deliberate? Or was it the other way around? The condition of Radovas's body suggests *something* backfired. A falling-out among thieves? Anyway, to anchor this spate of speculation to some sort of physical fact, I plan to get a list of every piece of equipment Soudha bought for his department, subtract from it everything they left there, and produce a parts list for their secret weapon. At this point my brilliance fails, and I plan to dump it on your uncle."

"Oh!" said Ekaterin. "He'll like that. He'll growl at you."

"Is that a good sign?"

"Yes."

"Hm. So, positing a secret-weapon sabotage-attack . . . how close are they to success? I keep coming back—sorry—to Foscol's odd behavior in providing that data packet of evidence against Tien. It seems to proclaim: it doesn't matter if the Komarrans are incriminated, because—fill in the blank. Because *why*? Because they will not be here to suffer the consequences? That suggests flight, which runs counter to the weapon hypothesis, which requires that they linger to use it."

"Or that they believed you would not be here to inflict the consequences," said Ekaterin. Had they meant Vorkosigan to die, too? Or . . . what?

"Oh, nice. *That's* reassuring." He bit rather aggressively into the last of his sandwich.

She rested her chin on her hand and regarded him with wry curiosity. "Does ImpSec know you babble like this?"

"Only when I'm very tired. Besides, I like to think out loud. It slows it down so I can get a good look at it. It gives you some idea of what living in my head is like. I admit, very few people can stand to listen at length." He shot her an odd sideways look. Indeed, whenever his animation slowed—which was not often—a gray weariness flashed underneath. "Anyway, you encouraged me. You sang *Hmm.*"

She stared in amused indignation and refused to rise to the bait.

"Sorry," he said in a smaller voice. "I think I'm a little disoriented just now." He gave her an apologetic grimace. "I actually came back here to rest. Is that not sensible of me? I must be getting old."

Both their lives were out of phase with their chronological ages, Ekaterin realized bemusedly. She now possessed the education of a child and the status of a dowager. Vorkosigan . . . was young for his post, to be sure. But this whole posthumous second life of his was surely as old as you could be at any age. "Time is out of joint," she murmured; he looked up sharply, and seemed about to speak.

Voices from the vestibule interrupted whatever he'd been about to say. Ekaterin's head turned. "Tuomonen, so soon?"

"Do you want to put this off?" Vorkosigan asked her.

She shook her head. "No. I want to get it over with. I want to go get Nikki."

"Ah." He drained his tea mug and rose, and they both went out to her living room. It was indeed Captain Tuomonen. He nodded to Vorkosigan, and greeted her politely. He had brought a female medtech with him, in the uniform of the Barrayaran military medical auxiliary, whom he also introduced. She carried a medkit, which she placed on the round table and opened. Ampoules and hyposprays glittered in their gel slots. Other first-aid supplies hinted at more sinister possibilities.

Tuomonen indicated Ekaterin should sit on the circular couch. "Are you ready, Madame Vorsoisson?"

"I suppose so." Ekaterin watched with concealed fear and some loathing as the medtech loaded her hypospray and showed it to Tuomonen to cross-check.

The medtech laid a second hypospray out at the ready, and pulled a small, burr-like patch off a plastic strip. "Would you hold out your wrist, Madame?"

Ekaterin did so; the woman pressed the allergy test patch firmly against her skin, then peeled it up again. She continued to hold Ekaterin's wrist while she marked time on her chrono. Her fingers were dry and cold.

Tuomonen dispatched the two guards to the perimeter, namely the hallway and the balcony, and set up a vid recorder on a tripod. He then turned to Vorkosigan, and with a rather odd emphasis, said, "May I remind you, Lord Vorkosigan, that more than one questioner can create unnecessary confusion in a fast-penta interrogation."

Vorkosigan gave him an acknowledging hand wave. "Quite. I know the drill. Go ahead, Captain."

Tuomonen glanced at the medtech, who stared closely at Ekaterin's wrist, then released it. "She's clear," the woman reported.

"Proceed, please."

At the medtech's direction, Ekaterin rolled up her sleeve. The hypospray hissed against her skin with a cold bite.

"Count backwards slowly from ten," Tuomonen told her.

"Ten," Ekaterin said obediently. "Nine . . . eight . . . seven . . ."

CHAPTER FOURTEEN

Two . . . one . . ." Ekaterin's voice, almost inaudible at first, grew more firm as she counted down.

Miles thought he could almost mark Ekaterin's heartbeats, as the drug flooded her system. Her tightly clenched hands loosened in her lap. Tension in her face, neck, shoulders, and body melted away like snow in the sun. Her eyes widened and brightened, her pale cheeks flushed with soft color; her lips parted and curved, and she looked up at Miles, beyond Tuomonen, with an astonished sunny smile.

"Oh," she said, in a surprised voice. "It doesn't *hurt*."

"No, fast-penta doesn't hurt," said Tuomonen, in a level, reassuring tone.

That isn't what she means, Tuomonen. If a person lived in hurt like a mermaid in water, till hurt became as invisible as breath, its sudden removal—however artificial—must come as a stunning event. Miles breathed covert relief that Ekaterin apparently wasn't going to be a giggler or a drooler, nor was she one of the occasional unfortunates in whom the drug released a torrent of verbal obscenities, or an almost equally embarrassing torrent of tears.

No. The kicker here is going to be when we take it away again. The realization chilled him. *But my God, isn't she beautiful when she is not in pain?* Her open, smiling warmth looked strangely familiar to him, and he tried to remember just when he'd seen that sweet air about her before. Not today, not yesterday . . .

It was in your dream.

Oh.

He sat back and rested his chin in his hand, fingers across

his mouth, as Tuomonen started down the list of standard neutral questions: name, birth date, parents' names, the usual. The purpose was not only to give the drug time to take full effect, but also to set up a rhythm of question-and-answer which would help carry the interrogation along when the questions, and answers, became more difficult. Ekaterin's birthday was just three weeks before his own, Miles noted in passing, but the War of Vordarian's Pretendership, which had so disrupted their mutual birth year in the regions around Vorbarr Sultana, had scarcely touched the South Continent.

The medtech had settled herself on a chair drawn up outside the conversation circle, out of the line of sight between interrogator and subject, but not, alas, entirely out of earshot. Miles trusted she had suitable top security clearances. He didn't know, and decided not to ask, if her gender represented delicacy on Tuomonen's part, tacit acknowledgment that a fast-penta interrogation could be a mind-rape. Physical brutality did not mix with fast-penta interrogation, which had helped to eliminate certain unsavory psychological types from successful careers as interrogators. But physical assault was not the only possible kind, nor even necessarily the worst. Or maybe she'd just been next up on the roster of available personnel.

Tuomonen moved on to more recent history. Exactly when had Tien acquired his Komarran post, and how? Had he known anyone in his department-to-be, or met with anyone in Soudha's group, before they'd left Barrayar? No? Had she seen any of his correspondence? Ekaterin, growing ever more cheerful in fast-penta elation, rattled on as confidingly as a child. She'd been so excited about the appointment, about the promised proximity to good medical facilities, certain she would get galactic-class help for Nikki at last. She had agonized over Tien's application and helped him to write it. Well, yes, written most of it for him. Serifosa Dome was fascinating, and their assigned apartment much larger and nicer than she'd been led to expect. Tien said the Komarrans were all techno-snobs, but she had not found them to be so . . .

Gently, Tuomonen led her back to the issue at hand. Just when had she discovered her husband's involvement in the embezzlement scheme, and how? She repeated the same story about Tien's midnight call to Soudha she had given Miles last night, larded with more extraneous details—among other things she insisted on giving Tuomonen a complete recipe for spiced brandied milk. Fast-penta did do odd things to one's memory, even though it did not, despite rumor, give one perfect recall. Her report of the overheard conversation sounded nearly verbatim, though. Despite his obvious fatigue, Tuomonen was skillful and patient, allowing her to ramble on at length, alert for the hidden gem of critical information in these flowing associations an interrogator always hoped would turn up, but usually didn't.

Her description of breaking into her husband's comconsole the following morning included the mulish side comment, "If Lord Vorkosigan could do it, *I* could do it," which at Tuomonen's alert query triggered an embarrassing detour into her views of Miles's earlier ImpSec-style raid on her own comconsole. Miles bit his lip and met Tuomonen's raised brows blandly.

"He did say he liked my gardens, though. Nobody else in my family wants to even look at them." She sighed, and smiled shyly at Miles. Dared he hope he was forgiven?

Tuomonen consulted his plastic flimsy. "If you didn't discover your husband's debts until yesterday morning, why did you transfer almost four thousand marks into his account on the previous morning?" His attention sharpened at Ekaterin's look of drunken dismay.

"He lied to me. Bastard. Said we were going for the galactic treatment. No! He *didn't* say it, damn it. Fool, me. I wanted it to be true so much. Better a fool than a liar. Is it? I didn't want to be *like* him."

Tuomonen sought enlightenment of Miles with a quick baffled glance. Miles blew out his breath. "Ask her if it was Nikki's money."

"Nikki's money," she confirmed with a quick nod. Despite the fast-penta wooze, she frowned fiercely.

"This make sense to you, my lord?" Tuomonen murmured.

"I'm afraid so. She had saved just that sum out of her household accounts toward her son's medical treatment. I saw the account in her files, when I was taking that, um, unfortunate tour. I take it that her husband, claiming to be using it for that purpose, instead relieved her of it to stave off his creditors." *Embezzlement indeed.* Miles exhaled, to bring his blood pressure back down. "Have you traced it?"

"Tien transferred it upon receipt to the Rialto Sharemarket Agency."

"There's no getting it back, I suppose?"

"Ask Gibbs, but I don't think so."

"Ah." Miles bit his knuckle, and nodded for Tuomonen to proceed. Now armed with the right questions, Tuomonen confirmed this interpretation explicitly, and went on to draw out all the intensely personal details about the Vorzohn's Dystrophy.

In exactly the same neutral tone, Tuomonen asked, "Did you arrange your husband's death?"

"No." Ekaterin sighed.

"Did you ask anyone, or pay anyone, to kill him?"

"No."

"Did you know he was to be killed?"

"No."

Fast-penta frequently made subjects bloody literal-minded; you always asked the important questions, the ones you were hot about, in a number of different ways, to be sure.

"Did you kill him yourself?"

"No."

"Did you love him?"

Ekaterin hesitated. Miles frowned. Facts were ImpSec's rightful prey; feelings, maybe less so. But Tuomonen wasn't quite out of line yet.

"I think I did, once. I must have. I remember the wonderful look on his face, the day Nikki was born. I must have. He wore it out. I can hardly remember that time."

"Did you hate him?"

"No . . . yes . . . I don't know. He wore that out too." She looked earnestly at Tuomonen. "He never hit me, you know."

What an obituary. *When I go down into the ground at last, as God is my judge, I pray my best-beloved may have better to say of me than, "He didn't hit me."* Miles set his jaw and said nothing.

"Are you sorry he died?"

Watch it, Tuomonen. . . .

"Oh, but it was such a relief. What a nightmare today would have been if Tien were still alive. Though I suppose ImpSec would have taken him away. Theft and treason. But I would have had to go see him. Lord Vorkosigan said I could not have saved him. There was not enough time after Foscol called me. I'm so glad. It's so ugly to be so glad. I suppose I should forgive Tien for everything, because he's dead now, but I'll never forgive him for turning me into something so ugly." Despite the drug, tears were leaking from her eyes now. "I didn't use to be this kind of person, but now I can't go back."

Some truths cut deeper than even fast-penta could soak. Expressionlessly, Miles reached past Tuomonen and handed Ekaterin a tissue. She blotted the moisture in owlish distress.

"Does she need more drug?" the medtech whispered.

"No." Miles made a hand-down gesture for silence.

Tuomonen asked some more neutral questions, till

something like his subject's original sunny and confiding air returned. *Yeah. Nobody should have to do this much truth all at once.*

Tuomonen looked at his flimsy, glanced uneasily at Miles, licked his lips, and said, "Your cases and Lord Vorkosigan's were found together in your vestibule. Were you planning to leave together?"

Shock and fury flushed through Miles in a hot wave. *Tuomonen, you dare—!* But the memory of sorting through all that mixed underwear under the eye of the ImpSec guard stopped his words; so, yes, it *could* have looked odd, to someone who didn't know what was going on. He converted his boiling words to a slow breath, which he let out in a trickle. Tuomonen's eyes flicked sideways, wary of that sigh.

Ekaterin blinked at him in some confusion. "I'd hoped to."

What? Oh. "She means, at the same time," Miles gritted through his teeth to Tuomonen. "Not together. Try that."

"Was Lord Vorkosigan planning to take you away?"

"Away? Oh, what a lovely idea. Nobody was taking me away. Who would? I had to take myself away. Tien threw my aunt's skellytum over the balcony, but he didn't quite dare throw me. He wanted to, I think."

Miles was diverted to brood on these last words. How much physical courage had it taken her, to stand up to Tien at the last? Miles did not underestimate just what nerve it took to face down large angry men who had the power to pick you up and pitch you across the room. Nerve and wit and never letting yourself get within arm's reach, nor blocked from the door. The calculations were automatic. And you had to stay in practice. For Ekaterin, it must have felt like landing a fully-loaded freight shuttle on her very first flying lesson.

Tuomonen, trying desperately for clarity and still with one eye on Miles, repeated, "Were you going to elope with Lord Vorkosigan?"

Her brows flew up. "No!" she said in astonishment.

No, of course not. Miles tried to recapture his first properly stunned reaction to the accusation, except that it now came out, *What a great idea. Why didn't I think of it?* which rather blunted the fine edge of his outrage. Anyway, she'd never have run off with him. It was all he could do to get a Barrayaran woman to walk down the street with a sawed-off mutie like him. . . .

Oh hell. Have you fallen in love with this woman, idiot boy?
Um. Yeah.

He'd been falling for days, he realized in retrospect. It was just that he'd finally hit the ground. He should have recognized the symptoms. *Oh, Tuomonen. The things we learn under fast-penta.*

He could finally see what Tuomonen was getting at, though, all complete. A nice neat little conspiracy: murder Tien, blame it on the Komarrans, run off with his wife over his dead body . . . "A most flattering scenario, Tuomonen," Miles breathed to the ImpSec captain. "Quick work on my part, considering I only met her five days ago. I thank you." *Was ever woman in this humor wooed? Was ever woman in this humor won? I think not.*

Tuomonen shot him a flat-lipped glower. "If my guard could think of it, and I could think of it, so could someone else. Best to knock the notion in the head as soon as possible. It's not as though I could fast-penta you. My lord."

No, not even if Miles volunteered. His known idiosyncratic reaction to the drug, so historically useful in evading hostile interrogation, also made it impossible for him to use it to clear himself of any accusation. Tuomonen was just doing his job, and doing it well. Miles leaned back, and growled, "Yeah, yeah, all right. But you're optimistic, if you think even fast-penta is fast enough to compete with titillating rumor. As a courtesy to his Imperial Majesty's Auditors' reputations, do have a word with that guard of yours after this."

Tuomonen didn't argue, or pretend to misunderstand. "Yes, my lord."

Temporarily undirected, Ekaterin was burbling along on her free-association tangent. "I wonder if the scars below his belt are as interesting as the ones above. I could hardly have got him out of his trousers in that bubble-car, I suppose. I had a chance last night, and I didn't even think of it. Mutie Vor. How does he do it . . . ? I wonder what it would be like to sleep with someone you actually liked . . . ?"

"Stop," said Tuomonen belatedly. She fell silent and blinked at him.

Just when it was getting really interesting . . . Miles quelled a narcissistic, or perhaps masochistic, impulse to encourage her to go on in this strain. He'd invited himself along on this interrogation to keep *ImpSec* from abusing its opportunities.

"I'm finished, my lord," Tuomonen said aside to him in a low voice. He did not quite meet Miles's eyes. "Is there anything else you think I should ask, or that you wish to ask?"

Could you ever love me, Ekaterin? Alas, questions of future probability were unanswerable, even under fast-penta.

"No. I would ask you to note, nothing she's said under fast-penta substantially contradicts anything she's told us straight out. The two versions are in fact unusually congruent, compared to other interrogations in my experience."

"Mine as well," Tuomonen allowed. "Very good." He motioned to the silently waiting medtech. "Go ahead and administer the antagonist."

The woman stepped forward, adjusted the new hypospray, and pressed it against the inside of Ekaterin's arm. The lizard-hiss of the anti-drug going in licked Miles's ears. He counted Ekaterin's heartbeats again, one, two, three . . .

It was a horribly vampiric thing to watch, as if life itself were being sucked out of her. Her shoulders drew in, her whole body hunched in renewed tension, and she buried her face in her hands. When she raised it again, it was flushed and damp and strained, but she was not weeping, merely utterly exhausted, and closed again. He had thought she would weep. *Fast-penta doesn't hurt, eh?* Couldn't prove it now.

Oh, Milady. Can I ever make you look that happy without drugs? Of more immediate importance, would she forgive him for being a party to her ordeal?

"What a very odd experience," Madame Vorsoisson said neutrally. Her voice was hoarse.

"It was a well-conducted interview," Miles assured the room at random. "All things considered. I've . . . seen much worse."

Tuomonen gave him a dry look, and turned to Ekaterin. "Thank you, Madame Vorsoisson, for your cooperation. This has been extremely useful to the investigation."

"Tell the investigation it is welcome."

Miles was not just sure how to interpret that one. Instead he said to Tuomonen, "That *will* be all for her, won't it?"

Tuomonen hesitated, obviously trying to sort out whether that was a question or an order. "I hope so, my lord."

Ekaterin looked across at Miles. "I'm sorry about the suitcases, Lord Vorkosigan. I never thought how it might look."

"No, why should you have?" He hoped his voice didn't sound as hollow as it felt.

Tuomonen said to Ekaterin, "I both suggest and request you rest for a while, Madame Vorsoisson. My medtech will stay with you for about half an hour, to be sure you're fully recovered and don't have any further drug reactions."

"Yes, I . . . that would probably be wise, Captain." Rubbery-legged, she rose; the medtech went to her side and escorted her off toward her bedroom.

Tuomonen shut down his vid recorder. He said gruffly, "Sorry about that last round of questions, my Lord Auditor. It was not my intention to offer an insult to either you or Madame Vorsoisson."

"Yeah, well . . . don't worry about it. What's next, from ImpSec's point of view?"

Tuomonen's weary brow wrinkled. "I'm not sure. I wanted to make certain I conducted this interrogation myself. Colonel Gibbs has everything in hand at the Terraforming offices, and Major D'Emorie hasn't called to complain yet about anything at the experiment station. What we *need* next, preferably, is for the field agents to catch up with Soudha and his friends."

"I can't be in all three places," Miles said reluctantly. "Barring an arrest coming through . . . the Professor is en route, and has had the advantage of a full night's sleep. You, I believe, have had none. My field instincts say this is the time to knock off for a while. Do I need to make that an order?"

"No," Tuomonen assured him earnestly. "You have your wrist-comm, I have mine . . . Field has our numbers and orders to report the news. I'll be glad to get home for a meal, even if it is last night's dinner. And a shower." He rubbed his stubbled chin.

He finished packing the recorder, exchanged farewells with Miles, and went off to consult with his guards, hopefully to apprise them of Madame Vorsoisson's change of status from suspect/witness to free woman.

Miles considered the couch, rejected it, and wandered into Ekaterin's—Madame Vorsoisson's. . . . Ekaterin's, dammit, in his mind if not on his lips—Ekaterin's workroom. Automatic lighting still sustained the assortment of young plantings on the trellised shelves in the corners. The grav-bed was gone; oh yes, he'd forgotten she'd had it removed. The floor looked remarkably inviting, though.

A flash of scarlet in the trash bin caught his eye. Investigating, he found the remains of the bonsai'd skellytum bundled up in a square of plastic sheeting, mixed with pieces of its pot and damp loose dirt. Curiously, he dug it out and cleared a place on Ekaterin's work table, and unrolled the plastic . . . botanical body bag, he supposed.

The fragments put him in mind of the soletta array and the ore ship, and also of a couple of the more distressing autopsies he'd recently reviewed. Methodically, he began to sort them out. Broken tendrils in one pile, root threads in another, shards of the poor burst barrel of the thing in another. The five-floor plunge had had something of the same effect on the liquid-conserving central structure of the skellytum as a sledgehammer applied to a watermelon. Or a needle-grenade exploding inside someone's chest. He picked out sharp potsherds, and made tentative tries at piecing the bits of plant into place, like a jigsaw puzzle. Was there a botanical equivalent of surgical glue, which could hold it all together again and allow it to heal? Or was it too late? A brownish tinge to the pale interior lumps suggested rot already in progress.

He brushed the damp soil from his fingers, and realized suddenly that he was touching Barrayar. This bit of dirt had come from South Continent, dug up, perhaps, from a tart old Vor lady's backyard. He dragged over the station chair from the comconsole, climbed precariously up onto it, and retrieved what proved to be an empty pan from an upper shelf. Safely on his feet again, he carefully gathered up as much of the soil as he could, and dumped it in the pan.

He stood back, hands on his hips, and studied his work so far. It made a sad pile. "Compost, my Barrayaran friend, you're destined to be compost, for all of me. A decent burial may be all I can do for you. Though in your case, that might actually be the answer to your prayers. . . ."

A faint rustle and an indrawn breath made him suddenly aware that he was not alone. He turned his head to find Ekaterin, on her feet again and pausing in the doorway. Her color looked better now than it had immediately after the interrogation, her skin not so puffy and lined, though she still looked very tired. Her brows were drawn down in puzzlement. "What are you doing, Lord Vorkosigan?"

"Um . . . visiting a sick friend?" Reddening, he gestured to his efforts laid out on her work bench. "Has the medtech released you?"

"Yes, she's just left. She was very conscientious."

Miles cleared his throat. "I was wondering if there was any way to put your skellytum back together. Seemed a shame not to try, seventy years old and all that." He drew back respectfully as she came up to the bench and turned over a fragment. "I know you can't sew it up like a person, but I can't help thinking there ought to be something. I'm afraid I'm not much of a gardener. My parents let me try, once, when I was a little kid, back behind Vorkosigan House. I was going to grow flowers for my Betan mother. Sergeant Bothari ended up doing the spade work, as I recall. I dug the seeds up twice a day to see if they'd sprouted yet. My plants did not thrive, for some reason. After that we gave up and turned it into a fort."

She smiled, a real smile, not a fast-penta grin. *We did not break her after all.*

"No, you can't put it back together," she said. "The only way is to start over. What I could do is take the strongest root fragments—several of them, to make sure," her long hands sorted through his pile, "and set them to soak in a hormone solution. And then when it starts to put out new growth, repot it."

"I saved the dirt," Miles pointed out hopefully. *Idiot. Do you know what an idiot you sound like?*

But she merely said, "Thank you." Following up on her words, she rummaged in her shelves and found a shallow basin, and filled it with water from the work bench's little sink. Another cupboard yielded a box of white powder; she sprinkled a tiny amount into the water and stirred it with her fingers. Taking a knife from her tool drawer, she trimmed the most promising root fragments and pushed them into the solution. "There. Maybe something will come of that." She stretched to set the basin carefully out of the way on the shelf Miles had had to reach by standing on the chair, and shook the pan of dirt into a plastic bag, which she sealed and put next to the basin. She then rolled up the decaying remains in their tarp again, to take over and shake into another bin; the plastic went back into the trash. "By the time I'd thought of this poor skellytum again, it would have gone out with the organic recycle, and been too late. I'd abandoned hope for it last night, when I thought I had to leave with just what I could carry."

"I didn't mean to burden you. Will it be awkward, to carry home on the jumpship?"

"I'll put it in a sealed container. By the time I reach my destination, it should be just about ready to replant." She washed and dried her hands; Miles followed suit.

Damn Tuomonen anyway, for forcing to Miles's consciousness a desire his back-brain had known very well was too unripe and out of season for any fruitful result. *Time is out of joint,* she'd said. Now he was going to have to deal with it. Now he was going to have to *wait.* How long? *How about till after Tien is buried, for starters?* His intentions were honorable enough, at least some of them were, but his timing was *lousy.* He shoved his hands deep into his pockets and rocked on his heels.

Ekaterin folded her arms, leaned against the counter, and stared at the floor. "I wish to apologize, Lord Vorkosigan, for anything I might have said under fast-penta that was not appropriate."

Miles shrugged. "I invited myself along. But I thought you could use a spotter. You did as much for me, after all."

"A spotter." She looked up, her expression lightening. "I had not thought of it like that."

He opened his hand and smiled hopefully.

She smiled briefly in return, but then sighed. "I'd been so frantic, all day, for ImpSec to be done so I could go get Nikki. Now I think they were doing me a favor. I dread this part. I don't know what to tell him. I don't know how much I *should* tell him about Tien's mess. As little as possible? The whole truth? Neither feels right."

Miles said slowly, "We're still in the middle of a classified case, here. You can't burden a nine-year-old boy with government secrets, or that kind of judgment call. I don't even know yet how much of this will eventually become public knowledge."

"Things not done right away get harder." She sighed. "As I'm finding now."

Miles drew up the comconsole chair for her, and motioned her into it, and pulled out the stool from under the work bench. He perched on it, and asked, "Had you told him you were leaving Tien?"

"Not even that, yet."

"I think . . . that for today, you should only tell him that his father suffered an accident with his breath mask. Leave the Komarrans out of it. If he asks for more details than you know how to deal with, send him to me, and I'll take the job of telling him he can't know, or can't know yet."

Her level look asked, *Can I trust you?* "Take care you don't stir up more curiosity than you quell."

"I understand. The problem of the whole truth is as much a question of when as what. But after we both get back to Vorbarr Sultana, I would like, with your permission, to take you to talk with Gr—with a close friend of mine. He's Vor, too. He had the experience of being in something like Nikki's position. His father died under, ah, grievous circumstances, when he was much too young to be told the details. When he stumbled across some of the uglier facts, in his early twenties, it was pretty traumatic. I'll bet he'll have a better feel than either of us for what to tell Nikki and when. He has a fine judgment."

She gave him a provisional nod. "That sounds right. I would like that very much. Thank you."

He returned her a half-bow, from his perch. "Glad to be of service, Madame." He'd wanted to introduce her to Gregor the man, his foster-brother, not Emperor Gregor the Imperial Icon, anyway. This might serve more than one purpose.

"I also have to tell Nikki about his Vorzohn's Dystrophy, and I can't put that off. I made an appointment for him at a clinic in Solstice for the day after tomorrow."

"He does not know he carries it?"

She shook her head. "Tien would never let me tell him." She studied him gravely. "I think you were in something like Nikki's position, too, when you were a child. Did you have to undergo a great many medical procedures then?"

"God, yes, years of 'em. What can I say that's useful? Don't lie about whether it's going to hurt. Don't leave him alone for long periods." *Or you, either . . .* There was finally something he *could* do for her. "Events permitting, may I ride along with you to Solstice and render what assistance I can? I can't spare your uncle to you—he's going to be buried in technical problems by day after tomorrow, if my parts list takes shape."

"I can't take you away from your duties!"

"My experience suggests to me that if Soudha hasn't been arrested by then, what I will be doing by day after tomorrow is spinning my mental wheels. A day away from the problems may be just what I will need to give me a fresh approach. You would be doing me a service, I assure you."

She pursed her lips doubtfully. "I admit . . . I would be grateful for the company."

Did she mean any company, generally, or his company particularly? *Down, boy. Don't even think about it.* "Good."

Voices drifted in from the vestibule: one of the guards, and a familiar rumble. Ekaterin jumped up. "My uncle is here!"

"He made very good time." Miles followed her into the hallway.

Professor Vorthys, his broad face wrinkled with concern, gave his valise over to the guard and folded his niece in his arms, murmuring condolences. Miles watched in exquisite envy. Her uncle's warm sympathy almost broke her down, as all of ImpSec's cool professionalism had not; Miles made a mental note. Cool and practical, that was the ticket. She dashed tears from her eyes, dispatched the guard with his case to Tien's old office as before, and led her uncle to the living room.

After a very brief conference, it was decided the Professor would accompany her to go collect Nikolai. Miles seconded this despite what he ironically recognized as his present lovesick mania for volunteerism. Vorthys had a family right, and Miles himself was too close to Tien's death. He was also swaying on his feet as the set of painkillers and stimulants he'd taken before lunch wore off. Taking a third dose today would be a bad mistake. Instead he saw the Professor and Ekaterin out, then checked in with ImpSec HQ in Solstice on the secured comconsole.

No new news. He wandered back toward the living room. Ekaterin's uncle was here; Miles should go, now. Collect his things and decamp to that mythical hotel he'd been gassing about for the last week. There was no room for him in this little apartment, with Vorthys reinstalled in the guest room. Nikki would need his own bed back, and he was damned if he was going to trouble Ekaterin to rustle up another grav-bed, or worse, for his Vor lordly use. What *had* she been expecting, when she'd ordered in that thing? He should definitely go. He was obviously not being as civilly neutral toward his hostess as he'd imagined, if that blasted guard could make whatever comment it had been that had set off Tuomonen on that list of embarrassing questions about the suitcases.

"Do you need anything, my lord?" The door guard's voice at Miles's elbow startled him awake.

"Um . . . yeah. Next time one of your boys comes over from Solstice HQ, have him bring me a standard military-issue bedroll."

In the meanwhile, Miles staggered over and curled up on the couch after all. He was asleep in minutes.

Miles awoke when the little party returned with Nikki. He sat up and managed to be reasonably composed by the time he had to face the boy. Nikki looked subdued and scared, but was not weeping or hysterical; he evidently turned his reactions inward rather than outward. Like his mother.

In the absence of female friends of Ekaterin's bearing casseroles and cakes in the Barrayaran manner, Miles caused ImpSec to supply dinner. The three adults kept the conversation neutral in front of Nikki, after which he went off to play by himself in his room, and Miles and the Professor retired to the study for a data-exchange. The new equipment found topside was indeed peculiar, including some power-transfer equipment heavy-duty enough for a small jumpship, parts of which had ripped apart, melted, and apparently exploded in a shower of plasma. The Professor called it, "Truly interesting," an engineering code-phrase that caught Miles's full attention.

In the middle of this, Colonel Gibbs reported in via comconsole. He smiled dryly at both Imperial Auditors, an expression which Miles was beginning to recognize as Gibbs's version of ecstasy.

"My Lord Vorkosigan. I have the first documented connection you were looking for. We've traced the serial numbers of a pair of hastings converters my Lord Vorthys's people found topside back through the chain to a Waste Heat purchase eight months ago. The converters were originally delivered to their experiment station."

"Right," breathed Miles. "Finally, more of a link than just Radovas's body. We have hold of the real string, all right. Thank you, Colonel. Carry on."

CHAPTER FIFTEEN

Ekaterin slept better than she'd expected to, but woke to the realization that she'd got through most of yesterday on adrenaline. Today, with its enforced wait for action, was going to be harder. *I've been waiting nine years. I can manage nineteen more hours.* Lying in bed allowed a kind of numb, foggy grief to descend, despite her release from the late chaos of Tien's life. So she rose, dressed carefully, ducked around the guard in her living room, made breakfast, and waited.

The Auditors stirred soon thereafter and came out gratefully for food, but carried off their coffee to the secured comconsole. She ran out of things to clean up, and went out to her balcony, but found the presence of another guard on post inhibited her from resting there. So she gave the guards coffee, and retreated to her kitchen, and waited some more.

Lord Vorkosigan emerged again. He fended off her offers of more coffee, and instead seated himself at her table. "ImpSec sent me the autopsy report on Tien this morning. How much do you want to know about it?"

The vision of Tien's congealed body, hanging in the frost, flashed in her memory. "Was there anything unexpected?"

"Not with respect to cause of death. They found his Vorzohn's Dystrophy, of course."

"Yes. Poor Tien. To spend all those years in a suppressed panic over his disease, only to die of another cause altogether." She shook her head. "So much effort, so *misplaced*. How far advanced was it, could they tell?"

"The nervous lesions were very distinct, according to the examiner. Though how they can tell one microscopic blob from another . . . The outward symptoms, if I interpret the medical jargon correctly, would have been impossible to conceal very soon."

"Yes. I think I knew that. It was the inward progress I wondered about. When did it start. How much of Tien's, oh, bad judgment and other behavior was his disease." Should she have somehow held on longer? *Could* she have? Until what other desperate denouement had played itself out?

"The damage builds slowly for a long time. Which parts of the brain are affected varies from person to person. For what it's worth, his seemed concentrated in the motor regions and peripheral nervous system. Though it may be possible to blame some of his actions on the disease, later, if a face-saving gesture is needed."

"How . . . politic. Face-saving for whom? I don't wish it."

He smiled a bit grimly. "I didn't think you did. But I have the unpleasant conviction that this case is going to shift from its nice clean engineering parameters into some very messy politics sooner or later. I never discard a possible reserve." He looked down at his hands, clasped loosely before him on the table. His gray sleeves imperfectly concealed the white bandages ringing his wrists. "How did Nikki take the news, last night?"

"That was hard. He started out—before I told him—trying to argue me into letting him stay and play another night. Getting passionate and sulking, you know how kids are. I so much wished I could simply let him go on, not having to know. I wasn't able to prepare him as much as I would have liked. I finally had to sit him down and tell him straight out, *Nikki, you have to come home now. Your Da was killed in a breath mask accident last night.* It just . . . wiped him blank. I almost wished for the whining back." Ekaterin looked away. She wondered what oblique forms Nikki's reactions might eventually take, and whether she would recognize them. Or handle them well. Or not . . . "I don't know how it's going to go in the long run. When I lost my mother . . . I was older, and we knew it was coming, but it was still a shock, *that* day, *that* hour. I always thought there would be more time."

"I've not yet lost a parent," said Vorkosigan. "Grandparents are different, I think. They are old, it's their destiny, somehow. I was shaken when my grandfather died, but my world was not. I think my father's was, though."

"Yes," she looked up gratefully, "that's the difference exactly. It's like an earthquake. Something that isn't supposed to move suddenly dumps you over. I think the world is going to be a scarier place for Nikki this morning."

"Have you hit him with his Vorzohn's Dystrophy news yet?"

"I'm letting him sleep. I'll tell him after breakfast. I know better than to stress a kid who has low blood sugar."

"Odd, I feel the same way about troops. Is there anything . . . can I help? Or would you prefer to be private?"

"I'm not sure. He doesn't have school today anyway. Weren't you taking my uncle out to the experiment station this morning?"

"Directly. It can wait an extra hour for this."

"I think . . . I would like it if you can stay. It's not good to make of the disease something all secret that's too awful to even talk about. That was Tien's mistake."

"Yes," he said encouragingly. "It's just a thing. You deal with it."

Her brows rose. "As in, one damn thing after another?"

"Yes, very like." He smiled at her, his gray eyes crinkling. Through whatever combination of luck and clever surgery, no scars marred his face, she realized. "It works, as tactics if not strategy."

True to his offer, Lord Vorkosigan drifted back into her kitchen as Nikki was finishing his breakfast. He lingered suggestively, stirring the coffee he took black and leaning against the far counter. Ekaterin took a deep breath and settled beside Nikki at the table, her own half-empty and cold cup a mere prop. Nikki eyed her warily.

"You won't be going to school tomorrow," she began, hoping to strike a positive note.

"Is that when Da's funeral is? Will I have to burn the offering?"

"Not yet. Your Grandmadame has asked that we bring his body back to Barrayar, to bury beside your uncle who died when you were little." Tien's mother's return message had come in by comconsole this morning, beamed and jumped through the wormhole-relays. In writing, as Ekaterin's had been, and perhaps for similar reasons; writing allowed one to leave so much out. "We'll do all the ceremonies and burn the offering then, when everyone can be there."

"Will we have to take him on the jumpship with us?" asked Nikki, looking disturbed.

From the side of the room Lord Vorkosigan said, "In fact, ImpS—the Imperial Civil Service will take care of all those arrangements, with your permission, Madame Vorsoisson. He will probably be back home before you are, Nikki."

"Oh," said Nikki.

"Oh," Ekaterin echoed. "I . . . I was wondering. I thank you."

He sketched a bow. "Allow me to pass on your mother-in-law's address and instructions. You have enough other things to do."

She nodded, and turned back to her son. "Anyway, Nikki . . . you and I are going to Solstice tomorrow, to visit a clinic there. We never mentioned this to you before, but you have a condition called Vorzohn's Dystrophy."

Nikki made an uncertain face. "What's *that*?"

"It's a disorder where, with age, your body stops making certain proteins in quite the right shape to do their job. Nowadays the doctors can give you some retrogenes that produce the proteins correctly, to make up for it. You're too young to have any symptoms, and with this fix, you never will." At Nikki's age, and on the first pass, it was probably not yet necessary to go into the complications it would entail for his future reproduction. She noticed dryly how she had managed to get through the long-anticipated spiel without once using the word *mutation*. "I've collected a lot of articles about Vorzohn's Dystrophy, which you can read when you want to. Some of them are too technical, but there are a couple I think you could get through with a little help." There. If she could avoid setting off his homework alarms, that ought to set up a reasonably neutral way to give him the information to which he had a right, and he could pursue it at his own pace thereafter.

Nikki looked worried. "Will it hurt?"

"Well, they will certainly have to draw blood, and take some tissue samples."

Vorkosigan put in, "I've had both done to me, what seems like a thousand times over the years, for various medical reasons. The blood draw hurts for a moment, but not later. The tissue sampling doesn't hurt because they use a medical micro-stun, but when the stun wears off, it aches for a while. They only need a tiny sample from you, so it won't be much."

Nikki appeared to digest this. "Do *you* have Vorzohn's thing, Lord Vorkosigan?"

"No. My mother was poisoned with a chemical called soltoxin, before I was born. It damaged my bones, mainly, which is why I'm so short." He wandered over to the table and sat down with them.

Ekaterin was expecting Nikki's next to be something along the lines of, *Will I be short?* but instead, his brown eyes widened in extreme worry. "Did she *die*?"

"No, she recovered completely. Fortunately. For us all. She's fine now."

He took this in. "Was she scared?"

Nikki, Ekaterin realized, had not yet sorted out just who Lord Vorkosigan's mother was, in relation to the people he'd heard about in his history lessons. Vorkosigan's brows rose in some bemusement. "I don't know. You can ask her yourself, someday, when—if you meet her. I'd be fascinated to hear the answer." He caught Ekaterin's unsettled gaze, but his eyebrows remained unrepentant.

Nikki regarded Lord Vorkosigan dubiously. "Did they fix your bones with retrogenes?"

"No, more's the pity. It would have been much easier on me, if it had been possible. They waited till they thought I was done growing, and then they replaced them with synthetics."

Nikki was diverted. "How d'you replace bones? How do you get them *out*?"

"Cut me open," Vorkosigan made a slicing motion with his right hand along his left arm from elbow to wrist, "chop the old bone out, pop the new one in, reconnect the joints, transplant the marrow to the new matrix, glue it up and wait for it to heal. Very messy and tedious."

"Did it hurt?"

"I was asleep—anesthetized. You're lucky you can have retrogenes. All *you* have to have are a few fiddling injections."

Nikki looked vastly impressed. "Can I see?"

After an infinitesimal hesitation, Vorkosigan unfastened his shirt cuff and pushed back his left sleeve. "That pale little line there, see?" Nikki stared with interest, both at Vorkosigan's arm and, speculatively, at his own. He wriggled his fingers, and watched his arm flex as the muscles and bones moved beneath his skin.

"I have a scab," he offered in return. "Want to see?" Awkwardly, he pushed up his pant leg to display the latest playground souvenir on his knee. Gravely, Vorkosigan inspected it, and agreed it was a good scab, and would doubtless fall off very soon now, and yes, perhaps there would be a scar, but his mother was very right to tell him not to pick it. To Ekaterin's relief, everyone then refastened their clothes and the contest went no further.

The conversation lagging after that high point, Nikki pushed a few last smears of groats and syrup artistically around the bottom of his dish, and asked, "Can I be excused?"

"Of course," said Ekaterin. "Wash the syrup off your hands," she called after his retreating form. She watched him—run, not walk—out, and said uncertainly, "That went better than I expected."

Vorkosigan smiled reassurance. "You were matter-of-fact, so you gave him no reason to be otherwise."

After a little silence Ekaterin said, "Was she scared? Your mother."

His smile twisted. "Spitless, I believe." His eyes warmed, and glinted. "But not, I understand, witless."

The two Auditors left for an on-site inspection of the Waste Heat experiment station shortly thereafter. Waiting carefully for a natural break in Nikki's quiet play in his room, Ekaterin called him in to her workroom to read the simplest and most straightforward article she had found on the subject of Vorzohn's Dystrophy. She sat him in her lap in her comconsole station chair, something she seldom did any more now he had become so leggy. It was a measure of his hidden unease this morning, she thought, that he did not resist the cuddle, nor her direction. He read through the article with fair understanding, stopping now and then to demand pronunciations and meanings of unfamiliar terms, or for her to rephrase or interpret some baffling sentence. If he had not been on her lap, she would not have detected the slight stiffening of his body as he read the line: . . . *later investigations concluded this natural mutation first appeared in Vorinnis's District near the end of the Time of Isolation. Only with the arrival of galactic molecular biology was it determined that it was unrelated to several old Earth genetic diseases which its symptoms sometimes mimic.*

"Any questions?" Ekaterin asked, when they'd finally wended to the end of the thing.

"Naw." Nikki elbowed off her lap and slid to his feet.

"You can read more whenever you want."

"Huh."

With difficulty, Ekaterin restrained herself from pursuing some more definite response from him, realizing she wanted it more for her sake than his own. *Are you all right, is it all right, do you forgive me?* He would not, could not, work through it all in an hour, or a day, or even a year; each day must have the challenge and response appropriate to it. *One damn thing after another*, Vorkosigan had said. But not, thank heavens, all things simultaneously.

The addition of Lord Vorkosigan to the expedition to Solstice made startling alterations in Ekaterin's carefully calculated travel plans. Instead of rising in the middle of the night to catch economy-class seats on the monorail, they awoke at a leisurely hour to take passage on an ImpSec suborbital courier shuttle which waited their pleasure, and would cover the intervening time zones with an hour to spare for lunch before Nikki's appointment.

"I love the monorail," Vorkosigan had confided apologetically at her first startled protest at the news of this change, sprung on her late in the evening when the two Auditors returned from their day's investigations. "In fact, I'm thinking of urging my brother Mark to invest in some of the companies trying to build more of them on Barrayar. But with this case heating up, ImpSec's made it pretty clear they would rather I did not travel by public transportation just now thank you very much my lord."

They also had two bodyguards. They wore discreet Komarran-style civilian clothes, which made them look exactly like a pair of Barrayaran military bodyguards in civvies. Vorkosigan seemed equally able to deal easily with them, or ignore them as though they were invisible, at will. He brought reports to read on the flight, but only glanced over them, seeming a little distracted. Ekaterin wondered if Nikki's restlessness broke his concentration, and if she ought to try and suppress the boy. But a quiet word from Vorkosigan at apogee won an excited Nikki an invitation to come forward and spend ten minutes in the pilot's compartment.

"How is the case going this morning?" Ekaterin asked him during this private interlude.

"Exactly as I predicted, unfortunately," he said. "ImpSec's failure to catch up with Soudha is growing more disturbing by the hour. I really thought they'd have nailed him by now. Between Colonel Gibbs's group, and that team of earnest ImpSec boys we have counting widgets out at the experiment station, my parts list is starting to take shape, but it will be at least another day before it's complete."

"Did my uncle like the idea?"

"Heh. He said it was tedious, which I already knew. And then he appropriated it from me, which I take to indicate approval." He rubbed his lips, introspectively. "Thanks to your uncle, we did get one spot of encouragement last night. He'd thought to confiscate Radovas's personal library, when we visited Madame Radovas, and we sent it off to ImpSec HQ for analysis. Their analyst confirmed Radovas's primary interest in jumpship technology and wormhole physics, which does not surprise me much, but then we got a bonus.

"Soudha or his techs did a superb job of erasing everyone's comconsoles before ImpSec got to them, but evidently no one thought of the library. Some of the technical volumes had notes entered in the margin boxes. The Professor was quite excited about the mathematical fragments, but more obviously, there were reminders to confide this or that thought or calculation to some names jotted next to them. Mostly members of the Waste Heat group, but also a couple of others, including one who appears to be one of the late members of the station-keeping crew at the soletta array. We're now positing that Radovas and his equipment, with inside help, had been smuggled up to the soletta for whatever it was they were trying to do, rather than being aboard the ore freighter. So was the soletta essential to what they were doing, or were they only using it for a test platform? ImpSec has agents out all over the planet today, questioning and requestioning colleagues, relatives, and friends of everyone on the soletta or having anything to do with their resupply shuttle. Tomorrow, I will get to read all *those* reports."

Nikki's return dried up this amiable flow of information, and they soon landed at one of ImpSec's own private shuttle-ports on the edge of the vast sealed city of Solstice. Instead of taking a public bubble-car, they were provided with a floater and driver, who took them down into the restricted tunnels by some dizzying back route that brought them to their destination in about two-thirds the time of the bubble-car system.

The first stop was a restaurant atop one of Solstice's highest towers, providing diners a spectacular view of the capital glittering halfway to the horizon; though the place was crowded, no one was seated near them while they ate, Ekaterin observed. The bodyguards did not join in the meal.

The menu had no prices, triggering a moment of panic in Ekaterin's heart. She had no way to direct Nikki, or herself, for that matter, to the cheaper selections. *If you have to ask, you can't afford it.* Her initial determination to argue possession of her portion of the bill with Vorkosigan sagged.

Vorkosigan's height and appearance drew the usual covert double-takes. For the first time in his company, she became aware of being mistaken for a couple or even a family. Her chin rose defensively. What, did they think him too odd to attach a woman? It was none of their business anyway.

The next stop—and Ekaterin was very grateful she did not have to navigate to it herself—was the clinic, a comfortable quarter hour early. Vorkosigan did not appear to notice anything in the least remarkable about the whole magic carpet ride, though Nikki had been enthusiastically diverted through-out. Had Vorkosigan planned that? The boy grew suddenly very much quieter as they took the lift-tubes up to the clinic lobby.

When they were ushered to the booth of an admissions clerk, Vorkosigan pulled up a chair for himself just behind Ekaterin and Nikki, and the bodyguards faded discreetly out of range. Ekaterin presented identification and civil service payment documentation, and all seemed to go smoothly, until they came to the information that Nikki's father was lately deceased, and the clinic comconsole demanded formal permissions from Nikki's legal guardian.

That thing is much too well programmed, Ekaterin thought, and embarked on an explanation of the distance to Tien's third cousin back on Barrayar, and the time-constrained need for Nikki's treatment to be completed before their return. The Komarran clerk listened with understanding and sympathy, but the comconsole program did not agree, and after a couple of attempts to override it, the clerk went off to fetch her supervisor. Ekaterin bit her lip and rubbed her palms on her trouser knees. To come so far, to be so close, to get hung up on some legal technicality *now* . . .

The supervisor, a pleasant young Komarran man, returned with the clerk, and Ekaterin gave her explanation again. He listened, and rechecked all the documentation, and turned to her with an air of earnest regret.

"I'm sorry, Madame Vorsoisson. If you were a Komarran planetary shareholder, instead of a Barrayaran subject, the rules would be very different."

"All Komarran planetary shareholders are Barrayaran subjects," Vorkosigan pointed out from behind her, in a bland tone.

The supervisor managed a pained smile. "I'm afraid that's not quite what I meant. The thing is, a similar problem came up for us just a few months ago, regarding treatment under quasi-emergency conditions of a Vor child of Komarr-resident Barrayarans. We went with what seemed to us to be the common-sense approach. The child's legal guardian later disagreed, and the judicial, er, negotiations are still going on. It proved to be a very costly error of judgment for the clinic. Given that Vorzohn's Dystrophy is a chronic and not an immediately life-threatening condition, and that you should in theory be able to obtain your legal permissions in a week or two, I'm afraid I'm going to have to ask you to reschedule."

Ekaterin took a deep breath, whether to argue or scream

she was not sure. But Lord Vorkosigan leaned past her shoulder and smiled at the supervisor.

"Hand me that read-pad, will you?"

The puzzled supervisor did so; Vorkosigan rummaged in his pocket and pulled out his gold Auditor's seal, which he uncapped and pressed to the pad, along with his right palm. He spoke into the vocorder. "By my order, and for the good of the Imperium, I request and require all assistance, to wit, suitable medical treatment for Nikolai Vorsoisson. Vorkosigan, Imperial Auditor." He handed it back. "See if that doesn't make your machine happier." He murmured aside to Ekaterin, "Just like swatting flies with a laser cannon. The aim's a bit tricky, but it sure takes care of the flies."

"Lord Vorkosigan, I can't . . ." Her tongue stumbled to a halt. *Can't what?* This wasn't like waffling over the lunch bill; Tien's benefits would be paying for Nikki's treatment, if only the Komarrans could be persuaded to disgorge it. Vorkosigan's offered contribution was entirely intangible.

"Nothing your esteemed uncle would not have done for you, if I could have spared him to you today." He gave her one of his ghost-bows, seated.

The supervisor's expression changed from suspicious to stunned as his comconsole digested this new data. "You are Lord Auditor Vorkosigan?"

"At your service."

"I . . . er . . . uh . . . in what capacity are you here, my lord?"

"Friend of the family." Vorkosigan's smile twisted just slightly. "Red tape cutter and general expediter."

To his credit, the supervisor managed not to gibber. He dismissed the clerk and sped them through processing, and himself escorted them upstairs and into the hands of the medtechs in the genetics department. He then vanished, but things ran amazingly quickly thereafter.

"It almost seems unfair," Ekaterin murmured, when Nikki was whisked away briefly by a tech to pee into a sampler. "I think Nikki just jumped the queue, there."

"Yes, well . . . I found last winter that an Auditor's seal had the same enlivening effect on ImpMil's veteran's treatment division, whose hallways are much draftier and drabber than these, and whose queue times are legendary. Quite miraculous. I was charmed." Vorkosigan's face grew more introspective, and sober. "I'm afraid I've not quite found my balance with this Imperial Auditor thing yet. What is the just use of power, what is its abuse? I could have ordered Madame

Radovas to be fast-penta'd, or ordered Tien to land us at the experiment station that first evening, and events would now be . . . well, I don't quite know what they would now be, except different than this. But I did not wish to . . ." He trailed off, and for just a flash, Ekaterin caught an impression of a much younger man beneath his habitual mask of irony and authority. *He is no older than me, after all.*

"Did you anticipate that problem with the permissions? I should have thought of it, I suppose, but they took all the information when I made the appointment, and didn't say anything, so I thought, I assumed—"

"Not specifically. But I hoped I might have a chance to do some little service or another today. I'm pleased it was so easy."

Yes, she realized enviously, he could just wave all ordinary problems out of his path. Leaving only the extraordinary ones . . . her envy ebbed. It occurred belatedly to Ekaterin that he too might feel some guilt about Tien's death, and that was why he was going to such lengths to assist Tien's widow and orphan. So intense a concern seemed unnecessary, and she wondered how to reassure him that she did not blame him without creating more awkwardness than she erased.

A battery of tests was completed upon Nikki in about half the time Ekaterin had mentally allotted for them. The Komarran physician met with them in her comfortable office very shortly thereafter; Vorkosigan dismissed the bodyguards to lurk in the corridor.

"Nikki's gene scan shows the dystrophy complex to be very much in the classic mode," the doctor told them, when Ekaterin and Nikki were seated side by side in front of her comconsole desk. Vorkosigan, as usual, took a backseat and just watched. "He has a few idiosyncratic complications, but nothing *our* lab can't handle."

She illustrated her talk with a holovid of the actual offending chromosomes, and a computer-generated vid of exactly how the retrovirus would deliver the splice that would work to supplement their deficiencies. Nikki did not ask as many questions as Ekaterin had hoped he would—was he intimidated, weary, bored?

"I believe our gene techs can have the retrovirus personalized for Nikki in about a week," the doctor concluded. "I'm going to have you return for the injection then, Nikki. Plan to stay overnight in Solstice for a recheck the following day, Madame Vorsoisson, and if possible, visit us again just before you leave Komarr. Nikki will need to be reexamined monthly thereafter for three months, which you can have done at a

clinic I will recommend to you in Vorbarr Sultana. We'll give
you a disk with all the records, and they should be able to
pick it up from there. After that, assuming all goes well, a
yearly checkup should suffice."

"That's all?" said Ekaterin, weak with relief.

"That's all."

"There was no damage yet? We are in time?"

"No, he's fine. It's hard to project, with Vorzohn's Dystrophy, but I would guess in his case the onset of detectable
gross cellular damage would have begun to appear in his late
teens or early twenties. You are in good time."

Ekaterin held Nikki's hand hard as they exited, her steps
firm, to keep her feet from dancing. With an, "Aw, Mama,"
Nikki extracted himself, and walked with independent dignity
beside her. Vorkosigan, his hands shoved deep in his gray trouser pockets, followed smiling.

Nikki fell asleep in the shuttle, with his head pillowed on
Ekaterin's lap. She watched him fondly, and stroked his hair,
lightly so as not to wake him.

Vorkosigan, sitting across from them with his reader on his
knees again, watched her in turn, and murmured, "Is it well?"

"It's well," she said softly. "But it feels so strange . . .
Nikki's illness has been the whole focus of my life for so
long. I gradually pared away all the other impossibilities to
concentrate wholly on this, the one main thing. It feels as
though I had been steeling myself to batter down some
unscalable wall. And then, when I finally took a deep breath
and put my head down and charged, it just . . . fell, all
in a heap, like that. And now I'm stumbling around in the
dust and the bricks, blinking. I feel very unbalanced. Where
am I now? *Who* am I now?"

"Oh, you'll find your center. You can't have mislaid it totally,
even if you have been revolving around other people. Give
yourself time."

"I thought my center was to be Vor, like the women before
me." She glanced across at him, feeling inarticulate and urgent.
"When I chose Tien . . . you have to understand, it *was* my
choice. My marriage was arranged, offered, but it wasn't forced.
I wanted it, wanted to have children, form a family, carry on
the pattern. Make my place in this, I don't know, generational
pageant."

"I am the eleventh of my name. I know about the Vor
pageant."

"Yes," she said gratefully. "It wasn't that I didn't choose

what I wanted, or gave away my center, or any of those things. But somehow, I didn't end up with the beautiful Vor pattern-weave I was trying to make. I ended up with this . . . tangle of strings." Her fingers wriggled in air, miming chaos.

His lips quirked, introspective and ironic. "I know tangles, too."

"But do you know—well, of course you would, but . . . The business with the brick wall. Failure, failure was grown familiar to me. Comfortable, almost, when I stopped struggling against it. I did not know achievement was so devastating."

"Huh." He was leaning back, now, his reader forgotten on his lap, regarding her with his entire attention. "Yes . . . vertigo at apogee, eh? And the reward for a job well done is another job, and what have you done for us lately, and is that *all*, Lieutenant Vorkosigan, and . . . yes. Achievement is devastating, or at least disorienting, and they don't warn you in advance. It's the sudden change of momentum and direction, I think."

She blinked. "How very strange. I expected you to tell me I was being foolish."

"Deny your perfectly correct perception? Why should you expect that?"

"Habit . . . I suppose."

"Mm. You can learn to enjoy the sensation of winning, you know, once you get over the initial queasiness. It's an acquired taste."

"How long did it take you to acquire it?"

He smiled slowly. "Once."

"That's not a taste, that's an addiction."

"It's one that would look well on you."

His eyes were uncomfortably bright. Challenging? She smiled in confusion, and stared out the port at the darkening Komarran sky as the shuttle began its descent. He rubbed his lips, not quite erasing their odd quirk, and returned his attention to his reports.

Uncle Vorthys met them at the apartment door, data disks in his hand and a vague distracted smile on his face. He gave Ekaterin's hand a warm grasp, and fended off Nikki's immediate attempt to appropriate him and carry him off to hear about the wonders of the ImpSec shuttle.

"Just a moment, Nikki. We shall go to the kitchen for dessert, and you can tell me all about it. Ekaterin. I've heard from the Professora. She's taken ship on Barrayar, and will be here in three days' time. I didn't like to tell you till she was sure she could get away."

"Oh!" Ekaterin almost jumped with delight, mitigated immediately by concern. "Oh, no, sir, do you meant to say you are dragging that poor woman through five wormhole jumps from Barrayar to Komarr for *me*? She gets so jumpsick!"

"It was Lord Vorkosigan's idea, actually," said Uncle Vorthys.

Vorkosigan put on a bright, trapped smile at this, and shrugged warily.

"Although I had fully intended to drag her here for my own sake," Uncle Vorthys continued, "at the end of the term. This just advanced the timetable. She does like Komarr, once she gets here and has a day to recover from the jump-lag. I thought you would like it."

"You shouldn't have—but oh, I do like it, very much."

Vorkosigan straightened at these words, and his smile relaxed into a self-satisfaction that amused her vastly. Ekaterin wasn't sure if she was reading the subtleties of his expression better now, or if he was concealing them less.

"If I get you a ticket, would you go out to meet her at the jump-point station?" Uncle Vorthys added. "I'm afraid I won't have time, and she hates traveling alone. You could see her a day earlier, and have some time together on the last leg downside."

"Certainly, sir!" Ekaterin almost shivered with the realization of how much she longed to see her aunt. She'd been living in Tien's orbit so long, she'd become used to her isolation as the norm. Ekaterin counted the Professora as one of the few non-disheartening relatives she possessed. A friend—an ally! The Komarran women Ekaterin had met were nice enough, but there was so much they didn't understand. . . . Aunt Vorthys might make acerbic comments, but she understood deeply.

"Yes, yes, Nikki—" said Uncle Vorthys. "Miles. When you are ready, I'll meet you in my room, and we can go over today's progress on the comconsole."

"Have we some? Is it interesting?"

Uncle Vorthys made a balancing gesture with his free hand. "I'd be interested in what pattern you see emerging, if any."

"At your convenience. Knock on my door when you're ready." Vorkosigan smiled at Nikki, gave the Professor a vague salutelike gesture, and withdrew.

Nikki, impatiently waiting his turn, now dragged his great-uncle off to the kitchen as promised; Ekaterin could only be grateful that of his day's events the ImpSec shuttle seemed to loom so much larger than the medical examinations. She followed, satisfied.

CHAPTER SIXTEEN

Early the next morning Miles, in shirt and trousers but bare-foot, stepped into the hallway with his toiletries case in hand. He must remind Tuomonen to return his medical kit. The ImpSec techs couldn't have found any interesting explosive devices in it, or he would have been informed by now. His bleary meditations suffered a check when he discovered Ekaterin, still dressed in a robe and with her hair in unusual but fetching disarray, leaning against the hall bathroom door.

"Nikki," she hissed. "Open this door at once! You can't hide all day in there."

A muffled young voice returned mulishly, "Yes, I can."

Lips tight, she tapped again, urgently but quietly, then jumped a little as she saw Miles, and clutched the neck of her robe.

"Oh. Lord Vorkosigan."

"Good morning, Madame Vorsoisson," he said civilly. "Ah . . . trouble?"

She nodded ruefully. "I thought yesterday went awfully easily. Nikki tried to insist he was too sick to go to school today, because of his Vorzohn's Dystrophy. I explained again it didn't work that way, but he got more and more stubborn. He begged to stay home. No, not just stubborn. Scared, I think. This isn't the usual malingering." She jerked her head toward the locked door. "I tried getting firm. It was not the right tactic. Now he's panicked."

Miles bent to glance at the lock, which was an ordinary mechanical one. Too bad it wasn't a palm lock; he knew some tricks with those. This one didn't even have screws, but some kind of rivets. It was going to take a pry bar. Or subterfuge . . .

"Nikki," called Ekaterin hopefully. "Lord Vorkosigan is out here. He needs to get washed and dressed, so he can go to work."

Silence.

"I'm torn," murmured Ekaterin in lower tones. "We're leaving in a few weeks. A few missed lessons wouldn't matter, but . . . that's not the point."

"I went to a private Vor school rather like his, when I was his age," Miles murmured back. "I know what he's afraid of. But I think your instincts are correct." He frowned thoughtfully, then set his case down and rummaged for his tube of depilatory cream, which he smeared liberally over his night's bristles. "Nikki?" he called more loudly. "Can I come in? I'm all over depilatory cream, and if I don't wash it off, it'll start eating through my skin."

"Won't he realize you can wash in the kitchen?" Ekaterin whispered.

"Maybe. But he's only nine, I'm gambling depilation is still a bit of a mystery."

After a moment Nikki's voice came, "You can come in. But I'm not coming out. And I'm locking it again."

"That's fair," Miles allowed.

Some rustling near the door. "Should I grab him when it opens?" Ekaterin asked, very dubiously.

"Nope. It would violate our tacit agreement. I'll go in, then we'll see what happens. At least you'll have a spy inside the gate, at that point."

"It seems wrong to use you so."

"Mm, but kids only dare defy those whom they really trust. The fact that I'm still mostly a stranger to him gives me an advantage, which I invite you to use."

"True enough. Well . . . all right."

The door opened a cautious crack. Miles waited. It opened a little wider. He sighed, turned sideways, and slipped through. Nikki shut it again immediately, and snapped the lock.

The boy was dressed for school, in his braided uniform of sober gray and maroon, but minus his shoes. The shoes presumably had been the sticking point, with their implicit commitment to going out. Nikki backed up and seated himself on the edge of the tub; Miles laid out his toiletries kit on the counter and rolled up his sleeves, trying to think fast before coffee. Or think at all. His eloquence had inspired his soldiers to face death, in the past, or so he dimly recalled. *Now let's try something really hard.* Playing for time and inspiration, he methodically brushed his teeth, by which time the depilatory had finished working. He washed off the resultant goo, rubbed his face dry with the towel, flung it over his shoulder, and leaned with his back against the door, slowly unrolling his sleeves and fastening his cuffs.

"So, Nikki," he said at last. "What's the trouble with going to school this morning?"

Moisture smeared around the boy's defiant eyes glistened when it caught the light. "I'm sick. I've got Vorzohn's thing."

"It's not catching. You can't give it to anybody." *Except for the way you got it.* From the blank look on Nikki's face, the idea of being dangerous to anyone else had never crossed his mind. Ah, the self-centeredness of childhood. Miles hesitated, wondering how to approach the real problem. For almost the first time, he wondered how certain aspects of his childhood had looked from his parents' point of view. The doubled vision was dizzying. *How the devil did I wind up on the enemy side?*

"You know," Miles essayed, "no one will even know you have it unless you tell them. It's not like they can smell it on you, eh?"

The mulish look redoubled. "That's what Mama said."

Scratch that trial balloon. There was an inherent problem in suggesting secrecy anyway, as Tien's life demonstrated. Suppressing a passing desire to strangle the boy for inflicting yet more distress on Ekaterin just now, Miles asked, "Have you had breakfast yet?"

"Yeah."

Starving him out or bribing him with food would be too slow, then. "Well . . . deal. I won't tell you you're blowing it all out of proportion if you won't tell me I don't understand."

Nikki glanced up from his seat, his attention arrested. *Yeah. See me, kid.* Miles considered, and immediately discarded, any argument that smacked of threat, that attempted to chivvy Nikki in the right direction by upping the pressure. For instance, the one that started out, *How do you ever expect to have the courage to jump through wormholes if you haven't the courage to face this?* Nikki was up against the wall now, driven into this untenable retreat. Upping the pressure would just squash him. The trick was to lower the wall. "I went to a private school a bit like yours. I can't remember a time I wasn't dealing with being a mutie Vor, in my classmates' eyes. By the time I was your age, I had a dozen strategies. Some of them were pretty counterproductive, I admit."

He'd gone through medical hell in his childhood with a stiff lip. But a few still-remembered playfellows, upon discovering

that his brittle bones made physical harassment too dangerous—to themselves, when they found they couldn't conceal
the evidence—had learned to reduce him to humiliated tears
with words alone. Sergeant Bothari, delivering Miles daily to
this academic purgatory, quickly made a routine of an expert
shakedown, relieving him of weapons ranging from kitchen
knives to a military stunner stolen from Captain Koudelka's
holster. After that, Miles had gone to war in a subtler fashion. It had taken almost two years to teach certain of his
classmates to leave him alone. Learning all round. Upon reflection, offering his own age nine-to-twelve solutions might not
be the best idea . . . in fact, letting Nikki even find out what
some of them had been could be a supremely bad idea. "But
that was twenty years ago, on Barrayar. Times have changed.
What exactly do you think your friends here will do to you?"

Nikki shrugged. "Dunno."

"Well, give me some guesses. You can't plan a strategy without good intelligence."

Nikki shrugged again. After a time he added, "It's not what
they'll do. It what they'll think."

Miles blew out his breath. "That's . . . a little tenuous for
me to work with, y'know. What you fear someone will think,
in the future. I usually have to use fast-penta to find out what
people really think. And even fast-penta won't tell me what
they're *going* to think."

Nikki hunched. Miles regretfully gave up the notion of telling
him that if he kept making those turtle-backed gestures, his
spine would freeze like that, just as Miles's had. There was
a faint, awful possibility the boy might believe him.

"What we need," Miles sighed, "is an ImpSec agent. Someone to scout unknown territory, not knowing what the strangers
they meet are going to do or think. Listen carefully, watch
and remember, report back. And they have to do it over and
over, in new places all the time. It's bloody daunting, the first
time."

Nikki looked up. "How do you know? You said you were
a courier."

Damn, the kid was sharp. "I'm, um, not supposed to talk
about it. You're not cleared. But do you think your school is
as dangerous as, say, Jackson's Whole, or Eta Ceta? Just to
pick a couple of, ah, random examples."

Nikki stared in silent and, Miles feared, justified scorn of
this adult floundering.

"Tell you something I did learn, though."

Nikki was drawn, or at least, looked up.

Go with it; he won't give you more. "It's not as daunting the second time. I wished later I could have started with the second time. But the only way to get to the second time is to do the first time. Seems paradoxical, that the fastest way to get to easy is through hard. In any case, I can't spare you an ImpSec agent to check out your school for antimutant activity."

Nikki snorted warily, alive to the least hint of patronization.

Miles's grin twisted in bleak appreciation. "Besides, it would be overkill, don't you think?"

"Prob'ly." Grouchy hunching.

"The ideal ImpSec scout would be someone who could blend in, anyway. Someone who knew the territory like that back of his hand, and wouldn't make dangerous mistakes out of ignorance. Someone who could keep his own counsel and not let his assumptions get in the way of his observations. And not get into fights, because it would blow his cover. Very practical people, the successful Imperial agents I've known." He eyed Nikki meditatively. *This was not going well. Try another.* "The youngest subagent I ever employed was about ten. It wasn't on Barrayar, needless to say, but I don't think you're any less bright or competent than she was."

"Ten?" said Nikki, temporarily startled out of his surly knot. "*She?*"

"It was for a spot of simple courier duty. She could pass unnoticed where a uniformed mercen—where a uniformed adult could not. Now, I'm willing to be your tactical consultant on this, ah, school-penetration mission, but I can't work without intelligence. And the best agent to collect it, in this case, is already in place. Do you dare?"

Nikki shrugged. But his lip-biting stony look had faded into one of speculation. "Ten . . . a *girl* . . ."

A hit, a very palpable hit. "I put her down on my ImpSec expenditures log as a local informant. She was paid, of course. Same rates as an adult. A small but measurable contribution to speeding that particular mission to a successful conclusion." Miles stared off into the middle distance for a moment, with an air of reminiscence of the sort which usually preceded long, boring adult stories. When he judged the hook was set, he feigned to come back to himself and smiled faintly at Nikki. "Well, that's enough of that. Duty drives. *I* haven't had breakfast. If you decide to come out, I'll be here for another ten minutes or so."

Miles unlatched the lock and let himself out. He didn't think Nikki had bought more than one word of his in three, though

for a change and in contrast to several of his historic negotiations, it had all been true. But at least he'd managed to
offer a line of retreat from an impossible position.

Ekaterin was waiting in the hall. He put his finger to his
lips and waited a moment. The door stayed closed, but the
lock did not click again. Miles motioned Ekaterin to follow,
and tiptoed away to the living room.

"Whew," said Miles. "I think that's the toughest audience
I've ever played to."

"What happened?" demanded Ekaterin anxiously. "Is he coming out?"

"Not sure yet. I gave him a couple of new things to think
about. He didn't seem as panicked. And it's going to get
really boring in there after a bit. Let's give him some time
and see."

Miles was just finishing his groats and coffee when Nikki
cautiously poked his head around the kitchen door. He lingered in the doorway, kicking his heel against the frame.
Ekaterin, seated across from Miles, put her hand to her lips
and waited.

"Where're my shoes?" asked Nikki after a moment.

"Under the table," said Ekaterin, maintaining, with obvious effort, a perfectly neutral tone. Nikki crawled under to
retrieve them, and sat cross-legged on the floor by the door
to put them on.

When he stood up again, Ekaterin said carefully, "Do you
want anyone to go with you?"

"Naw." His gaze crossed Miles's just briefly, then he slouched
into the living room to collect his school bag and let himself out the front door.

Ekaterin, turning back from her arrested half-rise from her
chair, sank down limply. "My word. I wonder if I ought to
call the school to make sure he arrives."

Miles thought it over. "Yes. But don't let Nikki know you
checked."

"Right." She swirled the coffee around in the bottom of her
cup, and added hesitantly, "How did you *do* that?"

"Do what?"

"Get him out of there. If it had been Tien . . . they were
both stubborn. Tien would get so frustrated with Nikki sometimes, not without cause. He would have threatened to take
the door down and drag Nikki to school; I would have run
around in circles placating, frantically afraid things would get
out of hand. Though they never quite seemed to. I don't know
if that was because of me, or . . . Tien would always be a

little ashamed later, not that he would ever apologize, but he would buy . . . well, it doesn't matter now."

Miles made a crosshatch pattern in the bottom of his dish with his spoon, hoping his desire for her approval was not too embarrassingly obvious. "Physical solutions have never come easily to me. I just . . . played with his mind, eased him out. I try never to take away somebody's face when I'm negotiating."

"Not even a child's?" Her lips quirked, and her brows flicked up in an expression he wasn't sure how to interpret. "A rare approach."

"So, maybe my tactics had the novelty of surprise. I admit, I did *think* of ordering my ImpSec minions into the breach, but it would have looked like a very silly order. Nikki's dignity wasn't the only one on the line."

"Well . . . thank you for being so patient. One doesn't normally expect busy and important men to take the time for kids."

Her voice was warm; she *was* pleased. Oh, good. He babbled in relief, "Well, I do. Expect it, that is. My Da always did, you see—take time for me. Later, when I learned not everyone's Da did the same, I just assumed it was only a trait of the *most* busy and *most* important men."

"Hm." She looked down at her hands, resting on either side of her cup, and smiled crookedly.

Professor Vorthys lumbered in, dressed for the day in his comfortable rumpled suit, scarcely more form-fitting than his pajamas. It was tailor-made garb, appropriate to his status as an Imperial Voice, but he must, Miles reflected, have driven his tailor to despair before coaxing *just* the fit he wanted, *With lots of room in the pockets*, as he'd once explained to Miles while the Professora rolled her eyes heavenward. Vorthys was stuffing data disks into these capacious compartments. "Are you ready, Miles? ImpSec just called to say they'll have an aircar and driver waiting for us at the West Locks."

"Yes, very good." With an apologetic smile to Ekaterin, Miles tossed off the last of his coffee and rose. "Will you be all right today, Madame Vorsoisson?"

"Yes, of course. I have a lot to do. I have an appointment with an estate law counselor, and any amount of sorting and packing . . . the guard won't have to go with me, will he?"

"Not unless you wish. We are leaving one man on duty here, by your leave. But if our Komarrans had wanted hostages, they could have taken me and Tien that first night." And bought themselves loads more trouble. If only they *had*,

Miles reflected regretfully. His case could be ever so much further along by now. Soudha was too damned smart. "If I thought you and Nikki were in any possible danger—" *I'd figure some way to use you for bait—* no, no. "If you are in the least uncomfortable, I'd be happy to assign you a man."

"No, indeed."

That faint smile again. Miles felt he could happily spend the rest of the morning studying all the subtle expressions of her lips. *Equipment lists. You're going to go study equipment lists.* "Then I bid you good morning, Madame."

Lord Auditor Vorthys, after his first survey of the new situation, had chosen to set up his personal headquarters out at the Waste Heat experiment station. Miles had to admit, the security there was great; no one was likely to blunder in by accident, or wander across its bleak surroundings unobserved. Well, he and Tien had, but the occupants had been distracted at the time, and Tien had apparently possessed a dire luck which amounted to antigenius. Miles wondered which had come first, for Soudha; had the administrative acquisition of such a perfect site for secret work triggered the idea for his shadow project, or had he had the idea first, and then maneuvered himself into the right promotion to capture control of the station? Just one of a long list of questions Miles was itching to ask the man, under fast-penta.

After the ImpSec aircar delivered the two Auditors, Miles went off first to check the progress of his, or rather, ImpSec Engineering Major D'Emorie's, inventory crews. The sergeant in charge promised completion of the tedious identification, counting, and cross-check of every portable object in the station before the end of today. Miles then returned to Vorthys, who had set up a sort of engineer's nest in one of the long upstairs workrooms in the office section, with roomy tables, lots of light, and a proliferating array of high-powered comconsoles. The Professor grunted greetings from behind a multicolored spaghetti-array of mathematical projections, glimmering above his vid-plate. Miles settled down in a comconsole station chair to study the growing list of real objects Colonel Gibbs claimed Waste Heat had paid for, but which were no longer to be found on Waste Heat's premises, hoping some subliminally familiar ordnance pattern might emerge.

After a while, the Professor shut off his holovid display and sighed. "Well, no doubt they built *something*. The topside crews picked up some more fragments yesterday, mostly melted."

"So does our inventory represent one something, destroyed

along with Radovas, or two somethings?" Miles wondered aloud.

"Oh, I should think two, at least. Though the second may not have been assembled yet. If one thinks it through from Soudha's point of view, one realizes he's been having a very bad month."

"Yes, if that whole mess topside wasn't some really bizarre suicide mission, or internecine sabotage, or. . . . and where *is* Marie Trogir, blast it? I'm not at all sure the Komarrans knew, either. When he talked to me, Soudha seemed to be angling to find out if I knew anything of her. Unless that was just more of his misdirection."

"Are you seeing anything in your inventory yet?" asked Vorthys.

"Mm, not exactly what I'm looking for. The final autopsy report on Radovas revealed some cellular distortions, in addition to the gross, and I use that term advisedly, damage. They reminded me a little of what happens to human bodies which have suffered a near-miss from a gravitic imploder beam. A hit, of course, is very distinctive, in a messy and violently-distributed way, but a near-miss can kill without actually bursting the body. I've been wondering since I first saw the cell scans if Soudha has reinvented the gravitic imploder lance, or some other gravitic field weapon. Scaling them down to personnel size has been an ongoing ambition of the weapons boffins, I know. But . . . the parts list doesn't quite jibe. There's a load of heavy-duty power transmission equipment among this stuff, but I'm damned if I see what they're transmitting it *to*."

"The math fragments found in Radovas's library intrigue me very much," said Vorthys. "You spoke to Soudha's mathematician, Cappell—what was your impression of him?"

"It's hard to say, now that I know he was lying through his teeth at me through the whole interview," said Miles ruefully. "I deduce that Soudha trusted him to keep his head, at a time when the whole team must have been scrambling like hell to complete their withdrawal. Soudha was very selective, I now realize, in just who he gated through to me." Miles hesitated, not just sure he could lay out the logic of his next conclusion. "I think Cappell was a key man. Maybe next after Soudha himself. Although the accountant, Foscol . . . no. I give you a foursome. Soudha, Foscol, Cappell, and Radovas. They're the core. I'll bet you Betan dollars to sand the farrago about a love affair between Radovas and Trogir was a complete fabrication, a convincing smoke screen they developed after the accident, to buy time. But in that case, where *is* Trogir now?" After a moment he added, "And were they planning to use their thing, or sell it? If sell, they'd almost have to find a customer out of the Empire. Maybe Trogir double-crossed everyone and took off with the specs to some high bidder. ImpSec's got a tight watch for our missing Komarrans on all the jump-point exits from the Empire. They only had a couple hours' start, they *can't* have got out before the lid clamped down. But Trogir had a two-week head start. She could be long gone by now."

Vorthys shook his head, declining to reason in advance of his data; Miles sighed, and returned to his list.

By the end of an hour, Miles was cross-eyed from staring at meters and meters of really supremely boring inventory read-outs. His mind wandered, revolving a plan to go attach himself like a hyperactive leech to *all* the field agents searching for the fugitive Komarrans. Sequentially, he supposed; he had learned not to wish to be twins, or any other multiple of himself. Miles thought of the old Barrayaran joke about the Vor lord who jumped on his horse and rode off in all directions. Forward momentum only worked as a strategy if one had correctly identified which way was *forward*. After all, Lord Auditor Vorthys didn't run around in circles; he sat composedly in the center and let it all come to him.

Miles's meditations on the proven disadvantages of cloning were interrupted when Colonel Gibbs called them. Gibbs was sporting a demure smile of amazing smugness. The Professor wandered over into range of the vid pickup and leaned on the back of Miles's chair as Gibbs spoke.

"My Lord Auditor. My Lord Auditor." Gibbs nodded to them both. "I've found something odd I expect you want. We finally succeeded in tracing the real purchase orders of Waste Heat's largest equipment expenditures. They have, over the last two years, bought five custom-designed Necklin field generators from a Komarran jumpship powerplant firm. I have the company's name and address, and copies of the invoices. Bollan Design— that's the builder—still has the tech specs on file."

"Soudha was building a jump ship?" Miles muttered, trying to picture it. "Wait a minute, Necklin rods come in pairs . . . maybe they broke one? Colonel, has ImpSec visited Bollan yet?"

"We did, to confirm the invoice forgery. Bollan Design appears to be a perfectly legitimate, though small, company; they've been in business about thirty years, which rather predates this embezzlement operation. They're unable to compete head to head with the major builders like Toscane

Industries, so they've specialized in odd and experimental designs and custom repairs of out-system and obsolete jumpship rods. Bollan as a company does not appear to have violated any regulation, and seems to have dealt with Soudha as a customer in all good faith. The invoices at the time they left Bollan were not yet altered; that was done when they arrived on Foscol's comconsole, apparently. Nevertheless . . . the chief design engineer who worked on the order directly with Soudha has not been to work for three days, nor did my field agent find him at home."

Miles swore under his breath. "Ducking fast-penta interrogation, you bet. Unless his body turns up dead in a ditch. Could be either, at this point. You have a detainment order out on him, I trust?"

"Certainly, my lord. Shall I download everything we've acquired so far this morning on your secured channel?"

"Yes, please," said Miles.

"Especially the tech specs," put in Vorthys over his shoulder. "After I look at them, I may want to talk to the people at Bollan who *are* still there. May I trouble ImpSec to be sure none of the rest of them go on an extempore vacation before I get in touch with them, Colonel?"

"Already been done, my lord."

Still looking smug, Gibbs signed off, to be replaced by the promised financial and technical data. Vorthys tried to foist the financial records off on Miles, who promptly filed them and went to look at Vorthys's tech readouts.

"Well," said Vorthys, when, after a cursory initial scan, he was able to pull up a holovid schematic, which rotated slowly and colorfully in three dimensions above his vid-plate. "What the hell is that?"

"I was hoping you'd tell me," Miles breathed, now hanging in turn over the back of Vorthys's station chair. "Sure doesn't look like any Necklin rod I've ever seen." The lines turning in air sketched out a shape like a cross between a corkscrew and a funnel.

"All the designs are slightly different," noted Vorthys, bringing up four more shapes to hang in series beside the first. "Judging by the dates, they were scaling up with each subsequent model."

According to the attached measurements, the first three were relatively smaller, a couple of meters long and a meter or so wide. The fourth was double the dimensions of the third. The fifth, probably four meters wide at the larger end and six meters in length. Miles pictured the size of the assembly room doors in the building next to this one. Wherever that last one had been delivered to—four weeks ago?—it hadn't been here. And one did not leave a delicate precision device like a Necklin rod out in the wind and rain.

"Those things generate Necklin fields?" said Miles. "What shape? With a pair of jumpship rods, the fields counter-rotate and fold the ship through five-space." He held his hands out parallel with each other, palm up, then pressed them inward. In the metaphor he'd been given, the field wrapped around its ship to create a five-space needle of infinitesimal diameter and unlimited length, to punch through that area of five-space weakness called a wormhole, and unfold again into three-space on the other side. He'd also been dragged through a more convincing mathematical demonstration, in his last term at the Academy, all details of which, never called on subsequently thereafter, had evaporated out of his brain shortly after the final exam. That was long before his cryo-revival, so it was one bit of memory loss he could not blame on the sniper's needle-grenade. "I used to know this stuff . . ." he muttered plaintively.

Despite this broad hint, the Professor did not break into an enlightening lecture. He just sat in his station chair, his chin cupped in his palm. After a moment, he leaned forward and called up a dizzying succession of data files from the probable-cause investigation. "Ah. Here it is." A wriggly graph appeared, flanked by a list of elements and percentages running down one side. A fast pass through the data from Bollan produced another, similar list. The Professor leaned back. "I'll be damned."

"*What?*" said Miles.

"I did not expect to get this lucky. That," he pointed to the first graph, "is an analysis of the composition of a very melted and distorted mass fragment we picked up topside. It has nearly the same composition fingerprint as this fourth device, here. The figures which are a tiny bit off are just the sort of lighter and more volatile elements I'd expect to lose in such a melt. Huh. I didn't think we'd *ever* be able to reconstruct the source of those blobs. Now we don't have to."

"If that was the fourth," said Miles slowly, "where's the fifth?"

The Professor shrugged. "The same place as the first, second, and third?"

"Do you have enough information from the inventory to reconstruct its power supply? At that point, we'd have the whole machine mapped, wouldn't we?"

"Mm, maybe. It will certainly supply some parameters. How much power? Continuous, or phased? Bollan had to know, to supply the proper coupler . . . ah." He noodled again with the specs and fell into a study of the complicated diagram.

Miles rocked impatiently on his heels. When he felt he could no longer maintain his respectful silence without the top of his head blowing off, he said, "Yes, but what does it *do*?"

"Just what it says, presumably. Generates a five-space distortion field."

"Which does what? *To* what?"

"Ah." The Professor sank back in his station chair and rubbed his chin ruefully. "Answering that may take a little longer."

"Can't we run comconsole simulations?"

"To be sure. But to get the right answer, one must first correctly frame the question. I want—humph!—a mathematical physicist specializing in five-space theory. Probably Dr. Riva, she's at the University of Solstice."

"If she's Komarran, ImpSec will object."

"Yes, but she's here on-planet. I've consulted her before, when I investigated a politically suspicious wormhole jump accident on the Sergyar route two years ago. She thinks sideways better than any of the other five-space people I know."

Miles was under the impression that all five-space math experts thought sideways to the rest of humanity, but he nodded understanding of the importance of this character trait.

"I want her; I shall have her. But before I drag her out of her comfortable academic routine, I think I want to visit Bollan in person. Your Colonel Gibbs is very good, but he can't have asked all the questions."

Miles considered denying personal ownership of ImpSec and anyone in it, but recognized ruefully that he was now identified as the authority on ImpSec among the Auditors just as Vorthys was identified as the engineering expert. *It's an ImpSec problem*, he pictured some future conclave of his colleagues concluding. *Give it to Vorkosigan*. "Right."

The trip to Bollan Design's plant did not prove as enlightening as Miles had hoped. A hop in a suborbital shuttle to a dome one Sector west of Serifosa soon brought Miles and Vorthys face-to-face with Bollan's upset owners. Since they'd already thrown open all their records to ImpSec that morning, they had little more to offer the Imperial Auditors. The administrative people knew only of financial and contractual details with Soudha's mythical "private research institute" that had supposedly ordered the work; some techs who'd worked in the fabrication shop had very little to add to the specs already in Vorthys's possession. If the missing engineer had been as innocent of the true identity of the customer and purpose of the device as were the rest of the Bollan employees, he'd have had no reason to flee; Bollan Design had committed no crime that Miles could identify.

However, the techs were able to recall dates of several visits from men answering to descriptions of Soudha, Cappell, and Radovas, definitely one from Soudha as recently as the previous week. Their supervisor had never included them in these conferences. They had been told never to discuss the odd Necklin generators outside their work group, as the devices were experimental and not yet patented, trade secrets soon to transmute into profit (or loss). The progression so far had looked a lot more like loss than profit.

The customers had always picked up the finished devices from the plant themselves, not had them delivered anywhere. Miles made a note to find out if Waste Heat had owned their own large transport, and if not, to have ImpSec check out recent lift-van rentals of anything big enough to have hauled those last two generators.

Nosing around the plant while the Professor went off to speak High Engineering to the bilingual, Miles felt himself increasingly drawn to the hypothesis that the chief designer had gone missing voluntarily. Upon closer examination it had been found that many of the man's personal notes had apparently gone with him. Bollan's plant security was not military grade, but it would be a stretch to imagine Soudha's hurried Komarrans first murdering the man, then smoothly and surgically removing quite so many comconsole records from quite so many locations without inside help. Anyway, Miles didn't wish the man dead in a ditch. He wished him very much alive, at the business end of Tuomonen's hypospray. That was the trouble, people *anticipated* fast-penta now. Modern conspirators were a lot more tight-lipped than back in the bad old days of mere physical torture. Three days ago, if someone had told Miles that Gibbs was going to hand him what amounted to complete design specs of Soudha's secret weapon on a platter, he would have been delighted to imagine his case nearly solved. Ha.

Miles and Vorthys arrived back at Ekaterin's apartment that night too late for dinner, but in time for a hand-made dessert obviously tailored to the Professor's tastes, involving chocolate, cream, and quantities of hydroponic pecans. They all sat around Ekaterin's kitchen table to devour it. Whatever Nikki had encountered from his playmates today, it hadn't been unpleasant enough to affect his appetite, Miles noted with approval.

"How was school today?" Miles asked him, ashamed to let such a deadly boring triteness fall from his lips, but how else was he supposed to find out?

"All right," Nikki said around a mouthful of cream.

"Think you'll have any trouble tomorrow?"

"Naw." The tone of his monosyllables had returned to its normal preadolescent adult-wary indifference; no more the breathy panicked edge of this morning.

"Good," Miles said affably. Ekaterin's eyes were smiling, Miles noted out of the corner of his own. *Good.*

When Nikki finished bolting his dessert and galloped off, she added wryly, "And how was work today? I wasn't sure if the extra hours represented progress, or the reverse."

How was work today. Her tone seemed to apologize for the prosaic quality of the question. Miles wondered how to explain to her that he found it altogether delightful, and wished she'd do it again. And again and . . . Her perfume was making his reptile-brain want to roll over and do tricks, and he wasn't even sure she was wearing any. This mind-melting mixture of lust and domesticity was entirely novel to him. Well, half novel; he knew how to handle lust. It was the domesticity that had ambushed his guard. "We have advanced to new and surprising levels of bafflement," Miles told her.

The Professor opened his mouth, closed it, then said, "That about sums it up. Lord Vorkosigan's hypothesis has proved correct; the embezzlement scheme was got up to support the production of a, um, novel device."

"Secret weapon," Miles corrected. "I said secret weapon."

The Professor's eyes glinted in amusement. "Define your terms. If it's a weapon, then what's the target?"

"It's so secret," Miles explained to Ekaterin, "we can't even figure out what it does. So I'm at least half right." He glanced after Nikki. "I take it once Nikki got into his usual routine, things smoothed out?"

"Yes. I'd been almost certain they would," said Ekaterin. "Thank you so much for your help this morning, Lord Vorkosigan. I'm very grateful that—"

Miles was saved from certain embarrassment by the chime of the hall door. Ekaterin rose and went to answer it and the Professor followed, blocking Miles from his planned counterbid,

*How did things go with the estate law counselor? I was sure
you could get on top of it.* The ImpSec guard was now on
post in the hallway, Miles reminded himself; he didn't need
to make a parade out of this. Tucking the line away in his
head for the next conversation-opener, he tapped open the
airseal door and wandered out onto the balcony.

Both sun and soletta had set hours ago. Only the city itself
gave a glow to the night. A few pedestrians still crossed
the park below, moving in and out of the shadows, hurry-
ing on their way to or from the bubble-car platform, or
strolling more slowly in pairs. Miles leaned on the railing
and studied one sauntering couple, his arm draped across
her shoulders, her arm circling his waist. In zero gee, a height
difference like that would cancel out, by God. And how did
the space-dwelling four-armed quaddies manage these
moments? He'd met a quaddie musician once. He was certain there must be a quaddie equivalent to a grip so humanly
universal . . .

His idle envious speculations were derailed by the sound
of voices within the apartment. Ekaterin was welcoming a
guest. A man's voice, Komarran accented: Miles stiffened as
he recognized the rabbity Venier's quick speech.

"—ImpSec didn't take as long to release his personal effects
as I would have imagined. So Colonel Gibbs said I might bring
them to you."

"Thank you, Venier," Ekaterin's voice replied, in the soft
tone Miles had come to associate with wariness in her. "Just
put the box down on the table, why don't you? Now, where
did he go . . . ?"

A clunk. "Most of it is nothing, styluses and the like, but
I figured you would want the vidclipper with all the holos
of you and your son."

"Yes, indeed."

"Actually, there is more to my visit than just cleaning out
Administrator Vorsoisson's office." Venier took a deep breath.
"I wanted to speak to you privately."

Miles, who had been about to reenter the kitchen from the
balcony, froze. Dammit, ImpSec had questioned and cleared
Venier, hadn't they? What new secret could he be about to
offer, and to Ekaterin of all people? If Miles entered, would
he clam up?

"Well . . . well, all right. Um, why don't you sit down?"

"Thank you." The scrape of chairs.

Venier began again, "I've been thinking about how awkward
your situation here has become since the Administrator's death.

I'm so very sorry, but I couldn't help being aware, watching
you over the months, that things were not what they should
have been between you and your late husband."

"Tien . . . was difficult. I didn't realize it showed."

"Tien was an ass," Venier stated flatly. "*That* showed. Sorry,
sorry. But it's true, and we both know it."

"It's moot now." Her tone was not encouraging.

Venier forged on. "I heard about how he played fast and
loose with your pension. His death has plunged you into a
monstrous situation. I understand you are being forced to return
to Barrayar."

Ekaterin said slowly, "I plan to return to Barrayar, yes."

He ought to clear his throat, Miles thought. Trip over a balcony chair. Pop back through the door and cry, *Vennie, fancy
meeting you here!* He began breathing through his mouth, for
silence, instead.

"I realize this is a bad time to bring this up, much too
soon," Venier went on. "But I've been watching you for
months. The way you were treated. Practically a prisoner, in
a traditional Barrayaran marriage. I could not tell how willing a prisoner you were, but now—have you considered staying
on Komarr? *Not* going back into your cell? You have this
chance, you see, to escape."

Miles could feel his heart begin to beat, in a free-form panic.
Where was Venier going with this?

"I . . . the economics . . . our return passage is a death
benefit, you see." That same wary softness.

"I have an alternative to offer you." Venier swallowed; Miles
swore he could hear the slight gurgle in his narrow neck.
"Marry me. It would give you the legal protection you need
to stay here. No one could force you back, then. I could
support you, while you train up to your full strength, botany
or chemistry or anything you choose. You could be so much.
I can't tell you how it's turned my stomach, to see so much
human potential wasted on that clown of a Barrayaran. I realize
that for you it would have to start as a marriage of convenience, but as a Vor, that's surely not an alien idea for you.
And it could grow to be more, in time, I'm certain it could.
I know it's too soon, but soon you'll be gone and then it will
be too late!"

Venier paused for breath. Miles bent over, mouth still open,
in a sort of silent scream. *My lines! My lines! Those were all
my lines, dammit!* He'd expected Vorish rivals for Ekaterin's hand
to come pouring out of the woodwork as soon as the widow
touched down in Vorbarr Sultana, but my God, she hadn't even

got off Komarr yet! He hadn't thought of Venier, or any other Komarran, as possible competition. He wasn't competition, the idea of Vennie as competition was laughable. Miles had more power, position, money, rank, all to lay at her feet when the time was finally ripe—Venier wasn't even taller than Ekaterin, he was a good four centimeters shorter—

The one thing Miles couldn't offer, though, was less Barrayar. In that, Venier had an advantage Miles could never match.

There followed a long, terrifying silence, during which Miles's brain screamed, *Say no, say no! say NO!*

"That's very kindly offered," Ekaterin said at last.

What the hell is that supposed to mean? And was Venier wondering the same thing?

"Kindness has nothing to do with it. I—" Venier cleared his throat again "—admire you very much."

"Oh, dear."

He added eagerly, "I've applied for the administrative position as head of terraforming here. I think I have a good chance. Because of the disruption in the department, HQ is surely going to be looking for some continuity. Or if the mud has splattered on the innocent as well as the guilty, I'll do whatever I have to do to get another shot, a chance to clear my professional reputation—I can make Serifosa Sector a showcase, I know I can. If you stay, I can get you voting shares. We could do it together; we could make this place a garden. Stay here and help build a world!"

Another long, terrifying silence. Then Ekaterin said, "I suppose you'd be assigned this apartment, if you succeeded to Tien's position."

"It goes with it," said Venier in an uncertain voice. Right, that wasn't a selling point, though Miles wasn't sure if Venier knew it. *I can hardly bear being in this place,* she'd said.

"You offer is kind and generous, Venier. But you have mistaken my situation, somewhat. No one is forcing me to return home. Komarr . . . I'm afraid these domes give me claustrophobia, anymore. Every time I pull on a breath mask, I'm going to think about the ugly way Tien died."

"Ah," said Venier. "I can understand that, but perhaps, in time . . . ?"

"Oh, yes. Time. Vor custom calls for a widow to mourn for one year." Miles could not guess what gesture, what facial expression, went with these words. A grimace? A smile?

"Do you hold to that archaic custom? Must you? Why? I never understood it. I thought in the Time of Isolation they tried to keep all women married all the time."

"Actually, I think it was practical. It gave time to be certain any pregnancy that might have been started could be completed while the woman was still under the control of her late husband's family, so they could be sure of claiming custody of any male issue. But still, whether I believe in formal mourning or not won't matter. As long as people think I do, I can use it to defend myself from—from unwanted suits. I so much need a quiet time and place to find my balance again."

There was a short silence. Then Venier said, more stiffly, "Defend? I did not mean my proposal as an attack, Kat."

"Of course I don't think that," she replied faintly.

Lie, lie. Of course she bloody well did. Ekaterin had experienced marriage as one long siege of her soul. After ten years of Tien, she probably felt about matrimony the way Miles felt about needle-grenade launchers. This was very bad for Venier. Good. But it was equally bad for Miles. Bad. Good. Bad. Good. Bad . . .

"Kat, I . . . I won't make a pest of myself. But think about it, think about all your alternatives, before you do anything irrevocable. I'll still be here."

Another awful silence. Then, "I don't wish to give you pain, who never gave me any, but it's wrong to make people live on false hopes." A long, indrawn breath, as if she was mustering all her strength. "No."

Yes!

And then, added more weakly, "But thank you so much for caring about me."

Longer silence. Then Venier said, "I meant to help. I can see I've made it worse. I really must be going, I still have to pick up dinner on the way home . . ."

Yes, and eat it alone, you miserable rabbit! Ha!

"Madame Vorsoisson, good night."

"Let me see you to the door. Thank you again for bringing Tien's things. I do hope you get Tien's job, Venier, I'm sure you could do it well. It's time they started promoting Komarrans into the higher administrative positions again . . ."

Miles slowly unfroze, wondering how he was going to slip past her now. If she went on to check Nikki, as she might, he could nip into her workroom without her seeing him, and pretend he'd been there all the time—

Instead, he heard her steps return to the kitchen. A scrape and rattle, a sigh, then a louder rattle as the contents of a box were, apparently, dumped wholesale into the trash chute. A chair being pulled or pushed. He inched forward, to peek around the door port. She had sat again for a moment, her hands pressed against her eyes. Crying? Laughing? She rubbed her face, threw back her head, and stood, turning toward the balcony.

Miles hastily backed up, looked around, and sat in the nearest chair. He extended his legs and threw back his head artistically, and closed his eyes. Dare he try to fake a snore, or would that be overdoing it?

Her steps paused. Oh, God, what if she sealed the door, locking him out like a strayed cat? Would he have to bang on the glass, or stay out here all night? Would anyone miss him? Could he climb down and come back in the front door? The thought made him shudder. He wasn't due for another seizure, but you never knew, that was part of what made his disorder *so* much fun. . . .

Her steps continued. He let his mouth hang slack, then he sat up, blinking and snorting. She was staring at him in surprise, her elegant features thrown into strong relief by the half-light from the kitchen. "Oh! Madame Vorsoisson. I must have been more tired than I thought."

"Were you asleep?"

His *Yes* mutated to a weak "Mm," as he recalled his promise not to lie to her. He rubbed his neck. "I'd have been half-paralyzed in that position."

Her brows drew down quizzically, and she crossed her arms. "Lord Vorkosigan. I didn't think Imperial Auditors were supposed to prevaricate like that."

"What . . . badly?" He sat all the way up and sighed. "I'm sorry. I'd stepped out to contemplate the view, and I didn't think anything when I first heard Vennie enter, and then I thought it might be something to do with the case, and then it was too late to say anything without embarrassing us all. As bad as the business with your comconsole all over again, sorry. Accidents, both. I'm not like this, really."

She cocked her head, a weird quirky smile tilting her mouth. "What, insatiably curious and entirely free of social inhibitions? Yes, you are. It's not the ImpSec training. You're a natural. No wonder you did so well for them."

Was this a compliment or an insult? He couldn't quite tell. Good, bad, good-bad-good . . . ? He rose, smiled, abandoned the idea of asking her about the estate law session, bid her a polite good night, and fled in ignominy.

CHAPTER SEVENTEEN

Ekaterin made an early start the following morning to meet her aunt inbound from Barrayar. The ferry from Komarr to the wormhole jump station broke orbit before noon Solstice time. Ekaterin settled into her private sleeper-cell aboard the ferry with a contented, guilty sigh.

It was just like Uncle Vorthys to have provided this comfort for her; he did nothing by halves. *No artificial shortages*, she could almost hear him enthusiastically booming, though he usually recited that slogan in reference to desserts. So what if she could stand in the middle of the cabinette and touch both walls. She was glad not to be rubbing shoulders with the crowds in the economy seats as she had done on her first passage, even if it was only an eight-hour flight from Komarr orbit to jump station dock. She had sat then between Tien and Nikki at the climax of a seven-day passage from Barrayar, and been hard-pressed to name which of them had been more tired, tense, and cranky, including herself.

If only she'd accepted Venier's proposal, she wouldn't be facing a repeat of that wearing journey, a point in his favor Vennie could not have guessed at. Just as well. She thought of his unexpected offer last night in her kitchen, and her lips twisted in remembered embarrassment, amusement, and an odd little flash of anger. How had Venier ever got the idea that she was available? In wariness of Tien's irrational jealousy, she'd thought she had tamped out any possible come-on signal from her manner long ago. Or did she really look so pitiful that even a modest soul like Vennie could imagine himself her rescuer? If so, that surely wasn't his fault. Neither Venier's nor Vorkosigan's enthusiastic plans for her future education and employment were distasteful to her, indeed, they matched her own aspirations, and yet . . . both somehow implied, *You can become a real person, but only if you play our game.*

Why can't I be real where I am?

Drat it, she was not going to let this churning mess of emotions spoil her precious slice of solitude. She dug her reader out of her carry-on, arranged the generous allotment of cushions, and stretched out on the bunk. At a moment like this, she could really wonder why solitary confinement was considered such a severe punishment. Why, no one could get *at* you. She wriggled her toes, luxuriating.

The guilt was for Nikki, left ruthlessly behind with one of his school friends, putatively so that he would miss no classes. If, as Ekaterin sometimes felt, she really did do nothing of value all day long, why did she have to inconvenience so many people to take over her duties when she left? Something didn't add up. Not that Madame Vortorren, whose husband was an aide to the Imperial Counsellor's Serifosa Deputy, hadn't seemed cordially willing to help out the new widow. Nor was adding Nikki to her household any great strain on its resources—she had four children of her own, whom she somehow managed to feed, clothe, and direct amidst a general chaos which never seemed to ruffle her air of benign absent-mindedness. Madame Vortorren's children had learned early to be self-reliant, and was that so bad? Nikki had been fended off in his plea to accompany Ekaterin with the reminder that the ferry pilots had strict rules against allowing passengers on the flight deck, and anyway, it wasn't even a jumpship. In reality, Ekaterin looked forward to a private time to talk frankly with her aunt about her late life with Tien without Nikki overhearing every word. Her pent-up thoughts felt like an over-filled reservoir, churning in her head with no release.

She could barely sense the acceleration as the ferry sped onward. She popped the book-disk the law counselor had recommended to her on estate and financial management into her viewer, and settled back. The counselor had confirmed Vorkosigan's shrewd guess about Tien's debts ending with his estate. She would be walking away after ten years with exactly nothing, empty-handed as she had come. Except for the value of the experience . . . she snorted. Upon reflection, she actually preferred to be beholden to Tien for nothing. Let all debts be canceled.

The management disk was dry stuff, but a disk on Escobaran water gardens waited as her reward when she was done with

her homework. It was true she had no money to manage as
yet. That too must change. Knowledge might not be power,
but ignorance was definitely weakness, and so was poverty.
Time and past time to stop assuming she was the child, and
everyone else the grownups. *I've been down once. I'm never
going down again.*

She finished one book and half the other, got in an exquisite
uninterrupted two-hour nap, and waked and tidied herself by
the time the ferry arrived and began maneuvering to dock.
She repacked her overnight bag, hitched up its shoulder strap,
and went off to watch through the lounge viewports as they
approached the transfer station and the jump point it served.

This station had been built nearly a century ago, when fresh
explorations of the wormhole had yielded up the rediscovery
of Barrayar. The lost colony had been found at the end of a
complex multijump route entirely different from the one through
which it had originally been settled. The station had undergone modification and enlargement during the period of the
Cetagandan invasion; Komarr had granted the ghem lords right
of passage in exchange for massive trade concessions through-
out the Cetagandan Empire and a slice of the projected profits of the conquest, a bargain it later came to regret. A quieter
period had followed, till the Barrayarans, graduates of the harsh
school of the failed Cetagandan occupation, had poured through
in turn.

Under the new Barrayaran Imperial management, the station had grown again, into a far-flung and chaotic structure
housing some five thousand resident employees, their families, and a fluctuating number of transients, and serving some
hundreds of ships a week on the only route to and from cul-
de-sac Barrayar. A new long docking bar was under construction, sticking out from the bristling structure. The Barrayaran
military station was a bright dot in the distance, bracketing
the invisible five-space jump point. Ekaterin could see half
a dozen ships in flight between civilian station and jump point,
maneuvering to or from dock, and a couple of local-space
freighters chugging off with cargoes to transfer at one of the
other wormhole jump points. Then the ferry itself slid into
its docking bay, and the looming station occluded the view.

The tedious business of customs checks having been got
through back in Komarr orbit before boarding, the ferry's passengers disembarked freely. Ekaterin checked her holocube map,
very necessary in this fantastic maze of a place, and went
off to ensure a hostel room for the night for herself and her

aunt, and to drop off her luggage there. The hostel room was small but quiet, and should do nicely to give poor Aunt Vorthys time to recover from her jump sickness before completing the last leg of her journey. Ekaterin wished she'd had such a luxury available on her own inbound passage. Realizing that the last thing the Professora would want to face immediately was a meal, Ekaterin prudently paused for a snack in an adjoining concourse cafe, then went off to wait her ship's docking in the disembarkation lounge nearest its assigned bay.

She selected a seat with a good view of the airseal doors, and faintly regretted not bringing her reader, in case of delays. But the station and its denizens were a fascinating distraction. Where were all these people going, and why? Most arresting to her eye were the obvious galactics, not-from-around-here in strange planetary garb; were they passing through for business, diplomacy, refuge, recreation? Ekaterin had seen two worlds, in her life; would she ever see more? Two, she reminded herself, was one more than most people ever got. *Don't be greedy.*

How many had Vorkosigan seen . . . ?

Her idle thoughts circled back to her own personal disaster, like a flood victim sorting through her ruined possessions after the waters have receded. Was the Old Vor ideal of marriage and family an intrinsic contradiction of a woman's soul, or was it just Tien who'd been the source of her shrinkage? It was not clear how to sort out the answer without multiple trials, and marriage was not an experiment she cared to repeat. Yet the Professora seemed to be proof of the possible. She had public achievement—she was a historian, teacher, scholar in four languages—she had three grown children, and a marriage heading for the half-century mark. Had she made secret compromises? She had a solid place in her profession—might she have had a place at the top? She had three children—might she have had six?

We are going to have a race, Madame Vorsoisson. Do you wish to run with your right leg chopped off, or your left leg chopped off?

I want to run on both legs.

Aunt Vorthys had run on both legs, reasonably serenely— Ekaterin had lived in her household, and didn't think she overidealized her aunt—but then, she'd been married to Uncle Vorthys. One's career might depend solely on one's own efforts, but marriage was a lottery, and you drew your lot in late adolescence or early adulthood at a point of maximum idiocy and confusion. Perhaps it was just as well. If people were too sensible, the human race might well come to an end. Evolution favored the maximum production of children, not of happiness.

So how did you end up with neither?

She snorted self-derision, then sat up as the doors slid open and people began trickling through. Most of the tide had passed when Ekaterin spotted the short woman with the wobbly step, assisted by a shipping line porter who saw her through the doors and handed her the leash of the float pallet holding her luggage. Ekaterin rose, smiling, and started forward. Her aunt looked thoroughly frazzled, her long gray hair escaping its windings atop her head to drift about her face, which had lost its usual attractive pink glow in favor of a greenish-gray tinge. Her blue bolero and calf-length skirt looked rumpled, and the matching embroidered travel boots were perched precariously atop the pile of luggage, replaced on her feet with what were obviously bedroom slippers.

Aunt Vorthys fell into Ekaterin's hug. "Oh! So good to see you."

Ekaterin held her out, to search her face. "Was the trip very bad?"

"Five jumps," said Aunt Vorthys hollowly. "And it was such a fast ship, there wasn't as much time to recover between. Be glad you're one of the lucky ones."

"I get a touch of nausea," Ekaterin consoled her, on the theory that misery might appreciate company. "It passes off in about half an hour. Nikki is the lucky one—it doesn't seem to affect him at all." Tien had concealed his symptoms in grouchiness. Afraid of showing something he construed as weakness? Should she have tried to . . . *It doesn't matter now. Let it go.* "I have a nice quiet hostel room waiting for you to lie down in. We can get tea there."

"Oh, lovely, dear."

"Here, why is your luggage riding and you walking?" Ekaterin rearranged the two bags on the float pallet and flipped up the little seat. "Sit down, and I'll tow you."

"If it's not too dizzy a ride. The jumps made my feet swell, of all things."

Ekaterin helped her aboard, made sure she felt secure, and started off at a slow walk. "I apologize for Uncle Vorthys dragging you all the way out here for me. I'm only planning to stay a few more weeks, you see."

"I'd meant to come anyway, if his case went on much longer. It doesn't seem to be going as quickly as he expected."

"No, well . . . no. I'll tell you all the horrible details when

we get in." A public concourse was not the venue for discussing it all.

"Quite, dear. You look well, if rather Komarran."

Ekaterin glanced down at her dun vest and beige trousers.
"I've found Komarran dress to be comfortable, not the least
because it lets me blend in."

"Someday, I'd love to see you dress to stand out."

"Not today, though."

"No, probably not. Do you plan on traditional mourning garb,
when you get home?

"Yes, I think it would be a very good idea. It might save
. . . save dealing with a lot of things I don't want to deal
with just now."

"I understand." Despite her jump sickness, Aunt Vorthys
stared around with interest at the passing station, and began
updating Ekaterin on the lives of her Vorthys cousins.

Her aunt had grandchildren, Ekaterin thought, yet still
seemed late-middle-aged rather than old. In the Time of Isolation, a Barrayaran woman would have been old at forty-
five, waiting for death—if she made it even that far. In the
last century, women's life expectancies had doubled, and
might even be headed toward the triple-portion taken for
granted by such galactics as the Betans. Had Ekaterin's own
mother's early death given her a false sense of time, and
of timing? *I have two lives for my foremothers' one.* Two lives
in which to accomplish her dual goals. If one could stretch
them out, instead of piling them atop one another . . . And
the arrival of the uterine replicator had changed everything,
too, profoundly. Why had she wasted a decade trying to play
the game by the old rules? Yet a decade at twenty did not
seem quite a straight trade for a decade at ninety. She needed
to think this through. . . .

Away from the docks and locks area, the crowds thinned
to an occasional passer-by. The station did not run so much
on a day-and-night rhythm, as on a ships in dock, everybody
switch, load and unload like mad because time was money,
ships out, quiet falls again pattern which did not necessarily
match the Solstice-standard time kept throughout Komarr local-
space.

Ekaterin turned up a narrow utility corridor she'd discovered earlier which provided a shortcut to the food concourse
and her hostel beyond. One of the kiosks baked traditional
Barrayaran breads and cannily vented their ovens into the
concourse, for advertising; Ekaterin could smell yeast and
cardamom and hot brillberry syrup. The combination was

redolent of Barrayaran Winterfair, and a wave of homesickness shook her.

Coming down the otherwise-unpeopled corridor toward them
along with the aromas was a man, wearing stationer-style dock-
worker coveralls. The commercial logo on his left breast read
SOUTHPORT TRANSPORT LTD., done in tilted, speedy-looking let-
ters with little lines shooting off. He carried two large bags
crammed with meal-boxes. He stopped short and stared in
shock, as did she. It was one of the engineers from Waste
Heat Management—Arozzi was his name.

He recognized her at once, too, unfortunately. "Madame
Vorsoisson!" And, more weakly, "Imagine meeting you here."
He stared around with a frantic, trapped look. "Is the Admin-
istrator with you . . . ?"

Ekaterin was just mustering a plan for, *I'm sorry, I don't
believe I know you?* followed by dancing around him blankly,
walking away without looking back, turning the corner, and
dashing madly for the nearest emergency call box. But Arozzi
dropped his bags, dug a stunner out of his pocket, and fumbled
it right way round before she'd made it any further than, "I'm
sorry—"

"So am I," he said with evident sincerity, and fired.

Ekaterin's eyes opened on a cockeyed view of the corridor
ceiling. Her whole body felt like pins and needles, and refused
to obey her urgent summons to move. Her tongue felt like a
wadded-up sock, stuffed in her mouth.

"Don't make me stun you," Arozzi was pleading with someone. "I will."

"I believe you," came Aunt Vorthys's breathless voice, from
just behind Ekaterin's ear. Ekaterin realized she was now aboard
the float pallet, half-sitting up against her aunt's chest, her
legs hung limply over the rearranged luggage in front of her.
The Professora's hand gripped her shoulder. Arozzi, after a
desperate look around, set his meal-boxes in her lap, picked
up the float pallet's lead, and started off down the corridor
as fast as the whining, overburdened pallet would follow.

Help, thought Ekaterin. *I'm being kidnapped by a Komarran
terrorist.* Her cry, as they turned down another corridor and
passed a woman in a food service uniform, came out a low
moan. The woman barely glanced at them. Not an unusual
sight, this, two very jumpsick transients being towed to their
connecting ship, or to a hostel, or maybe to the infirmary.
Or the morgue . . . Heavy stun, Ekaterin had been given to
understand, knocked people out for hours. This must be light

stun. Was this a favor? She could not feel her limbs, but she could feel her heart beating, thudding heavily in her chest as adrenaline struggled uselessly with her unresponsive peripheral nervous system.

More turns, more drops, more levels. Was her map cube still in her pocket? They passed out of passenger-country, into more utilitarian levels devoted to freight and ship repair. At last they turned in at a door labeled SOUTHPORT TRANSPORT, LTD. in the same logo style as on the coveralls, and AUTHORIZED PERSONNEL ONLY in larger red print. Arozzi led them around a turn, through some more airseal doors, and down a ramp into a large loading bay. It smelled cold, all oil and ozone and a sharp sick scent of plastics. They were at the outermost skin of the station, anyway, whatever direction they'd come. She'd seen the Southport logo before, Ekaterin realized; it was one of those minor, shoestring-budgeted local-space shipping companies that eked out a living in the few interstices left by the big Komarran family firms.

A tall, squarely-built man, also in worker's coveralls, trod across the bay toward them, his footsteps echoing. It was Dr. Soudha. "Dinner at last," he began, then he caught sight of the float pallet. "What the hell . . . ? Roz, what is this? Madame Vorsoisson!" He stared at her in astonishment. She stared back at him in muzzy loathing.

"I ran smack into her when I was coming away from the food concourse," explained Arozzi, grounding the float pallet. "I couldn't help it. She recognized me. I couldn't let her run and report, so I stunned her and brought her here."

"Roz, you fool! The last thing we need right now is hostages! She's sure to be missed, and how soon?"

"I didn't have a choice!"

"Who's this other lady?" He gave the Professora a weirdly polite, harried, how-d'you-do nod.

"My name is Helen Vorthys," said the Professora.

"Not Lord Auditor Vorthys's wife—?"

"Yes." Her voice was cold and steady, but as sensation returned Ekaterin could feel the slight tremble in her body.

Soudha swore under his breath.

Ekaterin swallowed, ran her tongue around her mouth, and struggled to sit up. Arozzi rescued his boxes, then belatedly drew his stunner again. A woman, attracted by the raised voices, approached around a stack of equipment. Middle-aged, with frizzy gray-blond hair, she also wore Southport Transport coveralls. Ekaterin recognized Lena Foscol, the accountant.

"Ekaterin," husked Aunt Vorthys, "who are these people? Do you know them?"

Ekaterin said loudly, if a little thickly, "They're the criminals who stole a huge sum of money from the Terraforming Project and murdered Tien."

Foscol, startled, said "What? We did no such thing! He was alive when I left him!"

"Left him chained to a railing with an empty oxygen canister, which you never checked. And then called *me* to come get him. An hour and a half too late." Ekaterin spat scorn. "An exquisite setup. Madame. Mad Emperor Yuri would have considered it a work of art."

"Oh," Foscol breathed. She looked sick. "Is this true? You're lying. No one would go out-dome with an empty canister!"

"You knew Tien," said Ekaterin. "What do you think?"

Foscol fell silent.

Soudha was pale. "I'm sorry, Madame Vorsoisson. If that was what happened, it was an accident. We intended him to live, I swear to you."

Ekaterin let her lips thin, and said nothing. Sitting up, with her legs swung out to the deck, she was able to get a less dizzying view of the loading bay. It was some thirty meters across and twenty deep, strongly lit, with catwalks and looping power lines running across the ceiling, and a glass-walled control booth on the opposite side from the broad entry ramp down which they'd come. Equipment lay scattered here and there around a huge object dominating the center of the chamber. Its main part seemed to consist of a wriggly trumpet-shaped cone made of some dark, polished substance—metal? glass?—resting in heavily padded clamps on a grounded float cradle. A lot of power connections slotted in at its narrow end. The mouth of the bell was more than twice as tall as Ekaterin. Was this the "secret weapon" Lord Vorkosigan had posited?

And *how* had they ever got it, and themselves, past the ImpSec manhunt? ImpSec was surely checking every shuttle that left the planetary surface—now, Ekaterin realized. This thing could have been transported weeks ago, before the hunt even started. And ImpSec was probably concentrating its attention on jumpships and their passengers, not on freight tugs trapped in local space. Soudha's conspirators had had years to develop their false ID. They acted as though they owned this place—maybe they did.

Foscol spoke to Ekaterin's fraught silence, almost as tight-lipped as Ekaterin herself. "We are not murderers. Not like you Barrayarans."

"I've never killed anyone in my life. For not-murderers, your body count is getting impressive," Ekaterin shot back. "I don't know what happened to Radovas and Trogir, but what about the six poor people on the soletta crew, and that ore freighter pilot—and Tien. That's eight at least, maybe ten." *Maybe twelve, if I don't watch my step.*

"I was a student at Solstice University during the Revolt," Foscol snarled, clearly very rattled by the news about Tien. "I saw friends and classmates shot in the streets, during the riots. I remember the out-gassing of the Green Park Dome. Don't you dare—a Barrayaran!—sit there and make mouth at me about murder."

"I was five years old at the time of the Komarr Revolt," said Ekaterin wearily. "What do you think I ought to have done about it, eh?"

"If you want to go back in history," the Professora put in dryly, "you Komarrans were the people who let the Cetagandans in on us. Five million Barrayarans died before the first Komarran ever did. Crying for your past dead is a piece of one-downsmanship a Komarran cannot win."

"That was longer ago," said Foscol a little desperately.

"Ah. I see. So the difference between a criminal and a hero is the *order* in which their vile crimes are committed," said the Professora, in a voice dripping false cordiality. "And justice comes with a sell-by date. In that case, you'd better hurry. You wouldn't want your heroism to spoil."

Foscol drew herself up. "We aren't planning to kill anyone. All of us here saw the futility of *that* kind of heroics twenty-five years ago."

"Things don't seem to be running exactly according to plan, then, do they?" murmured Ekaterin, rubbing her face. It was becoming less numb. She wished she could say the same for her wits. "I notice you don't deny being thieves."

"Just getting some of our own back," glinted Foscol.

"The money poured into Komarran terraforming doesn't do Barrayar any direct good. You were stealing from your own grandchildren."

"What we took, we took to make an investment for Komarr that will pay back incalculable benefit to our future generations," Foscol returned.

Had Ekaterin's words stung her? Maybe. Soudha looked as though he was thinking furiously, eyeing the two Barrayaran women. *Keep them arguing,* Ekaterin thought. People couldn't argue and think at the same time, or at least, a lot of people she'd met seemed to have that trouble. If she could keep them talking while her body recovered a little more from the stun, she could . . . what? Her eye fell on a fire and emergency alarm at the base of the entry ramp, maybe ten steps away. Alarm, false alarm, the attention of irate authorities drawn to Southport Transport . . . Could Arozzi stun her again in less than ten steps? She leaned back against her aunt's legs, trying to look very limp, and let one hand curl around the Professora's ankle, as if for comfort. The novel device loomed silently and mysteriously in the center of the chamber.

"So what are you planning to do," Ekaterin said sarcastically, "shut down the wormhole jump and cut us off? Or are you going to make—" Her voice died as the shocked silence her words had created penetrated. She stared around at the three Komarrans, staring at her in horror. In a suddenly smaller voice she said, "You can't do that. Can you?"

There was a military maneuver for rendering a wormhole temporarily impassable, which involved sacrificing a ship—and its pilot—at a mid-jump node. But the disruption damped out in a short time. Wormholes opened and closed, yes, but they were astrographic features like stars, involving time scales and energies beyond the present human capacity to control. "You can't do that," Ekaterin said more firmly. "Whatever disruption you create, sooner or later it will become passable again, and then you'll be in twice as much trouble as before." Unless Soudha's conspiracy was just the tip of an iceberg, with some huge coordinated plan behind it for all of Komarr to rise against Barrayaran rule in a new Komarr Revolt. More war, more blood under glass—the domes of Komarr might give her claustrophobia, but the thought of her Komarran neighbors going down to destruction in yet another round of this endless struggle made her sick to her stomach. The revolt had done vile things to Barrayarans, too. If new hostilities were ignited and went on long enough, Nikki would come of an age to be sucked into them. . . . "You can't hold it closed. You can't hold out here. You have no defenses."

"We can, and we will," said Soudha firmly.

Foscol's brown eyes shone. "We're going to close the wormhole *permanently*. We'll get rid of Barrayar forever, without firing a shot. A completely bloodless revolution, and there will be nothing they can do about it."

"An engineer's revolution," said Soudha, and a ghost of a smile curved his lips.

Ekaterin's heart hammered, and the echoing loading bay seemed to tilt. She swallowed, and spoke with effort: "You're planning to shut the wormhole to Barrayar with the Butcher of Komarr and three-fourths of Barrayar's space-based military forces on *this side*, and you actually think you're going to get a *bloodless* revolution? And what about all the people on Sergyar? You are idiots!"

"The original plan," said Soudha tightly, "was to strike at the time of the Emperor's wedding, when the Butcher of Komarr and three-fourths of the space forces would have been safely in Barrayar orbit."

"Along with a lot of innocent galactic diplomats. And not a few Komarrans!"

"I cannot think of a better fate for all the top collaborators," said Foscol, "than to be locked in with their lovely Barrayaran friends. The Old Vor lords are always saying how much better they had it back in their Time of Isolation. We're just giving them their wish."

Ekaterin squeezed the Professora's ankle and climbed slowly to her feet. Upright, she swayed, wishing her unbalance really were artistic fakery to put the Komarrans off-guard. She spoke with deadly venom. "In the Time of Isolation, I would have been dead at forty. In the Time of Isolation, it would have been my job to cut my mutant infants' throats, while my female relatives watched. I guarantee at least half the population of Barrayar does not agree with the Old Vor lords, including most of the Old Vor ladies. And you would condemn us all to go back to that, and you dare to call it bloodless!"

"Then count yourself lucky you're on the Komarran side," said Soudha dryly. "Come on, folks, we have work to do, and less time than ever to do it. Starting from now, all sleep shifts are canceled. Lena, go wake up Cappell. And we have to figure out how to lock these ladies down safely out of the way for a while."

The Komarrans were no longer waiting for the Emperor's wedding to provide their ideal tactical moment, it appeared. *How close* were they to putting their device into action? Close enough, it appeared, that even the arrival of two unwanted hostages wasn't enough to divert them.

Aunt Vorthys was trying to sit up straighter; Arozzi's eye had returned to the boxes of cooling food at his feet. Now.

Ekaterin launched herself forward, barreling into Arozzi and dashing onward. Arozzi swung around after her, but was temporarily distracted by a blue boot, thrown with surprising accuracy if limited strength by Aunt Vorthys, which bounced off the side of his head. Soudha and Foscol both began sprinting after her, but Ekaterin made it to the alarm and yanked down the lever hard, hanging on it as Arozzi's wavering stun beam found her. It hurt more, this time. Her hands spasmed open, and she fell. The first beat of the klaxon smote her ears before the shock and blackness took her away again.

Ekaterin opened her eyes to see her aunt's face, sideways. She realized she was lying with her head on the Professora's lap. She blinked and tried to lick her lips. Her body was all pins and needles and deep aches. A wave of nausea wrenched her stomach, and she struggled to lean sideways. A couple of spasms did not result in vomiting, however, and after a muffled belch, she rolled back. "Are we rescued?" she mumbled. They did not look rescued to her. They appeared to be sitting on the floor of a tiny lavatory, chilly and hard.

"No," said the Professora in a tone of disgust. Her face was tense and pale, with red bruises showing in the soft skin of her face and neck. Her hair was half down, straggling over her brow. "They gagged me, and dragged us both over behind that thing. The station squad burst in all right, but Soudha made all sorts of fast-talk apologies. He claimed it was an accident when Arozzi stumbled into the wall, and agreed to pay some enormous fine or another for turning in false alarms. I tried to make a noise, but it didn't do any good. Then they locked us in here."

"Oh," said Ekaterin. "Drat." Oversocialized, maybe, but stronger words seemed just as inadequate.

"Just so, dear. It was a good try, though. For a moment, I thought it would work, and so did your Komarrans. They were very upset."

"It will make the next try harder."

"Very likely," agreed her aunt. "We must think carefully what it ought to be. I don't think we can count on a third chance. Brutality does not seem to come naturally to them, but they do act very stressed. I don't believe those are safe people, just now, for all that they know you. When do you think we will be missed?"

"Not very soon," said Ekaterin regretfully. "I sent a message to Uncle Vorthys when I first got in to the station hostel. He may not expect another till we fail to get off the ferry tomorrow night."

"Something will happen then," said the Professora. Her tone of quiet confidence was undercut when she added more faintly, "Surely."

Yes, but what will happen between now and then? "Yes," Ekaterin echoed. She stared around the locked lavatory. "Surely."

CHAPTER EIGHTEEN

Professor Vorthys's requested experts were due to arrive at the Serifosa shuttleport at nearly the same early hour as Ekaterin departed for her connection with the jump station ferry, so Miles managed to invite himself along on what would otherwise have been a family farewell. Ekaterin did not discuss last night's visit from Venier with her uncle; Miles had no opportunity to urge her, *Don't accept any marriage proposals from strangers while you're out there.* The Professor loaded her with verbal messages for his wife, and got a goodbye hug. Miles stood with his hands shoved in his pockets, and nodded a cordial safe-journey to her.

What Miles thought of as the *Boffin Express*, a commercial morning flight from Solstice, landed a short time later. The five-space expert, Dr. Riva, turned out to be a thin, intense, olive-skinned woman of about fifty, with bright black eyes and a quick smile. A stout, sandy young man she had in tow whom Miles first pegged as an undergraduate student was revealed as a mathematics professor colleague, Dr. Yuell.

A high-powered ImpSec aircar waited to whisk them directly out to the Waste Heat experiment station. When they arrived, the Professor led them all upstairs to his nest, which seemed to have acquired more comconsoles, stacks of flimsies, and tables littered with machine parts overnight. To everyone's discomfort, but not to Miles's surprise, ImpSec Major D'Emorie took formal recorded oaths of loyalty and secrecy from the two Komarran consultants. Miles thought the loyalty oath was redundant, since neither academic could have held their current posts without having taken one previously. As for the secrecy oath . . . Miles wondered if either of the Komarrans had noticed yet that they had no way of leaving the experiment station except by ImpSec transport.

The five of them all then sat down to a lecture conducted by Lord Auditor Vorthys, which seemed halfway between a military briefing and an academic seminar, with a tendency to drift toward the latter. Miles wasn't sure if D'Emorie was there as participant or observer, but then, Miles didn't have much to say either, except to confirm one or two points about the autopsies when he was cued by Vorthys. Miles wondered again whether he might be more useful elsewhere, such as out with the field agents; he could hardly be less useful here, he realized glumly as the mathematical references began flying over his head. *When you folks convert all that to the pretty colored shapes on the comconsole, show me the picture. I like my storybooks to have pictures in them.* Perhaps he ought to go back to school for two or three years himself, and brush up. He consoled himself with the reflection that it was seldom he found himself in company who made him feel this stupid. It was probably good for his soul.

"The power that's fed into the—I suppose we can call it the horn—of the Necklin field generator is pulsed, definitely pulsed," Vorthys told the Komarrans. "Highly directional, rapid, and adjustable—I almost want to say, tunable."

"That's so very odd," said Dr. Riva. "Jumpship rods have a steady power—in fact, keeping unwanted fluctuations out of the power is a major design concern. Let's try some simulations with the various hypotheses . . ."

Miles woke up, and bent closer, as the assorted theories began to take visible form as three-dimensional vector maps above the vid-plate. Professor Vorthys provided some limiting parameters based on the projected nature of the power supply. The boffins did indeed produce some pretty pictures, but except for aesthetic considerations involving color contrasts, Miles didn't see what was to choose among them.

"What happens if somebody stands in front of the directional five-space pulses from that thing?" he asked at last. "At various distances, say. Or runs an ore freighter in front of it."

"Not much," said Riva, staring at the whirls and lines with an intensity at least equal to Miles's. "I'm not sure it would be good for you on the cellular level to be that close to any power generator of this magnitude, but it is, after all, a *five-space* field pulse. Any three-space effects would be due to some defocus on the fringe, and doubtless take the energy form of gravitational waves. Artificial gravity is a five-space/three-space interface phenomenon, as is your military gravitic imploder lance."

D'Emorie twitched slightly, but trying to keep a five-space physicist from knowing about the principles of the imploder lance was an exercise in futility right up there with trying to keep weather secret from a farmer. The best the military could hope for was to keep the engineering details under wraps for a time.

"Could it be, I don't know . . . that we're looking at *half* the weapon?"

Riva shrugged, but looked interested rather than scornful, so Miles hoped it wasn't a stupid question. "Have you determined if it is meant to be a weapon at all?" she said.

"We've got some very dead people to account for," Miles pointed out.

"That, alas, does not necessarily require a weapon." Professor Vorthys sighed. "Carelessness, stupidity, haste, and ignorance are quite as powerfully destructive of forces as homicidal intent. Though I must confess a special distaste for intent. It seems so unnecessarily redundant. It's . . . *anti*-engineering."

Dr. Riva smiled.

"Now," said Vorthys, "what I want to know is what happens if you aim this device *at* a wormhole, or, possibly, activate it while jumping *through* a wormhole. One would in that case also have to take into account effects due to the Necklin field it was traveling inside."

"Hmm . . ." said Riva. She and the sandy-haired youth went into close math-gibberish-mode, punctuated by some reprogramming of the simulation console. The first colorful display was rejected by them both with the muttered comment, "*That's not right.* . . ." A couple more went by. Riva sat back at last, and ran her hands through her short curls. "Any chance of taking this home to sleep on overnight?"

"Ah," said Lord Auditor Vorthys. "I'm afraid I was unclear to you over the comconsole last night. This is something in the nature of a crash program, here. We have reason to suspect time could be of the essence. We're all here for the duration, till we figure this out. No data leave this building."

"What, no dinner at the Top of the Dome in Serifosa?" said Yuell, sounding disappointed.

"Not tonight," Vorthys apologized. "Unless someone gets really inspired. Food and bedding will be supplied by the Emperor."

Riva glanced around the room, and by implication the facility. "Is this going to be the ImpSec Budget Hostel again? Bedrolls and ready-meals?"

The Professor smiled wryly. "I'm afraid so."

"I should have remembered that part from the last time. . . . Well, it's motivation of a sort, I suppose. Yuell, that's enough of this comconsole for now. Something's not right. I need to pace."

"The corridor is at your disposal," Professor Vorthys told her cordially. "Did you bring your walking shoes?"

"Certainly. I did remember *that* from our last date." She stuck out her legs, displaying comfortable thick-soled shoes, and rose to go off to the hallway. She began walking rapidly up and down, murmuring to herself from time to time.

"Riva claims to think better while walking," Vorthys explained to Miles. "Her theory is that it pumps the blood up to her brain. My theory is that since no one can keep up with her, it cuts down on the distracting interruptions."

A kindred spirit, by God. "Can I watch?"

"Yes, but please don't talk to her. Unless she talks to you, of course."

Both Vorthys and Yuell returned to fooling with their comconsoles. The Professor appeared to be trying to refine his hypothetical design for the missing power-supply system for the novel device. Miles wasn't sure but what Yuell was playing some sort of mathematical vid game. Miles leaned back in his station chair, stared out the window, and addressed his imagination to the question, *If I were a Komarran conspirator with ImpSec on my tail and a novel device the size of a couple of elephants, where would I hide it?* Not in his luggage, for damn sure. He scratched out ideas on a flimsy, and drew rejecting lines through most of them. D'Emorie studied the Professor's work and reran some of the earlier simulations.

After about three-quarters of an hour, Miles became aware that the echo of soft rapid footsteps from the corridor had ceased. He rose, and went and poked his head out the door. Dr. Riva was seated on a window ledge at the end of the corridor, gazing pensively out over the Komarran landscape. It fell away toward the stream, here, and was much less bleak than the usual scene, being liberally colonized by Earth green. Miles ventured to approach her.

She looked up at him with her quick smile as he neared, which he returned. He hitched his hip over the low ledge, and followed her gaze out the sealed window, then turned to study her profile. "So," he said at last. "What are you thinking?"

Her lips twisted wryly. "I'm thinking . . . that I don't believe in perpetual motion."

"Ah." Well, if it had been easy, or even just moderately difficult, the Professor would not have called for reinforcements, Miles reflected. "Hm."

She turned her gaze from the scenery to him, and said after a moment, "So, you're really the son of the Butcher?"

"I'm the son of Aral Vorkosigan," he replied steadily. "Yes." Her version of the perpetual question was neither the accidental social blunder of Tien, nor the deliberate provocation of Venier. It seemed something more . . . scientific. What was she testing for?

"The private life of men of power isn't what we expect, sometimes."

He jerked up his chin. "People have some very odd illusions about power. Mostly it consists of finding a parade and nipping over to place yourself at the head of the band. Just as eloquence consists of persuading people of things they desperately want to believe. Demagoguery, I suppose, is eloquence sliding to some least moral energy level." He smiled bleakly at his boot. "Pushing people uphill is one hell of a lot harder. You can break your heart, trying that." Literally, but he saw no point in discussing the Butcher's medical history with her.

"I was given to understand that power politics had chewed you up."

Surely she could not see scars through his gray suit. "Oh," Miles shrugged, "the prenatal damage was just the prologue. The rest I did to myself."

"If you could go back in time and change things, would you?"

"Prevent the soltoxin attack on my pregnant mother? If I could only pick one event to change . . . maybe not."

"What, because you wouldn't want to risk missing an Auditorship at thirty?" Her tone was only faintly mocking, softened by her wry smile. What the devil had Vorthys told her about him, anyway? She was highly aware, though, of the power of an Emperor's Voice.

"I almost arrived at thirty in a coffin, a couple of times. An Auditorship was never an ambition of mine. That appointment was a caprice of Gregor's. I wanted to be an admiral. It's not that." He paused, and drew in breath, and let it out slowly. "I've made a lot of grievous mistakes in my life, getting here, but . . . I wouldn't trade my journey now. I'd be afraid of making myself smaller."

She cocked her head, measuring his dwarfishness, not missing his meaning. "That's as fair a definition of satisfaction as any I've ever heard."

He shrugged. "Or loss of nerve." Dammit, he'd come out here to pick *her* brain. "So what do you think of the novel device?"

She grimaced, and rubbed her hands slowly, palm to palm. "Unless you want to posit that it was invented for the purpose of giving headaches to physicists, I think . . . it's time to break for lunch."

Miles grinned. "Lunch, we can supply."

Lunch, as threatened, was indeed military-issue ready-meals, though of the highest grade. They all sat around one of the tables in the long room, pushed aside chunks of equipment to make space, and tore off the wrappers from the self-heating trays. The Komarrans eyed their food dubiously; Miles explained how it could have been much worse, getting a giggle from Riva. The conversation became general, touching on husbands and wives and children and tenure and an exchange of scurrilous anecdotes about the fecklessness of former colleagues. D'Emorie had a couple of good ones about early ImpSec cases. Miles was tempted to top them with a few about his cousin Ivan, but nobly refrained, though he did explain how he'd once sunk himself and his personal vehicle in several meters of arctic mud. This led to the subject of the progress of Komarran terraforming, and so by degrees back to work. Riva, Miles noticed, grew quieter and quieter.

She maintained her silence as they all took to the comconsoles again after lunch. She did not resume her pacing. Miles watched her covertly, then less covertly. She reran several simulations, but did not play with further alterations. Miles knew damn well one couldn't hurry insight. This kind of problem-solving was a lot more like fishing than like hunting: waiting patiently and, to a degree, helplessly, for things to rise up out of the depths of the mind.

He thought about the last time he'd been fishing.

He considered Riva's age. She'd been in her teens at the time of the Barrayaran conquest of Komarr. In her twenties at the time of the Revolt. She'd survived, she'd endured, she'd cooperated; her years under Imperial rule had been good, including an obviously successful life of the mind, and a single marriage. She'd compared children with Vorthys, and spoken of an eldest daughter's upcoming wedding. No Komarran terrorist, she.

If you could go back in time and change things . . .

The only moment in time you could change things was the elusive *now*, which slipped through your fingers as fast as you could think about it. He wondered if she was thinking about that right now, too. Now.

Now, the Professora's ship from Barrayar would be getting ready for its final wormhole jump. Now, Ekaterin's ferry would be approaching the jump-point station. Now, Soudha and his crew of earnest techs would be doing . . . what? Where? Now, he was sitting in a room on Komarr watching a quietly brilliant woman who had stopped thinking.

He rose, and went to touch Major D'Emorie on his green-uniformed shoulder. "Major, can I have a word with you outside."

Surprised, D'Emorie shut down his comconsole, where he'd been checking out some question about available power transformers Vorthys had put to him. He followed Miles into the hall and down the corridor.

"Major, do you have a fast-penta interrogation kit available?"

D'Emorie's brows rose. "I can check, my lord."

"Do so. Get one and bring it to me, please."

"Yes, my lord."

D'Emorie went off. Miles lingered by the window. It was twenty minutes before D'Emorie returned, but he had the familiar case in his hand.

Miles took it. "Thank you. Now I would like you to take Dr. Yuell for a walk. Discreetly. I'll let you know when you can come back in."

"My lord . . . if it's a matter for fast-penta, I'm sure ImpSec would want me to observe."

"I know what ImpSec wants. You may be assured, I will tell them what they need to know, afterward." Turnabout, hah, for all those briefings with vital pieces missing Lieutenant Vorkosigan had once endured . . . life was good, sometimes. Miles smiled a little sourly; D'Emorie, intelligently, veered off.

"Yes, my Lord Auditor."

Miles stood aside for D'Emorie to exit with Dr. Yuell. When he entered the long room, he locked the door after himself. Both Professor Vorthys and Dr. Riva looked up at him in puzzlement.

"What's that for?" Dr. Riva asked, as he set the case on the table and opened it.

"Dr. Riva, I request and require a somewhat franker

conversation with you than the one we had earlier." He held up the hypospray and calibrated the dosage for her estimated body mass. Allergy check? He didn't think he needed it, but it was standard operating procedure; if he didn't have to guess, he didn't have to guess wrong. He tore off a test-dot from the coiled strip of them and walked over to her station chair. She was too startled to resist at first when he took her hand, turned it over, and pressed the tester to the inside of her wrist, but she jerked back her arm at the prickle. He let it go.

"Miles," said Professor Vorthys in an agitated voice, "what is this? You can't fast-penta . . . Dr. Riva is my invited guest!"

That wording was one step away from the sort of Vor challenge that used to result in duels, in the bad old days. Miles took a deep breath. "My Lord Auditor. Dr. Riva. I have made two serious errors of judgment on this case so far. If I'd avoided either of them, your nephew-in-law would still be alive, we'd have nailed Soudha before he got away with all his equipment, and we would not now all be sitting at the bottom of a deep tactical hole playing with jigsaw puzzles. They were both at heart the same error. The first day we toured the Terraforming Project, I did not insist on Tien landing the aircar here, though I wanted to see the place. And on the second night, I did not insist on a fast-penta interrogation of Madame Radovas, though I wanted to. You're the failure analyst, Professor; am I wrong?"

"No . . . But you could not have known, Miles!"

"Oh, but I could have known. That's the whole point. But I didn't choose to do what was necessary, because I did not want to appear to use or abuse my Auditorial power in an offensive way. Especially not on here on Komarr, where everyone is watching me, the son of the Butcher, to see what I'll do. Besides, I spent a career fighting the powers-that-be. Now I am them. Naturally, I was a little confused."

Riva's hand was to her mouth; there was no hive or red streak on the inside of her arm. Well and good. Miles returned to the table and picked up the hypospray.

"Lord Vorkosigan, I do not consent to this!" said Riva stiffly as he approached her.

"Dr. Riva, I did not ask you to." His left hand guarded his right as in knife-play; the hypospray darted in to touch her neck even as she turned and began to rise from her chair. "It would be too cruel a dilemma." She sank back, glaring at him. Angry, but not desperate; she was divided in her own mind, then, which had doubtless saved them both the embarrassment of him chasing her around the room. Even at her age and dignity she could probably outrun him if she were truly determined to do so.

"Miles," said the Professor dangerously, "it may be your Auditorial privilege, but you had better be able to justify this."

"Hardly a privilege. Only my duty." He stared into Riva's eyes as her pupils dilated and she sank back limply in her chair. He didn't bother with the standard opening litany of neutral questions while waiting for the drug to cut in, but merely watched her lips. Their thin tension slowly softened to the stereotypical fast-penta smile. Her eyes remained more focused than those of the usual subject; he bet she could make this a lengthy and circuitous interrogation, if she chose. He'd do his best to cut that circuit as short as possible. The shortest way across a hostile District was around three sides.

"This was a really interesting five-space problem that Professor Vorthys set you," Miles observed to her. "Sort of a privilege to be brought in on it."

"Oh, yes," she agreed cordially. She smiled, frowned, her hands twitched, then her smile settled in more securely.

"Could be prizes and academic preferment, when it's all sorted out at last."

"Oh, better than that," she assured him. "New physics only come along once in a lifetime, and usually you're too young or too old."

"Strange, I've heard military careerists make the same complaint. But won't Soudha get the credit?"

"I doubt it was Soudha who thought of it. I'd bet it was the mathematician, Cappell, or maybe poor Dr. Radovas. It should be named after Radovas. He died for it, I suspect."

"I don't want anybody else to die for it."

"Oh, no," she agreed earnestly.

"What did you say it was, again, Professor Riva?" Miles did his best to pitch his voice like a bewildered undergraduate's. "I didn't understand."

"The wormhole collapsing technique. There ought to be a better name for it. I wonder if your Dr. Soudha calls it something shorter."

Lord Auditor Vorthys, who'd been watching with slit-eyed disapproval, sat slowly upright, his eyes widening, his lips moving.

The last time Miles had felt his stomach behave like this, he'd been on a combat drop from low orbit. *Wormhole collapsing technique? Does this mean what I think it does?*

"Wormhole collapsing technique," he repeated blandly, in his best fast-penta interrogator style. "Wormholes collapse, but

I didn't think anything people could do could cause them to. Wouldn't it take an awful lot of power?"

"They seem to have found a way around that. Resonance, five-space resonance. Amplitude augmentation, you see. Shut it down forever. Don't think it would work in reverse, though. Can't be anti-entropic."

Miles glanced at Vorthys. The words obviously meant something to *him*. Good.

Dr. Riva waved her hands dreamily in front of her. "Higher and higher and higher and—boop!" She giggled. It was a very fast-penta'ish sort of giggle, the disturbing sort which suggested that on some other level, in her drug-scrambled brain, she was not giggling at all. Maybe she was screaming. As Miles was. . . . "Except," she added, "that there's something very wrong somewhere."

No lie. He walked over and picked up the hypospray of antagonist, and glanced up at Vorthys. "Anything you want to add while she's still under? Or is it time to go back to normal mode?"

Vorthys still had an abstracted, inward look, his mind obviously ratcheting over everything he'd learned during the investigation in light of this new, revolutionary idea. He glanced up and over at the goofily grinning Riva. "I think we need all our wits about us." His brows drew down in something like pain. "One sees, of course, why she hesitated to confide her theory to us. In case it *is* right . . ."

Miles walked over to Riva with the second hypospray. "This is the fast-penta antagonist. It will neutralize the drug in your system in less than a minute."

To his astonishment, she threw up a restraining hand. "Wait. I had it. I could almost see it, in my mind . . . like a vid projection . . . energy transfers, flowing . . . field reservoir . . . wait."

She closed her eyes and leaned her head back; her feet tapped gently and rhythmically on the floor. Her smile came and went, came and went. Her eyes popped open at last, and she stared briefly and intently at Vorthys. "The keyword," she intoned, "is *elastic recoil*. Remember it." She glanced at Miles and held out a languid arm. "You may proceed, my lord." She giggled again.

He applied the hypospray over the blue vein inside her proffered elbow; it hissed briefly. He gave her an odd little half-bow, and stepped back, and waited. Her loose limbs tightened; she buried her face in her hands.

After about a minute, she looked up again, blinking. "What did I just say?" she asked Vorthys.

"Elastic recoil," he repeated, watching her intently. "What does it mean?"

She was silent a moment, staring at her feet. "It means . . . I compromised myself for nothing." Her lips thinned bitterly. "Soudha's device doesn't work. Or at any rate, it doesn't work to collapse a wormhole." She sat up, and shook herself out, stretching, the sense of her body doubtless coming back to her as the last of the antagonist chased through her system. "I thought that stuff would make me sick."

"Reactions vary wildly from subject to subject," said Miles. Indeed, he'd never seen one quite like *that* before. "A woman we interrogated the other day said she found it very restful."

"It had the *strangest* effect on my internal visualizations." She stared at the hypospray with speculative respect. "I may try it on purpose someday."

I want to be there if you do. Miles had a sudden exciting vision of using the drug to augment his own insights—instant brains!—then remembered to his extreme disappointment that fast-penta didn't work like that on him.

Riva glanced at Miles. "If I ever get out of a Barrayaran prison. Am I under arrest now?"

Miles chewed his lip. "What for?"

"Isn't violating loyalty and security oaths treason?"

"You haven't violated any security oath. Yet. As for the other . . . when two Imperial Auditors say they didn't see something, it can become remarkably invisible."

Vorthys smiled suddenly.

"I thought you were sworn to tell the truth, Lord Auditor."

"Only to Gregor. What we tell the rest of the universe is negotiable. We just don't advertise the fact."

"That, alas, is true." Vorthys sighed.

"How will you explain the missing drug doses to ImpSec?"

"One, I am an Imperial Auditor, I don't have to explain anything to anyone. Least of all ImpSec. Two, we used it experimentally to enhance scientific insight. Which I gather is the truth, so I return to Go *and* collect my tokens."

Her lips twisted up in a genuine, if wryly baffled, smile. "I see. I think."

"In short, this never happened, you are not under arrest, and we have work to do. For my curiosity, though, before I call our junior colleagues back in—can you give me a quick synopsis of your chain of reasoning? In nonmathematical terms, please."

"It's only *in* nonmathematical terms so far. If I can't run some real numbers in under this—well, I'll just have to dismiss it as an interesting hallucination."

"You were convinced enough to dry up on us."

"I was stunned. Not so much convinced as breathless."

"With hope?"

"With . . . I don't quite know." She shook her head. "I may yet be proved wrong, and it wouldn't be the first time. But you are familiar, I assume, with examples of positive feedback loops in resonant phenomena—sound, for example?"

"Feedback squeals, yes."

"Or a pure note that breaks a wineglass. And in structures— you know why soldiers must break step when marching across a bridge? So that the resonance of their steps doesn't collapse the structure?"

Miles grinned. "I actually saw that happen once. It involved a squad of Imperial Junior Scouts, a flag ceremony, a wooden footbridge, and my cousin Ivan. Dumped twenty really obnoxious teenage boys into a creek." He added aside to the Professor, "They wouldn't let me march with my squad that evening because, they said, my height would mess up their symmetry. So I was watching from the back benches. It was glorious. I think I was about thirteen, but I'll treasure the memory forever."

"Did you see it coming, or did it take you by surprise?" asked the Professor curiously.

"I saw it coming, though not, I admit, very far in advance."

"Hm."

Riva's brows twitched; she licked her lips and began. "Wormholes resonate in five-space. Very slightly, and at a very high rate. I *believe* that the function of Soudha's device is to emit a five-space energy pulse precisely tuned to the natural frequency of a wormhole. The pulse's power is low, compared to the latent energies involved in the wormhole's structure, but if properly tuned it might—no, *would*, gradually build up the amplitude of the wormhole's resonance until it exceeded its phase boundaries and collapsed. Or rather, I think Soudha's group thought it must collapse. What I think actually happened is more complex."

"Elastic recoil?" Vorthys prodded hopefully.

"In a sense. What *I* think happened is that the pulse amplified the resonance energies until the phase boundaries recoiled, and the energy was abruptly returned to three-space in the form of a directed gravitational wave."

"Good God," said Miles. "Do you mean to say Soudha's found a way to turn an entire wormhole into a giant imploder lance?"

"Mmmm . . ." said Riva. "Er . . . maybe. What I don't know is if that was what he *meant* to do. The first theory made more political sense to me . . . as a Komarran. It quite seduced me. I wonder if they were seduced as well? If he *did* mean the wormhole to act as a sort of imploder lance, I don't see that he's found a way to aim it. I think the gravitational pulse was returned back along the initial path. I don't know if Radovas committed suicide, but I'm very much afraid he may have shot himself."

"My word," breathed Vorthys. "And the ore ship—"

"If their test platform was indeed aboard the soletta array, the involvement of the ore ship was sheer bad luck. Bad timing. It blundered into the gravitational pulse and was ripped apart, then was funneled toward and struck the soletta array and thoroughly confused the issue. If the device was aboard the ore ship—well, same result."

"Including the confusion," said Vorthys ruefully.

"But . . . but there's still something very wrong. You have presumably calculated most of the energy vectors involved in the soletta accident?

"Over and over."

"You trust the numbers you gave me?"

"Yes."

"And you've put limits on what energies the device can have transferred, over various lengths of time."

"There are some fairly strict and obvious engineering limits to its potential peak power output," agreed Vorthys. "What we don't know is how long they could run it."

"Well," the five-space physicist took a deep breath, "unless they were running it for weeks, and Radovas and Trogir were seen downside much later than that, I think you've got more energy out of the wormhole than went into it."

"From where?"

"Presumably from the wormhole's deep structure. *Somehow.* Unless you want to posit that Soudha has invented perpetual motion as well, which is against my religion."

Vorthys was looking wildly excited. "This is wonderful! Miles, call Yuell. Call D'Emorie. We *must* check those numbers."

When D'Emorie returned with Yuell, all the tech folk were too entranced with the breakthrough regarding the novel device to broach any embarrassing questions about where the fast-penta had gone. D'Emorie would doubtless think to ask later; Miles would be bland and uninformative, he decided. Riva clearly didn't want to waste time and mental energy on anger when there was physics to be had, but if she decided to be pissed at him later, he would grovel as needed. For now, Miles sat back, watched, and listened, feeling that he understood perhaps one sentence in three.

So did Soudha now imagine that he possessed a wormhole collapser—or a giant imploder lance? He had stolen much of the technical data from the accident investigation; he had a lot of the same numbers Vorthys did, and the same amount of time to look them over. While simultaneously managing a complex evacuation of some dozen persons and several tons of equipment, Miles reminded himself. Soudha had been rather busy. Of course, *he* hadn't had to waste time reconstructing the plans of his device from scattered specs.

But the gravitational backlash from the test wormhole near the soletta array must have surprised Radovas—however briefly—and Soudha. The accident had stopped their research, brought Auditors down upon them, compelled their flight. It made no sense, none, to posit the destruction of the soletta as deliberate sabotage and suicide. If one wanted to blow up Barrayarans, there were much more inviting targets around. Such as the military stations guarding each wormhole exit from Komarr local space. As an imploder lance variant, the device wasn't going to make a very useful military weapon till they figured out how to aim it at someone besides themselves. Though if one could set it up in secret aboard a military station, turn it on, and flee before the blast occurred . . .

Had Soudha figured out what had happened yet? He had data, yes, but his five-space man was dead. Arozzi was only a junior engineer, and Cappell the math man did not show any special brilliance in his academic record. Vorthys had been able to tap the top five-space expert on the planet, not to mention Yuell the Wonderboy, who, Miles noted, was just at this moment arguing math with Vorthys and winning. Given the data and enough time, Radovas might have made the same conceptual breakthrough as Riva, but Soudha in his flight was not equipped to. Unless he'd found a replacement for Radovas . . . Miles made a note to tell ImpSec to check for the disappearance of any other Komarran five-space experts in the last weeks.

Soudha's flight, Miles decided, had to be following one of three logic branches. Either they had abandoned all and fled, or they'd withdrawn to hide, painfully rebuild their safe base, and try again another day. *Or* they had moved up their timetable and elected to risk all on an early strike of some kind. Miles wondered if they'd put what should have been a technically-driven decision to a vote. They were Komarrans, after all, and apparently volunteers. Amateur conspirators, not that it was exactly a licensed trade. Option One didn't feel right, given what Miles had seen so far. Option Two seemed more likely, but gave ImpSec time enough to do their job. The Komarrans might have thought so too.

If you're going to worry, worry about Option Three. There was a lot to worry about, in Option Three. Panicked and desperate people were capable of very strange moves indeed; look at some of the incidents in his own career.

"Professor Vorthys. Dr. Riva." Miles had to repeat himself, more loudly, before they looked up. "So you aim this device at a wormhole, and switch it on, and it starts pumping in energy. At some point, it builds up to a break-point and bounces back at you. What happens if you turn it off before that point?"

"I am not certain," said Riva, "that that wasn't exactly what happened. The backlash may have been triggered by either exceeding the phase boundaries, or by Radovas turning off the pulse source. It is unclear if the phase-boundary deaugmentation is discontinous or not."

"So . . . once activated, the device may become in effect its own dead-man switch? Turning it off sets it off?"

"I'm not sure. It would be a good point to test."

From a suitable distance. "Well . . . if you figure it out, please let me know, eh? Carry on."

After a moment to either digest his question, or wait to see if he'd pop out with any other interruption, the conversation around the table returned to its original polyglot of English, mathematics, and engineering. Miles settled back, feeling anything but reassured.

If Soudha had perfected his device with an eye to using the wormholes as power sources to blow up the military stations that guarded them, as a surprise opening for a shooting war . . . the way to do it would be to blow up all six at once, coordinated with a Komarr-wide uprising on the scale of the ill-fated Komarr Revolt. Miles was not totally pleased with ImpSec's performance in this case so far, but Soudha's had been a small group, running close to the ground. The signs of a massive revolt brewing must be too widespread for even ImpSec to miss. Besides, the chief conspirators were all of an age to have been through that once. Anyone who'd experienced the debacle of the Komarr Revolt on the Komarr side had reason to mistrust their fellows almost as much as they mistrusted Barrayarans. The last people Soudha would want in on his plot were a bunch more Komarrans. And . . . they didn't have six devices. They'd had five, the fourth was destroyed, and the three earlier ones seemed to have been smaller-scale prototypes.

It was like having a gun with one bullet in it. You'd want to pick your target very carefully.

Suppose Soudha still imagined he possessed a wormhole-collapser, albeit one with a few bugs in the design. There were six active wormholes in Komarr local space, but Miles hadn't any doubt which one Soudha would go for.

The sole jump to Barrayar. *Cut us off at one stroke, yeah.* From a Komarran viewpoint *that* was a plot worth all of these five years of devotion, all the sweat and risk: closing Barrayar's only gate to the galactic wormhole nexus. A bloodless revolution, by God, sure to appeal to these tech types. They'd return Komarr to the good old days of its glory a century ago—and Barrayar to its bad old days, in a new Time of Isolation. Whether everyone, or indeed, anyone on either Komarr or Barrayar wanted to go there or not. Did the conspirators imagine they'd be permitted to *live*, once the truth was unraveled?

Probably not. But if Riva spoke straight, the process was not reversible; the wormhole, once collapsed, could not be reopened. The deed would be done, and no tears or prayers would undo it. Like an assassination. Soudha and his friends might imagine themselves as a new and more effective generation of Martyrs, content to be enshrined after death. They had seemed too practical, but who knew? One could be hypnotized by the hard choices in ways that had nothing to do with one's intelligence.

Yes. Miles now knew where the Komarrans were going, if they weren't there already. The civilian—or the military? No, the civilian transfer station which served the wormhole jump to Barrayar.

You just sent Ekaterin there. She's there now.

So was the Professora, and so were several thousand other innocent people, he reminded himself. He fought panic, to follow out his thread of thought to the end. Soudha might have a bolthole of some kind set up on the station, prepared perhaps months or years in advance. He would plan to set up his novel device, aim it at the wormhole, draw power from—where? If from the station, someone might notice. If they mounted it aboard a ship (and it had to have been on some kind of ship to get out there), they could draw ship's power. But traffic control and the Barrayaran military were unlikely to tolerate any ship hanging around the wormhole without a filed flight plan, from which it had better not deviate.

Ship, or station? He had insufficient data to decide. But if
Soudha had not seriously modified his device, the plot which
began with a bloodless plan to collapse the wormhole could
end in the bloody chaos of a major disaster to the transfer
station. Miles had seen space disasters on various scales. He
didn't want to ever see another.

Miles could imagine a dozen different scenarios from the
data they had in hand, but only this one gave him no time
or room to be wrong. *Go.* He reached for the secured
comconsole and punched up ImpSec Komarr HQ at Solstice.

"This is Lord Auditor Vorkosigan. Give me General Rathjens,
immediately. It's an emergency."

Vorthys looked up from the long table. "What?"

"I've just figured out that if there's any action coming up,
it's got to be at the transfer station by the Barrayar jump."

"But Miles—surely Soudha would not be so foolish as to
try again, after his initial disaster!"

"I don't trust Soudha in any way. Have you heard from
Ekaterin or your wife?"

"Yes, Ekaterin messaged when you were out getting your,
ah, supplies. She'd reached her hostel safely and was off to
meet the Professora."

"Did she leave a number?'

"Yes, it's on the comconsole—"

General Rathjen's face appeared above the vid-plate. "My
Lord Auditor?"

"General. I have new data suggesting our escaped Komarrans
are at or are heading for the Barrayar Transfer Station. I want
a max-penetration ImpSec search-sweep for them on the station and aboard any in-bound traffic, to commence as quickly
as possible. I want ImpSec courier transport for myself out
to there as fast as you can scramble it. I'll give you the details
once I'm en route. When all that's in motion, I want to send
a tight-beam personal message to, um—" he did a quick search
"—this number."

Rathjens's brows rose, but he said only, "Yes, my Lord Auditor. I'll be most interested in those details."

"Indeed you will. Thanks."

Rathjens's face vanished; in a few moments, the tight-beam
link blinked its go-ahead.

"Ekaterin," Miles spoke rapidly and with all his will into
the vid pickup, as if he might so speed the message. "Take
the Professora and get yourselves aboard the first outbound
transport you can find, any local space destination—Komarr
orbit, one of the other stations, anywhere. We'll arrange to

pick you both up later and get you home right and tight. Just get yourselves off the station, and go at once."

He hesitated over his closing; no, this was not the time or place to declare, *I love you*, no matter what dangers he imagined threatening her. By the time this message arrived, she might well be back in her hostel room, with the Professora listening over her shoulder. "Be careful. Vorkosigan out."

As Miles rose to go, Vorthys said doubtfully, "Do you think I should go with you?"

"No. I think you all should stay here and figure out what the hell happens when somebody tries to turn that infernal device off. And when you do, please tight-beam me the instructions."

Vorthys nodded. Miles gave the lot of them an ImpSec analyst's salute, which was a vague wave of the hand in the vicinity of one's forehead, turned, and strode for the door.

CHAPTER NINETEEN

Ekaterin watched morosely as the sonic toilet ate her shoes with scarcely a burp.

"It was worth a try, dear," said Aunt Vorthys, glancing at her expression.

"There are too many fail-safe systems on this space station," Ekaterin said. "This worked for *Nikki*, on the jumpship coming out here. What an uproar there was. The ship's steward was so upset with us."

"My grandchildren could make short work of this, I'll bet," agreed the Professora. "It's too bad we don't have a few nine-year-olds with us."

"Yes," sighed Ekaterin. *And no.* That Nikki was safely back on Komarr right now was a source of liberating joy in some secret level of her mind. But there ought to be some way to sabotage a sonic toilet that would light up a station tech's board and bring an investigation. How to turn a sonic toilet into a weapon was just not in Ekaterin's job training. *Vorkosigan* probably knew how, she reflected bitterly. Just like a man, to be underfoot in her life for days and then a quarter of a solar system away when she really needed him.

For the tenth time, she felt the walls, tried the door, inventoried their clothes. Practically the only flammable item in the room was the women's hair. Setting a fire in a room in which one was locked did not much recommend itself to Ekaterin's mind, though it was a possible last resort. She stuck her hands in the wall slot and turned them, letting the sonic cleaner loosen the dirt, and the UV light bathe away the germs, and the air fan, presumably, whisk their little corpses away. She drew her hands out again. The engineers might swear the system was more effective, but it never made her feel as fresh as an old-fashioned water wash. And how were you supposed to put a baby's bottom in the thing? She glowered at the sanitizer. "If we had any kind of a tool at all, we ought to be able to do *something* with this."

"I had my Vorfemme knife," said the Professora sadly. "It was my best enameled one."

"Had?"

"It was in my boot-sheath. The boot I threw, I believe."

"Oh."

"You don't carry yours, these days?"

"Not on Komarr. I was trying to be, I don't know, modern." Her lips twisted. "I do wonder about the cultural message in the Vorfemme knife. I mean, yes, it made you better armed than the peasants, but never as well-armed as the two-sword men. Were the Vor lords afraid of their wives getting the drop on them?"

"Remembering my grandmother, it's possible," said the Professora.

"Mm. And my Great-Aunt Vorvayne." Ekaterin sighed, and glanced worriedly at her present aunt.

The Professora was leaning on the wall with one hand supporting her, looking still very pale and shaky. "If you are done with the attempted sabotage, I think I would like to sit down again."

"Yes, of course. It was a stupid idea anyway."

The Professora sank gratefully onto the only seat in the tiny lavatory, and Ekaterin took her turn leaning on the wall. "I am so sorry I dragged you into this. If you hadn't been with me . . . One of us *must* get away."

"If you see a chance, Ekaterin, take it. Don't wait for me."

"That would still leave Soudha with a hostage."

"I don't think that's the most important issue, just now. Not if the Komarrans were telling the truth about what that great ugly thing out there does."

Ekaterin rubbed her toe over the smooth gray deck of the lav. In a quieter voice, she asked, "Do you suppose our own side would sacrifice us, if it came to a standoff?"

"For this? Yes," said the Professora. "Or at any rate . . . they certainly ought to. Do the Professor and Lord Auditor Vorkosigan and ImpSec *know* what the Komarrans have built?"

"No, not as of yesterday. That is, they knew Soudha had built something—I gather they had almost managed to reconstruct the plans."

"Then they *will* know," said the Professora firmly. And a little less firmly, "Eventually . . ."

"I hope they won't think we ought to sacrifice ourselves, like in the Tragedy of the Maiden of the Lake."

"She was actually sacrificed by her brother, as the tradition would have it," said the Professora. "I do wonder if it was quite so voluntary as he later claimed."

Ekaterin reflected dryly on the old Barrayaran legend. As the tale went, the town of Vorkosigan Surleau, on the Long Lake, had been besieged by the forces of Hazelbright. Loyal vassals of the absent Count, a Vor officer and his sister, had held out till the last. On the verge of the final assault, the Maiden of the Lake had offered up her pale throat to her brother's sword rather than fall to the ravages of the enemy troops. The very next morning, the siege was unexpectedly lifted by the subterfuge of her betrothed—one of their Auditor Vorkosigan's distant ancestors, come to think of it, the latterly famous General Count Selig of that name—who sent the enemy hurriedly marching away to meet the false rumor of another attack. But it was, of course, too late for the Maiden of the Lake. Much Barrayaran historical sympathy, in the form of plays and poems and songs, had been expended upon the subsequent grief of the two men; Ekaterin had memorized one of the shorter poems for a school recitation, in her childhood. "I've always wondered," said Ekaterin, "if the attack really had taken place the next day, and all the pillage and rape had proceeded on schedule, would they have said, 'Oh, that's all right, then'?"

"Probably," said Aunt Vorthys, her lips twitching.

After a time, Ekaterin remarked, "I want to go home. But I don't want to go back to Old Barrayar."

"No more do I, dear. It's wonderful and dramatic to read about. So nice to be able to read, don't you know."

"I know girls who pine for it. They like to play dress-up and pretend being Vor ladies of old, rescued from menace by romantic Vor youths. For some reason they never play *dying in childbirth*, or *vomiting your guts out from the red dysentery*, or *weaving till you go blind and crippled from arthritis and dye poisoning*, or *infanticide*. Well, they do die romantically of disease sometimes, but somehow it's always an illness that makes you interestingly pale and everyone sorry and doesn't involve losing bowel control."

"I've taught history for thirty years. One can't reach them all, though we try. Send them to my class, next time."

Ekaterin smiled grimly. "I'd love to."

Silence fell for a time, while Ekaterin stared at the opposite wall and her aunt leaned back with her eyes closed. Ekaterin watched her in growing worry. She glanced at the door, and said at last, "Do you suppose you could pretend to be much sicker than you really are?"

"Oh," said Aunt Vorthys, not opening her eyes, "that would not be at all difficult."

By which Ekaterin deduced that she was already pretending to be much less sick than she really was. The jump-nausea seemed to have hit her awfully hard, this time. Was that gray-faced fatigue really all due to travel-sickness? Stunner fire could be unexpectedly lethal for a weak heart—was there a reason besides bewilderment that her aunt had not tried to struggle or cry out under Arozzi's threats?

"So . . . how is your heart, these days?" Ekaterin asked diffidently.

Aunt Vorthys's eyes popped open. After a moment, she shrugged. "So-so, dear. I'm on the waiting list for a new one."

"I thought new organs were easy to grow, now."

"Yes, but surgical transplant teams are rather less so. My case isn't that urgent. After the problems a friend of mine had, I decided I'd rather wait for one of the more proven groups to have a slot available."

"I understand." Ekaterin hesitated. "I've been thinking. We can't do anything locked in here. If I can get anyone to come to the door, I thought we might try to feign you were dangerously sick, and get them to let us out. After that—who knows? It can't be worse than this. All you'd have to do is go limp and moan convincingly."

"I'm willing," said Aunt Vorthys.

"All right."

Ekaterin fell to pounding on the door as loudly as she could, and calling the Komarrans urgently by name. After about ten minutes of this, the lock clicked, the door slid back, and Madame Radovas peeked in from a slight distance. Arozzi stood behind her with his stunner in his hand.

"What?" she demanded.

"My aunt is ill," said Ekaterin. "She can't stop shivering, and her skin is getting clammy. I think she may be going into shock from the jump-sickness and her bad heart and all this stress. She has to have a warm place to lie down, and a hot drink, at least. Maybe a doctor."

"We can't get you a doctor right now." Madame Radovas peered worriedly past Ekaterin at the limp Professora. "We could arrange the other, I guess."

"Some of us wouldn't mind having the lav back," Arozzi muttered. "It's not so good, all of us having to parade up and down the corridor to the nearest public one."

"There's no other safe place to lock them up," said Madame Radovas to him.

"So, put them out in the middle of the room and keep an eye on them. Stick them back in here later. One's sick, the other has to take care of her, what can they do? It's no good if the old lady dies on us."

"I'll see what I can do," said Madame Radovas to Ekaterin, and closed the door again.

In a little while she came back, to escort the two Barrayaran women to a cot and a folding chair set up at the edge of the loading bay, as far as possible from any emergency alarm. Ekaterin and Madame Radovas supported the stumbling Professora to the cot, and helped her lie down, and covered her up. Leaving Arozzi to guard them, Madame Radovas went off and returned with a steaming mug of tea and set it down; Arozzi then turned the stunner over to her and returned to his work. Madame Radovas drew up another folding chair and sat down a few prudent meters away from her captives. Ekaterin supported her aunt's shoulders while she drank the tea, blinked gratefully, and sank back with a moan. Ekaterin made play of feeling the Professora's forehead, and rubbing her chill hands, and looking very concerned. She stroked the tousled gray hair, and stared covertly around the loading bay she'd merely glimpsed before.

The device still sat in its float cradle, but more power lines snaked across the floor to it now; Soudha was overseeing the attachment of one such cable to the awkward array of converters at the base of the horn. A man she did not recognize busied himself in the glass-walled control booth. At his gestures, Cappell drew careful chalk lines on the deck near the device. When he finished, he consulted with Soudha, and Soudha himself took the float cradle's remote control, stepped back, and with exquisite care set the cradle to lift, move forward till it almost touched the outer wall, and gently land again in precise alignment with the chalk marks. The horn was now aimed not quite square-on with the inner door of the large freight lock. Were they getting ready to load it aboard a ship, and take it out to point at the wormhole? Or could they use it right from here?

Ekaterin drew her map cube from her pocket. Madame Radovas sat up in alarm, aiming the stunner, saw what it was, and settled back uneasily, but did not move to take the map from her. Ekaterin checked the location of the Southport Transport docks and locks; the company had leased three loading bays in a line, and Ekaterin was not sure just which she was now in. The three-dimensional vid projection did not supply any exterior orientation, but she rather thought they were on the same side of the station as the wormhole, which might well put this lock in line-of-sight to it. *I don't think there's very much time left at all.*

In addition to the ramp by which she'd entered and the door to the lavatory, there appeared to be two other airsealed exits from the bay. One was clearly a personnel lock to the exterior, next to the freight lock. Another went back into a section which might be offices, if this was indeed the center bay of the three. Ekaterin mentally traced a route through it to the nearest public corridor. Several Komarrans had come and gone through that door; perhaps they were all camping back there. In any case, it seemed more heavily populated than the door she'd come in. But closer. The control booth was a dead end.

Ekaterin eyed her fellow-widow. Strange to think that their different domestic paths had brought them both to the same place in the end. Madame Radovas looked tired and worn. *This has been a nightmare for everyone.*

"How do you imagine you're going to get away, after this?" Ekaterin asked her curiously. *Will you take us along?* Surely the Komarrans would have to.

Madame Radovas's lips thinned. "We hadn't planned to. Till you two came along. I'm almost sorry. It was simpler before. Collapse the wormhole and die. Now it's all possibilities and distractions and worries again."

"Worries? Worse than expecting to die?"

"I left three children back on Komarr. If I were dead, ImpSec would have no reason to . . . bother them."

Hostages all round, indeed.

"Besides," said Madame Radovas, "I voted for it. I could do no less than my husband did."

"You took a *vote*? On what? And how do you divide up Komarran-style voting shares in a revolt? You had to have taken everyone along—if anyone who knew anything had been left to be questioned under fast-penta, it would have been all up."

"Soudha, Foscol, Cappell, and my husband were considered the primary shareholders. They decided I had inherited my husband's voting stock. The choices were simple enough— surrender, flee, or fight to the last. The count was three to one for this."

"Oh? Who voted against it?"

She hesitated. "Soudha."

"How *odd*," said Ekaterin, startled. "He's your chief engineer now—doesn't that worry you?"

"Soudha," said Madame Radovas tartly, "has no children. He wanted to wait and try again later, as though there would be a later. If we do not strike now, ImpSec will shortly hold all our relatives hostage. But if we close the wormhole and die, there will be no one left for ImpSec to threaten with their harm. My children will be safer, even if I never see them again." Her eyes were bleak and sincere.

"What about all the Barrayarans on Komarr and Sergyar who will never see their families again? Cut off, not ever knowing their fate . . ." *Mine, for instance.* "They'll be the same as dead, to each other. It will be the Time of Isolation all over again." She shivered in horror at the cascading images of shock and grief.

"So be glad you're on the good side of the wormhole," Madame Radovas snapped. At Ekaterin's cold stare, she relented a little. "It won't be like your old Time of Isolation at all. You have a fully developed planetary industrial base, now, and a much larger population, which has experienced a hundred-year-long inflow of new genes. There are plenty of other worlds which scarcely maintain any galactic contact, and they get along just fine."

The Professora's eyes slitted open. "I think you are underestimating the psychological impact."

"What you Barrayarans do to each other, afterwards, is not my responsibility," said Madame Radovas. "As long as you can never do it to *us* again."

"How . . . do you expect to die?" asked Ekaterin. "Take poison together? Walk out an airlock?" *And will you kill us first?*

"I expect you Barrayarans will take care of those details, when you figure out what happened," said Madame Radovas. "Foscol and Cappell think we will escape, afterwards, or that we might be permitted to surrender. *I* think it will be the Solstice Massacre all over again. We even have our very own Vorkosigan for it. I'm not afraid." She hesitated, as if contemplating her own brave words. "Or at any rate, I'm too tired to care anymore."

Ekaterin could understand *that*. Unwilling to murmur agreement with the Komarran woman, she fell silent, staring unseeing across the loading bay.

Dispassionately, she considered her own fear. Her heart beat, yes, and her stomach knotted, and her breath came a bit too fast. Yet these people did not frighten her, deep down, nearly as much as she thought they ought to.

Once upon a time, shortly after one of Tien's unfathomable uncomfortable jealous jags had subsided back to whatever fantasy world it came from, he'd earnestly assured her that he had thrown his nerve disruptor (illegally owned because he did not carry it in issuance from their District liege lord) from a bridge one night, and got rid of it. She hadn't even known he'd possessed it. These Komarrans were desperate, and dangerous in their desperation. But she had slept beside things that scared her more than Soudha and all his friends. *How strange I feel.*

There was a tale in Barrayaran folklore about a mutant who could not be killed, because he hid his heart in a box on a secret island far from his fortress. Naturally, the young Vor hero talked the secret out of the mutant's captive maiden, stole the heart, and the poor mutant came to the usual bad end. Maybe her fear failed to paralyze her because Nikki was her heart, and safe away, far from here. Or maybe it was because for the first time in her life, she owned herself whole.

A few meters away across the loading bay, Soudha crossed again to the novel device, aimed the remote at the float cradle, and adjusted its position fractionally. Cappell called some question from the other side of the bay, and Soudha set the remote down on the edge of the cradle and paced along one of the power cables, examining it closely, till he reached the wall slot Cappell was fussing over. They bent their heads together over some loose connection or other. Cappell yelled a question to the man in the glass booth, who shook his head, and went out to join them.

If I think about this, the chance will be gone. If I think about this, even my mutant's heart will fail me.

Had she the right to take this much risk upon herself? *That* was the real fear, yes, and it shook her to her core. This wasn't a task for her. This was a task for ImpSec, the police, the army, a Vor hero, anyone but her. *Who are not here.* But oh, if she tried and failed, she failed for all Barrayar, for all time. And who would take care of Nikki, if he lost both parents in the space of barely a week? The safe thing to do was to wait for competent grownup male people to rescue her.

Like Tien, yeah?

"Are you getting any warmer now, Aunt Vorthys?" Ekaterin asked. "Have you stopped shivering?" She rose, and bent over her aunt with her back to Madame Radovas, and pretended to tuck the blanket tighter, while actually loosening it. Madame Radovas was shorter than Ekaterin, and slighter, and twenty-five years older. *Now*, Ekaterin mouthed to the Professora.

Moving smoothly but not suddenly, she turned, paced toward Madame Radovas, and flung the blanket over the woman's head as she jumped to her feet. The chair banged over backward. Another two paces and she was able to wrap her arms around the smaller woman, pinning her arms to her side. The stunner's beam splashed, buzzing, on the deck at their feet, and the nimbus made Ekaterin's legs tingle. She lifted Madame Radovas off her feet and shook her. The stunner clattered to the deck, and Ekaterin kicked it toward her aunt, who was fighting to get upright on her cot. Ekaterin flung the blanket-muffled Komarran woman away from her as hard as she could, turned, and sprinted for the float cradle.

She snatched up the remote control and spun away toward the glass control booth as fast as her legs could push her, her sweating bare feet firm against the smooth surface. The men at the wall outlet shouted and started toward her. She didn't look back.

She galloped around the corner and up the two stairs to the booth in one leap. She batted frantically at the door control pad. The door took forever to slide shut; Cappell was almost to the steps before she was able, after two tries with her shaking fingers, to activate the lock. Cappell hit the door with a resounding thud and began pounding on it.

She did not, dared not, look back to see what was happening to the Professora. Instead, she raised the remote and pointed it through the glass at the float cradle. The controls included six buttons and a four-pronged knob. She'd never been good at this sort of coordination. Fortunately, subtlety was not her object now.

The third stab of her fingers on a button found the *up* vector. All too slowly, the float cradle began to rise off the loading bay deck. Perhaps there were some sort of sensors in it which kept it level; the first four combinations she tried seemed to do nothing. Finally, she was able to make the thing begin to rotate. It bumped into the catwalks above, making nasty grinding noises. Good. Power cables snapped off and whipped around; the strange man barely dodged the spitting sparks. Soudha was screaming, trying to jump up at the glass wall in front of her. She could barely hear him. The glass, after all, was supposed to stand up to vacuum. He scrambled back and aimed a stunner at her. The beam splashed harmlessly off the window.

At last, she was able to make the sensor program appear on the remote's little readout. She canceled its running instructions, and then the cradle became more lively. She'd achieved an almost 180-degree rotation, bottom to top. Then she turned the cradle's power off.

It was only about a four-meter drop from the catwalks to the deck. She had no idea what material the huge horn was fabricated from. She anticipated having to try a couple of times, to achieve some dent or crack Soudha could not repair in the day it would take for her and her aunt to be missed at the ferry. Instead, the bell burst like—like a flower pot.

The boom shook the bay. Shards big and small skittered off across the deck like shrapnel. One jagged piece whanged past centimeters from Soudha's head and smacked into the booth's glass, and Ekaterin ducked involuntarily. But the glass held. Amazing material. She was glad the device's horn hadn't been cast of it. Laughter bubbled out of her throat, bravura berserker joy. She wanted to destroy a *hundred* devices. She turned on the float cradle's power again and bounced the smashed remains on the deck a few more times, just because she could. *The Maiden of the Lake fires back!*

The Professora was sitting on the deck by the far wall, bent over. Not running away, not even close to making an escape. Not good. Madame Radovas was on her feet and had recovered her stunner. Cappell the mathematician was beating on the control booth's door with a meter-long high-torque wrench he'd found somewhere. Arozzi, his face running with blood from a flying piece of horn-shrapnel, dissuaded him before he rendered it unopenable; Soudha came running up with a handful of electronic tools, and he and Arozzi disappeared below the door's window. Scratchy sounds penetrated by the door lock, more sinister even than Cappell's frantic blows.

Ekaterin caught her breath and looked around the control booth. She couldn't empty the air from the loading bay, her aunt was out there, too. There, there was the comconsole. Should she have gone for it first? No, she was doing this in the right order. No matter how screwed up ImpSec's response was, no matter how misapplied or incompetent their tactics, they could not possibly lose Barrayar now.

"Hello, Emergency?" Ekaterin panted as the vid-plate activated. "My name is Ekaterin Vorsoisson—" She had to stop, as the automated system tried to route her to her choice of traveler's aids. She rejected Lost & Found, selected Security, and started over, not certain she'd reached a human yet, and praying it would all be recorded. "My name is Ekaterin

Vorsoisson. Lord Auditor Vorthys is my uncle. I'm being held prisoner, along with my aunt, by Komarran terrorists at the Southport Transport docks and locks. I'm in a loading bay control booth right now, but they're getting the door open." She glanced over her shoulder. Soudha had defeated the lock; the airseal door, bent from Cappell's efforts with the wrench, whined and refused to retreat into its slot. Soudha and Arozzi put their shoulders to it, grunting, and it inched open. "Tell Lord Auditor Vorkosigan—tell ImpSec—"

Then the swearing Soudha slipped sideways through the door, followed by Cappell still clutching his wrench. Laughing hysterically, tears running down her cheeks, Ekaterin turned to face her fate.

CHAPTER TWENTY

Miles barely restrained himself from pressing his face to his courier ship's airlock window, while waiting for the tube seals from the jump station to finish seating themselves. When the door hissed open at last he swung himself through in one motion, to land on his feet with a thump, and glare around the hatch corridor. His reception committee at the private lock, the ranking ImpSec man aboard and a fellow in blue-and-orange civilian security garb, both braced to attention after only the briefest beat of surprise at his height—he could tell by the way their eyes had to track downward to meet his face—and appearance.

"Lord Auditor Vorkosigan," the strained-looking ImpSec man, Vorgier, acknowledged Miles. "This is Group-Commander Husavi, who heads Station Security."

"Captain Vorgier. Commander Husavi. Are there any new developments in the situation in the last," he glanced at his chrono, "fifteen minutes?" Almost a full three hours had passed since the first message from Vorgier had turned his journey from Komarr orbit into this viscous nightmare of suppressed panic. Never had an ImpSec courier ship seemed to move so slowly, and since no amount of Auditorial screaming at the crew could change the laws of physics, Miles had perforce seethed in silence.

"My men, backed by those of Commander Husavi, are almost into position for our assault," Vorgier assured him. "We believe we can get an emergency tube seal into place over the outer door of the airlock containing the Vor women before, or almost before, the Komarrans can evacuate the air. The moment the hostages are retrieved, our armored men can enter the Southport bay at will. It will be over in minutes."

"Too bloody likely," snapped Miles. "Several engineers have had several hours to prepare for you. These Komarrans may be desperate, but I guarantee they are not stupid. If I can think of putting a pressure-sensitive explosive in the airlock, so can they."

What a set of mental images Vorgier's words conjured—a tube seal misapplied or applied too late to the outer skin of the station, Ekaterin's and the Professora's bodies blown outward into space—some space-armored ImpSec goon missing his catch—Miles could almost hear his embarrassed, bass *Oops* over the audio link now, in his mind's ear. Such a blessing that Vorgier hadn't confided these details earlier, when Miles would have had all those hours en route to reflect upon them, stuck aboard his courier ship. "The Vor ladies are not expendable. Madame Dr. Vorthys has a weak heart, her husband Lord Auditor Vorthys tells me. And Madame Vorsoisson is—just not expendable. And the Komarrans are the least expendable of all. We want them alive for questioning. Sorry, Captain, but I mislike your plan."

Vorgier stiffened. "My Lord Auditor. I appreciate your concern, but I believe this will be most quickly and effectively concluded as a military operation. Civilian authority can help best by staying out of the way and letting the professionals do their job."

The ImpSec deck had dealt him two men in a row of exceptional competence, Tuomonen and Gibbs; why, oh why, couldn't good things come in threes? They were supposed to, dammit. "This is *my* operation, Captain, and I will answer personally to the Emperor for every detail of it. I spent the last ten years as an ImpSec galactic agent and I've dealt with more damned *situations* than anyone else on Simon Illyan's roster and I know just *exactly* how fucked-up a *professional* operation can get." He tapped his chest. "So climb down off your Vor horse and brief me properly."

Vorgier looked considerably taken aback; Husavi tamped out a smile, which told Miles all too much about how things had been going here. To Vorgier's credit, he recovered almost instantly, and said, "Come this way, my Lord Auditor, to the operations center. I'll show you the details, and you can judge for yourself."

Better. They started off down the corridor, almost quickly enough for Miles's taste. "Has there been any change or increase in power-draw into the Southport Transport area?"

"Not yet," Husavi answered. "As you ordered, my engineers shut down their lines to just that necessary to run their life support. I don't know how much power the Komarrans are able to tap from the local system freighter they have docked there. Soudha has said if we try to capture or remove the ship, they'll open the airlock on the Vor ladies, so we've waited. Our remote sensors don't indicate any unusual readings from there yet."

"Good." Baffling, but good. Miles could not imagine why the Komarrans hadn't switched on their wormhole-collapsing device yet, in a last-ditch effort to accomplish their long-sought goal. Had Soudha figured out its inherent defect? Corrected it, or tried to? Was it not quite ready yet, and the Komarrans even now frantically preparing it? In any case, once it was powered up they were all in deep-deep, because the Professor and Riva had concluded, with some pretty unreassuring hand-waving, something like a fifty percent probability of an immediate gravitational back-blow from the wormhole the moment it was switched off, ripping the station apart. When Miles had inquired what the technical difference was between *a fifty-fifty chance* and *we don't know*, he hadn't got a straight answer from them. Further theoretical refinements had come to an abrupt halt, when the news had come through about the stand-off here; the Professor was on his way now to the jump point, just a few hours behind Miles.

They turned a corner and entered a lift-tube. Miles asked, "What's the current status of the station evacuation?"

Husavi replied, "We've waved off all incoming ships that could be diverted. A couple had to dock in order to refuel, or they couldn't have made it to an alternate station." He waited till they'd exited into another corridor before continuing. "We've managed to remove most of the transient passengers and about five hundred of our nonessential personnel so far."

"What story are you giving them?"

"We're telling them it's a bomb scare."

"Excellent." *And effectively true.*

"Most are cooperating. Some aren't."

"Hm."

"But there's a serious problem with transportation. There are simply not enough ships in range to remove everyone in less than ten hours."

"If the power-draw to the Southport bay spikes suddenly, you'll have to start shuttling people over to the military station." Though Miles was by no means sure the gravitational event, if it occurred, wouldn't suck in and damage or destroy the military station as well. "They'll have to help out."

"Captain Vorgier and I discussed this possibility with the

military commander, my lord. He wasn't happy with the prospect of a sudden influx of, um, randomly selected, uncleared persons onto his station."

Miles bet not. "I'll speak with him." He sighed.

Vorgier's "operations center" turned out to be the local ImpSec offices; the central communications chamber did indeed bear a passing resemblance to a warship's tactics room, Miles had to allow. Vorgier called up a holovid display of the Southport docks and locks area, one with rather better technical detail than the one Miles had spent the last hour studying. He ran over the expected placement of his men and the projected timing and technique of his assault. It wasn't a bad plan, as assaults went. In his youth, out on covert ops, Miles had come up with things just as bravura and idiotic on equally short notice. All right . . . more idiotic, he admitted ruefully to himself. *Someday, Miles,* his boss ImpSec Chief Simon Illyan had once said to him, *I hope you live to have a dozen subordinates just like you.* Miles hadn't realized till now that had been a formal curse on Illyan's part.

Vorgier's sales pitch kept fading out in Miles's mind, displaced by an instant-replay of the recording of the last message from Ekaterin, which Vorgier had thoughtfully supplied Miles by tight-beam. He'd memorized every nuance of it in the last three hours. *I'm in a loading bay control booth—they're getting the door open—* She hadn't said anything about the novel device. Unless some report had been going to follow the *Tell Lord Vorkosigan—tell ImpSec—*part, which had been so rudely interrupted by the red-faced Soudha's paw abruptly descending on the comconsole control. Nothing could be seen in the fuzzy background, however computer-enhanced, but the dull control booth. And the mathematician, Cappell, gripping a wrench he looked ready to use for something other than tightening bolts, but evidently hadn't; ImpSec had received vids via the loading bay airlock's safety channel of both women being bundled alive into it, before Soudha had cut off the signal feed. Those brief images too burned in Miles's brain.

"All right, Captain Vorgier," Miles interrupted. "Hold your plan as a possible last resort."

"To be implemented under what circumstances, my Lord Auditor?"

Over my dead body, Miles did not reply. Vorgier might not understand it wasn't a joke. "Before we start blowing walls down, I want to try to negotiate with Soudha and his friends."

"These are Komarran terrorists. Madmen—you can't negotiate with them!"

The late Baron Ryoval had been a madman. The late Ser Galen had been a madman, without question. And the late General Metzov hadn't exactly been rowing with both oars in the water, either, come to think of it. Miles had to admit, there had been a definite negative trend to all those negotiations. "I'm not without experience in the problem, Vorgier. But I don't think Dr. Soudha is a madman. He's not even a mad scientist. He's merely a very upset engineer. These Komarrans may in fact be the most sensible revolutionaries I've ever met."

He stood a moment, staring unseeing at Vorgier's colorful, ominous tactical display, the logistics of the station evacuation warring in his head with guesses about the Komarrans' state of mind. Delusion, political passion, personality, judgment . . . visions of Ekaterin's terror and despair spun in his back-brain. If so spacious a containment as a Komarran dome gave her claustrophobia . . . *stop it.* He pictured a thick sheet of glass sliding down between him and that personal maelstrom of anxiety. If his authority here was absolute, so was his obligation to keep his thinking clear.

"Every hour buys lives. We'll play for time. Get me a channel to the military station's commander," Miles ordered. "After that, we'll see whether Soudha will answer his comconsole."

The deliberately blank chamber in which Miles sat might as easily have been on the nearby military station, or a ship lying several thousand kilometers off-station, as the few hundred meters from the Southport bay it actually was. Soudha's location, when his face formed at last over the vid-plate, was not so anonymous; he sat in the same glass-walled control booth from which Ekaterin had sent her alarm. Miles wondered what techs were monitoring the corridors for moves on ImpSec's part, and who was keeping a nervous finger on the personnel airlock's outer door control. Had they arranged it as a deadman's switch?

Soudha's face was drawn and sincerely weary, no more the bland bluff liar. Lena Foscol sat tensely to the right of his station chair on a rolling stool, looking like some frumpy vizier. Madame Radovas too looked on, her face half-shadowed behind him, and Cappell stood off to the side, almost out of focus. Good. A Komarran stockholders' voting quorum, if he read the signs right. At least they honored his Imperial Auditor's authority to that extent.

"Good evening, Dr. Soudha," Miles began.

"You're out here?" Soudha's brows rose as he took in the lack of transmission lag.

"Yes, well, unlike Administrator Vorsoisson, I got out of my chains at the experiment station alive. I still don't know if you intended me to survive."

"He didn't really die, did he?" Foscol interrupted.

"Oh, yes." Miles made his voice deliberately soft. "I got to watch, just as you arranged. Every filthy minute of it. It was a remarkably ugly death."

She fell silent; Soudha said, "This is all beside the point now. The only message we want to receive from you people is that you have the jumpship ready to transport us to the nearest neutral space—Pol, or Escobar—whereupon you will get your Vor ladies back. If it's not that, I'm cutting this com."

"I have a few pieces of free information for you, first," said Miles. "I don't think they're ones you anticipate."

Soudha's hand hovered. "Go on."

"I'm afraid your wormhole-collapser no longer qualifies as a secret weapon. We caught up with your specs on file at Bollan Design. Professor Vorthys invited Dr. Riva, of Solstice University, in to consult. Are you aware of her reputation?"

Soudha nodded warily; Cappell's eyes widened. Madame Radovas stared wearily. Foscol looked deeply suspicious.

"Well, putting together your specs, the data from the soletta accident, and Riva's physics—there was a mathematician by the name of Dr. Yuell in there too, if the name means anything to you—the Empire's top failure analyst and the Empire's top five-space expert have concluded that you did not, in fact, manage to invent a wormhole-collapser. What you managed to invent was a wormhole-boomerang. Riva says that when the five-space waves amplified the wormhole's resonance past its phase boundaries, instead of collapsing, the wormhole returned the energy to three-space in the form of a gravitational pulse. Tangling with this pulse was what destroyed the soletta array and the ore ship, and—I'm sorry, Madame Radovas—killed Dr. Radovas and Marie Trogir. The probable-cause crew finally found her body a few hours ago, I regret to report, wrapped up in some of the wreckage they'd retrieved almost a week back."

Only a puff of breath from Cappell marked his grief, but water glittered in his eyes. *Check*, thought Miles. *I thought he'd protested too much.* Nobody looked surprised, merely oppressed.

"So if you succeed in getting your thing working, what you will actually do is destroy this station, the five thousand or so people aboard, and yourselves. And tomorrow morning, Barrayar will still be there." Miles let his voice fall to a near whisper. "All for nothing, and less than nothing."

"He lies," said Foscol fiercely into the shocked silence. "He lies."

Soudha gave a weird snort, ran his hands through his hair, and shook his head. Then, to Miles's dismay, he laughed out loud.

Cappell stared at his colleague. "Do you really think that's why? That it malfunctioned like that?"

"It would explain," began Soudha. "It would explain . . . oh, God." He trailed off. "I thought it was the ore ship," he said at last. "Interfering somehow."

"I should also mention," Miles put in, still uneasily watching Soudha's odd reaction, "that ImpSec has arrested all the Waste Heat personnel and their families you left back at the Southport Transport facility at Solstice. And then there are all your other relatives and friends, the innocents who knew nothing. The hostage game is a bad game, a sad and ugly game that's a lot easier to start than end. The worst versions I've seen ended up with neither side in control, or getting anything they wanted. And the people who stand to lose the most in it frequently aren't even playing."

"Barrayaran threats." Foscol lifted her chin. "Do you think, after all this, we can't stand up to you?"

"I'm sure you can, but for what reason? There aren't too many prizes left in this mess. The biggest one is gone; you can't shut off Barrayar. You can't keep your secret or shield anyone you left behind on Komarr. About the only thing you can do now is kill more innocent people. Great goals can call for great sacrifices, yes, but your possible rewards are steadily shrinking." Yes, that was it; don't raise the pressure, lower the wall.

"We did not," husked Cappell, rubbing his eyes with the back of his hand, "go through all this just to deliver the weapon of the century straight into Barrayaran hands."

"It's already there. As a weapon, it appears to have some fundamental defects, so far. But Riva says there's evidence you got more power out of the wormhole than you put into it. This suggests possible future peaceful, economic uses, when the phenomena are better understood."

"Really?" said Soudha, sitting up. "How did she figure? What are her numbers?"

"Soudha!" said Foscol reprovingly. Madame Radovas winced, and Soudha subsided, albeit reluctantly, staring at Miles through narrowed eyes.

"On the other hand," Miles continued, "until further research assures us that collapsing a wormhole is indeed quite impossible, none of you are going anywhere, and especially not to any other planetary government. It's one of those ugly military decisions, y'know? And I'm afraid it's mine." *The Vor ladies are not expendable*, he'd told Vorgier. Was he lying then, or now? Well, if he couldn't figure it out, maybe the Komarrans wouldn't either.

"You are all headed, inexorably, for a Barrayaran prison," he went on. "The devil's bargain part about being Vor, which a lot of people including some Vor overlook, is that our lives are made for sacrifice. There is no threat, no torture, no slow murder you can apply to two Barrayaran women that will change your outcome."

Was this the right tack? Above the vid-plate their listening images were undersized, a little ghostly, hard to read. Miles wished he were having this conversation face-to-face. Half the subliminal clues, of body language, of the subtle nuances of expression and voice, were washed out in transmission and unavailable to his instincts. But handing himself over to them in person to augment their hostage collection could only have served to stiffen their wavering resolve. The memory of a woman's hand, slipping through his fingers into a screaming fog, flickered through his mind; his fists clenched helplessly in his lap. *Never again, you said. Not expendable, you said.* He watched the Komarrans' faces intently for all flickers of expression he could get, reflections of truth, lies, belief, suspicion, trust.

"There are advantages to prisons," he went on persuasively. "Some of them are comfortably furnished, and unlike graves, sometimes, eventually, you can get out of them again. Now, I am willing, in exchange for your peaceful surrender and cooperation, to personally guarantee your lives. Not, note, your freedom—that will have to wait. But time passes, old crises are succeeded by new ones, people change their minds. Live ones do, anyway. There are always those amnesties, in celebration of this or that public event—the birth of an Imperial heir, for instance. I doubt any of you will be forced to spend as much as a full decade in prison."

"Some offer," said Foscol bitterly.

Miles let his brows rise. "It's an honest one. You have a better hope of amnesty than Tien Vorsoisson does. That ore freighter pilot will enjoy no visits from her children. I reviewed her autopsy, did I mention? All the autopsies. If I have a moral qualm, it's that I'm bargaining away the rights of the dead soletta-keepers' families to any justice for their slain. There ought to be civil trials for manslaughter over this."

Even Foscol looked away at these words.

Good. Go on. The more time he burned, the better, and they were tracking his arguments; as long as he could keep Soudha from cutting the com, he was making some twisty sort of progress. "You bitch endlessly about Barrayaran tyranny, but somehow I don't think you folks took a vote of all Komarran planetary shareholders, before you attempted to seal—or steal—their future. And if you could have, I don't think you would have dared. Twenty years ago, even fifteen years ago, maybe you could have counted on majority support. By ten years ago, it was already too late. Would your fellows really want to close off their nearest market now, and lose all that trade? Lose all their relatives who've moved to Barrayar, and their half-Barrayaran grandchildren? Your trade fleets have found their Barrayaran military escorts bloody useful often enough. Who are the true tyrants here—the blundering Barrayarans who seek, however awkwardly, to include Komarr in their future, or the Komarran intellectual elitists who seek to exclude all but themselves from it?" He took a deep breath to control the unexpected anger which had boiled up with his words, aware he was teetering on the edge with these people. *Watch it, watch it.* "So all that remains for us is to try and salvage as many lives as possible from the wreckage."

After a little time, Madame Radovas asked, "How would you guarantee our lives?" They were the first words she had spoken, though she had listened intently throughout.

"By my order, as an Imperial Auditor. Only Emperor Gregor himself could gainsay it."

"So . . . why won't Emperor Gregor gainsay it?" asked Cappell skeptically.

"He's not going to be happy about any of this," Miles answered frankly. *And I'm going to have to give him the report, God help me.* "But . . . if I lay my word on the line, I don't think he'll deny me." He hesitated. "Or else I will have to resign."

Foscol snorted. "How nice for us, to know that after we are dead, you will resign. What a consolation."

Soudha rubbed his lips, watching Miles . . . watching his truncated image, Miles reminded himself. He was not the only one missing body cues. The engineer was silent, thinking . . . what?

"Your word?" Cappell grimaced. "Do you know what a Vorkosigan's word means to us?"

"Yes," said Miles levelly. "Do you know what it means to me?"

Madame Radovas tilted her head, and her quiet stare became, if possible, more focused.

Miles leaned forward into the vid pickup. "My *word* is all that stands between you and ImpSec's aspiring heroes coming through your walls. They don't need the corridors, you know. My *word* went down on my Auditor's oath, which holds me at this moment unblinking to a duty I find more horrific than you can know. I only have one name's oath. It cannot be true to Gregor if it is false to you. But if there's one thing my father's heartbreaking experience at Solstice taught, it's that I'd better not put my word down on events I do not control. If you surrender quietly, I can control what happens. If ImpSec has to detain you by force, it will be up to chance, chaos, and the reflexes of some overexcited young men with guns and gallant visions of thwarting mad Komarran terrorists."

"We are not terrorists," said Foscol hotly.

"No? You've succeeded in terrifying *me*," Miles said bleakly. Her lips thinned, but Soudha looked less certain.

"If you unleash ImpSec, the consequences will be your doing," said Cappell.

"Almost correct," Miles agreed. "If I unleash ImpSec, the consequences will be my responsibility. It's that devil's distinction between being in charge and being in control. I'm in charge; you're in control. You can imagine how much this thrills me."

Soudha snorted. One corner of Miles's mouth tilted up in unwilling response. *Yeah, Soudha knows all about that one, too.*

Foscol leaned forward. "This is all a smoke screen. Captain Vorgier said they were sending for a jumpship. Where is it?"

"Vorgier was lying for time, which was his clear duty. There will not be a jumpship." Shit, that did it. There were only two ways this could go now. *There were only two ways it could go before.*

"We have a pair of hostages. Do we have to space one of them to prove we're serious?"

"I believe you are deathly serious. Which one gets to watch, the aunt or the niece?" Miles asked softly, settling back again. "You claim to not be mad terrorists, and I believe you. You're not. Yet. You are also not murderers; I actually accept that all the deaths you've left in your wake were accidents. So far. But I also know that line gets easier to slip over with practice. Please observe that you have now gone as far as you can without turning yourselves into a perfect replica of the enemy you set out to oppose."

He let those last words hang in the air for a time, for emphasis.

"Vorkosigan's right, I think," said Soudha unexpectedly. "We've come to the end of our choices. Or to the beginning of another set. One that isn't the set I signed up for."

"We have to stick together, or it's no good," said Foscol urgently. "If we have to space one of them, I vote for that hell-cat Vorsoisson."

"Would you do it with your own hands?" said Soudha slowly. "Because I think I decline."

"Even after what she did to us?"

What in God's name did gentle Ekaterin do to you? Miles kept his expression as blank as he could, his body still.

Soudha hesitated. "Seems it made no difference after all."

Cappell and Madame Radovas both began to speak at once, but Soudha held up a restraining hand. He blew out his breath like a man in pain. "No. Let us continue as we began. The choice is plain. Stop now—unconditional surrender—or call Vorkosigan's bluff. Now, it's no secret to you I thought the time to go into hiding for a later try was before we ever left Komarr."

"I'm sorry I voted against you the last time," Cappell said to Soudha.

Soudha shrugged. "Yeah, well . . . If we're going to quit, the time's come."

No, it hasn't, Miles thought frantically. This was too abrupt. There was time for another ten hours of chit chat at the very least. He wanted to slide them to surrender, not stampede them to suicide. Or murder. If they believed him about the defects of their device, as they appeared to, it must soon occur to them that they could hold the whole station hostage, if they didn't mind the self-immolating aspect. Well, if they weren't going to think of that themselves, far be it from him to point it out. He leaned back in his station chair, and chewed on the side of his finger, and watched, and listened.

"There's no benefit in waiting, either way," Soudha went on. "The risk increases every minute. Lena?"

"No surrender," said Foscol sturdily. "We go on." And more bleakly, "Somehow."

"Cappell?"

The mathematician hesitated a long time. "I can't stand that Marie died for nothing. Hold out."

"Myself . . ." Soudha let his big square hand fall open. "Stop. Now that we've lost surprise, this goes nowhere. The only question is how long it takes to arrive." He turned to Madame Radovas.

"Oh. My turn already? I didn't want to go last."

"Yours would be the tie-breaking vote in any case," said Soudha.

Madame Radovas fell silent, staring out the control booth's glass—at the airlock door, across the bay? Miles's gaze could not help following hers; her turn back caught him at it, and he flinched.

You've done it now, boy. Ekaterin's life and your soul's oath ride on a frigging Komarran shareholders' debate. How did you let this happen? This wasn't in the plans. . . . His eye relocated, and ignored, the code on his comconsole that would launch Vorgier and his waiting troops.

Madame Radovas's gaze returned to window. She said, to no one in particular, "Our safety before always depended on secrecy. Now even if we get to Pol or Escobar, or further, ImpSec will follow us. There would not ever be a safe time to give up our hostages. In exile or not, it will be prisoners, always prisoners. I'm tired of being a prisoner, of hope or fear."

"You were not a prisoner!" said Foscol. "You were one of us. I thought."

Madame Radovas looked across at her. "I supported my husband. If I hadn't—he would still be alive. Lena, I'm *tired.*"

Foscol said tentatively, "Maybe you should rest, before deciding."

The look she got from Madame Radovas in return for that line made her drop her eyes, and look away.

Madame Radovas said to Soudha, "Do you believe him, about the device not working?"

Soudha frowned deeply. "Yes. I'm afraid so. Or I would have voted differently."

"Poor Barto." She stared at Miles for a long time in an almost detached wonder.

Encouraged by her apparent dispassion, he asked curiously, "Why is your vote the tie-breaker?"

"The scheme was my husband's idea, originally. This obsession has dominated my life for seven years. His voting share was always considered the greatest."

How very Komarran. Then Soudha had actually been the second-in-command, forced into the dead man's shoes . . . it was all amazingly irrelevant now. *Maybe they'll name it after him. The Radovas Effect.* Belike. "We are both heirs, of a sort, then."

"Indeed." The widow's lips twisted. "You know, I will never forget the look on your face when that fool Vorsoisson told you there was no place on his forms for an Imperial order. I almost laughed out loud, despite it all."

Miles smiled briefly, scarcely daring to breathe.

Madame Radovas shook her head in disbelief, but not, he thought, of his promises. "Well, Lord Vorkosigan . . . I'll take your word. And find out what it's worth." She searched the faces of each of her three colleagues, but when she spoke, she looked at him. "I vote to stop now."

Miles waited tensely for signs of dissension, protest, internal revolt. Cappell struck his fist on the booth's glass wall, which reverberated, and turned away, his features working. Foscol buried her face in her hands. After that, silence.

"That's it, then," said Soudha, bleakly exhausted. Miles wondered if the news of the device's inherent defect had sapped his will more than any argument. "We surrender, on your word for our lives. Lord Auditor Vorkosigan." He squeezed his eyes shut and opened them again. "Now what?"

"A lot of sensible slow moves. First I gently detach ImpSec from its vision of a heroic assault. They were getting pretty worked up, out here. Then you inform the rest of your group. Then disarm whatever booby-traps you've set, and pile any weapons you may possess well away from yourselves. Unlock the doors. Then sit down quietly on the loading bay floor with your hands behind your heads. At that point, I'll let the boys in." He added prudently, "Please avoid sudden movements, that sort of thing."

"So be it." Soudha cut his comm; the Komarrans winked out. Miles shuddered in sudden disorientation, alone again in his little sealed room. The screaming man behind the glass wall in his mind was getting out a battering ram, it felt like.

Miles opened the channel on his comconsole and ordered a medical squad to accompany the arresting officers from ImpSec and Station Security, who were to be armed with stunners and stunners only. He repeated that last command a couple of times, to be sure. He felt as if he'd spent a century in his station chair. When he tried to stand up, he nearly fell over. Then he ran.

Miles's only compromise with Vorgier's anxiety for the Imperial Auditor's personal safety was to march down the ramp into the Southport loading bay behind instead of in front of the security team. The ten or so Komarrans, sitting cross-legged on the floor, twisted around to watch as the Barrayarans entered. After Miles came the tech squad, which spread out looking for booby-traps, and behind them the medical team with a float pallet.

The first thing which caught Miles's eye after the live target inventory was the upside-down float cradle in the middle of the bay, atop a pile of tangled wreckage. He was able, barely, to recognize it from the diagrams he'd seen back on Komarr as the fifth novel device. His heart lifted at this inexplicable, welcome sight.

He walked around it, staring, and came up to where Soudha was being frisked down and restrained. "My goodness. Your wormhole-collapser appears to have met with an accident. But it won't do you any good. We have the plans."

Cappell and a man Miles recognized as the engineer who'd fled from Bollan Design stood nearby, glowering at him; Foscol struggled into earshot, barely controlled by her female arresting officer.

"It wasn't us," sighed Soudha. "It was *her*."

A jerk of his thumb drew Miles's attention to the inner door of the bay's personnel airlock. A metal bar was placed crookedly across the airseal door's jamb; the ends were melted onto door and wall respectively.

Miles's eyes widened, and his lips parted in breathless anticipation. "Her?"

"The bitch from hell. Or Barrayar, which is almost the same thing to hear her tell it. Madame Vorsoisson."

"Remarkable." The source of several oddly tilted responses on the Komarrans' part to his recent negotiations began at last to come clear to Miles. "Um . . . *how?*"

All three Komarrans tried to answer him at once, with a medley of blame-casting which included a lot of phrases like, *If Madame Radovas hadn't let her out, If you hadn't let Radovas let her out, How was I supposed to know? The old lady looked sick to me. Still does. If you hadn't put the remote down right in front of her, If you hadn't left the damned control booth, If you had just moved faster, If you had run for the float cradle and cut the power, So why didn't you think of that, huh?* by which Miles slowly pieced together the most glorious mental picture he'd had all day. All year. For quite a long time, actually.

I'm in love. I'm in love. I just thought I was in love, before. Now I really am. I must, I must, I must have this woman! Mine, mine, mine. Lady Ekaterin Nile Vorvayne Vorsoisson Vorkosigan, yes! She'd left nothing here for ImpSec and all the Emperor's Auditors to do but sweep up the bits. He wanted to roll on the floor and howl with joy, which would be most undiplomatic of him, under the circumstances. He kept his face neutral, and very straight. Somehow, he didn't think the Komarrans appreciated the exquisite delight of it all.

"When we stuffed her in the airlock I *welded* it shut," said Soudha morosely. "I wasn't going to let her do us a *third* time."

"Third time?" Miles said. "If that was the second, what was the first?"

"When that idiot Arozzi first brought her down here, she damn near blew the whole thing right then by hitting the emergency alarm."

Miles glanced aside at the alarm on the nearby wall. "And then what happened?"

"We had a sudden influx of station accident control. I thought I'd never get rid of them."

"Ah. I see." *How curious. Vorgier never mentioned that part. Later.* "You mean we've spent the last five hours scrambling to evacuate this station for nothing?"

Soudha smiled sourly. "You coming to me for sympathy, Barrayaran?"

"Heh. Never mind."

Most of the prisoners were formed up and marched out; with a gesture, Miles ordered Soudha to be held behind.

"Moment of truth, Soudha. Have you booby-trapped this thing?"

"There is a motion-sensitive charge attached to the outer door. Opening it from this side should not set it off."

With iron self-control, Miles watched as an ImpSec tech torched off the metal bar. It fell to the deck with a clang. He paused in one last moment of sick fear.

"What are you waiting for?" asked Soudha curiously.

"Just pondering the depth of your political ingenuity. Suppose this is set to go off and snatch our prize from us at the last."

"Now? Why? It's over," said Soudha.

"Revenge. Manipulation. Maybe you figure to drive me berserk and trigger a repeat of the Solstice Massacre all over again, writ somewhat smaller. That could be a propaganda coup. Whether it would be worth spending your lives for is all in your point of view, of course. Properly massaged, the incident could help start a new Komarr Revolt, I suppose."

"You have a really twisted mind, Lord Vorkosigan," said Soudha, shaking his head. "Was it your upbringing, or your genetics?"

"Yes." Miles sighed. After a brief moment of reflection, Miles waved the guards on, and Soudha was marched out after his colleagues.

After a go-ahead nod from the Imperial Auditor, the tech tapped the control pad. The inner door whined, sticking halfway. Miles pressed it gently sideways with his boot, and it shuddered open.

Ekaterin was on her feet, between the inner door and the Professora, who sat on the deck wearing her niece's vest over her own bolero. Ekaterin's face bore a red bruise, her hair was hanging every which way, her fists were clenched, and she looked perfectly demented and altogether gorgeous, in Miles's personal opinion. Smiling broadly, he held out both his hands and leaned inside.

She glared back at him. "About time." She stalked past, muttering in a voice of loathing, "Men!"

After the briefest lurch, Miles managed to convert his open arms into a smooth bow toward the Professora. "Madame Dr. Vorthys. Are you all right?"

"Why, hello, Miles." She blinked at him, gray faced and very chilled-looking. "I've been better, but I believe I'll survive."

"I have a float pallet for you. These sturdy young men will help you to it."

"Oh, thank you, dear."

Miles stood back and waved the medtechs forward. The Professora looked perfectly content to be whisked aboard the medical pallet and covered with warm wraps. A cursory examination and a few words of debate resulted in a half-dose of synergine for her, but no IV; then the pallet rose into the air.

"The Professor will be here shortly," Miles assured her. "In fact, he'll likely be along before you both are done at the station infirmary. I'll see he gets sent straight on to you."

"I'm so pleased." The Professora motioned him nearer; when he bent over her, she grabbed him by the ear and planted a kiss on his cheek. "Ekaterin was wonderful," she whispered.

"I know," he breathed. His eyes crinkled, and she smiled back.

He stepped back from the pallet to Ekaterin's side, hoping her aunt's example might inspire her—he wouldn't mind salvaging *some* little show of appreciation—"You didn't seem surprised to see me," he murmured. The pallet started off, under the guidance of a medtech, and he and Ekaterin followed in procession; the ImpSec technicians politely waited till they'd cleared the chamber to plunge in to the airlock to disarm the charge.

Ekaterin shoved a strand of hair back over one ear with a hand that trembled only slightly. Red bruises glared on her arms, too, as her sleeve slid back. Miles frowned at them. "I knew it had to be our side," she said simply. "Or else it would have been the *other* door."

"Eh. Quite." Three hours, she'd had, to contemplate that possibility. "My fast courier was slow."

They turned up the next corridor in reflective silence. Gratifying as it might have been to have her fling herself into his arms and weep relief into—well, if not his shoulder, at least the top of his head—in front of that herd of ImpSec fellows, he had to admit he admired this style even more. *So what is this thing you have about tall women and unrequited love?* His cousin Ivan would doubtless have some cutting things to say—he growled in anticipation, in his mind. He would deal with Ivan and other hazards to his courtship later.

"Do you know you saved about five thousand lives?" he asked her.

Her dark brows drew down. "What?"

"The novel device was defective. If the Komarrans had managed to get it started, the gravitational back-blow from the wormhole would have taken out this station just like the soletta array, possibly with as few survivors. And I shudder at the thought of the property damage bill. To think how Illyan used to complain about my equipment losses back when I was just covert ops. . . ."

"You mean . . . it didn't work after all? I did all that for *nothing*?" She stopped short, her shoulders sagging.

"What do you mean, nothing? I've met Imperial generals who completed their entire careers with less to show for them. You should get a bloody medal, *I* think. Except that this whole thing is going to end up so classified, they're going to have to invent a whole new level of classification just to put it in. And then classify the classification."

Her lips puffed, not quite mirthfully. "What would I do with so useless an object as a medal?"

He thought bemusedly of the contents of a certain drawer at home in Vorkosigan House. "Frame it? Use it as a paperweight? Dust it?"

"Just what I always wanted. More clutter."

He grinned at her; she smiled back at last, clearly beginning to come off her adrenaline jag, and without breaking down, either. She drew breath and started forward again, and he kept pace. She had met the enemy, mastered her moment, hung three hours on death's doorstep, all that, and she'd

emerged still on her feet and snarling. Oversocialized, hah.
Oh, yeah, Da, I want this one.

He stopped at the door to the infirmary; the Professora vanished within, borne off by her medical minions like a lady
on a palanquin. Ekaterin paused with him.

"I have to leave you for a time and check on my prisoners. The stationers will take care of you."

Her brow wrinkled. "Prisoners? Oh. Yes. How *did* you get
rid of the Komarrans?"

Miles smiled grimly. "Persuasion."

She stared down at him, one side of her lovely mouth curving up. Her lower lip was split; he wanted to kiss it and make
it well. *Not yet. Timing, boy. And one other thing.*

"You must be very persuasive."

"I hope so." He took a deep breath. "I bluffed them into
believing that I wouldn't let them go no matter what they did
to you and the Professora. Except that I wasn't bluffing. We
could not have let them go." There. Betrayal confessed. His
empty hands clenched.

She stared at him in disbelief; his heart shrank. "Well, of
course not!"

"Eh . . . what?"

"Don't you know what they wanted to do to Barrayar?" she
demanded. "It was a horror show. Utterly vile, and they
couldn't even see it. They actually tried to tell me that collapsing the wormhole wouldn't hurt anyone! Monstrous fools."

"That's what I thought, actually."

"So, wouldn't you put *your* life on the line to stop them?"

"Yes, but I wasn't putting my life—I was putting yours."

"But I'm Vor," she said simply.

His smile and his heart revived, dizzy with delight. "True
Vor, milady," he breathed.

A female medtech was approaching, murmuring anxiously,
"Madame Vorsoisson?" Miles yielded to her shepherding
motions, gave Ekaterin an analyst's salute, and turned away.
He was humming, off-key, by the time he rounded the first
corner.

CHAPTER TWENTY-ONE

The station infirmary personnel insisted on keeping both Vor women overnight, a precaution with which neither argued. Despite her exhaustion Ekaterin did get dispensation to go pick up her valise from her never-used hostel room, under the watchful eye of a very young ImpSec guard who called her "Ma'am" in every sentence and was determined to carry her luggage.

One message waited on her hostel room's comconsole: an urgent order from Lord Vorkosigan for her to take her aunt and flee the station at once, delivered in a tone of such intense conviction as to almost send her scurrying off despite its obviously outdated content. Instructions only, she noted; no explanations whatsoever. He really must have once held military command. The contrast between this strained, forceful lord and the almost goofy geniality of the young man who'd bowed her out of the airlock bemused her; which was the real Lord Vorkosigan? For all his apparently self-revealing babble, the man remained as elusive as a handful of water. *Water in the desert.* The thought popped unbidden into her mind, and she shook her head to clear it.

After she returned to the infirmary, Ekaterin sat up for a while with her aunt, waiting for the Professor. Uncle Vorthys arrived in the next hour. He was unusually breathless and subdued as he sat on the edge of his wife's bed and embraced her. She hugged him back, tears starting in her eyes for almost the first time in this whole night's ordeal.

"You shouldn't frighten me like that, woman," he told her in mock severity. "Running around getting kidnapped, thwarting Komarran terrorists, putting ImpSec out of a job . . . Your premature demise would entirely disarrange my selfish plan to drop dead first and leave you to pick up after me. Kindly don't do that!"

She laughed shakily. "I'll try not to, dear." The patient gown she wore was not a very flattering fashion, but her color did look rather better, Ekaterin thought. Synergine, hot liquids, warmth, quiet, and safety were working to banish her more alarming symptoms without further medical intervention, so that even her anxious husband was fairly quickly reassured. Ekaterin let her aunt tell him most of the story of their harrowing hours with the Komarrans, only putting in a few murmurs of correction when she waxed too flattering of her niece's part in it all.

Ekaterin reflected with bleak envy on the nature of a marriage that its principals could regard as prematurely threatened after a mere forty-plus years. *Not for me. I've lost that option.* The Professor and the Professora were surely among the fortunate few. Whatever personal qualities it took to achieve this happy state, it was abundantly plain to Ekaterin that she did not possess them. So be it.

The Professor's booming voice and precise academic diction returned to usual as he proceeded to harry the medtechs, unnecessarily, on his wife's behalf. Ekaterin intervened to suggest firmly that what Aunt Vorthys needed most now was *rest*; after one last disruptive pass through the private room, he took himself off to find Lord Vorkosigan and tour the late battlefield at the Southport locks. Ekaterin didn't think she could ever sleep again, but after she cleaned up and crawled into her own infirmary bed, a medtech brought her a potion and invited her to drink it. Ekaterin was still complaining muzzily that such things didn't work for her when the bed sheets seemed to suck her right down.

Whether due to the potion, exhaustion, sheer nervous collapse, or the absence of a nine-year-old demanding services, she slept late. The restful residue of the morning, spent chatting desultorily with her aunt, had drifted toward noon when Lord Vorkosigan trooped into the infirmary room. He was clean as a cat and his fine gray suit was crisp and fresh, though his face was traced with fatigue. He carried an enormous and awkward flower arrangement under each arm. Ekaterin hurried to help relieve him of them, sliding them onto a table before he dropped them both.

"Good day, Madame Dr. Vorthys, you're looking much better. Excellent. Madame Vorsoisson." He ducked his head at her, and his white grin winked.

"Wherever did you find such gorgeous flowers on a space station?" Ekaterin asked, astonished.

"In a shop. It's a Komarran space station. They'll sell you anything. Well, not *anything*—that would be Jackson's Whole. But it stands to reason, with all the people meeting and greeting and parting through here, that there would be a market niche for this sort of thing. They grow them right here on the station, you know, along with all their truck garden vegetables. Why do they call them truck gardens, I wonder? I don't think they ever grew trucks in them, even back on Old Earth." He dragged over a chair and sat down near her, at the foot of the Professora's bed. "I believe that dark red fuzzy thing is a Barrayaran plant, by the way. It made me break out in hives when I touched it."

"Yes, bloody puffwad," she agreed.

"Is that its name, or a value judgment?"

She smiled. "I believe it refers to the color. It comes from South Continent, on the western slopes of the Black Escarpment."

"I was at the Black Escarpment for winter training once. Happily, these things must have been buried under several meters of snow at the time."

"How shall we ever get them home, Miles?" said the Professora, half laughing.

"Don't burden yourself," he recommended. "You can always give them to the medtechs when you leave."

"But they must be very expensive," said Ekaterin in worry. Ridiculously so, for something they could only enjoy for a few hours.

"Expensive?" he said blankly. "Automated weapons-control systems are expensive. Combat drop missions which go wrong are very expensive. These are cheap. Really. Anyway, it supports a business, which is good for the Imperium. If you get a chance, you ought to ask for a tour of the station's hydroponics section before you leave. I'd think you'd find it pretty interesting."

"We'll see if there's time," said Ekaterin. "It's been such a bizarre experience. It's strange to realize I'm not even late getting back to pick up Nikki yet. Just a few more days to complete his treatment, and I'm done with Komarr."

"Do you have everything in hand for that? Everything you need? Your aunt," he nodded at the Professora, "is with you now."

"I expect I'll be able to handle anything that comes up this time," Ekaterin assured him.

"I expect you will." That scimitar smile flickered over his face again.

"We only missed the ship we were originally scheduled to take this morning because Uncle Vorthys insisted we wait and travel back to Komarr with him in his fast courier. Do you know when that will be? I should send a message to Madame Vortorren."

"He has a few chores here yet. ImpSec Komarr sent us out a special squad of boffins and techs to clean up and document that mess you made in the Southport loading bay—"

"Oh, dear. I'm sorry—" she began automatically.

"No, no, it was a beautiful mess. Couldn't have made a better one myself, and I've made a few. Anyway, he will be overseeing them, and then returning to Komarr to set up a secret scientific commission to study the device, explore its limits and all that. And HQ sent me some high-powered interrogators whom I wanted to personally brief before they took charge of my prisoners. Captain Vorgier wasn't too happy that I wouldn't let any of his local people question our conspirators, but I've already declared all details of this case need-to-know under my Auditor's seal, so he's out of luck." He cleared his throat. "Your uncle and I have decided I get the job of going straight back to Vorbarr Sultana from here and making the preliminary report to Emperor Gregor in person. He's only been getting ImpSec digests."

"Oh," she said, startled. "Leaving so soon . . . ? What about all your things—you shouldn't go off without your seizure stimulator, should you?"

Half self-consciously, he rubbed his temple; the white bandages were gone from his wrists, she noticed, leaving only pale red rings of new scars. To add to his collection, presumably. "I had Tuomonen pack up all my kit and send it out here with the crew from HQ. It arrived a couple of hours ago, so I'm all set. Good old ImpSec, they do piss me off sometimes. Tuomonen is going to get a major black mark, because the conspiracy in Serifosa Terraforming took place on his watch, and he never caught it, even though it was really the Imperial Accounting Office which should have been the first line of defense. And that idiot Vorgier is getting a commendation. There is no justice."

"Poor Tuomonen. I liked him. Isn't there anything you can do about that?"

"Mm, I turned down a chance to be in charge of ImpSec's internal affairs, so no, I think I'd better not."

"Will he keep his post?"

"It's uncertain at this time. I told him if he finds his military career at a stand, to look me up. I think I'm going to be able to use a good trained assistant in this Auditor job. The work will be irregular, though. The trend of my life."

He sucked thoughtfully on his lower lip, and glanced across at her. "The reclassification of this case from a peculation scam to something far more serious also affects what you can tell Nikki, I'm afraid. It's all headed into a security black hole as fast as we can stuff it in there, and it's going to stay there for quite some time. There will, therefore, be no public prosecutions and no need for you to testify, though ImpSec may be around for another interview or two—*not* under fast-penta. In retrospect, I'm very relieved I played it as close to my chest as I did. But for Nikki, and all Tien's relatives, and anyone else, the story is going to have to remain that he died in a simple breath mask accident from being caught outside with a low reservoir, and you don't know any more details than that. Madame Dr. Vorthys, this is for you, too."

"I understand," said the Professora.

"I am both relieved, and disturbed," said Ekaterin slowly.

"In time, the security considerations will soften. You will have to rejudge the problem then, when, well, when many things may have changed."

"I did wonder if, for Nikki's name's honor, I ought to try to pay back the Imperium all the bribe money Tien received."

He looked startled. "Good God, no. If anyone owes anything, it's Foscol. *She* stole it in the first place. And we certainly won't be getting anything back from her."

"Something is owed," she said gravely.

"Tien settled his debt with his life. He's quits with the Imperium, I assure you. In the Emperor's Voice, if necessary."

She took this in. Death did wipe out debt. It just didn't erase the memory of pain; time was still required for that healing. *Your time is your own, now. That* felt strange. She could take all the time she wanted, or needed. Riches beyond dreams. She nodded. "All right."

"The past is paid. Please notify me about Tien's funeral, though. I wish to attend, if I can." He frowned. "I too owe something there."

She shook her head mutely.

"In any case, do call me when you and your aunt get back to Vorbarr Sultana." He glanced again at the Professora. "She and Nikki *will* be staying with you for a time, yes?" Ekaterin was not quite sure if that was phrased as a question or a demand.

"Yes, indeed." Aunt Vorthys smiled.

"So here are all my addresses." He spoke again to Ekaterin, and handed her a plastic flimsy. "The numbers for the Vorkosigan residences in Vorbarr Sultana, Hassadar, and Vorkosigan Surleau, for Master Tsipis in Hassadar—my man of business, I believe I mentioned him to you—he usually knows where to get hold of me in a pinch, when I'm out in the District—and a drop-number through the Imperial Residence, which will *always* know how to reach me. Any time, day or night."

Aunt Vorthys leaned back, with her finger on her lips, and regarded him with growing bemusement. "Do you think those will be enough, Miles? Perhaps you can think of three or four more, just to be sure?"

To Ekaterin's surprise, he flushed a little. "I trust these will suffice," he said. "And of course, I should be able to reach you through your aunt, right?"

"Of course," murmured Aunt Vorthys.

"I'd like to show you over my District sometime," he added to Ekaterin, avoiding the Professora's eye. "There's a great deal to see there you might find of interest. There's a major forestry project going on in the Dendarii Mountains, and some radiation reclamation experiments. My family owns several maple syrup and winery operations. There's botany all over the damn place, in fact; you can hardly move without tripping over a plant."

"Perhaps later on," said Ekaterin uncertainly. "What *will* happen to the Terraforming Project, as a result of all this mess with the Komarrans?"

"Mm, not too much, I now suspect. The security classification is going to limit the immediate public political repercussions."

"In the long run, too?"

"Though the amount of money that was stolen from Serifosa Sector's budget was huge from the viewpoint of a private individual, from the standpoint of the bureaucracy it wasn't that big a bite. There are nineteen other Sectors, after all. The damage to the soletta array is actually going to be the biggest bill."

"Will the Imperium repair it properly? I've so hoped they would."

He brightened. "I had this great idea about that. I'm going to pitch it to Gregor that we should declare the soletta repair—

and enlargement—as a wedding present, from Gregor to Laisa and from Barrayar to Komarr. I'm going to recommend its size be nearly doubled, adding the six new panels the Komarrans have been begging for since forever. I think this mischance can be turned into an absolute propaganda coup, with the right timing. We'll shove the appropriation through the Council of Counts and Ministers quickly, before Midsummer, while everyone in Vorbarr Sultana is still sentimentally wound up for the Imperial Wedding."

She clapped her hands in enthusiasm, then paused in doubt. "Will that work? I didn't think the crusty old Council of Counts was susceptible to what Tien used to call *romantic drivel.*"

"Oh," he said airily, "I'm sure they are. I'm a cadet member of the Counts myself—we're only human, after all. Besides, we can point out that every time a Komarran looks up—well, half the time—they'll see this Barrayaran gift hanging overhead, and know what it's doing to create their future. The power of suggestion and all that. It could save us the expense of putting down the *next* Komarran conspiracy."

"I hope so," she said. "I think it's a lovely idea."

He grinned, clearly gratified. He looked over at the Professora, and away, shifted around, and drew a small packet from his trouser pocket. "I don't know, Madame Vorsoisson, whether Gregor will give you a medal or not, for your quick thinking and cool response in the Southport bay—"

She shook her head. "I don't need—"

"But I thought you should have something to remember it all by. This." He stuck out his hand.

She took the packet and laughed. "Do I recognize this?"

"Probably."

She unfolded the familiar wrapping and opened the box to reveal the little model Barrayar from the jeweler's shop in Serifosa, now on a slender chain of braided gold. She held it up; it spun in the light. "Look, Aunt Vorthys," she said shyly, and handed it across for inspection and approval.

The Professora examined it with interest, squinting a trifle. "Very fine, dear. Very fine indeed."

"Call it the Lord Auditor Vorkosigan Award for Making His Job Easier," said Vorkosigan. "You really did, you know. If the Komarrans hadn't already lost their infernal device, they would never have surrendered, even if I'd talked myself blue. In fact, Soudha said something to that effect during our preliminary interrogations last night, so you may consider it

confirmed. If not for you, this station would be in a million
hurtling pieces by now."

She hesitated. Should she accept—? She glanced at her aunt,
who was smiling at her benignly and without apparent
misgivings about the propriety of it. Not that Aunt Vorthys
was particularly passionate about propriety—that indifference
was, in fact, one of the qualities which made her Ekaterin's
favorite female relative. *Think on that.* "Thank you," she said
sincerely to Lord Vorkosigan. "I will remember. And I do
remember," she added.

"Um, you're supposed to forget the unfortunate part about
the pond."

"Never." Her lips curved up. "It was the highlight of the
day. Was it some sort of psychic precognition that you laid
this by?"

"I don't think so. Chance favors the prepared and all that.
Fortunately for my credit, from the outside most people can't
tell the rapid exploitation of a belatedly recognized opportunity from deep-laid planning." He positively smirked as she
slid the chain over her head. "You know, you're the first girlfr—
female friend I've had I've ever succeeded in giving Barrayar
to. Not for lack of trying."

Her eyes crinkled. "Have you had a great many girlfriends?"
If he hadn't, she'd have to dismiss her whole gender as con-
genital idiots. The man could charm snakes from their holes,
nine-year-olds from locked bathrooms, and Komarran terrorists from their bunkers. Why weren't females following him
around in herds? Could no Barrayaran woman see past his
surface, or their own cocked-up noses?

"Mmm . . ." A rather long hesitation. "The usual progression, I suppose. Hopeless first love, this and that over the years,
unrequited mad crushes."

"Who was the hopeless first love?" she asked, fascinated.

"Elena. The daughter of one of my father's Armsmen, who
was my bodyguard when I was young."

"Is she still on Barrayar?"

"No, she emigrated years ago. Had a galactic military career
and retired with the rank of captain. She's a commercial ship-
master now."

"Jumpships?"

"Yes."

"Nikki would be so envious. Um . . . what exactly is this
and that? If I may ask." Would he answer?

"Er. Well. Yes, I think you should, all things considered.
Better sooner than later, belike."

He was growing terribly Barrayaran, she thought; that use of *belike* was pure Dendarii mountain dialect. This outburst of confidences was at least as entertaining as putting him on fast-penta might be. Better, given what he'd said about his weird reaction to the drug.

"There was Elli. She was a free mercenary trainee when I first met her."

"What is she now?"

"Fleet Admiral. Actually."

"So she was this. Who was that?"

"There was Taura."

"What was she, when you first met her?"

"A Jacksonian body-slave. Of House Ryoval—very bad news, House Ryoval used to be."

"I must ask more about those covert ops missions of yours sometime . . . So what is she now?"

"Master Sergeant in a mercenary fleet."

"The same fleet as, um, the this?"

"Yes."

Her brows rose, helplessly. Her Aunt Vorthys was leaning back with her finger over her lips again, her eyes alight with laughter; no, the Professora clearly wasn't going to interfere with this. "And . . . ?" she led him on, beginning to be immensely curious as to how long he'd keep going. Why in the world did he think all this romantic history was something she ought to know? Not that she would stop him . . . nor would Aunt Vorthys, apparently, not for a bribe of five kilos of chocolates. But her secret opinion of her gender began to rise.

"Mm . . . there was Rowan. That was . . . that was brief."

"And she was . . . ?"

"A technical serf of House Fell. She's a cryo-revival surgeon in an independent clinic on Escobar, now, though, I'm happy to say. Very pleased with her new citizenship."

Tien had protected her proudly, she reflected, in the little Vor-lady fortress of her household. Tien had spent a decade protecting her so hard, especially from anything that resembled growth, she'd felt scarcely larger at thirty than she'd been at twenty. Whatever it was Vorkosigan had offered to this extraordinary list of lovers, it hadn't been protection.

"Do you begin to notice a trend in all this, Lord Vorkosigan?"

"Yes," he replied glumly. "None of them would marry me and come live on Barrayar."

"So . . . what about the unrequited mad crush?"

"Ah. That was Rian. I was young, just a new lieutenant on a diplomatic mission."

"And what does she do, now?"

He cleared his throat. "Now? She's an empress." He added, under the pressure of Ekaterin's wide stare, "Of Cetaganda. They have several, you see."

A silence fell, and stretched. He shifted uneasily in his chair, and his smile flicked on and off.

She rested her chin in her hand, and regarded him; her brows quirked in quizzical delight. "Lord Vorkosigan. Can I take a number and get in line?"

Whatever it was he'd been expecting her to say, it wasn't that; he was so taken aback he nearly fell off his chair. Wait, she hadn't meant it to come out sounding quite like— His smile stuck in the *on* position, but decidedly sideways.

"The next number up," he breathed, "is 'one.'"

It was her turn to be taken aback; her eyes fell, scorched by the blaze in his. He had lured her into levity. His fault, for being so . . . luring. She stared wildly around the room, groping for some suitably neutral remark with which to retrieve her reserve. It was a space station: there was no weather. *My, the vacuum is hard out today. . . .* Not that, either. She gazed beseechingly at Aunt Vorthys. Vorkosigan observed her involuntary recoil, and his smile acquired a sort of stuffed apologetic quality; he too looked cautiously to the Professora.

The Professora rubbed one finger thoughtfully over her chin. "And are you traveling back to Barrayar on a commercial liner, Lord Vorkosigan?" she asked him affably. The mutually alarmed parties blinked at her in suffused gratitude.

"No," said Vorkosigan. "Fast courier. In fact, it's waiting for me right now." He cleared his throat, jumped to his feet, and made a show of checking his chrono. "Yes, right now. Professora, Madame Vorsoisson, I trust I shall see you both back in Vorbarr Sultana?"

"Yes, certainly," said Ekaterin, barely avoiding breathlessness.

"I will look forward to it with great fascination," said the Professora piously.

His smile went crooked in trenchant appreciation of her tone; he backed out with a flourishing, self-conscious bow, a courtly effect slightly spoiled by his caroming off the door-jamb. His quick steps faded down the corridor.

"A nice young man," observed Aunt Vorthys, into a room seeming suddenly much emptier. "A pity he's so short."

"He's not so short," said Ekaterin defensively. "He's just . . . concentrated."

Her aunt's smile grew maddeningly bland. "I could see that, dear."

Ekaterin lifted her chin in what remained of her dignity. "I see you are feeling very much better. Shall we go ask about that hydroponics tour?"

MILES VORKOSIGAN/NAISMITH:
HIS UNIVERSE AND TIMES

Chronology	Events	Chronicle
Approx. 200 years before Miles's birth	Quaddies are created by genetic engineering.	*Falling Free*
During Beta-Barrayaran War	Cordelia Naismith meets Lord Aral Vorkosigan while on opposite sides of a war. Despite difficulties, they fall in love and are married.	*Shards of Honor*
The Vordarian Pretendership	While Cordelia is pregnant, an attempt to assassinate Aral by poison gas fails, but Cordelia is affected; Miles Vorkosigan is born with bones that will always be brittle and other medical problems. His growth will be stunted.	*Barrayar*
Miles is 17	Miles fails to pass physical test to get into the Service Academy. On a trip, necessities force him to improvise the Free Dendarii Mercenaries into existence; he has unintended but unavoidable adventures for four months. Leaves the Dendarii in Ky Tung's competent hands and takes Elli Quinn to Beta for rebuilding of her damaged face; returns to Barrayar to thwart plot against his father. Emperor pulls strings to get Miles into the Academy.	*The Warrior's Apprentice*

Chronology	Events	Chronicle
Miles is 20	Ensign Miles graduates and immediately has to take on one of the duties of the Barrayaran nobility and act as detective and judge in a murder case. Shortly afterwards, his first military assignment ends with his arrest. Miles has to rejoin the Dendarii to rescue the young Barrayaran emperor. Emperor accepts Dendarii as his personal secret service force.	"The Mountains of Mourning" in *Borders of Infinity* *The Vor Game*
Miles is 22	Miles and his cousin Ivan attend a Cetagandan state funeral and are caught up in Cetagandan internal politics. Miles sends Commander Elli Quinn, who's been given a new face on Beta, on a solo mission to Kline Station.	*Cetaganda*
Miles is 23	Now a Barrayaran Lieutenant, Miles goes with the Dendarii to smuggle a scientist out of Jackson's Whole. Miles's fragile leg bones have been replaced by synthetics.	"Labyrinth" in *Borders of Infinity*
Miles is 24	Miles plots from within a Cetagandan prison camp on Dagoola IV to free the prisoners. The Denarii fleet is pursued by the Cetagandans and finally reaches Earth for repairs. Miles has to juggle both his identities at once, raise money for repairs, and defeat a plot to replace him with a double. Ky Tung stays on Earth. Commander Elli Quinn is now Miles's right-hand officer. Miles and the Dendarii depart for Sector IV on a rescue mission.	"The Borders of Infinity" in *Borders of Infinity* *Brothers in Arms*

Chronology	Events	Chronicle
Miles is 25	Hospitalized after previous mission, Miles's broken arms are replaced by synthetic bones. With Simon Illyan, Miles undoes yet another plot against his father while flat on his back.	*Borders of Infinity*
Miles is 28	Miles meets his clone brother Mark again, this time on Jackson's Whole.	*Mirror Dance*
Miles is 29	Miles hits thirty; thirty hits back.	*Memory*
Miles is 30	Emperor Gregor dispatches Miles to Komarr to investigate a space accident, where he finds old politics and new technology make a deadly mix.	*Komarr*